ABOUT THE AUTHOR

Carol Westron is a successful short story writer turned novelist. Fascinated by psychology and history, Carol writes crime novels set both in contemporary and Victorian times. Her books are predominantly set in the South of England, where she now lives.

Crime Series set on the South Coast

The South Coast Crime books form an overlapping series of police procedurals where characters and events from one series interact and impact on the other, mirroring real life, where police personnel often work over a large area within their county.

The Fragility of Poppies is set in the fictional south coast town of Galmouth and is a spin-off from the South Coast Crime police procedurals.

Books in the South Coast Crime series:

The Terminal Velocity of Cats
(Mia Trent Scene of Crimes) published 2013

About the Children
(Serious Crimes Team) published 2014

The Fragility of Poppies
(Serious Crimes Team) published 2016

Karma and the Singing Frogs
(Mia Trent Scene of Crimes) to be published 2017.

The books are separate and all stand by themselves.

The Fragility of Poppies

Carol Westron

To Andrew
  Happy Birthday
Carol Westron

pentangle
press

Copyright © 2016 Carol Westron

Carol Westron has asserted her right under the Copyright, Designs and Patents Act, 1988 to be identified as the author of this work.

This book is sold subject to the condition that it shall not, by way of trade or otherwise, be lent, resold, hired out, or otherwise circulated without the publisher's prior consent in any form of binding, cover other than that in which it is published and without similar condition including this condition being imposed on the subject purchaser.

All the characters in this publication are fictional and any resemblance to real persons, living or dead is purely coincidental.

ISBN 978-1530757268
Book design by The Art of Communication www.artofcomms.co.uk
First published in the UK 2016 by Pentangle Press www.pentanglepress.com

Dedication

To Jo

Your favourite of all my books with all my love.

Thank you for being my daughter.

X

Acknowledgements

Thank you to The Art of Communication for a great lay-out and another stunning cover.

Thank you Jack Halsall for the original cover photograph.

Thanks to my Pentangle Press colleagues: Wendy Metcalfe for some sharp-eyed editing and Christine Hammacott for her help and advice and for being such a great writing mate who is always there for me.

Thank you Lizzie Hayes, a wonderful friend and a brilliant editor, who has supported, encouraged and promoted me and is going to keep me writing Golden Age of Crime articles for a very long time to come.

Thanks to all my friends and readers for your support and encouragement.

All my love and thanks to my family, without whom nothing that I've achieved would be possible or worthwhile. Thank you for being there for me, Peter, Jo, Jack & Adam, Paul, Claire, Oliver & Henry, Alan, Lyndsey, Thomas, Tabitha & Pippa.

but i have seen
death's clever enormous voice
which hides in a fragility
of poppies...

e.e.cummings

Chapter 1: Annie

NOVEMBER 2011

"Remember your poppy, dear." The lady behind the newsagent's counter nudges the tray towards me.

"Of course." Our village isn't the sort of place where you say, *'I don't like paper flowers.'* It's best to conform. Round here, artists are regarded with suspicion anyway.

"How's your husband? Is he on the hunt for the missing girl?" She leans forward, eager to chat.

"Yes." I try for non-committal. The police get nasty when Detective Inspector's wives are quoted... or misquoted... gossiping about sensitive cases.

"Dreadful business."

"Yes." No one could deny that the disappearance of three young, local girls in the past six months is dreadful, but I've been a cop's wife for ten years and I try to compartmentalise. Otherwise the horrors Rick sees will dominate both our lives.

"No question this time that someone's gone off with her," persists the shop lady. "Poor little mite. It's not like that first girl who went missing."

"No." I stick to monosyllables, concentrating on getting them in the right place.

When the first girl disappeared everyone assumed she was a runaway. She was sixteen and sexually active. She didn't get on with her parents and she'd run off many times before. The police had looked but they hadn't suspected foul play. Everybody had expected her to turn up when it suited her. That changed when a second girl vanished, three months later.

Now another child has gone. The three month interval has taken on a sinister significance and the lost children are getting younger every time.

"A lot of people from the village are helping with the search," says the newsagent. "Have you heard how it's going?"

"I'm sorry. I don't know any more than you do." This is totally true. Rick hasn't been home for the last two days. He's been working non-stop since Katie disappeared.

Another customer enters the newsagents and I escape.

I wish I could join the search for Katie. It would be good to trudge along in wordless comradeship with other people who, for a few hours, have shelved their everyday lives because they wish to help. But again I'm hampered by the rulebook, which says a DI's wife must stay away from criminal investigations, in case, in some way, evidence gets compromised.

I walk the mile home with thoughts of the missing child mingling with the poignancy of the poppies and my own dark memories. Poppies used to be a recurring theme for me. I thought I'd finished with them but now the frail, indomitable flowers are back, burning in the centre of my mind.

To my surprise, by the time I reach my house, the pain of loss and the symbolism of the Flanders flower has combined with the recent memory of a glory of poppies in a wild garden we'd visited in Devon. That had been before the second girl went missing. It was a time when we were happy.

Sparkling with inspiration, I go straight up to my attic studio.

Hours later I step back and survey my work. A border of dull red, paper poppies melt into fragile, quickening life and the central body of the canvas is a flame of scarlet, flaunting flowers.

There have only been a few occasions in my life when I've considered my canvas on the first day of creation and known that what I've done is unequivocally good. Today I look at my work and love it.

I know when I come to it cold there'll be things I want to change, but now I need caffeine, food and reconnection with the world.

A mug of coffee and bacon sandwich later, I think about Rick and wonder how he's doing. I can't phone him. The chances are he'll be busy and if I interrupt anything important his boss will give him hell. DCI Newton's a good friend to Rick but I've always had the impression that he thinks that wives should neither be seen nor heard, which probably explains why he's been divorced three times.

I glance at the clock. There's five minutes until the ten o'clock news.

I go upstairs and draw the curtains. My studio window is open to release the fumes of oil paint. I shut it, smelling the acrid smoke of Guy Fawkes' bonfires, so different from the richer, softer smell of burning autumn leaves. From somewhere near the village, a rocket arcs through the darkness and explodes in a shower of stars.

Downstairs, I pour myself a glass of wine and turn on the television.

'A spokesman for Galmouth CID confirmed that, this afternoon, police officers discovered three bodies in a hut in Elmwash Woods.' Pictures flash up of thick woodland and a wooden hut, painted camouflage green. The bright yellow of the police tape jars against the muted background. I understand why the police hadn't found the hut before. In spring and summer it would have been hidden by thick leaves.

The hut in Elmwash is replaced by a photograph of Katie's smiling face.

'Police are not able to confirm the identity of the deceased at this time, but fears have increased for the safety of ten-year-old Katie Cavendish, who vanished two days ago from the garden of her home just outside Galmouth. Two other girls have disappeared from the Galmouth area within the past six months: Emma Brown, aged thirteen, and Hannah Summers, sixteen.' Their pictures appear next to Katie's. They are all fair-haired and exceptionally beautiful.

They go through the whole story. When Hannah went missing the wreath of flowers left beside a Galmouth bus shelter held no significance; nor did the ankle chain that was posted to the local newspaper. It was a cheap, mass-produced thing with no obvious link to Hannah.

Three months later Emma disappeared. This generated a full-scale hunt. She was, by all accounts, an innocent thirteen-year-old and happy at home. The wreath of flowers occurred again, this time in the park that Emma walked through as a short-cut home. Two days later, her hair jewels were received by the Galmouth Daily News.

That was in August. For the last three months Rick has been part of the team working on the case. As a rule he doesn't talk about his work but this case is different, so much a part of him that he couldn't leave it behind. He told me that he was certain a known sex offender, a man called Ernest Clift, was responsible, but Clift was a sly bastard who covered his tracks and they didn't have enough solid evidence. Rick has hauled Clift in several times, questioned him to the legal limit and let him go.

This week, when Katie disappeared, a wreath of roses was left by her front gate.

There are tears in my eyes as I watch the news broadcast through. Then I switch off the television and sit, waiting for Rick to come home. I know he might not turn up tonight but I can't just go to bed.

To pass the time, I pick up a sketchbook and pencil and fill the pages with line drawings of swirling poppy shapes.

It's after one in the morning and my sketchbook's almost full when I hear the front door open. I get up and go into the hall. Rick's there, taking off his coat. His face is white and shuttered and every movement is heavy with exhaustion.

"Hello you." I cross the hall and put my arms around him. He stands stiff and unyielding, not I think because he's rejecting me but because the hold on his emotions is too tight.

"The bodies in Elmwash Woods? It's them, isn't it?" I say.

"Yeah, though we'll need DNA tests to confirm about Emma and Hannah before the coroner can say so formally." His voice is rigidly controlled. "The bodies are badly decomposed."

"You saw them?" I hug him tighter.

"I found them."

"But why were you there?" As a senior CID officer he should have been in the Incident Room co-ordinating the search.

"I wanted to be out there, not sitting behind a desk. And I'd had a tip about the woods... I'd put out word I wanted to know what Clift had been up to the last few days, and an informer told me he'd been seen around there... so I pushed for a thorough search on foot... The hut windows were boarded up from inside and the door was padlocked, but I had this feeling, so I told one of the uniformed guys to cut the chain. As soon as I opened the door the smell hit me and I knew. They were laid out on boxes covered in red velvet and there were flowers... fresh roses and lilies... arranged around them."

"Oh Rick!" I'm shaking but he's like carved stone.

"I had to go in. No time to wait for SOCO. From the doorway Katie looked like she was sleeping. I had to be sure I couldn't save her... then I got near and saw what the bastard had done to her."

Chapter 2: Annie

NOVEMBER 2015

The Devon sun soaks into us, as if this were some more exotic shore, but the beach colours are soft and subtly shaded. My senses are filled with Impressionist images. I hear the hiss and rustle of the waves and children shouting as they play.

Our hands are intertwined and Rick is whistling softly, *Annie's Song*.

I jerk awake. The dream disappears. I'm alone in the winter darkness, achingly aware of the emptiness beside me in the double bed.

I hear a car door slam and check the time: ten minutes to eleven. It's Rick's off-duty weekend and I know one of the younger cops had planned a birthday booze-up. I'm surprised Rick's home so early, or home at all, nowadays he often stays at the Station house.

The car drives off and I drift back to near sleeping until I hear him staggering up the stairs. He stops outside my door. That puzzles me. For the last few months he's slept in the spare room. "You okay?" I call.

The door bangs open and he's silhouetted by the light from the hall. It's strange that I feel scared straight away. I've never been scared of Rick; angry, hurt and bitter but never scared. "Rick? What's wrong?"

I'm hurled back. His hand is round my throat. I'm struggling for breath. He's glaring down at me. His dark eyes are staring and his face is twitching, like he's having some sort of fit. "This will sort you, you fucking frigid bitch."

The pressure on my throat tightens. I put my hands up, trying to claw free. A blow cracks across my cheek. The light from the hall shimmers and dims before my eyes. His weight pinions me. The sweet staleness of his breath makes me gag but I can't turn my head away. He prises my legs apart. Rams home. The screams I can't utter are swelling in my head. Rick can't be doing this.

At last he rolls away from me. I draw in a shuddering breath, gulp, and choke it back. If I am very still and very quiet perhaps he won't do anything else to me.

He's snoring, a heavy, rasping sound. I turn my head towards him. I expect to see a stranger lying there. But it's Rick.

Inch by inch I slither from the bed, then I grab my robe and flee to the bathroom. Once there I ease the door shut and slide the bolt in place. It's not enough. I upturn the linen basket and jam it between bath and door.

With my back against the wall I slide down to the floor. My throat and head hurt and it throbs underneath where he... I feel sick.

I lean forward and rest my head upon my knees. Time flows around me.

At last I regain awareness. Rick could wake and find me here, trapped and powerless. That spurs me into movement. I force myself to my feet and into the shower. Then I huddle into the protection of jogging bottoms, high-necked jumper and my sturdiest underwear. The clothes are warm from the airing cupboard but I can't stop shivering.

The clock strikes two as I ease open the bathroom door. It makes me jump and I fight the urge to scurry back into my stronghold. The light makes me feel vulnerable and I twist the dimmer switch to mute the brightness. I tiptoe along the shadowed hall, senses at screaming point. All the sounds of the old house are magnified.

I flee up the stairs to my attic studio and shift a cupboard to bar the door. A bottle of white spirit falls and rolls across the room. The noise on the wooden boards is like the rumble of thunder. I freeze, and listen until I'm sure there's no movement downstairs.

I can't spend all night cringing at every sound. By morning I'd be a mad woman in my attic. I've got to make sure he can't come after me. I rummage through the drawers. At last I find the thing I'm looking for. The old handcuffs Rick gave me years ago, when I was using confinement as my theme. I turn them over, fingering the cold, smooth metal, not convinced I dare to do this.

It's hard to push the cupboard aside and go downstairs. Harder to enter the bedroom. Rick's still sprawled on his back, deep in drunken sleep.

A spike of anger skewers through me. I fasten one of the handcuff bracelets round his wrist. He mutters and I halt, trapped in the moment. Then, in one swift movement, I clip the handcuffs to the steel bedhead.

I back across the bedroom, run along the corridor, then upstairs to the sanctuary of my studio once again.

Chapter 3: Annie

Eight hours later, in the sane light of morning, the events of the night have the macabre unreality of a dream. I stand on the landing, stare at the closed door, and listen to Rick groan his way back to consciousness.

I want to run. To seek the safety of my mother's house. I could leave the handcuff key downstairs and the front door on the latch, and phone his mate, Bob, to come and sort him.

Rick's blasphemies blend into coherent speech, "Annie, where are you? Annie, I need you!" His voice is shrill with panic.

Oh Rick, how could we have let things come to this?

"Annie, help me." The whimpered words tear through me more fiercely than a scream. Rick's always been terrified of being trapped.

No way can I leave him there like that. I take a deep breath, place my trembling fingers on the handle and push open the bedroom door.

The curtains aren't drawn and the room is full of the grey light of a wet morning. It stinks of drink, sweat and fear. Rick's eyes are fixed on me; they hold the terror of a snared animal. "Annie, what's happening? Was it you who cuffed me? Why?"

I stare at him. "Don't you remember what you did last night?"

"No." He shakes his head and winces. "Look, just tell me how I'm supposed to have fucked up this time."

Even as I curl inside myself, some part of me appreciates the irony of his choice of words. "You... hurt me." The word I should use stays trapped within my mind.

The last trace of colour drains from his face. "I hurt you? How? What did I do?" He struggles to sit up. The movement makes him retch. "Annie, get me free."

I don't move.

"Annie... please... I'm going to throw up."

I cross the room towards him. I know I should be ready to run in case he turns on me, but I'm filled with numbing desolation, as if I've nothing left worth fighting for. I fumble the key into the lock and turn it until the quietest of clicks proclaims he's free. He swings clear of the bed and makes a staggering dash for the en-suite.

I shut the door on him and clear up the mess.

I remove the handcuffs from the bed and thrust them out of sight in the back of a clothes drawer.

I open the windows to air the room.

I strip the stained and crumpled bedding.

I hold it at arm's length and go downstairs.

I bundle it into the washing machine.

I turn the dial to intensive wash.

I make a pot of tea and sit, drinking mug after mug, while I watch the clock tick round from eleven to half-past.

Eventually I hear Rick on the stairs. He enters the kitchen slowly, moving like everything hurts. He's dressed in vest and jeans and, under the dark stubble, his olive-brown complexion is tinged with green. He holds out his hand to me but I look away, avoiding eye contact. He sits down at the table and cradles his head between his hands. "I'm sorry, I still can't remember what happened last night."

"That's convenient."

"Annie, I swear I can't remember. Please tell me what I did."

'This will sort you, you fucking frigid bitch,' the remembered words roar in my mind. Again I feel his weight pinioning me, his hand on my throat, his sour breath in my face... the pain.

He pours himself a cup of stewed tea and pushes paracetamol capsules through their foil covering: one, two, three, four. I wonder if he expects me to protest. I say nothing and he gags them down.

"Annie, whatever I did, I'm sorry. Can't we at least try to sort it out?"

"No." I'm too tired and afraid and hurt to talk.

We sit in silence. Outside, the November clouds release their steel grey spite and hurl fist loads of hail at the windows.

"Your mother's picked a lousy day for her lunch party." Rick rubs his goose-pimpled arms.

"Yes."

"I suppose you'd rather I didn't come with you?"

"What do you think?"

I go upstairs to the bedroom and through to the en-suite. The medicine cabinet has been the target of a police raid. I look in disgust at the mess of boxes and powders that have tipped into the wash-basin and onto the floor. The room reeks of sick.

Back in the bedroom I pack a case, then take my make-up and luncheon-party clothes into the main bathroom to change. My mother has old-fashioned standards and usually I'd wear a skirt, but today I want to stay covered up. I dress and spend more time than usual on my make-up, trying to brighten my sallow cheeks and conceal the dark shadows beneath my eyes. Before I go downstairs I conceal my figure-hugging trousers and polo-necked top under a jacket, and do up all the buttons.

Rick's sitting in the kitchen; still looking as if death would be his preferred next move. He spots the case I'm carrying and stands up. "Are you coming back?"

Fear sweeps through me. If I say 'no' will he use physical force to make me stay? I sidle across the kitchen, measuring the distance to the door.

Chapter 4: Annie

Rick doesn't come after me. He lets me go without another word. I slide through the door, slam it shut and run to my car. Heart pumping fast, I jump in and drive away.

As I turn out of the drive I take a last glance in the rear mirror and choke back a sob. I've always loved our home. It's an ex-farmhouse, too big for just us two, we bought it when we were first married, ready for when we decided to start a family.

I watch my hands clench on the steering wheel and moderate my speed along the mud-slicked country lanes.

I'm thirty-six next birthday and Rick's already there; if we're not ready to start that family soon we never will be. I remind myself that argument is over. I keep forgetting we can't be a couple any more.

When we married, a lot of people were negative. They said we were too different to make a go of it. But for years we'd seemed okay, both busy with our jobs and separate lives. Me working my way up through the art teaching ranks and getting the odd promising show put on, and Rick making Detective Inspector before he was thirty. We didn't mix much with each other's friends, and family get-togethers could be iffy too, but together we were good.

My mother was always the most determined critic of our marriage. For that matter, she still is. She never thought that Rick was good enough for me. She cited statistics about divorce in the police force and her prejudices were confirmed when Bob Borrow's wife took their three children and left him. Rick, of course, took Bob's side. He spent a lot of time supporting his mate and they both made bitter jibes about Bob's wife. I'd got on well with Pat Borrow and tried to explain her side of the story to Rick, but he wouldn't listen.

Last year I decided Time's wingèd chariot was about to

run us down and we should start the deferred family. At first I couldn't believe he'd changed his mind and didn't want children, now or ever. I'd tried the lot: reasoning, cajoling, begging, arguing and good old-fashioned seduction, but he'd remained stubborn. So six months ago I'd put a ban on sex. If he didn't love me enough to father my child, why should he screw me whenever it suited him?

I started it in anger, but the heat had hardened into a cold shell of bitterness. Bereavement is back within me in fresh force and with it a guilt that makes me cringe. I shouldn't have withdrawn from him, not without telling him why I need a baby so desperately. If I'd tried harder, surely I could have made him understand.

I drive by instinct through country lanes and small villages. This isn't the quickest way to Bellmead, the village where I grew up, but it's comforting in its familiarity.

I pass through Saronholt slowly. A few months ago, the Residents' Committee campaigned to have the speed limit reduced to ten miles an hour. It's a very posh village that mustn't be disturbed by traffic noise. Today a lot of people are gathered on the village green, milling around the War Memorial cross and trampling on the sprays of poppies that the wind has blown across the damp grass. The crowd includes several uniformed police officers, so I guess it must be the Saronholt Fun Run, which is held annually in memory of a local dignitary.

In Bellmead I pass the place that was my childhood home with eyes averted, unwilling to look at the four starter homes now standing on the site. I don't blame Mother for selling. When my sister and I moved out, the house and grounds were too much for a widow living on her own. She'd been pleased that the money she gained meant she could be generous to me and Elaine when we needed deposits for our homes.

There's a banner outside the church: *Congratulations on your Wedding, Susanne and Peter*. Fourteen years ago a similar banner had read Annie and Rick.

I turn through the entrance of Mother's retirement estate, stop the car and cry.

How did it happen? When did our marriage fall apart? The answer is there before me, so simple I must have known it all along. It came to a head with my demands to have children, but the trouble started the day Rick found that hut in Elmwash Woods. And it went into free-fall with the death of Ernest Clift.

It's hard to remember that time, it's distorted with tension, fear and pain. After Rick found the dead girls he had Clift in and questioned him again. But somehow, in some strange way, as days went past, Clift started to call the shots; turning up whenever he wanted and offering himself for interview. And, for some reason, Rick couldn't tell him to sod off.

Then it was over. In that last interview, something happened, although Rick never told me what. Clift left the police station. He bought flowers and made them into a garland, which he placed around his neck. He'd waited on the footbridge that spans the road, just along from the police car park. He must have known Rick always turned that way to come home. Afterwards witnesses said he'd had his binoculars trained on the road.

When Rick's car approached he jumped.

The car was a write-off and so was Ernest Clift.

Chapter 5: Rick

Annie walks away from me and I let her go. There's nothing I can do to make her stay. What the hell did I do to her? She said I hurt her. I always swore I'd never hurt my wife. I've seen too much of it. But she wouldn't have said it if it wasn't true. And there was the way she was moving; Annie never stands closed in on herself like that.

Instinct takes me up to her studio. It smells of paint, white spirit and her perfume. The chair I always used has been pushed into a corner. It's piled with old magazines and holiday brochures. I spot one for the place in Devon where we stayed years ago. I shift the brochures and sit down. I've got to remember what I did last night.

I remember the first part of the evening. It was someone's birthday so we went to this Mexican restaurant and we were drinking Tequila. I'd never had it before and I didn't like it much. It made me feel strange.

I remember how hot the room was and how crowded. I spent most of the time outside. After a while I gave up on the evening and flagged down a passing cab.

I remember the drive home… at least sort of. Outside the car the lights were playing funny tricks, slithering past like satin streamers, then exploding into a cascade of sharp stars that hurt my eyes.

I remember getting out of the car and fumbling for my door key.

I force myself to concentrate on what came next but still there's nothing. This frustrates me. I've never believed people who claimed they couldn't remember what they'd done when they were slaughtered. Whatever the psychologists say, short of head injury, I don't believe in convenient amnesia.

The truth is I don't rate psychologists. It's no good whinging. When bad things happen you get through it and carry on. The psychologist they sent me to four years ago kept saying I had to talk about the trauma I'd been through. As if it would help to sit round talking about Elmwash and Ernest Clift and the way he died.

I shouldn't have started thinking about Clift. The door in my mind has opened and he's loose inside my head, with all his evil and his ugliness. I hear his voice, *'You can't escape me, Richard'* and brace myself to see his smashed and bleeding face. But the words merge into my voice and I'm yelling, *'You fucking frigid bitch.'*

I see Annie's face, white and terrified. I feel my hand on her throat.

I remember what I did to her.

I realise the phone is ringing. I think, *'Annie,'* and almost fall down the attic stairs in my rush to answer it. "Hello?"

"Guv? It's Kelly. You're needed at the Station straight away."

Just what I need to make this lousy day complete.

"Guv? Are you still there?"

"Yeah. What's happened?"

"Missing child."

There's no avoiding that one. "Okay, I'm on my way."

It takes me a long time to get ready but I can't go into work until I've showered and shaved. I make myself black coffee and force down a few plain biscuits. It's the only way I can safely drive. I ought to leave Annie a note, but I don't know what to say.

I drive the ten miles into town slowly, concentrating on every move. In Galmouth, as I approach the road-bridge, tension sends stabs of pain through my already aching head. If I go round the long way, Ernest Clift has won... *'I've got friends, good friends, that will carry on for me.'*

Today Clift has won. I do a U-turn and drive the long way into work.

I try to slip into the room without interrupting the briefing, but Detective Superintendent Roebuck gives me an evil look and everyone else turns round to stare.

"About time," says Roebuck.

"Sorry sir." I slide towards a chair.

"Don't make yourself comfortable. We're finished here. We've got to get out and make the most of the light. It's going quickly with this rain."

The way he glares, I guess the weather's down to me as well.

"Sorry sir," I say again, but this time I let an arsey note show through.

I see his weasel face flush. "Go to Saronholt. Report to DCI Lane."

"What's going down, sir?"

"I can't waste time getting stragglers up to speed. I've got a Media Conference. DCI Lane will fill you in." He throws the last words over his shoulder as he leaves. Most of the team disperses and only Bob Borrow and DC Louisa Kelly are left.

"I love the way the bastard goes for you," says Bob. "Like it's your fault we're not moving fast. He only turned up to sound off to the Press."

I shrug. I've just been bloody stupid. I'm on career gridlock and I've made matters worse by pissing off Roebuck.

Bob's still moaning, "He had no business calling you down like that in front of everyone. Kelly, you got your notebook handy? Don't want you to misquote me."

Kelly ignores him. "I've organised some sandwiches, Guv."

The words are polite but her tone's heavy with contempt. That shows how negligible she thinks I am these days. Kelly's got everything going for her. She's black, she's beautiful and she's bloody smart, with a good degree that puts her on the Fast Track. She plans to get to the top, and she doesn't care who she tramples over on the way. She's Superintendent Roebuck's protégé and his snitch on the rest of CID.

I need to eat. I follow Bob across the room and pick up

a sandwich.

"It's sardines," Bob warns, spraying me with crumbs and fishy breath.

"Bloody hell." I put it back again. "What's going down, Bob?" I'm sure there's something under the surface that no-one's telling me.

He shrugs. "Missing kid. Makes everyone edgy."

"Right. I'll get out to Saronholt." I could hang round here and push Bob to tell me more details, but if I do Kelly will report to Roebuck and we'll both be in the shit.

Bob nods, and I think he looks relieved. "Roebuck told me to tie up a few things here. I'll see you later, mate."

"Yeah, see you." It scares me how paranoid I'm getting. He's my best mate and I'm certain he's not levelling with me.

Chapter 6: Annie

"Annie, are you all right?" The thumping on the inside of my skull resolves itself into a tapping on my side window.

I scrub at the tears and switch on a bright smile as I wind the window down. "Maris. Hi. I didn't see you there."

"Are you all right?" she repeats tenaciously.

"I'm fine. More important, how are you?" I look meaningfully at the vast curve of her belly.

Her freckled face breaks into a broad smile. "I'm very well."

"Surely you should be on maternity leave by now?" Maris is in charge of Graphics at the Art College and I hold a similar post in Fine Art.

"I don't want to leave until I have to. There's no sense in sitting round at home." The brisk reply strikes me as unlike Maris but recently she's changed a lot.

"Where are you going?" Actually I can guess; this is a cul de sac.

"To your mother's. I saw her in the Post Office and she invited me for lunch. My car's being serviced so I had to walk, but it's worth it. It's so nice to meet some interesting people. Since Mummy went away it's very quiet at home."

I'm thrown by her describing my family as interesting. After one family Christmas, Rick swore that if being boring was a criminal offence, all my relations would be banged up for life. A wave of pain flows through me as I think of Rick.

"You're not all right!" exclaims Maris. "Annie, what's wrong?"

"Nothing." As I speak, the heavens roar mockingly. "Get in."

"It's only round the corner."

"You'll still get wet." I lean over and open the door, aware of my mother's annoyance if I allow her nine-months-

29

pregnant guest to arrive soaked to the skin.

She trundles round, clambers in and turns to gaze into my face. Maris has colourless eyes and an unnervingly flat stare.

"Annie, tell me what's wrong. Why were you crying?"

"I wasn't."

"He hit you," she says with gentle certainty.

"What?" I stare at her.

"Your face is bruised."

I wrench the rear view mirror across to look. In the bathroom I'd missed the faint tell-tale mark on my left cheek.

Maris puts her arms around me. "I'm here, Annie. I'll look after you."

"I'm okay." I pull myself away and retrieve my handbag to make repairs.

"You could get him into a lot of trouble if you reported him for hitting you."

The police are a close-knit family who watch each other's backs but they jump from a great height on those who get found out.

"I didn't say Rick hit me. I bumped it in the studio... something fell off a shelf."

She puts a hand on my knee. "Just remember I'm here for you."

"Put your seat belt on. Mother will be annoyed if we're late."

Obediently she pulls the seat belt around her, stretching it to its limit, and slots it in. "Yes. I saw Neil's car go past a few minutes ago."

"Neil? Oh God she hasn't invited him?" Neil is the College's Head of Sculpture, Fine Art and Graphics and I'm his deputy.

"She said she had. Don't you want him to come? You and Neil seem so close."

There's no way I can explain the delicate past-present balance of my relationship with Neil. "We go back a long way."

"Not as far back as you and I do." She bites her lower lip. "Are you in love with him?"

I stare at her. I feel a tremor of wild laughter welling up in me, but it can't get past the lump that blocks my throat. I swallow hard. "No, I'm not in love with Neil."

"I'm glad."

That's strange. It's not as if Maris likes Rick. I hunt for something safe to talk about and settle for the weather. "It's an awful day for the Saronholt Fun Run."

"The Fun Run?" She looks puzzled. "No, that's next week."

"But I saw them all gathered on the village green."

"Oh that's not for the Fun Run. That must be the search party."

"Search party?"

"Yes. They were talking about it in the Co-op when I popped in a few minutes ago. Someone said a little girl had disappeared. She's probably been abducted like those other girls were a few years ago."

She seems to mistake my horror for forgetfulness because she adds, "Surely you remember? Those girls the police found dead in Elmwash Woods."

"Yes, I remember," I say.

Chapter 7: Rick

"You look bloody awful. Why don't you bugger off home?"

I'm hardly through the door of the Church Hall we're using as an Incident Room before DCI Lane's trying to get rid of me.

"I'm fine, sir." That's a lie. I feel jumpy, like my wiring's snarled up and giving me small electric shocks. "Superintendent Roebuck told me to come out here."

Lane scowls at me, like a man deciding what to do with an unwanted present from someone he can't afford to offend. "Do you know what we've got here?"

"Missing child, sir. Superintendent Roebuck said you'd fill me in."

Lane nods towards the Incident Board with its photo of a small, plump, fair-haired girl. "Stacie Frewer, aged seven. Last reported sighting around eleven this morning."

He pauses. His gimlet eyes are boring straight through me and I'm sure he's got something else to say. It's not like him to bugger around, that's Roebuck's game. Lane goes straight to the point, it's one of the few good things about him. That and the fact he plays no favourites, he just hates everyone. He's a big man and the extra weight he carries makes him look older than he is. He's a good cop, I've got to give him that, but he's not a patch on Will Newton. Will was the best DCI I've ever known and a bloody good friend.

"Yes sir?" I prompt him to say what's on his mind.

"Come with me." Lane leads me outside the hall, out of earshot of all the listeners. "Whoever took Stacie left a bunch of flowers under her swing. So Superintendent Roebuck reckons the Elmwash killer's back."

It's burn out time. The world roars in on me. There's a thudding like a giant heartbeat in my brain. From an echoing distance I hear my voice yelling, "But he's dead! The fucking bastard's dead!"

I keep shouting until I run out of breath. I'm shaking and my mouth is dry. Slowly awareness trickles through my mind that I've blown the last shreds of my career.

Will Newton's voice echoes in my memory: *'One day, Rick, you're going to go too bloody far.'* I'd always got away with it with Will because he was on my side, but Will's been dead over three years now.

I realise Lane's still waiting. "Sorry sir," I say.

"Yeah. I didn't think you'd be thrilled about it. That's why I brought you out here. Don't need you supplying entertainment for that lot." He glares in the direction of the small windows in the hall door and I see a few watching cops duck out of sight. He turns back to me. "Now you got that out your system, you can bloody listen to me."

"Yes sir. I'm sorry."

"I don't need apologies. I need a DI that'll pull his weight. I know it ain't easy for you. You're the only senior cop left round here who worked on the Elmwash case."

He pauses, as if waiting for me to say something. I guess he just wants a routine, 'yes sir,' but there's something I need to know. "Sir, you weren't around here then, but you must have checked out the case. Do you think Clift was the Elmwash killer?"

I see him consider, weighing his words, and brace myself, expecting a thundering rebuke, but he says quietly, "The truth is, I don't know. He was a nasty bit of work. It made sense he'd be a suspect but there wasn't enough to charge him, much less get those wimps at the CPS to prosecute. The main evidence for him being the Elmwash killer was that the crimes stopped when he died." He pauses, then continues, "Until now."

I feel sick but I stick to what I know. "Clift was the Elmwash killer. It's over."

"I hope so. Please God little Stacie will turn up okay.

But if she doesn't and things pan out the way Superintendent Roebuck thinks, it's gonna get nasty. People will say the case was closed when the real killer's still out there."

"You said there were flowers left under the swing?"

"Yeah, along with a pink hair-ribbon and a kid's bracelet... little beads on an elastic thread. Stacie's father says the ribbon's hers but not the bracelet. He says he's never seen that before."

"That makes no sense." The Elmwash killer took jewellery from the kids he killed, but he sent it on to the newspapers to stir things up.

"None of it makes any bloody sense. The main thing that you've got to decide right now is if you've got any doubts that you can cope. If that's the case, tell me here and now and you can go home on sick leave. I'll square it with the Superintendent."

Whatever the outcome, I can't walk away. "I'm up to it, sir. I don't want to go on leave."

Chapter 8: Annie

"Arianne. At last." Mother offers me a cool, scented cheek. "No Richard?"

"He's not well."

"I see." Her tone makes it clear she's diagnosed the source of his indisposition. She turns to Maris, "My dear, you didn't walk, did you? You naughty girl. I hope you haven't tired yourself."

"I'm quite well, thank you, Mrs Carstairs. My car's in for servicing but Annie picked me up before it was raining." Maris squeezes my arm affectionately, then she hands Mother a small box of Co-op chocolate creams. "These are for you."

"Thank you, dear." Mother doesn't actually hold the plebeian box between finger and thumb but she looks as if she'd like to. "I must say Maris, you're looking very well. Quite blooming isn't she, Arianne?"

"Yes."

"And how's your dear mother, Maris?"

"Poor Mummy. When I visit her she always gets upset. I suppose it's because she misses me so much. So I don't like to go and see her very often."

"Never mind, dear. It's an excellent Care Home and she seems very comfortable. And at least your mother will see her grandchild before she dies. I've been waiting so long for Arianne to make me a grandmother that I've quite given up hope and, of course, she's much older than you."

"Not that much, only two years. Anyway you're already a grandmother three times over," I protest. My gaze travels to where Elaine, my sister, is standing by the buffet table, in obvious disagreement with her own teenage daughter.

Mother fixes me with the look that makes me think of blue ice. "But not through you, Arianne. You've become such a career woman. I knew how it would be when you insisted on marrying Richard. No-one could describe him as a steady family man. I pray you never regret it."

Dizziness engulfs me. The drawing room lights swirl in and out of focus. My mother's voice oozes past but the words don't make sense. A grip on my arm steers me across the room and a chair under my knees forces me to sit. A glass is thrust into my hand. I take an unwary gulp and choke as the brandy burns my throat.

"You're better now," says Maris.

"Yes." I achieve a sort of smile.

How could I have been stupid enough to think I could stay with Mother even for a night? I could never tell her what Rick had done to me.

"Annie my sweet, no Rick with you?" Neil looms over us, cutting off the room.

"No."

"Not a family-gathering sort of guy?" Neil gets a note of sympathy into his voice that doesn't match the malicious amusement in his smile.

"I wouldn't have put you down as the family-gathering sort either."

"I'll do a great deal for one of Sonia's lunches. All the best delicacies Waitrose can provide. Anyway, it's not my family that's gathered here."

It's easier to deal with Neil when he's not looking down on you literally as well as in every other way. I stand up and the brandy slops over my fingers.

"On the hard stuff, Annie? That's not like you."

Maris glares at him. "I gave it to Annie. She felt faint."

"That's not like you either, Annie. You're not doing a Maris on us are you?"

"What are you talking about?"

"You know what I mean, my love. If you're pregnant break it to me gently, because without you the Art Department would undoubtedly sink into chaos."

"I'd hardly be drinking brandy if I was pregnant." I spoil

the effect of my words by abandoning the glass.

Neil seems unabashed. "That's a relief, but you must have noticed there's a lot of it about. The whole College seems to be full of waddling women."

Maris lumbers to her feet and hurries off. I must admit 'waddle' is entirely appropriate. "You've embarrassed her."

Neil grins and sheds his affectation. "At least I've got rid of her. It's bad enough having to put up with her in the department without her cropping up at the weekends."

"I could say the same for you. I have to put up with your crap all week. I don't need to meet you at my mother's house."

"Bitch," he complains. "That's completely different. I'm one of your mother's favourite people. Even you must admit she prefers me to Rick or Philip."

I glance towards my brother-in-law, who's trying to restrain his boisterous sons and rebellious daughter. My sister has distanced herself from them and is talking to some of Mother's Bridge cronies.

"She prefers you because you're not married to either of her daughters."

"That's an interesting theory. Pity we can't try it out. Unless you're thinking of leaving Rick?" He tilts my chin upwards and I know he's sussed out the bruise.

I try to meet his ice-grey gaze and fail. Neil is tall and fair, ostentatiously good-looking and well aware of it. A lot of female students fancy him and it's rumoured he screws around the College, although nothing has been proved.

I move into the attack, "You're just nasty about Maris because she wouldn't pose naked for you to sculpt her."

He shrugs. "It was stupid of me to ask her. I should have known Maris wouldn't see beyond the personal. All I wanted was to sculpt that wonderful curved shape of the full womb. In the end, young Chloe sat for me. She was grateful for the fee."

"I thought you had some trouble there." Not that it's

my business; Chloe specialises in sculpture and she's Neil's protégé.

"Just a misunderstanding with her boyfriend. You know what these foreign boys are like."

"Josef's a good kid." Josef is one of my Fine Art students and very talented.

"It got sorted." He nods towards Maris who's standing with a group of elderly women. "Do me a favour, Annie, and talk her into starting Maternity Leave. It's doing my head in not being sure whether she's going to turn up each morning. Knowing her, she'll go into labour at the most inconvenient moment, probably halfway through the lecture by the Visiting Artist next week."

"That would be grotesquely appropriate."

He looks puzzled then laughs. "Considering who she claims the father is? True, but I can do without that sort of irony."

The last time a famous artist came to College had been nine months ago. Neil had worked like crazy to get it fixed, then he'd been felled by gastric flu. I'd had time to greet our guest before I'd gone down with the same nasty bug. It had been left to Maris to entertain him, which she'd done with remarkable success.

Neil shakes his head. "It's incredible to think of Maris dragging him back to Holy Cottage and ravishing him. It proves the age of miracles isn't past."

There had been a lot of ribald amusement about the cottage name. "It's nothing to do with religion, it's a corruption of 'holly' because holly bushes used to grow there."

"Corruption's about right," comments Neil.

"It hasn't done her career any good."

The distinguished guest had died a month later, at another University on his tour. He'd had a heart attack, following an interactive session with a Post-grad student.

"True," Neil agrees with gloomy satisfaction.

I don't protest he's being mean. We both know Maris is neither talented nor dedicated to her art. Neil is both of these and increasingly desperate for success.

"I wish I'd met the guy," continues Neil. "I mean how did he manage to do it?"

"Do what?"

"Screw Maris. I'd have sworn she didn't like men. The Virgin Maris, that's what everyone calls her."

"You're really sick."

And so am I, at least I think I might be at any moment. The room is stifling and, for the first time, I know how Rick feels when he's scared of being trapped.

I mutter, "See you," and head for the door.

My brother-in-law is the only person not socially engaged.

"Phil, could you tell Mother discreetly that I've gone. I don't want to disrupt her party but I'm not feeling well."

"Of course. Can I ask what's wrong? Sonia and Elaine will want to know."

"It's nothing, just a bug."

"Is that what Rick's got? I'll enjoy telling them that. They're sure he's got a hangover." He grins at me and I smile wanly back. He's a kind man and I've always liked him, even if he is a bit on the dull side.

"Tell Mother not to ring me tonight. I'll phone her soon." I grab my bag and leave.

As I drive through the village, it strikes me I don't know where I'm going. I pull into the lay-by near the park to think things through. I can't tell Mother or Elaine and I can't go home. I feel a moment of disorientation, near to panic. I remind myself that I'm an independent woman with cash and credit cards in my purse. I'll go to a hotel.

A niggling doubt slithers through my mind. I open my bag and peer inside. Then I rummage. I turn the contents out onto the passenger seat. No purse. I've left it on the kitchen worktop. Now I really don't know what to do.

39

I get out of my car and walk across the sodden grass. I reach the children's playground, sit on the roundabout and kick-start myself into motion. I try to imagine going home, slipping in and grabbing my purse. I can't do it. My logical mind tells me I've got to go back sometime, but not yet.

I've got to work out where I go from here. The thought of leaving my home hurts but I couldn't bear to live there alone. Anyway the house doesn't really matter. Losing Rick hurts more than giving up any place or possession.

I carry on pushing my foot against the ground, turning the roundabout round and round and round.

Chapter 9: Annie

'Too late.' The words of defeat whisper through my mind, haunting me, draining me of hope. In the Christian Church despair is a mortal sin and I have never been nearer despair than this. Not even when my dad died. The guilt returns. Could I have done something... anything... to prevent this happening?

After Clift's suicide Rick had to take sick leave and they insisted he saw a psychologist for trauma counselling. He and the psychologist were definitely not a match made in Heaven. He didn't like her and I'm pretty sure she didn't take to him. He told me once that she talked down to him the way my mother does. When he said that I realised how bitterly he resented me urging him to stick with the counselling.

In the end the psychologist said he could return to work. I'm not sure if Rick played her. He's clever although he isn't always wise. I suspect DCI Newton had a hand in it; he never had time for things like counselling and I think he pulled some strings to get Rick back to work. Not that I'll ever know now. Will Newton died a few months after Rick went back to work. He had a heart attack and was gone before the paramedics arrived. I know Rick was devastated by Will's death. He cared more for him than he does his own father. But he wouldn't talk about it or let me comfort him. He built a barricade around his emotions and I was locked outside.

I come back to the present. The rain has started again. In my haste to get away I'd left my jacket at Mother's house and now I'm chilled and drenched. I look round the park and, with a jolt of fear, I realise a gang of youths are lurking in the bushes. Rick has told me these village parks are often the haunts of teenagers dealing drugs.

I walk to the exit, trying to keep up a façade of nonchalance. Neil's Ferrari is parked behind my car and

Maris is sitting in his passenger seat. The window slides down and she says, "Annie, are you all right?"

"Yes."

"I told you she would be," says Neil. "What are you doing cavorting in the rain?"

"Finding out what it feels like to drown." I speak the truth and they accept it as illusion. One advantage of conceptual art is that you can do the strangest things and pass them off as research. "Why are you here, Neil?"

"I got lumber... your mother asked me to drop Maris home. When she spotted your car she insisted I pulled over. She was scared you were ill."

I smile at Maris. "Thanks but I'm okay."

"I was really worried, especially when those boys came past and gave us such funny looks."

"They probably thought you were plain-clothes police keeping watch on the drug dealers."

"How the other half lives," drawls Neil. "I suggest we move on before we get involved in a drugs bust. They might think Maris has got a half-ton of heroin hidden under that floral tent." He turns back to me, taking in the details of my closely defined boobs. "You, on the other hand, are definitely not concealing anything."

"Sleazy bastard," I respond amiably. It's no good letting Neil get to you.

Maris turns red and gets out of the car with more speed than grace. "Goodbye Neil. Annie can take me home."

"Suit yourselves. See you tomorrow." He drives away.

Maris takes my keys. "I'll drive, you're not up to it."

I dislike her bossy manner but I'm too tired to argue.

Holy Cottage is half a mile up a rough track. As we bounce and slither along I eye Maris' bulk and pray, *'Please God, today's been bad enough, don't make me have to deliver a baby too.'*

It's a shabby cottage and the garden is a swamp. Maris

sees me looking round and sighs. "It's so hard to cope."

"Why don't you sell and move nearer town?"

She stares at me blankly. "Why should I?"

"There'd be more to do and you'd be nearer your friends."

"I don't have any friends, apart from you. I like it here. Come in."

Inside, the cottage is old fashioned and dingy. It smells stuffy and damp.

"Straight up for a hot bath." Maris missed her vocation, she'd have made a formidable nanny in Victorian times.

I follow her up the narrow stairs and into the bathroom. She turns on an ancient geyser, which pops with alarming vigour as it bursts into life. A few moments later, hot water steams as it hits the discoloured enamel of the bath.

"I'll put the fire on in Mummy's room, then it will be nice and warm when you get out." She hands me a towel and leaves.

I'm terrified by the geyser but I manage to turn it off and add cold water until the bath is usable. I undress and climb in and try to relax, but I'm too tense. I've no idea where to go or what to do, tonight, or in the days and nights to come.

When Maris said, *'I don't have any friends,'* I'd felt a rush of protest and pity, but I'm no better off. I've got no one to turn to.

Maris' mummy's bedroom is full of dark, old-fashioned furniture. It smells of lavender air freshener, old person and incontinence. The towel is stiff and rough. I scour myself dry and see myself in the long mirror. The flush of the bath is fading and the bruises on my neck look very dark.

I hear a sound behind me. Maris is standing there watching me. I feel embarrassed.

"There's food downstairs." She leaves as quietly as she arrived.

I get clothes from my case and dress as quickly as I can.

Maris has lit a fire in the living room. I sit in one of the shabby armchairs, my eyes watering from the smoke.

"Is pizza and red wine okay for you, Annie?"

"It's brilliant." I'm surprised. I'd put Maris down as a tea and sandwiches person.

"I put prawns on it, I know you get the woman to put some on when you buy it at College for lunch."

My pleas for extra shellfish is a joke between me and the cafeteria staff.

"That's because I don't often eat fish at home. It makes Rick ill, so I only have it when he's out." Rick used to love fish but he'd become allergic to it after a vicious bout of food poisoning when we'd been on honeymoon in Greece.

"Now you'll be able to have fish any time you want." Maris sounds pleased for me.

"I guess." The portion I'm chewing feels claggy in my mouth.

Chapter 10: Annie

The rain lashes at the windows making them rattle. Maris gets up and draws the curtains. "This wretched rain. It's made the whole house damp. The cellar has got an inch of water in it."

I've been smelling that underlying dampness all along, but now it triggers buried memories. "When I came here before, it was to a party, wasn't it?"

"Yes. My eighth birthday party. I had a pink dress. Mummy made it specially."

It's as if a tap turns in my memory and a stream of images flows through. I recall this room; how dark and scary it had seemed, especially the glass cabinet with its hunting rifles. I'd wondered which of them had killed the moulting deer whose head was mounted on the wall. The guns are still here but now the deer is bald.

I remember joining in the party games, aware of being the oldest and trying not to push too hard or jump too high; Maris, clumsy and lumpy; Elaine, darting like a glistening dragonfly. Suddenly the other children are back in my mind. Twins, close to my age, but something had gone wrong when they were born and they were no bigger than four-year-olds. Maris' mummy kept trying to coax them to take their places in the games but they would not be chivvied. They stood in the corner, watching us with wary eyes. The boy had a wet patch on his trousers and the girl had got her finger up her nose.

"What happened to your brother and sister?"

"They died."

"I'm sorry." I'm ashamed of my callous forgetfulness.

She looks surprised, then smiles. "Don't be sad. It was a long time ago."

Her smile brings the other memory, the end of the party.

Mother returned, and Elaine ran out to spring into the car. I stopped to say 'thank you' to Maris' mummy and saw Maris standing in the doorway, sandy and stout in her pink frilly dress. She was fingering the silver locket we'd given her and there was desolation in her eyes.

I went back and hugged her. "Thank you, Maris, we've had a lovely time." And her plump face had lit up in a smile.

Maris' pressure on my arm pulls me back into the present. "It was nice when we were best friends at Junior School."

That's not the way I remember it. I see it as me walking the school playground with my mates and this short, fat shadow materialising with amazing speed and attaching itself to me with the tenacity of plastic glue.

"I always thought it was Fate we should be friends. As if we were meant to be together. Didn't you?"

The honest answer is, 'No,' but I compromise with, "It's a long time ago."

"I missed you when you went to Secondary School. I came round to see you every day but you were never there."

I don't answer. Mother and Elaine are good liars and they'd come through for me.

"Of course that was when your daddy died, so I expect you were a bit upset."

"A bit." Desolation sludges through me, as cold and cruel as on the day Dad had his heart attack and died. In looks I was Dad's girl, as Elaine is Mother's image. It was Dad who took me on vigorous country walks and taught me the rough-and-tumble sports. Mother took me to the ballet and to concerts. They'd both encouraged me to love art.

"It was because of you I decided to do art," says Maris. "I wanted to be with you."

I move free of the hand that's pawing at my arm and drain my glass. The wine hits my brain and sends it staggering. Maris leans forward to refill.

"I'd better not. I've got to drive."

"Where to?"

"I don't know! I meant to go to a hotel but I've left my purse and credit cards at home." To my dismay my voice wobbles into a pathetic wail.

"You can stay here."

I stare at her, instinctively rejecting the idea.

"At least for tonight. You can't go back to him."

The way the room's swaying I can't go anywhere.

She strokes my arm. "He hurt you, didn't he?"

I nod, struggling with another bout of tears.

"Tell me." She leans forward and puts her arms around me.

I sob out my story, cradled against the swell of her womb, and, under my bruised cheek, I feel her baby move.

Suddenly I'm appalled at what I've done. I shouldn't have told her. This is between Rick and me. "Maris, you mustn't tell anyone what I said."

"I'll always do what's best for you, Annie." She smiles but I don't feel reassured.

"Where's your TV?"

"I haven't got one. I've never seen the need. What did you want to watch?"

"I was hoping to catch the news."

I try to keep my manner casual but Maris must read my thoughts. "Surely you're not still worrying about your husband?" She spits the last two words.

"It's not that simple."

Maris scowls and stomps out to the kitchen.

She hasn't drawn the curtains across the small window at the corner of the room. I stagger to my feet and go to it. It's draughty and I shiver as I stare at the cold, wet night. I wonder if the child has been found. I hope she's tucked up safely in her bed, well scolded and warmly hugged.

Maris returns and stands next to me. "She's not been found. I expect she's dead."

"How do you know they haven't found her?"

"I listened to the news on my kitchen wireless."

If she'd told me that, I could have gone with her and heard the news first-hand. Rick must be part of the investigation. I know Elmwash will be burdening his mind but I wonder if he's thinking of me as well.

I turn back to the window and silently pray for the missing child, her family and for all those who are trying to find her.

I get out my phone to check for messages but the screen is blank. "I can't get any reception."

Maris shrugs. "Why would you want to?" she asks and refills my glass.

Chapter 11: Annie

I surface from sleep as deep as drowning and discover I'm lying naked in Maris' mummy's bed. Disgust banishes my drowsiness and I get up.

I've no real knowledge of how I got to bed, just a drifting memory of feeling giddy and sleepy, and Maris helping me upstairs. I said, "You must be careful... remember the baby," but my speech was as slurred as my footsteps.

I reclaim last night's towel to wrap round me as I head for the bathroom. I open the bedroom door and find Maris standing there and almost lose the towel in my fright.

"I've brought you a cup of tea."

"Thanks." I take it and put it on the dressing table.

"Drink it while it's hot." She stands in the doorway watching me. I consider pushing past her but you can't shove a pregnant woman with any force.

"I'll put some clothes on." I abandon washing and slide into my pants and trousers then fumble on my bra. Her stare makes me uncomfortable. "I was pretty out of it last night, I'm sorry I was a pest."

"You weren't. It's nice having you here." She speaks in an emotionless monotone. "You're very beautiful."

"Not me. It's Elaine who's beautiful, she takes after Mother." I pull on my jumper and feel more secure.

"No, you've always been more beautiful than them."

Socks and boots in place I'm armoured against her gaze. "Is there any news about the missing child?"

"They haven't found her." She sounds bored. I get the impression she considers my obsession as tedious and absurd.

Before work I drop Maris at the garage to pick up her car, then I fit in a quick trip home to collect my purse. I won't have my options limited to Holy Cottage again.

Rick's car's not in the drive and the security system's on. I grab my purse and run.

As I drive to work my mobile beeps and I pull over to check my messages. There's just one text: ANNIE, R U OK? PLEASE LET ME KNOW. RICK.

I hesitate then text back, I AM OK. R U?

It's a full teaching day and I'm glad of it. At mid-morning break, when I return to my office, I find Josef waiting.

"Annie, may I speak with you?"

"Come in and sit down." I wait until he has done so, then ask, "What's the problem?"

"The last assignment. I must ask you for an extension."

"I was thinking that." The assignment's overdue. Our degree courses are ratified by a nearby university and we have to keep the standard high.

"I am sorry, Annie, things are difficult." He passes a hand over his thin, sallow face and I think how tired he looks.

"What's wrong?"

"Chloe, she has had the baby. A little boy, Joseph, named after me but spelt the English way."

"Congratulations."

"Thank you. Unfortunately it is not easy. The baby, he cries a lot, and Chloe cries also. She is, I think, depressed."

No wonder Josef looks shattered. "What about you?"

He looks surprised. "Me? I am well, just tired. The baby does not sleep."

"Hasn't Chloe got family that can help?"

"No."

I don't pursue the subject. Josef has no family. From early infancy he was brought up in a Romanian orphanage. He's here on a four-year permit to study in Britain, with charitable funding to pay his fees.

"Have you still got your job at the supermarket, Josef?"

"There was some trouble. They do not want me to be there any more."

"Has Chloe spoken to Neil?"

"No."

"Why not? He's her tutor and he's got more clout than me."

"I do not like her talking to Neil about private things. I do not trust him. Annie, do you think they will send me away?"

It takes a moment for me to understand. "Back to your own country you mean? Of course not. Why should they?"

"Because I have done something wrong."

"Don't be silly, Josef. Getting a girl pregnant isn't against the law, not if she's over sixteen." Josef's in his late-twenties, eight years older than Chloe, but my guess is he's the innocent in that team.

"Many people do not like me."

"They're jealous because you're likely to get a First. Don't worry about the assignment. Take some paternity leave. Are you going back to Chloe now?"

"Yes. It will take two hours to get home. I do not like to be away from them. The place where we are living, it is not nice to have a baby there. There is a woman who is not normal. Chloe says she is a loony, so we have to watch the baby all the time."

"For God's sake, where are you living?"

He eyes me warily. "It is an old house where nobody wants to live. Soon they will pull it down and build flats."

"You're in a squat? How far away is it?"

"At Elmwash. It is a village about eight miles from here. It seems a long way when you are tired."

I suppress a shiver at the unexpected mention of Elmwash and say, "I bet it does. What's the bus service like?"

"I have no money for that. I will walk."

"If you wait an hour I'll give you a lift. You'll still be home earlier than walking."

Someone knocks on my door. I open it and find Maris, plate in hand. "You weren't in for break so I got you some salmon sandwiches. I got the canteen woman to make them especially for you." She makes it sound ludicrously intimate.

"Maris, thank you, but I must get on. I'm sure Josef would appreciate the food. He walked in from Elmwash this morning. He and Chloe have got a little boy."

She gives Josef a glance of sour malice. "Congratulations, I suppose, although I don't know how you'll cope. The poor child hasn't got much chance in life, has it?"

I steer her out of the door. "Goodbye, Maris."

She slams off down the corridor. Her walk is as near a stalk as a heavy-based, wobbly toy can reasonably achieve.

I turn to grin at Josef.

He doesn't return my smile. "You see, people do not like me."

"No," I say, "That one's down to me."

Chapter 12: Rick

I spend the morning in Saronholt's village school. It's a Victorian building, small and poky, with high windows that make you feel like the walls are closing in. I'm stuck with the job of questioning bewildered little kids and tearful teachers. If that isn't grief enough, Roebuck's landed me with his top snitch, Louisa Kelly, and I can't say a word against her or I'll get done for racism and sexism, when the truth is I don't like the two-faced bitch.

I feel really rough. It's my own fault. I didn't finish working until after midnight, then I went with Bob to the Station House for the night and we drank too much again.

Stacie's teacher's a middle-aged woman who holds a wad of tissues to dab at her eyes and lips. She's told us Stacie's a quiet child, not top of the class or near it, but willing and well behaved. The Frewers moved to Saronholt when Stacie was a baby and Mr Frewer is a school governor.

"What about Mrs Frewer?" I ask.

"She doesn't mix much. I suppose you'd call her shy. But she always dresses Stacie beautifully." The teacher indicates the display labelled *'Our Autumn Fair.'*

I drag myself out of my chair and take a closer look. I spot Stacie's plump little figure in the first few photographs; she looks anxious and she's wearing a pink dress. "Why isn't Stacie in the later pictures?"

The teacher's lips compress into a thin line. "Her mother took her home."

"Why was that?"

"She had a little accident and had to go home to change."

"You mean she wet herself?"

The teacher looks offended. "Yes."

"How did her parents take that?"

"Her mother didn't say much but Terence... Mr Frewer

was wonderful. He's so patient with Stacie. Tell me, how's he... they...how are they?"

"They're still hoping for the best," says Kelly.

"They must be devastated." This time the 'he' is out of her speech if not her mind. "Everyone says Stacie's been taken like those girls in Elmwash Woods." She presses the tissues against her lips and starts to sob.

"Please don't upset yourself," says Kelly and I think how weird it is that her voice is comforting while her face is an ebony mask of contempt. She turns her gaze on me and her expression doesn't change.

I mutter, "Excuse me," and leave.

I walk across the playground, steering clear of the newsboys. My mobile's in my pocket and I finger it, longing to ring through to Annie, just to hear her voice. I got her text this morning but I didn't answer about how I was doing. Now I get the phone out and tap in the reply, 'NOT GREAT.'

I note the silence when I walk into the Incident Room. Not many people meet my eyes. I guess they reckon looking might be catching and I'm the local leper. Everyone thinks we're at the start of another spate of murders. They believe we got it wrong about Elmwash and stopped looking while the bastard's still out there.

Bob hurries across to me. "You okay, Rick?"

"Yeah."

He nods to where Roebuck's standing. "The Superintendent wants to see you."

I go across the room and Roebuck greets me with, "Rick. How are you?"

What's with everybody constantly checking on my health? "I'm fine."

"Anything helpful at the school?"

"No sir."

"It's time we considered the worse-case scenario. Stacie is probably dead and my predecessor made a mistake in winding down the Elmwash investigation."

"It was no mistake. Clift was the Elmwash murderer."

Roebuck's face gets even thinner as all the lines turn down. "I understand you're convinced of that but there was no forensic evidence to tie him to the hut."

I can't argue about that, and I know SOCO went over the whole hut inch by inch.

"And we have to consider the evidence of the flowers," continues Roebuck.

Now that's different. The Incident Room Board has been updated and I've already checked out about the flowers but I decide to play dumb and let the Superintendent tell me for himself. "These flowers... you reckon they were left in place of the kid, like the ones at Elmwash were?"

"Yes, exactly the same. These were left in the garden under Stacie's swing."

"What flowers were they? Where did they come from?"

"Poppies... silk ones. They came from the War Memorial just opposite Stacie's house."

"You mean some bastard went and nicked them from the middle of the village in broad daylight before he grabbed Stacie?" I don't bother to cover my incredulity. If the Elmwash killer had taken that sort of chance we'd have probably had him when the first Elmwash girl disappeared, certainly he'd have taken no more than two.

It's clear Roebuck resents my disbelief. He scowls and answers stiffly, "The strong winds recently blew a lot of the poppies around the village green. Stacie's father said that several had blown into his front garden and his wife had picked them up and put them in a pile in the back garden."

I shake my head. "The Elmwash killer always bought flowers, expensive ones. He'd have felt using second-hand ones didn't show the kids enough respect."

I'm deep in my thoughts and don't plan my words. I hear some of the cops mutter, "Get real." I suppose it does sound weird, talking about respect after what he did to those girls, but there's no way I can explain the knowledge I gained of Ernest Clift.

Roebuck says curtly, "As you claim to be the expert, it's time you had another look at Elmwash Woods."

"Elmwash?"

"Is there a problem? If you can't handle it...?"

"No problem sir." My headache notches up a few degrees, like someone's tightening a steel band around my head.

"Take Constable Kelly and have a look around."

We're at Kelly's car when Bob catches up with us. "I had a word with Roebuck and he says I can come along to lend a hand."

"Cheers Bob."

"Anyway you forgot the keys to turn off the alarm."

"Oh yeah. Thanks mate." After they cleared the contents of the hut, they surrounded it with wire fencing and put in an alarm system to keep out the scum who thought a bit of the hut would make a nice souvenir.

"They should flatten the place," says Bob.

"That's not going to happen."

"Yeah, I know. Roebuck reckons they'll discover new evidence that'll lead to an arrest."

I scowl at him. "Not unless they plan to go into hell and arrest Ernest Clift."

Chapter 13: Annie

Elmwash House won't need pulling down for redevelopment, a few more weeks of rain and it will wash away. Once it was an impressive country house with elegant grounds but now the only evidence of past glory is the slime-grey sheet of water that was the ornamental lake. Elmwash Woods is part of this estate.

I pull up outside the house and Josef says, "Please, you will come in? Chloe will like to see you."

"I don't want to disturb her." Chloe's never been keen on me.

"She will want to thank you." He indicates the four carrier bags of shopping I stopped to get en route.

Inside the house it stinks of decay and water is running down the walls. Josef leads me along the dim corridors. As we approach the end room I hear Chloe screech, "Get out of here, you loony bitch."

A door opens and a woman sidles past me. She has a ravaged face and her wild hair is streaked with grey.

Chloe is sitting on a mattress in the middle of the room, breastfeeding her baby.

"Hello, Chloe. Congratulations."

"You reckon?" Her spiky hair is greasy and her face looks small and white.

"You've got a beautiful baby."

"And he's got a beautiful nursery hasn't he?"

It's obvious they've done their best. The room has been draped with throws and blankets, but nothing can overcome the chill wetness.

"I've bought you some things. I hope you don't mind."

"Beggars can't be choosers, can they?"

"Chloe, that is not nice," Josef protests.

"Oh sorry, am I spoiling your creeping?"

"Annie is being kind."

"Brown-nose boy."

As I turn to leave, Chloe's bitching voice carries on, "Josef, sod off. Leave me alone. I don't need you. I don't need anyone." Her face crumples and she starts to cry.

Josef sits beside her and puts his arms around her and the baby. He's crying too.

I'm overwhelmed by pity but I say, "It's a good job I bought a box of tissues." I crouch down beside them and offer a handful of tissues to each. After a few minutes snivelling, order is restored.

Chloe says, "Sorry I was rude but it's not what you want for your kid, is it?"

"No, it's not."

"But that's no reason I should take it out on you."

"That's okay. Please accept the stuff I've bought. It's nothing much."

Two of the carriers hold very basic food and Josef points towards the camp stove. "I can cook."

Chloe manages an almost cheerful smile, "He's really good, even on that thing."

"Definitely a keeper," I say. "I've got some bits for the baby."

I lay out a selection of baby clothes and disposable nappies.

"That's great, thanks." She fingers them with obvious pleasure while Josef looks at her tenderly

The last bag holds a box of chocolates. "Don't eat them all at once," I warn her.

"I know, otherwise it'll go through my milk and give baby Joe gutache. I got a book out the library. I want to do this baby thing right."

"The Student Welfare Officer should be able to help."

"No! No social workers. They'd take one look at this place and put Joey in Care."

"But what about the Health Visitor, doesn't she check on you?"

"It's easy enough to blag them. They're not fussed about coming out, as long as you take the baby to them regular and don't argue with what they say. The student health service don't give a shit, they're more into counselling abortions than having kids. Please Annie, don't interfere. You can't trust any of them: Social Workers, the Pigs, the Immigration gits, they're all bastards."

"As long as you promise to tell me if you can't cope."

"I promise. Do you want to hold the baby?"

Baby Joseph cuddles against my neck. I rub my cheek against his fluffy hair and kiss him. He's adorable and I feel my heart tighten with desperate tenderness.

I've got to give him back now, before it hurts too much to let him go. I pass him over. "May I come and visit you again?"

"Yeah, I'd like that," and then, as if surprised, "I really would."

As I drive back past Elmwash Woods I see a number of cars parked in a lay-by and several people with cameras and recording equipment milling round as if they're waiting for something... has the missing child been found here in the woods? I feel a cold claw of fear rake through me. I suppress my shudder and accelerate past.

I'm late back to College. I rush into my office and find Maris sitting there.

"I've been waiting for you."

"I've got a seminar." I grab my notes and head back towards the door.

"You're angry with me."

"Yes."

"Why?"

I find it hard to believe she doesn't know. "You were unkind to Josef."

"He shouldn't be in our country and they shouldn't have

had that child. It was irresponsible."

I don't bother to argue the immigration issue, there's no point; there's no argument that can part Maris from her prejudices, she's the most intolerant, self-righteous person I've ever known. However, I can't let her dismissal of baby Joseph pass without protest. "But the baby's here now and they're doing their best, and he's a little darling," I think of the screwed up face, the button nose, and the dark slanting eyes. "He's adorable."

"Most babies are, if you like that sort of thing."

Whatever else little Joseph lacks, he's got parents who love him. It horrifies me to think what sort of life Maris' baby is doomed to lead. I wonder if I ought to talk to someone and warn them of my concerns

She hauls herself to her feet. "I'm going home now."

"Are you okay?" I ask, in duty bound.

"I'm tired. Are you coming home with me tonight?"

"No thank you." I don't know what I'm going to do but I'm not going back to Holy Cottage.

She rummages in her bag, brings out a small, plastic bottle and presses it into my hand. "I brought these with me. I thought they might be useful if you decided to go back to your house."

"What are they?"

"Sleeping pills. Use as many as you need." She leaves.

That's crazy! Does she think I'm going to lie in a drugged sleep when Rick could come after me again? I consider throwing the pill bottle in my waste bin but that would be irresponsible, so I shove it into my bag to dispose of later.

Chapter 14: **Rick**

When we arrive at Elmwash Woods we find the Press have got there ahead of us. They start flashing cameras and shouting questions the second we get out the car. I push past them and go into the woods. Kelly can make a politically correct statement or Bob can deck the bastards, I don't give a shit. Out of sight, deep inside the shelter of the trees, I get my bottle out of my pocket and gulp it down.

I remember Will Newton telling me, when I first joined CID, that flat half-bottles were best for keeping hidden in a coat pocket. At the time that shocked me. I still know it's wrong but at least it gets me walking through those woods.

I walk, head down, hands deep in pockets, holding onto the bottle. The trees are bare and the wood is very quiet. I stumble on the rutted path. Kelly's grip on my arm stops me from going down. "You okay, Guv?"

"Yeah, thanks."

"What's the matter, Kelly? Getting nervous?" says Bob. "If you want someone to hold your hand it'd best be me. The DI's married and his wife's the possessive type."

Kelly removes her support from my arm.

Bob carries on trying to needle her. "It's a creepy place this, ain't it, Kelly? Don't suppose you've done much stuff like this before? Being fast-track you spend more time in networking than detective work."

I should intervene and tell him to shut his lairy mouth but it's all I can do to hold myself together and we haven't even reached the bloody hut. If Kelly decks him, he'll deserve it, and I'll swear it was an unfortunate accident.

Of course she doesn't hit him, she's way too smart for that, but she gives him an arsey look, like she'll remember him when she's Assistant Chief Constable and he's pulling sergeant's long-service pay.

"Here we are. Elmwash Mausoleum. Nice ain't it?" I realise that Bob's as scared as I am about being here again.

The shed that was so well concealed stands out clearly now. Deep inside the defensive wire there's a bunch of white roses lying propped against the hut door.

In my head I hear the whispered words, *'I've got friends, good friends, who will carry on for me.'*

The crack of a branch warns me that somebody's lurking in the shelter of the trees.

Chapter 15: Annie

Life must go on even when the bits that matter have fallen apart. Late that afternoon I go in search of Neil. A London gallery is about to show a joint exhibition of our work. My stuff's up there, ready to hang, but I suspect Neil's been busy and hasn't even packed his sculpture yet.

He's over-running on his lecture. I slip into the hall and listen, although I've heard most of it before.

"So you see, as artists, you must use the visual expressions of suffering, other people's and your own. A good artist needs to develop psychological insight. Gillian Wentworth, the artist who's visiting us tomorrow has done some powerful studies of soldiers suffering from Post Traumatic Stress. I advise you to study them. Here's an example of body language I recorded this afternoon." He activates the screen. "It's a news broadcast about the child that went missing yesterday. Look at the mother, head down, arms folded, not meeting anyone's eyes. And the father, so tense, and that forced smile. Contrast them with the police, the professionals, concerned but detached."

He smiles at me. "You ought to ask Annie about that, her husband's a cop. He investigated the last big local murder case. The Press called it the Elmwash Mausoleum Case. There was a programme about it last month, very interesting study in ritual abuse. So Annie, is your husband on this new enquiry?"

I don't answer. I'm focused on the recording. *"This afternoon police sent officers to Elmwash woods."*

"Earth calling Annie, is Rick working on this one?"

"Yes." My eyes are on the screen, where Rick is walking into the woods, followed by a young black woman and a man I think is Bob. Rick keeps his face turned away from the reporters' shouted questions and flashing cameras, but

I know the way Rick moves and I recognise the tilt of his dark head and, even from that fleeting glimpse, I know he's hurting.

"You reckon that's Rick? At that distance it could be just about anyone. Thanks folks, you'd better be moving, we've over-run."

"The room empties and Neil looks hopefully at me. "How about you take my Adult Ed. class tonight? It's not as if there's going to be anyone waiting for you at home."

"What do you mean?" I feel colour flare in my cheeks.

He looks surprised. "Rick's liable to be out late looking for this missing kid."

"Is there any news about her?"

"I'm afraid not, but on a later news flash they said something about there being an incident in Elmwash Woods."

"Incident? What sort of incident?"

"I've no idea. The cop in charge was being pretty cagey. You will take my class for me, won't you? I've still got a lot to do for my half of our exhibition."

"I'm sorry, I can't."

Neil sighs. "More fool me for mentioning Elmwash Woods. See you tomorrow."

The car park is well lit but there are small islands of darkness where the amber glow of the lamps doesn't reach. My car's in the shadows. I click the remote and jump straight in, spilling books onto the front passenger seat. I lock the doors, the way Rick always warns me to do.

I know where I'm going. It was sorted the moment I saw that television image of Rick in Elmwash Wood. I'm heading home, even though I'm desperately afraid.

Rick's car's still not there and the house is in darkness. As I go round, closing curtains and turning on the lights I discover a scene of Rick-created desolation. Shedding bag, jacket and high-heeled boots, I go through the rooms like a housewifely hurricane, as if I'm purging the house of its collaborative guilt.

When I come back to comparative sanity I realise I'm shattered and starving. I shove a homemade frozen meal into the microwave and set a tray to eat in front of the television. While I eat I watch the News.

Most of the stuff about Stacie has been said before, and there are no real developments, except for whatever happened in Elmwash Woods. Rick's boss, Detective Superintendent Roebuck, comes on screen for the briefest of interviews, confirming that there was an incident near the vicinity of the hut. Police officers had questioned a man but nobody has been arrested. He says absolutely nothing. In my frustration, I think how like a weasel he looks, thin-faced and cold-eyed. I open the drinks cabinet to pour myself a glass of wine and notice the whisky bottle is empty.

I don't drink spirits, so the whisky consumption is down to Rick. He's always liked a drink, most policemen do, but that was beer with the boys after his shift and never more than a pint if he was driving. Only in the last few years has he drunk whisky in any quantity. I start shaking. How could my husband have turned into an alcoholic without me noticing?

Chapter 16: Annie

I sit in the living room, wondering what to do. I've sorted my bedroom and made sure I've got a cupboard positioned handy to block the door. But I can't go to bed before Rick comes home. I can't lie up there waiting to hear the car draw up; waiting to hear him moving round the house. I've got to stay up, fully dressed, my mobile ready in my pocket until he gets in.

The problem is I have no idea when he's due back or if he'll come at all.

The sound of a car lurching to a halt produces a conflict of feelings: relief that waiting is over, and gut-clenching fear. I stand up and move to the hall to meet him. I hear him struggle to get his key into the lock. My fear intensifies. What if he's drunk again?

When he gets in he's stumbling and I'm not sure if he's drunk or very tired.

"Hi," he says.

"Hi. Have you eaten?" My voice comes out calmer than I feel.

"I'm not hungry but I could do with a cup of tea."

"Go and sit down. I'll make it."

I dunk a teabag into a large mug and when it's brewed I add milk and sugar and take it into the living room. I put it on the coffee table and step back.

"Thanks." He fumbles to pick up the mug and the hot liquid slops over his fingers. "Shit!"

I wince. How easily could he turn on me again?

"I'm sorry… I didn't mean… Annie, could you get me something for my head? It's bloody killing me."

"You shouldn't take painkillers when you've been drinking." I know it's unwise to argue with him but the words slip out.

"I haven't been drinking, I swear. Not since I threw up in those bloody woods."

That gets through my defences. "I saw you on the News. Was it very bad, going back there?"

"Yeah."

"I'll get you some paracetamol." I fetch two pills and a glass of water. "That's all you should have. It's not safe to take more." I head towards the door.

"Annie, don't go, please."

I pause. If he wants to talk things through I can't throw away the chance. I sit opposite him, the coffee table between us. "Do you want to talk about it?"

"Yeah, please." He pauses, as if marshalling his thoughts. "Right from the start, it was creepy in those woods. Like there was someone lurking, watching us. I think Bob and Kelly felt it too."

I stare at him. I'd expected him to talk about what he'd done on Sunday night. Does he still not remember? Or does he think this case is more important?

"Who's Kelly?" I ask.

"Louisa Kelly, she's a detective constable. She's Roebuck's favourite snitch."

There was a time when we told each other all about our work and colleagues but that's long past. "Is it the same? The hut and everything?"

"They've covered it in alarms and wire to keep off sightseers."

"I'm surprised they didn't pull it down, like the West's house."

"Cromwell Road was a special case. It needed all sorts of permits to get it flattened and only after the trial was over. The Elmwash hut's not as high profile and there was no trial, so officially it's still a crime scene. Of course all the contents are in storage." He sounds more confident talking about stuff he knows.

"What happened today?" I ask.

He shudders. "Outside the hut there were these flowers, right inside the wire, white ones, some sort of roses. That freaked me out. For a moment I thought…"

He doesn't need to continue. I know he'd thought Ernest Clift had returned to put garlands on his mausoleum again.

"I thought… I heard…" He's shaking.

"It's okay, Rick, it's over. Where did the flowers come from? Was it a tribute to the girls?"

He shudders and I add hastily, "I mean from their parents or somebody like that."

He nods.

"What happened then? The TV report said something about a minor incident."

"It could easily have been a major incident. Someone was standing in the undergrowth and Bob went all macho and jumped him."

"Brilliant." It's the kind of thing I've come to expect of Bob.

"Bob had him down on the ground and they were rolling over, thumping each other. I tried to get them apart and one of them clobbered me in the guts." He gives an unconvincing grin. "That's when the booze and I parted company."

I put my hand out, then think better of it and draw back again.

"Kelly got them sorted. She's bloody tough that girl. The guy was Emma Brown's dad, the second girl to go. I didn't recognise him. He's aged twenty years. He comes to that bloody hut with flowers every day. He's even got this special hook and line to put the flowers through the wire. He said sometimes you get yobs up there. That's why, when he heard us coming, he stepped off the path to keep clear."

"Poor man."

"Yeah. I spent a couple of hours with him. For some reason the poor bastard wanted to talk to me. He's lost everything… it's broken his marriage… he's lost his job… he's on alcohol rehab… the lot…"

We sit in silence. I feel trapped in the space between us, afraid that anything I say will provoke him. At last I force myself into movement. I stand up, murmur, "Goodnight," and hurry upstairs. Once in my bedroom I barricade my door.

Chapter 17: Annie

"You're late," snarls Neil as I walk past his open office door.

Ostentatiously I consult my watch. "No I'm not."

"Well you're not early."

I spoil the fight by giggling. Neil's a master at any game that involves moving the goal post faster than the ball. "You having a good day?" I enquire.

"Bloody marvellous." He smiles at me, that rueful, mischievous grin that even now reminds me why I fell for him when I was a First Year student and he was a part-time tutor working for his PhD. As he turns his head he winces.

I go in and perch on the edge of his heavily laden desk. "What's wrong?"

"I did my neck in packing crates for the exhibition. And I still haven't got them done."

"Have you seen your doctor?"

"I'll make an appointment for later on today, if I can fit it in."

"Why shouldn't you?"

He lists off reasons on his fingers, like he's talking to a backward child, "Because we've got a visiting artist. I've been angling for Gillian Wentworth to come here for too long to bugger it up now. Because Wesley Arnold's decided to sacrifice a turkey in Studio One and MacIntyre from Health and Safety is threatening to close us down. Because Maris isn't in, so I've got to sort her classes as well."

"Why isn't Maris in?"

"Sara said she'd phoned the office to say she'd had the baby yesterday."

"Oh God, I should have checked on her. She said she was feeling tired. Is she all right? And the baby? Do you know what hospital she's in?"

"No idea."

"You selfish bastard!"

He looks cynical. " Methinks the lady is protesting a bit too much. Let's be honest, Maris isn't the sort of person anyone really cares about."

It takes no time to track down the quote but longer to acknowledge the truth of Neil's words. "It's so sad that no-one cares about her."

"Yes, but that's what she is, sad." Then, in an obvious attempt at reconciliation, "I think Sara said she'd had a boy."

"I'll check her out later. Did you know that Chloe and Josef have got a baby boy?"

"Yes, I heard."

"They're really struggling. As their personal tutors we should support them."

"Talk to Student Welfare, it's nothing to do with me. The last time I tried to help, Josef gave me aggro and I haven't got the time or patience to deal with more. I've got to sort out some sort of replacement for Maris."

"I'll see if Lucy George will come back and take over Graphics for a while."

"Old Lucy? But she was about a hundred when she retired!"

"Sixty-four actually and she didn't really want to go."

"She won't want to come back either, not to help me out."

"There's no harm in trying."

"Don't forget the Health and Safety guy's prowling round. I wish you'd control your bloody geniuses."

This time I have no grounds for offence. "Wesley's not a genius, he's an annoying little prat with a fixation about raw meat. I'll sort him."

In the Department office, Sara, the secretary, tells me the little she knows about Maris. "She phoned this morning and said she'd had a little boy. She didn't say where she was but I phoned the hospital to ask what ward so I could send some flowers from the department and they said they hadn't got her there. Must be some private place, I guess."

"I suppose there's nothing more we can do." I must apologise to Neil, it's clear that the lack of information isn't down to him not bothering.

"Not unless you fancy putting your sexy detective husband onto it." She giggles. "He can interrogate me any time he wants."

I turn my back on her and punch in Lucy's number. "Lucy? Hi, it's Annie Evans. Is there any chance of you doing some supply work for us? Maris had her baby last night and we need someone with your expertise to stand in for her."

A belligerent snort echoes down the line. "Bit late to be phoning for a replacement now. That useless twerp should have arranged maternity cover for her from seven months."

"It's not Neil's fault. Maris insisted on staying on."

Another noise of derision. "I dare say, dozy little creep. Is Joan Hammond still second-in-command in Graphics?"

"Yes, but I don't think she's up to organising things." Joan Hammond is incapable of organising cake making in a WI baking class.

"No, but I can work with her."

"Then you'll do it?"

"I didn't say that. I haven't got any wish to oblige Neil Walder."

I try to recover the position. "Didn't I explain? Neil's hurt his neck and I'm pretty sure the doctor will tell him to take sick leave."

"Hmm. So you're in charge and I'd be dealing with you?"

"Probably." I cross my fingers. Neil doesn't go off sick unless he's three-quarters dead.

"I'll think about it. How's your gorgeous husband?"

"A bit stressed. He's on the hunt for the missing child."

There's a brief silence while Lucy thinks this through. Her relationships with her ex-colleagues range through contemptuous loathing to irritable tolerance, but she has met Rick at staff parties and exhibitions and has formed a passion for him that I can only hope is motherly.

"It won't help Rick if you're run off your feet. He'll need your support, especially if the kiddie turns up dead. All right, I'll do it, but make sure that twerp doesn't think I'm doing it for him."

"Neil's not such a twerp that he'd think that."

This time a snort of laughter reaches me. "I've got arrangements to make but I'll be in tomorrow."

"Brilliant." I put the phone down and inform Sara, "Lucy George will be back for a few weeks."

"Oh joy." She puts down her novel and starts work.

Chapter 18: Annie

The dead turkey's a dead goose but otherwise Neil's got it right. I stand in Studio One and stare at the rotting bird nailed to a rough wooden cross. I wonder how long it's been on the premises. Wesley must have deliberately kept it out of my sight. So why did the idiot boy have to choose the day we had a visiting artist to display it?

I go to the store cupboard and grab a large bucket. "Put it in there and get it out of here." I thrust the bucket at Wesley.

"Fuck off!" He throws the bucket away and it clatters across the studio. He looks very menacing as he steps towards me. He's covered in tattoos and piercings, and dressed in biker's leathers.

I've played this wrong. There are other students watching. I should have dealt with the matter privately. It's crazy to send away my witnesses but I say crisply, "You lot take a break."

Reluctantly they drift towards the door.

When we're alone, I repeat, "I'm sorry, Wesley, but it's got to go. The Health and Safety Officer is looking to close us down."

"Fucking wanker."

"Move it, Wesley."

"You fucking bitch."

That level of abuse to a member of staff could get him excluded, but I don't want that. Wesley's been let down enough in his young life.

He's standing too close, fists clenched. I hear again the words, *'This will sort you, you fucking frigid bitch.'*

"Back off, Wesley. You can't win this one." Amazingly my voice sounds calm. "Either you take that disgusting bird out of here or I do, but if you come one inch closer to me I'll have you permanently excluded."

He stares at me, then takes a reluctant step back.

"Okay Wes, let's both calm down and talk this through."

"I've not finished working with it yet and a new one won't look the same." My gentler tone has worked and he sounds more pleading than aggressive.

"How about you take it into the grounds? But make it somewhere discreet, not the front lawn or the playing fields. You can set up there but I'd advise you to finish it soon, it's beginning to decompose."

"That's the idea."

I shudder. "And use the bucket. If you drip blood around the College it'll be us who're nailed up."

He stares out of the window. "It's pissing down."

"You can borrow this." I salvage an old golf umbrella from the still-life pile.

He stares at me, sullen and miserable.

"Go on, Wes. All the best crucifixions take place out of doors." Which, I have good reason to know, simply isn't true.

"So what about yourself?" Gillian Wentworth smiles at me as I pour tea and pass her the cream cakes.

"Me?"

"Yes, you. All day you've shown me your students' work and hardly mentioned your own. If I hadn't seen your exhibitions, I'd know nothing about your art."

"But you're here to look at the students' work not mine."

"Maybe, but most places I go the tutors ask for crits. You're a well-behaved lot here. All the part-time lecturers waited until I'd finished with the students and you didn't ask at all." There's a note of reproof in her voice and I wonder if she thinks I'm too arrogant to ask her opinion.

"I'd love a crit from you."

Of all the visiting artists we've had she's the most inspirational. She's middle-aged with straight grey hair, and her stocky, square-set frame is dressed in trousers and sweatshirt. Her talk had been succinct, but her enthusiasm glowed through every word. Her tour around the studio and her crits of Second and Third Year Work had been tough but positive and the whole College is buzzing with creative energy.

"I've got time now," she offers.

"I don't keep much work in College. I've got a studio at home."

"Lucky woman. I'm surprised Neil didn't tell you to bring work in for the day. Even in his agony he managed to show me his latest work while you were off collecting his model and her partner and baby."

"Neil did tell me a few days ago, but I forgot." I realise how rude this sounds and say hastily, "I'm glad I got Chloe and Josef in to hear your crits."

It was worth the journey to see how they brightened up when they got back to work and to their friends. I'd noticed Chloe looking for Neil and explained he'd got a doctor's appointment. Seeing her disappointment, I'd over-emphasised the severity of his neck trouble, which was cowardice rather than kindness on my part.

"I'd have been interested to hear your crit of Neil's piece."

Gillian grins. "He was surprisingly nervous about showing it to me but I told him it was excellent. It reminds me of his best work, that sculpture of the pregnant woman he did several years ago, but I don't think this work is so emotionally profound."

I don't want to follow this through but it will look odd if I don't.

"Yes?" Oh God! That tight, disinterested word must have blown my cover wide open. What's worse, like a novice painter, I can't let bad alone. "His present sculpture is very powerful."

"Yes, but not as strong as the Death Camp sculpture. Except of course she isn't going to the Gas Chamber she's walking to the operating theatre to have an abortion."

I feel the blood draining from my face. I look at Gillian and see realisation dawn.

Chapter 19: Rick

I didn't bring a bottle with me today. That's down to Graham Brown, little Emma's dad. When we were talking he warned me not to wreck my life the way he'd done.

I thought it was too late for that but I said, "Don't worry about me."

"It's going to be hard for you if it all starts up again."

I thought it would be even harder for him and his estranged wife and the families of the other Elmwash kids. "The man who killed Emma is dead. It's over, Graham."

"I hope you're right. For your sake as well as ours. I saw the way they slanted it on the News last night. If they get half a chance they'll bloody crucify you."

I don't know whether to be relieved or pissed off when Lane puts me onto directing search operations in the field. He says they need someone senior to make sure the search teams check out the animal sanctuary inch by inch. Thermal imaging is useless with all those animals giving off body heat.

We spend hours turning over the bloody place by hand. We go through every building slowly and methodically. Even when we've finished I don't feel comfortable. A place like that has so many nooks and crannies it's impossible to be sure we've covered everywhere.

I don't meet the owner or her helper, who lives in a caravan next to her bungalow. They'd been interviewed before I got there and decide to stay indoors. I think that's odd. The owner was co-operative enough. She'd allowed us access to all the outbuildings, but I'd expected her to be out there to check we didn't scare her precious pets. Although, to be honest, I'm not sure which way round the scaring goes. I have to get really heavy with the uniformed guys before they'll search the stables, donkey field and pigsties.

I try to keep focused but I can't help thinking of Annie. I hate her being frightened of me. Last night there were a couple of times when I thought we were getting closer. I should have told her how sorry I am about what I did to her but I was afraid she'd tell me we're finished. I make up my mind, tonight I'll try to get home early and sober and talk to her and beg her to give me another chance. But if she says she wants us to split up, I won't argue. I'll move out straight away.

Chapter 20: Annie

Gillian looks at me anxiously. "I'm sorry. I didn't mean to upset you."

"It's okay. It was a long time ago."

"I wonder, would you like me to call round tonight and see your studio? I could give you a real crit then."

"I'd love that." It's the greatest honour she could offer me. Then I think of Rick and imagine him coming in, drunk and abusive. "But it's rather awkward... my husband..." I stammer to a halt and try again, "My husband's a policeman. He's working on a missing child case and when he comes in he..."

"Wants you to himself? That's understandable."

"It's not that exactly..." This is far too personal to explain.

Gillian rescues me. "Why don't you bring samples of your work to my hotel? We can have dinner together."

"I'd love to. I don't know why you're being so kind to me."

"I like to back my fancy." She glances out of the window, "I'm glad your college doesn't go in for landscape sculpture. It's still pouring down out there."

I remember Wesley.

"Oh God, I forgot! There's still one Second Year left for you to crit."

I run Wesley to earth, summon Gillian, formidable in her fisherman's yellow waterproof, introduce her and stand back to watch the crit. I learn a lot, and not just about the art of depicting crucified and rotting birds. Beneath her warm interest I see Wesley slough off his ill-mannered bravado, once I even hear him laugh.

"Interesting work," she says at last. "But, if you'll take my advice, you'll move away from these images of misery and despair. Take that foreign lad, Josef, strangely enough his work has a quality of joy that sets him apart from the rest."

"Always fucking Josef," mutters Wes.

Gillian doesn't comment but I can see that she's picked up on this as fast as I have. "We're talking about you, not Josef. You've got an original mind but you've got to discipline it and not hide behind these dreary clichés. Don't be afraid to admit to yourself if you've made a mistake." She winks at him. "No need to admit it to the other buggers though. I'll be off now. Annie, I'll see you later."

She squelches away through the mud.

I survey my leather-clad black sheep and he stares back defensively. He has offered all the available shelter to his canvas and he's drenched.

"Tomorrow you'd better work in the old bike shed. No-one uses it."

"Thanks but I think I've finished. I'm pissed off with this goose. Thanks for getting Gillian to come out and crit me. I didn't expect that."

"No problem. But we'll have to find somewhere suitable to dump that goose or we'll be overrun by rats."

"I'll put it in the big bin."

"Make sure it's well wrapped in bin liners. Have you got any spare clothes?"

"Yeah."

"Get the goose sorted and go and change, then come to my room."

Twenty minutes later he knocks on my office door. He's changed into dry black jeans and black pornographic tee-shirt, and looks so miserable I abandon formality. "Cheer up Wes. It's not that bad."

"You going to throw me out?"

"Throw you out? Of College, you mean? Of course not."

He says in a sort of rush, "Sorry I was lairy to you."

"And I'm sorry I called you down in front of the others,

but why put that goose on show today?"

"The wankers in the studio... they said I wouldn't dare."

"Wes, you are an idiot." And so am I for not guessing he'd been set up.

"I know. It shook me when you went for me like that. I mean you're not like the other tutors, always bitching about fuck all."

"It was the goose. I don't like mouldering meat."

"I'm a vegetarian," he admits.

That makes me laugh. "Sit down, Wes, I want to talk to you."

Reluctantly he obeys. I've been his Personal Tutor for two and a half years. He's the youngest student in the Second Year, only just eighteen, with divorced and dysfunctional parents who'll give him anything money can buy and little else. Too clever for his own good, he's a whiz-kid who did five A-levels at fifteen. When he joined us there was this garbage in the local paper about *'Boy Genius Opts for Art'*.

"It's hard work trying to live up to people's expectations, isn't it, Wes?" His lower lip quivers, he bites down on it and nods. "Why don't you give yourself a break and have some fun?"

He shrugs. "I don't know how."

It's not just what he says but the bewilderment behind the words that brings a lump to my throat. "Do your parents know how you feel, Wes?"

"They don't care. Dad's long gone. He's in France, shacked up with this woman. Mum used to say he only went with her because she's slim and beautiful and Mum wasn't any more because she'd had Serena and me. Her figure really went when she had me. She said I was enormous and the ugliest kid that she'd ever seen, not like Serena who was always fucking beautiful." He laughs suddenly, "But I wasn't half as ugly when I was a kid as when I started tattooing and getting the studs put in. She told me it made her sick to look at me and she wished I'd died and Serena lived."

I struggle to conceal my horror. Wesley has always been troublesome, so I'd studied his background more closely than most of my study group. I knew his older sister had died of kidney failure, caused by anorexia, when Wesley was only ten, but I hadn't realised how hideous his home life must have been.

"Are you still living with your mother, Wes?"

"No. I've got a flat. Dad gives me an allowance... conscience money, I guess."

"Have you tried talking to your dad?"

"He doesn't give a shit about me. Mum said so all along."

This is one screwed up kid. He does all his crying deep inside and all his bleeding too, but even he can't hold back on the shivering that's taking him apart.

"Are you okay?"

"I don't feel that good."

I set out on a quick guilt trip. "You've probably caught a chill in the rain."

"No, it's my arm... bit of do it yourself tattooing that's gone bad. It'll clear up."

"Show me."

His leather jacket's draped over his shoulders. He pulls it aside to reveal his swollen, inflamed arm. "Wes, that looks awful! You need to get it sorted."

"I'll go down to A & E."

"Do you want me to take you?" I try not to sound half-hearted, even though I know that queuing in Casualty will make me short of time for meeting Gillian.

"No, ta all the same. I'll go on the bike."

"You can't ride a motorbike with your arm like that."

"I'll manage. If I leave it here some bastard'll pinch it."

He hesitates in the doorway. "Thanks, Annie."

I know I should insist on driving him. "Be careful, Wes."

Chapter 21: Annie

I make a bargain with God. If Rick comes in before I go to visit Gillian I'll phone her and excuse myself, then I'll try to get him to talk things through.

In my studio I sort the work I'll take with me if I go. There's one box file that I keep skirting round. I say to myself, *'I can't show her that. It's rubbish, morbid and self-indulgent.'* This is Pandora's box file, containing all the grief and guilt that I must not release upon the world. I set up equipment and run through.

A day in late summer.

A man walking along a lane, a young girl beside him, his child, his flesh, blood and bone, his spirit and ambition. They are easy together, each happiest in the other's company. They are laughing and stepping out with easy strides.

Out into the country where they hear the Combine Harvester buzzing in the field. Everything is bright like it's been fresh painted in acrylics.

Dad laughs. "You see, love, God's an artist."

He bends to touch a poppy; his fingertips caress the brilliant petals.

"I've often thought these must be the lilies of the field the Bible talks about. They're beautiful, aren't they? So bright and delicate and fragile-looking but they thrive on disruption, a bit like your mother thrives on angry words."

He and Mother had quarrelled before we'd gone out.

"Are you and Mother cross with each other, Dad?"

He smiles at me and strokes my cheek, much as he'd caressed the poppy. "Not really, Annie. Nothing that matters. You'll find that's the way it is with love, it looks like it's so easy to destroy but it always comes back, just like the poppies."

We walk on, along the lanes that interweave and never

84

seem to end.

"Hang on a minute, love. Give me time to get my breath."
"What's wrong, Dad?"
"It's nothing, just a touch of indigestion."
"Can I do anything Dad?"
"No. I've taken some tablets. It'll be better in a minute."
…"Dad, are you all right?"
"Now don't fuss, there's a good girl."
…"Should I get some help, Dad?"
"No need for all that bother, it'll pass."
…"Dad, what's wrong? Daddy, speak to me!"
"Maybe you'd best go and get someone my love…"
Running, faster, stumbling, breath catching on the sobs in my throat. Tears sting my face. 'Oh please, God, please God, please.' On and on, no help anywhere.
"Please, it's my daddy. Help me please."
We found him lying in the field. He'd crushed the harvest poppies where he fell.

I don't remember the funeral. Autumn came and went. On Armistice Day, Mother had to take me out of church because I was sobbing uncontrollably.

Tears are running down my face as I repack the box and place it ready to go, next to the oil painting of poppies I'd done four years ago. It was painted long after I created the conceptual poppy stuff but it draws on the same experience. I've never shown this painting, although it's one of the best things I've done. The associations are too painful: not just Dad's death but the death of those three children; I did it on the day Rick discovered the hut in Elmwash woods.

I shower, change and do my make-up. I'm spinning out time, waiting for Rick.

I've got everything in the car when I hear the phone. I run back and gasp, "Hi."

"Annie? You sound out of breath. Not disturbing anything am I?"

"What do you want, Neil?"

"I hoped you'd come over and help me to pack up my sculpture."

"Sorry, I'm busy." I slam the phone down and reread the note I've placed on the notice board: 'Rick. Gone to dinner with a visiting artist, see you later, Annie.' I insert 'love' as the penultimate word.

"Lovely work," says Gillian.

Lovely work and lovely meal and lovely wine, lots and lots of it.

"You've got a nice little College. I hope you'll set up a regular contact. I'd like to see how some of the students progress."

"That would be brilliant. Neil will be thrilled."

"You and Neil are very close, aren't you?"

"We go back a long way and he's helped my career."

"But have you ever considered which is the horse and which the cart?"

I try to work this out, fail, and ask, "What do you mean?"

"No matter how slick the cart is it's the horse that pulls it, unless of course they're both headed down hill."

"What?"

"I'm trying to warn you not to allow Neil to hold you back."

I've known for some time that Neil's career has reached a plateau but I won't admit this to someone who has a lot of clout in the art world. "Neil doesn't hold me back. He's a fine artist and an exceptional teacher. The College may be small but he's turned the Art Department into one of the best in the country, even though the powers that be are only interested in pouring money into Technology and Business Studies."

"That's true. It is exceptionally dynamic, at least as far as Sculpture and Fine Art are concerned."

I agree with her omission of our third department, Maris and dynamic are not words that belong in the same dictionary.

Gillian returns her focus to my work. "What you said about Neil is true of you as well, you're a fine artist and an inspirational teacher. The only thing you lack is guts."

"Pardon?"

"You're afraid of revealing pain, your own or anyone else's, and that can make your work superficial. Although you do steer away from the more obvious mistakes, like that silly child and his unpleasant bird."

I don't like being compared to Wes and I don't like knowing it's justified. I pass her my poppy work and walk out of the room.

I go down to the reception area. It's time to decide whether to call a taxi or stay at the hotel. I get out my mobile and phone my home number.

As it rings I whisper, *'God, give me a break. Let Rick be there and fit to talk.'*

It switches to the answer phone. "Rick, it's me. If you're there, please pick up."

No response. I ring off and try again. *'Okay God, I'm giving you one last chance, so get your act together.'*

This time I inform the answer phone, "Hi Rick. I've been drinking so I'm staying here tonight. If you need me you can get me at the Clarence Hotel. 'Bye."

I book a room and return to Gillian's suite.

She greets me with a joyous smile. "I knew you had it in you. I have influence with a London Gallery that specialises in projected images and I'm sure they'll give you a show. This is the work that could start you towards the top."

Chapter 22: Rick

By five o'clock the light's pretty useless. We've done a fair day's work, although the results have all been negative. The local ponds have been dragged and we've made a start on checking out the back garden wells. I leave my second-in-command to wind up the search.

I have to report back to the Station. Afterwards, as I head home, I pull over at the hospital flower stall to buy Annie some roses. The ones I choose are dark red and velvety. They remind me of a dress she used to wear.

I'm almost back to the car when I hear the sound of a skid. A kid in black leather has lost control of his motorbike. He hits one car and goes right over it to land on the bonnet of the next.

There's a second's silence when all the world is still. Then life starts up again and someone screams. I run to the motorcyclist, half climb on the car and check him out. He's limp and unresponsive. Through the visor his open eyes are staring vacantly.

The paramedics arrive. "It's okay, we'll take over now."

I watch as they work on him. Suddenly his face blends into the elderly pouched face of Ernest Clift, which in its turn smashes into a squashed mess of blood, bone and brain as it hits my windscreen.

I stagger a few steps backwards and sit down on the kerb. I duck my head between my knees and wait until the faintness passes. When I open my eyes the first thing I see are the scattered roses in the gutter.

The Accident Investigation guy is new to this district and doesn't recognise me. I don't tell him who I am, even though it means they keep me hanging round the hospital for hours. The two car drivers are in shock and I'm the nearest thing to a coherent witness they've got.

One of the Casualty nurses brings me a cup of tea. She says how grateful the Accident Investigation Officer feels; few people could have coped with such an unpleasant sight and been able to recount the details accurately. She warns me that shock could set in later. I feel like a hypocrite as I thank her and say I'll be fine.

It's close to eleven when I get free of the hospital and head home. My romantic flower gesture's lying in the gutter but at least I'm still sober, even if I don't feel great.

Annie's car's not on the drive. I feel a spasm of fear that makes me wince. *'I know where you live. I've seen your pretty wife.'* For years I've lived in dread of something happening to her.

As soon as I get indoors I see her note stuck to the message board. I read it and feel relieved. At least she's safe. I wonder if the *'love'* inserted in different coloured ink, as an obvious afterthought, is a good sign or bad.

I check out the answerphone. She won't be back tonight. I'd been holding myself together but now I feel disintegration start. I go up to the spare room... my room since Annie refused to sleep with me... pull the suitcase from under the bed and get out the bottle of whisky I keep there.

Chapter 23: Annie

I wake up too late to go home before work and I feel glad I've brought a suitable change of clothes, but when I walk into the departmental office I wish I'd skived off for the day. The atmosphere's distinctly nasty. Lucy is listing all the changes Maris has made and scowling at Neil, who has lost his usual indifference to her attitude. He's in a foul mood and holding his head at a funny angle, which actually isn't funny because he's obviously in pain.

"Where's Sara?" I ask.

"Off sick," says Neil. "She went home in tears because someone upset her."

I follow the direction of his glare. "Lucy, what did you say to her?"

"I merely commented on the state of her desk. That girl has no idea of order."

"She manages if she's left to work in her own way." For the money the College pays we can't expect better than Sara and, in the past, we've had a great deal worse. "Lucy we're grateful to you for stepping into the breach but I asked you to keep things running, not to close the departmental office. Sara isn't your responsibility."

I half expect her to walk out on us and, from the blistering look he's giving me, Neil thinks the same. Instead she gives me a grim smile and says, "So keep my nose out? Fair enough, I'll try."

I pick up the phone and call Sara. "Hi Sara. This is Annie. I understand you had a few problems?... Of course that upset you... Yes, I know you're sensitive... The thing is poor Neil's in agony but he can't go home when we're so short staffed. Is there any chance of you coming back in? We wouldn't expect you to work very fast, just keep things running... Thanks, you're a star."

As I put the phone down, Neil says cynically, "I like the bit about not working very fast. A snail with arthritis could work quicker than she does."

Lucy gives a snort of agreement. It's a unique moment, the first time I've known them to agree on anything.

"Neil, what did the doctor say?" I ask.

"It's the usual problem. It'll ease off in a day or so. It's one of the hazards of the job. It comes from lifting heavy stuff."

That's true of the recurring problem, but Neil has obviously forgotten I'd witnessed the original injury, seventeen years ago. It was an alcoholic post-exhibition party and he was swinging from a chandelier that didn't take his weight.

"Yes, I was there the first time you hurt it. Don't you remember I went to hospital with you in the ambulance?"

He gives me a look that says 'bitch' or 'snitch' or both, and I realise his sense of humour isn't at its best.

"Do you feel as rotten as you look?"

He picks up the mirror that Sara keeps handy on her desk and studies his face. "Marginally worse."

"Then go home. I'll take your Second and Third Years with mine. The part time staff can take the First Year and other groups."

"Are you sure?"

"Of course."

"Thanks. I've got a meeting with Health and Safety but I'll go home after that."

"You can tell them Wesley probably won't be in for a while, he's got a badly infected arm. I told him to go to A&E."

"It's probably a symptom of mad turkey disease," says Neil.

"Wesley? Is he the boy with the large motorbike?" The concern in Lucy's voice makes us both turn to look at her.

"That's right. Why?"

91

"I heard a local News bulletin. It said a teenage motorcyclist had been killed outside the hospital yesterday evening."

"Wesley!" I feel the blood draining from my face.

"There's no reason to assume it's him," protests Neil. "Lucy, did you pick up the kid's name?"

"No, the broadcaster said they couldn't give out a name until the parents had been informed."

"Wesley's father and his new family live in France," I whisper.

"Oh God!" says Neil.

"You've changed your tune, haven't you?" snaps Lucy.

He glares at her. "Just because I don't want dead birds mouldering round the department doesn't mean I wish the kid any harm."

"I'd better get on," I say and head blindly towards the door.

I teach the first session with a heavy, spiked weight pressing in the centre of my chest. Death's the one situation that's totally unredeemable. I feel guilty that I hadn't insisted on driving him to A&E.

It's late in the morning when Sara puts her head round the studio door and says, "Visitors in your office, Annie. It's to do with Wesley Arnold."

"Who is it?" I demand, but she's already gone.

I enter my office and a smartly dressed, middle-aged man stands to greet me. I'm surprised. Surely they'd send an uniformed officer? I look past him to the sweet-faced, fair young woman holding a baby and on again to the boy with his arm in a sling.

"Wesley!" I say and the entire room spins round.

'*Okay God, that's one I owe you,*' I acknowledge in my head.

"Mrs Evans? I'm Mark Arnold, Wesley's dad," the man's hand engulfs mine.

"You came?"

"Of course I came. The minute we heard the message you left on our phone yesterday evening. We dumped the other two kids with Francoise's mum and caught the Eurostar. This is my wife, Francoise."

She smiles at me and Wesley's dad carries on, " We surprised this useless article still in bed. When Francoise saw the state of his arm she made me take him straight to Casualty."

I stare at Wes and the lump in my throat threatens to suffocate me.

He misinterprets my silence. "Don't look at me like that, Annie. I know I promised to get it fixed yesterday, but there was hassle outside the hospital. Some guy came off his bike and topped himself, so I left it."

"I heard about the accident. I thought it was you."

"And that freaked you out?"

"Of course it did."

"Sorry."

"So you should be," says Wesley's dad. He smiles at me. "Thanks for being so good to Wes."

"You're welcome." It had been easy to access Mark Arnold's name and number from Wesley's file before I left College yesterday but hard to decide whether I ought to contact him.

"I didn't realise Wesley needed me. His mother told me he didn't want to see me, that he blamed me for his sister's death."

"That is enough, Mark," says Francoise, her eyes on Wesley.

At her words Wesley turns to face her, the baby crows triumphantly and makes a snatch at his lip ring. Very gently he prises her hand away and pretends to nibble her fingers while she shrieks in delight.

He looks across at me and says, "Thanks Annie."

"I thought you might swear at me for interfering."

93

"No, that's them others, you're alright."

"The doctor said Wesley's arm's infected and if we're not careful he could be seriously ill," says Mark Arnold. "Would it be all right if he came home with us?"

"Sounds good to me. You could take an extended Christmas break, Wes, and come back fully fit in the New Year. You'd better come along to the studio and get any paints and stuff you need."

"I'll pass on that."

It's not what he says, it's the tight note in his voice. He's chickening out, because yesterday they'd seen him called down. Give it a month and he could have real problems coming back.

"There's one thing you could do for me before you go. I'd really appreciate it."

"What's that?" He doesn't exactly leap into my trap.

"Come in and go through yesterday's critique. It will help some of the less able students."

"I can't. I mean I'm not feeling very good."

"Just five minutes," I persist.

"No, I..."

His stepmother says quietly, "I think, Wesley, you ought to do as Annie asks."

He looks like a trapped animal as he crosses the room to join me. I catch Francoise's gaze and she smiles.

"Your stepmother's lovely," I say to Wesley as we walk down the corridor.

"Yeah. I've got two more little half-sisters I've never met and Dad and Francoise say they really want me." He stops outside the studio. "Annie, I don't want to do this."

"Five minutes," I promise and shove him through the door.

The work time has turned into a gossip session, which dies away as we come in.

"I'm glad to see you're all working so hard," I say. "Right, people, we're going to do something a bit different for this one. First I want to thank Wes for joining us..."

I'm interrupted by giggles from a few creeps who think they know when I'm being snide. I glare them into silence. "As I was saying, I want to thank Wesley for joining us when he's ill. He's going on sick leave but he's agreed to go over his work with us first. Wes, what do you think of your work this year?"

Wesley stares gloomily at the dead goose picture and it looks dismally back at him. "A lot of it's crap."

There's a murmur of agreement from those who've had to share a studio with the goose but Josef says, "Wesley's work is powerful and brave."

I smile at him. "Thank you, Josef. I agree with you. Has anyone else got anything to say?... No? Then, as Wesley seems to be his own harshest critic, I suggest we go straight on to Gillian's crit. It was too wet to set up a camcorder outside so I took notes which Gillian elaborated when we got together last night."

I read the crit concluding with Gillian's words, "I do not like much of the subject matter that Wesley chooses to depict but I admire the skill of his painting, his excellent brushwork and the savage honesty of his art. He has great potential."

In the stunned silence Wesley grabs the paper from my hand and stares at it.

The applause starts with Josef's loud, determined hand beats but slowly the others pick it up. I see Wesley gnawing at his lower lip, more moved than he wants to show.

When it finishes, he manages a creditably cheeky grin and says, "Ta," to the other students, then to me, " I guess I'd better take that painting gear with me after all."

Chapter 24: Rick

I wake up when they're well into the post-mortem. They've got to the bit that requires drilling through the centre of my head. The pain helps me suss out I'm not dead and whoever's doing the drilling is doing it from inside. I make it to my feet, do an urgent pit-stop at the cloakroom, then out to the kitchen. I drink half a gallon of water followed by black, sweet, instant coffee and manage to choke down paracetamol.

When I get to the Incident Room, Roebuck sends for me. He looks down his nose like he's trying to decide what stone I was under before I crawled into his office.

"You're late."

"Sorry, sir."

He glares at me and I think he's going to take me off the case. I don't want that, not until we know about the kid and whether the link to Elmwash is for real. To my surprise he says, "I've got two important jobs for you. The Family Support Officer has had to take some leave. Can you liaise with the Frewers until she gets back?"

"Yes sir." That's shoving me right into the heart of the case.

"And there's something else. You know the Elmwash investigation inside out. I want you to interview the witnesses in this case and review the evidence to see if you can spot anything significant."

"Significant, sir?"

"Anything that ties this in with the Elmwash case."

"The Elmwash killer's dead."

"No, Ernest Clift is dead. I trust you'll approach this with an open mind. Take Detective Constable Kelly with you, it's best to have a woman on the job."

What would he know about having a woman on the job? "Yes sir."

I stride back through the main room. "Kelly! You're with me."

As she stands up, several papers slither from her desk. At the door I glance back and see her trying to sort them.

"Kelly!" I bellow. "I haven't got all day!"

I'm halfway down the village street when Kelly catches up with me. I see her expression and feel glad someone else is pissed off too.

I decide to leave the Frewers until last and get a feel for the background. As we work our way round the village I drop into a routine explanation, 'This is just a follow-up, sometimes details come back after the first shock wears off.'

We drink cups of tea and coffee and listen to how wonderful Terry Frewer is and how devoted he is to Stacie and how Cindy Frewer always dresses her beautifully, sometimes she'd change her two or three times a day.

We're about to enter the village grocery shop when Kelly says, "Guv, there's a girl in there. Her mother owns the shop. This girl, Vicki, is fourteen and she used to baby-sit for the Frewers. Yesterday I got the feeling she had something she wanted to say but she wasn't happy talking to me."

"Funny that."

"I thought if you gave her an opening, maybe she'd tell you. She's the sort with an eye for the guys."

"If I said that you'd call me a sexist bastard. Okay, you keep the woman talking and I'll try out my charm."

Kelly's look makes it clear I'm not the only one who can do dumb insolence.

The kid in the shop is plump and skimpily dressed. I see her appraising me as we enter. Kelly diverts the older woman by ordering sandwiches for the Incident Room and the girl goes across to tidy the magazines.

I follow her. "You're Stacie's baby-sitter, aren't you?"

"Used to be." She looks across to where her mother and Kelly are standing.

"Vicki? What you saying to that cop?" the woman's

voice breaks in.

"Nothing."

I smile at the woman. "I was wondering if I could use your lav?"

She doesn't look happy but she says, "Alright. Vicki, show him where to go."

It's not just an excuse. I'm desperate for a pee. When I come out of the cloakroom Vicki's still waiting, just outside the door. She giggles. "You feeling better for that? I thought you were making up a reason to get me on my own."

"I did want to talk to you."

"I know." She moves closer.

I sidestep. "Tell me about Stacie and her parents."

"Stacie's dead, isn't she?"

"I don't know."

"I bet someone took her away and did terrible things to her. Like those other girls in that wood. They had all about it on tele..."

I break in, "What's Stacie like?"

She considers, then answers in a softer tone, "Sweet, always trying to please people, especially her mum and dad."

"But?" I prompt her.

"But she wasn't very good at getting stuff right."

"Why's that?"

"She was a bit slow... and clumsy... and sort of young for her age."

"What were her parents like when she got things wrong?"

"Her mum yelled sometimes, nothing special, just what mums do."

"And her stepdad?"

She shrugs. "He didn't yell but he was more nasty than her mum."

"Everyone says how kind he was to Stacie."

"He's a filthy, lying bastard."

"In what way?" Another shrug and a sullen, scowling look. "Come on, Vicki, you can tell me."

She pouts at me provocatively. "I'll tell you if you're friendly. Guys ought to be friendly. Especially when they've got a girl alone." She leans towards me and her boobs brush against my chest. She's wearing a low-cut top and she's bloody well endowed.

I step backwards and end up hard against the cigarette boxes. And I mean hard in every sense. God Annie, what have you done to me that I can get my bollocks in a twist because of a close encounter with a teenage slapper?

"You should be at school, shouldn't you?" I say.

"Mum kept me home. She don't like being in the shop alone, not with a psycho wandering round the place. Anyway, school's boring. They don't teach you nothing real." She puts her hand up towards my face and I slap it away.

"You don't have to pretend. I know you fancy me." She moves even closer.

"You ready, Guv?" For the first time ever I'm glad to hear Kelly's voice.

"Yeah, let's get out of here."

"Talk about needing danger money," I say when we're back in the street.

"She give you anything, Guv?"

I don't plan to share the anatomical details. "She's obviously got a grudge against Terence Frewer."

"What did she say about him?"

"That he's a filthy, lying bastard."

Kelly shrugs. "That could mean she propositioned him and he blew her away. He seems a decent enough bloke and she's a little tart." She looks across the street. "Stacie's teacher's waving. I think she wants a word."

"That's all I need. You see to her while I talk to the Frewers' next door neighbour."

She grins at me. "You sure you don't need me as chaperone?"

"Cut the comedy and do your bloody job."

"Yes, sir." She turns on her heel and walks away.

Chapter 25: Rick

The old girl who lives next door to the Frewers must be nearly eighty. She's white-haired, plump and impossible to hurry.

At last I steer her onto business. "You saw Stacie in the garden on Sunday?"

"Yes, I saw her in the morning, near her swing. So pretty she looked, in that pink shiny dress she had a few months ago when she was a bridesmaid. I thought to myself, 'you must be off somewhere special today.'"

"Somewhere special?"

"To his family I expect, his mother or his sister. He likes Stacie to do him credit."

"You get on well with the Frewers?"

"Very well. Terry helps me sometimes with odd jobs. He even sorted out my TV aerial for me. I'm getting too old to go clambering round in the loft so Terry slipped through from his side and saw to it."

"What about Mrs Frewer?"

"Cindy often pops over for a chat. She says it's like having a grandma living next door. She hasn't got any family of her own you see, just Terry and poor little Stacie. And Stacie's always in here, going down my sweetie jar. But don't tell her dad that, he thinks she has too many sweets. I told Cindy it's just puppy fat, she'll grow out of it." Her triple chins wobble and she presses a hand to her mouth to suppress a sob.

I look out the window but all I can see is a six-foot wooden fence. "Where did you see Stacie from?"

"I was upstairs, in my bedroom. Do you want to see?"

"Please."

The old girl wheezes up the stairs, panting her explanation as she goes. "I was out on Saturday. My great-nephew got married and I was partying until late. So on Sunday I thought

I'd have a lie in."

I stare out of the window at the garden next door. It leads into a field and then to woodland. The swing is near the end and is sheltered by a fancy open-sided shed.

"Bit wet for playing in the garden, wasn't it?"

"She loves that swing. That's why Terry had the shelter put up for her. Still I did think it was daft her being out there in that pretty dress. She must have been frozen."

"What time was it when you saw her?"

"I can't be sure. I was sleepy. I only got up to spend a penny."

"And you're sure you didn't hear anything?"

"No." Her billowy face quivers. "If only I'd looked out at the right time."

Kelly's standing on the pavement, outside the Frewers' house. She's got the hard-done-by look of someone who's been kept waiting in the rain.

"What did the old bat want?" I nod towards the school.

"To give me a file of stuff Stacie did, pictures and class diary, that sort of thing. I don't think there's much in it for us. I dropped it back to the Incident Room. I didn't think it would be a good idea to take it into the Frewers' house."

"Yeah, that wouldn't be great." It takes less than that to send anxious parents over the edge.

We head up the Frewers' front path. Terence Frewer is looking out. He opens the door and ushers us into the hall. "Is there any news?"

"I'm afraid not, sir. I'm Detective Inspector Evans. I'll be keeping you informed until DS Carling is able to resume work as your Liaison Officer."

He holds out his hand to me. "Pleased to meet you, Inspector."

He's in his early forties, fair-haired with an open friendly manner. He's taller than me and strongly built. I loosen my grasp before the handshake becomes a test of strength. "This is Detective Constable Kelly."

He smiles at Kelly. "We met yesterday. Constable Kelly, could you find good use for a towel?"

She pushes her wet hair out of her face. "That's okay, sir. I'll stand and drip."

"Perhaps we could go and join your wife?" I say. "She must be wondering what's happening."

He seems surprised by the reminder and the smile wavers, then he pins it back in place. "Of course. She's in here."

The living room's old-fashioned and formal, dominated by a large piano. There are two tall, free-standing plant pots, one at the edge of the bay window and the other shoved in a dark corner. I wonder what it did to deserve punishment.

Cindy Flower doesn't look more than a kid herself. She sits cowering in the circle of her husband's embrace as he perches on the arm of her chair.

"Have you found her?" Her voice is high-pitched and breathless.

He hugs her closer to him. "Hush. There's no news yet."

"No new developments but we'll keep you informed," I say.

"We'll have to hope the TV appearance works," he says.

I see Stacie's mum shrink even deeper inside herself. "TV appearance?" I query.

"It's all very well you people saying you'll keep us informed but it seems you need to put each other in the picture." The words are snide but he says it with a smile.

"Mr and Mrs Frewer want to do a media appeal. It's scheduled for late this afternoon," says Kelly in my ear.

"I see." I look at the fragile young woman and wonder how she'll cope. I think she's conscious of my stare. She looks up and I see violet eyes much the same shade as the dark shadows that surround them. Terence notes the look and tightens his grip upon his wife until there's no space between them.

I sit down and say, "With your permission we're going

to run through everything again." Cindy is chewing at a strand of her long hair. I see her flinch and I carry on quickly, "I know it's painful but we've found that people's recall after a few days is often useful."

"To see if we contradict ourselves?" says Terry.

"To see if you remember anything else." I meet his smile with my own.

"Can we offer you anything before we start? Tea, coffee, or something stronger?"

I follow the gesture of his outstretched hand and focus on the open drinks cabinet. "No thank you, sir."

Kelly says, "I'd love a cup of tea. How about I give you a hand to make it, Cindy?"

I guess she reckons Cindy's more likely to open up to her when they're alone. Nice theory, trouble is the poor kid's looking like she's being invited by a panther to step into the jungle and sort out some tasty snacks.

Terry urges Cindy to stand. "That's right, love. Make some sandwiches too. It will keep you occupied." She stares at him blankly, then she goes with Kelly.

"She's taking it badly," he tells me in a confidential tone. I think 'You stupid bastard, of course she bloody is.'

"You're sure you won't join me?" He pours himself a double whisky.

"No, thank you sir. If we can confirm the information that's in these reports. You're an accountant, I believe?"

"Chief Accountant at Sanders and Goodenough, the office stationery firm."

"In Central London? That's quite a distance to travel every day. Do you have a flat in London?"

"Oh no. Nowadays I do a lot of work on-line but I've always preferred to get home every night. I don't like to leave my wife alone too much. She needs looking after."

"Looking after?"

"She's not strong and things get too much for her. That's one of the reasons we bought this house in a quiet village. It's the sort of place with good, old-fashioned virtues that you don't get in towns and cities any more. I'm not sure you'd understand, you strike me as an Inner City sort of man."

I ignore the sneer. "There can be a lot of jealousy in villages. Can you think of anyone who's got a grudge against you?"

He shakes his head. "No, I get on well with everyone. Anyway I can't believe that anyone would take Stacie because they wanted to hurt me."

"You'd be surprised what some people will do to get at someone who's upset them." Ernest Clift's pouched face slithers across my mind. "What about Stacie's real father? Is he still on the scene?"

"Her real father? Oh, you mean her biological father? No, he's dead."

"I see. And you married Stacie's mother when Stacie was a baby? It must feel like she's your own then?"

"Yes, of course. She is mine. I adopted her."

"I've heard how good you are about helping at the school. You must be very proud of Stacie."

"Of course," he repeats, but this time I get the flicker of something else.

Not for the first time, I think Family Liaison Officer is a weird sort of job. You're supporting the family and yet you're investigating them. Often a kid's death is down to a family member, but there's been nothing so far to suggest the Frewers have hurt Stacie.

"Was it usual for you to stay away from Church with Stacie while her mum went alone?"

"I was tired, but I felt that someone ought to put in an appearance. People like us have obligations."

I've got my back to the window, facing into the house, and I see what Terry Frewer can't... Cindy steps through the door, she looks around the room and her eyes meet mine. In all the years I've been doing this lousy job I've spoken to many parents whose kids have gone astray, although most times, thank God, they turn up again okay. I thought I'd seen the full range of reactions when a kid disappears: pain, terror, self-blame, anger and disbelief, But never before have I seen such total emptiness.

Chapter 26: Rick

My shock at Cindy's expression must show on my face. Frewer turns round swiftly but, like a ghost, Cindy's already gone.

I speak quickly, before he can ask me what I saw. "Your wife likes going to Church? She's keen on village events?"

He doesn't answer. As far as I'm concerned he doesn't need to. The questions we asked in the village have made it clear that Cindy's accepted only in a despising sort of way.

"It says in the reports that you last saw Stacie about eleven o'clock when she went outside to play. Wasn't it wet for that?"

"You obviously haven't got children or you'd know you can't keep them inside all the time."

"But she was dressed in her party frock." I look towards the gold-framed photograph on the piano, Stacie as a bridesmaid, wearing a pink, frilly dress. It's the photo that's been circulated to the media.

"The swing is in a sheltered part of the garden."

"And you didn't go out to check on Stacie?"

Dull red colour seeps into his cheeks. "I've been into this already. If you'd read the reports you'd know I went to sleep. I was tired. I work hard."

Too tired to look after his daughter? Perhaps he feels more guilt than he's letting show and that's why he's got such attitude. Whatever. There's no point in pushing that point any further. "And the bracelet that was found under the swing, you're sure it isn't Stacie's?"

"Of course it isn't! I wouldn't allow my daughter to wear such a common tawdry bit of rubbish."

It's interesting how vehement he is, but that may just be his snobbery coming out. Fingerprint testing has shown that the bracelet had been wiped clean, although the ribbon had the fingerprints of Stacie and her parents, which makes sense if they'd tied it for her.

I nod to the piano. "Who's the pianist in the family?"

"Me." He sits down on the silk-draped stool and runs his fingers lovingly across the piano's polished veneer. "It's the piano my parents bought me when I was a boy." He frowns. "It's dusty. Cindy hasn't been up to housework the last few days."

And Annie calls Bob a male chauvinist.

"What about Stacie? Is she learning the piano?"

"She's just started lessons."

"Does she like it?"

"Of course."

"That's good. It's no use forcing kids to do stuff that needs lots of work if they don't enjoy it."

"Indeed? Tell me, Inspector, do they include these bog-standard child psychology courses as part of your training?"

He's close to losing his temper. He jerks to his feet and the drape on the piano stool comes with him. As he thrusts it back over the stained upholstery I see his hands are trembling.

"As a matter of fact they do... give psychology courses I mean. After all we've got to deal with a lot of kids who've been abused."

What the hell's got into me? When relations of a victim are rude or aggressive it's usually a reaction to their pain and you smooth things over. I've dealt with more bereaved families than most because my bosses claim I'm good at it. But this guy's getting to me. I want to prise up the glossy cover he's put on things and see what's wiggling underneath. But maybe it's not him, perhaps it's me. I'm in a bastard of a mood and taking it out on anyone I can.

I get my reaction. Terry Frewer's mouth tightens and a muscle twitches in his cheek. "Don't talk like that! Do you have any idea what hell it is for me? If I'd looked after her better I'd still have my little girl!" On the last words he covers his face with his hands.

It's not just the acting, which I'd rate as bad. Over the years I've seen plenty of genuinely bereaved people who feel they've got to make a display of their grief and who come across as phoney. What hits me is the look that swept across his face before he started whinging. It's not directed at me but towards the piano with the picture of Stacie on top of it. It's not a look of grief or even anger. It's sullen resentfulness.

The women come back in, Kelly carrying a tray. Terry's still snivelling but Cindy doesn't go to him. She lingers by the door looking like she wants out, which makes two of us.

"Kelly, pour Mr Frewer his tea while Mrs Frewer shows me Stacie's bedroom."

Terry emerges from behind his hands. "I can do that. I don't want my wife upset."

"No, you stay there, sir. You need to keep calm for that TV broadcast. I'll look after Mrs Frewer."

She accompanies me out of the room and I follow her upstairs. She walks with shoulders rounded, arms folded across her chest. Despite her childlike figure she moves like a sick old woman. Pity engulfs me and I think, 'I can't do this any more.'

Stacie's room is pink and white and full of fluffy toys. The atmosphere is heavy with scented airspray and yet there's a stale smell underneath. A lot of old houses smell damp in winter.

"Have you got a loo I can use?" I've been drinking tea and coffee all morning with the people we interviewed.

She nods to a door. I push it open and find Stacie's got an en-suite bathroom, patterned in pink and silver. As I close the bathroom door a wave of dizziness sweeps through me. I feel like shit. I want to go home, crawl into bed and stay there forever.

Before I leave the bathroom I take a look around. I know the house has been searched but I want to get my own impressions about the way they live. I check out the airing cupboard; it's full of pink, frilly bed linen and a pile of plastic sheets.

When I go back, Cindy's sitting on Stacie's bed. A battered brown teddy is on her lap, she's cuddling it to her and rocking gently side to side.

I sit down on the bed next to her. "You were at Church when Stacie went missing, and you stayed on afterwards?"

"I stayed to help with coffee."

"But Terry and Stacie were at home?"

"Terry was tired. And he wanted to be sure that Stacie was dressed up ready to visit her auntie."

"Does her dad often get her sorted?"

She makes a dismissive gesture. "I'd laid Stacie's things out and he said he'd take the chance to run through the piano piece she was going to play for her auntie."

"She's good at the piano?" It doesn't match with the rest of her profile.

"Terry says she can do it if she tries but I'm not sure she can. I think she takes after me and I'm not musical."

"Me neither. I used to have trumpet lessons at school and my old man used to knock me across the room when I wouldn't practise, then he'd belt me even harder when I did."

"Terry doesn't hit Stacie."

I'm about to say I didn't mean it like that when I realise she's put emphasis on the word 'hit.' It makes me wonder what Terry does do when people anger him.

"I understand you were late getting home?"

"Mrs Barnes, that's the churchwarden's wife, said it was my turn to do the washing up. I knew I'd be late but I didn't argue. I'm not much good at standing up to people. Then there was this old lady who needed taking home. She's a bit confused and people get impatient with her, so I took her."

"The bracelet we found under the swing, your husband says that didn't belong to Stacie?" I don't know why I think the bracelet matters but it's still there in the back of my mind.

"No, but I might not have known. If Stacie made it at school or a friend gave it to her, she might not show me. She'd know her father wouldn't let her wear a cheap bead

109

bracelet. He always wants us to look smart."

There's something else I want to ask but I'm scared it will destroy her fragile composure. I take a deep breath and say, "There were some silk poppies in your back garden. Did you put them there?"

"Yes. They were blowing round the village green outside our house... they looked messy and Terry was cross. He told me to clear them up and throw them in the bin."

Her hands are twisting convulsively in her lap and I reach out and hold them gently to still their trembling. "But you didn't throw the poppies away?" I ask.

"No, it seemed wrong... disrespectful... so I put them in the garden and weighted them down with a stone so they wouldn't blow around again." She turns those amazing eyes on me and asks, "You're married aren't you?"

"Yeah." My wedding ring's on the hand that covers both of hers.

"Does your wife do everything you tell her to?"

"No." Where the hell did that come from?

"You're lucky."

I used to think so. Every day I'd think 'you fucking lucky bastard,' but then the luck stopped and the fucking too.

"About Stacie's biological father? Terry said he was dead?"

"Her real dad you mean? Yes, he died before she was born. In a car crash. Without Terry to look after me I don't know what I'd have done."

"Was Terry a family friend?" I've checked their ages in the file: she's twenty-four and he's forty-three.

"Oh no, nothing like that. Terry was my boss. It was my first job when I left school and he was so kind to me when Robbie died."

"What was Stacie's dad like?"

"Robbie? He was sweet," her voice lilts with remembered happiness. "He was always laughing, always full of fun. We never had any money but it didn't matter, not when we were together with our baby on the way." She hugs the battered teddy and I know it came from him.

"Cindy? Are you all right?" Terry Frewer's voice echoes up the stairs.

She seems to draw inside herself. She goes to a cupboard and locks the teddy in.

I open the door and yell down, "Everything's fine."

"Thank you. You've been kind," she says. It's as if she's talking from behind a shield.

"About the Press Conference, it's a hassle but you don't have to be afraid."

She smiles at me like I've said something incredibly stupid. "Don't worry about me. I'm not afraid of anything, not now."

Chapter 27: Annie

Invigorated by Wesley's safe return, I move into hyperdrive. I give Neil the good news and urge him to go home, promising to send round a couple of responsible students who are willing to help pack up his sculptures for cash-in-hand. That sorted, I ask Sara if she could phone round the Maternity Units to track down Maris and get the latest news. I think it's an imposition but she seems pleased to do it.

It's half-day for mainstream students and I'm free, although I have a pile of paperwork. I leave College promptly at one o'clock and stop off to buy a present for Maris' baby.

When I get home, I check the answerphone. There are my messages from last night and one from Mother, demanding to know whether I have recovered from Sunday's indisposition. Dutifully I ring back and hit lucky because she's not in. I leave a placatory message.

When I go into the living room I can smell the heavy, sweet scent of whisky and I know Rick was drinking again last night.

I get out my paperwork. A slim book takes my eye. Gillian gave it to me before we said goodnight. It's the book that accompanied her recent exhibition and I guess she's using it to drive home her point about standing up to be counted. Last night, tired and somewhat drunk, I'd put it aside to consider when my brain was more in gear. I look at it now and see the images of men and women scarred by violence. Gillian has called it simply, PTS.

I turn the pages. Gillian's images of young soldiers aren't exploitative but they are filled with pain. In a curious way her art reminds me of Stanley Spencer, who immortalised the suffering of the First World War. I guess trauma and pain are timeless. But for me there's something else, something truly terrible: I've seen the same expression on Rick's face, the same tightness in his body.

As I read Gillian's notes about Post-Traumatic Stress, I discover trauma can be buried so deep it takes years to show itself.

As always when I need sanctuary, I flee to my studio. At last I truly understand what Gillian meant when she said my work lacked guts. I'm not hiding any more. I'm obsessed by the memory of a thin-faced girl, sitting cross-legged on bright bedding, suckling her baby in a sordid squat. I've no photos to work from but the image burns so clearly I know I can do this from memory.

As I think about Chloe, it occurs to me that I could be three days pregnant. I gave up taking the Pill some time ago. How stupid of me not to think of that before. I know it's a long-shot but I wish I hadn't drunk so much last night.

Starting new work is scary. Especially when I'm determined to take no prisoners. It takes a while for me to be drawn in but suddenly I'm there.

It's three hours later when I return to the present with a stiff neck and sense of inner peace. I step back to survey my new work and feel reasonably satisfied.

I've backed into the corner that's cluttered by Rick's chair. He used to curl up there so we could be together while I worked. He'd read a book, play on his iPod or fill out papers, but often, when I glanced across, he'd be watching me.

I stumble over the pile of holiday brochures lying on the floor beside the chair. The last totally good time we'd had together was our Devon holiday. A few weeks ago I sent for the brochure for the hotel we'd stayed in. I'd considered asking Rick if he'd go back there with me to try and sort things out.

I flee to the kitchen to track down coffee and cake. There's a new message on the answer phone: "Rick? It's Dorothy Planter, from next door to your mum. There's trouble with your dad. He's got upset about going into that Home place.

The Social Worker says she'll be back in an hour or so to see if he's being more reasonable. You'd best get over here and help your mum."

The message had been left nearly an hour ago. I could try and contact Rick but I don't like to when he's on a missing child hunt. Surely I can deal with this for him?

I scribble a note: 'Gone to see your mum,' and head off.

I've never felt comfortable with Rick's mum and dad. His mum's always pleasant but I know she doesn't like me. I can tell by the flickering looks she gives me when she thinks I'm not watching. At least Rick's dad has made it clear how he feels. 'There's that snobby bitch.' And I know, in his dementia, he's saying out loud what he's always thought.

In the afternoon the terraced street isn't crowded and I manage to park close to their house. The door is opened by Rick's mum's neighbour, a solid, square woman with tightly-permed, dyed-black hair. She has sharp eyes and a sharp nose and a sharp disapproving glare.

"Good afternoon, Mrs Planter."

Reluctantly she steps back to let me squeeze past. "Tris, it's your Rick's wife."

"Hi Tris. Rick's tied up at work so I came instead."

"Tied up at work when his mum needs him!" snorts Mrs Planter. There's a murmur of agreement from the other neighbours, who seem to have come in to watch the fun.

"You can't expect him to drop everything when there's a kiddie missing," says Tris. "Thanks for coming, Annie, though I don't know there's much you can do."

"What's wrong?"

"It's Tom. He's due to go into Respite Care. Every six weeks they take him for a few days to this old people's home. It helps me to cope the rest of the time, you see."

"Yes, Rick told me about that. What's the problem?"

"He's being stubborn. He doesn't want to go. Seems to think he's a child again, being evacuated." She indicates an official looking woman. "The Social lady went and got a nurse from the Home to help her, but they say they can't actually force him to go. If he doesn't he'll lose his place until next time."

I should have contacted Rick but it's too late now. I say to the Social Services lady, "Let me try, please."

"Please hurry. I've got other clients to see."

Rick's mum looks troubled. "Don't take offence if he's rude, will you?"

"I won't." I slip into the small square sitting room. "Hello, Tom."

The room is stuffy and it smells of old age and piss. When I first knew him he was a big man but now he's stooped and frail. He looks up at me with puzzled, watery eyes. "Mummy? Oh Mummy don't make me go."

I force out the words, "You've got to. It's for your own good."

"Please Mummy. I don't want to. Please don't make me go." His voice has lost its grown man maturity and pitched back into quavery childhood.

"You've got to go, but in a little while you can come back again."

"You promise?"

"Yes."

I hold out my hand and he levers himself up and takes it. His fingers are cracked and dry.

He shuffles beside me out into the hall and the worst of the smell comes with him. Rick's mum must have cleared the neighbours because she's standing there alone. She puts his jacket round his shoulders and his moist blue eyes drift over her with no sign of recognition. I urge him outside and into the Social Worker's car. As I prise my hand free he puts up his face for a kiss. I make brief contact with the leathery cheek. He puts his arms around me and draws me towards him. The wetness of his lips on my cheek makes me feel sick.

There's a puzzled look upon his face. "Aren't you going to tell me to be good?"

"Be good and do what the ladies tell you."
"I love you Mummy."
"I love you too." It isn't easy but I say the words.

Chapter 28: Annie

I return to the house and Rick's mum greets me with a smile. "Thank you."

"You're welcome. Now you can enjoy your break."

"Yes, as long as he doesn't make too much fuss and they bring him back."

"They bring him back and lumber you again?" I'm too shocked to be tactful.

She shrugs. "It's going to upset them when they realise that he's wet through the pad again. He's very nasty about being changed you know."

I feel ashamed that I didn't know and full of admiration for my mother-in-law who carries such a burden day after weary day. "How do you stand it?"

"I don't know. Sometimes I don't think I do. We've had carers in but he won't let them near him, so sometimes, when he wets himself, I pretend I haven't noticed. And sometimes when he yells for me I pretend I haven't heard. Are you in a hurry or would you like a cup of tea?"

"That would be great."

"Come on upstairs. I'll air the sitting room later when I'm sure the coast is clear."

It's years since I've been in Tris' bedroom. She's transformed it into a bright, comfortable bedsit, complete with kettle and mini-fridge.

She smiles at my surprise. "Rick helped me decorate. It's one advantage of Tom not being able to get upstairs any more."

"Does Rick know how bad it's got?"

"I don't think so. I try and keep it from him. He does enough already and it would only worry him. He's a great one for worrying."

That pricks my conscience. "I must phone home to let

Rick know everything's okay before he hears Mrs Planter's message."

There's no answer when I ring home, so I leave a message on the answer phone. While Tris makes the tea I look around her room. The contents of her bookshelves surprise me. There's a lot of children's classics and contemporary women's fiction but also DVDs of ballets and biographies of dancers.

"Do you like dance?" I ask.

"Oh yes. When I was a little girl I always dreamed of being a dancer but my mum didn't approve of that sort of thing." Her smile is rueful. "Mum used to say I got my fancy notions from my father. I don't think she had any regrets while Papa was alive but after he died she found it very hard. She tried to pretend I wasn't half-Italian. She wouldn't let anyone call me Beatrice. And, of course, after I married Tom he used to sneer at me. He'd say I had Wop blood in me."

I say hesitantly, "Tris, I don't want to be rude but why did you marry Tom?"

Miraculously, she doesn't seem offended. "My mum was very ill. She knew she hadn't got long left and she wanted to see me settled. She died three weeks after my wedding."

"I see."

Tris never talked much about her family and all Rick knew about his grandfather was that his name had been Guiseppe and he'd been a POW. He'd returned to England some years after the War to marry Tris' mum. He'd died when Tris was five. From the few photographs Rick's seen, it seems he's taken his looks from his grandfather. I think Tris looks subtly Italian too. In the past few years her slenderness has become thinness and her dark hair is spiced with grey, but she's still a remarkably beautiful woman.

I turn back to the bookshelves and realise she's got a lot of art books. Most of them are the things beginners buy when they want to educate themselves but there's also a catalogue of my last significant exhibition. I look at Tris enquiringly.

"Last year, when Tom was in Respite, I went up to see your art show in London." She sounds apologetic, as if she thinks I might object.

I'm surprised and touched. "What did you think of it?"

"I didn't really understand it, it's no good pretending I did. But I liked the way the slides went round in a circle, so you could make up a different story in your head depending which way round you looked at them."

That sounds like a pretty fair critique to me. "I've got some new stuff on soon. May I take you and tell you about it? We could have dinner and go to the ballet afterwards." She looks startled and I'm afraid I've offended her. "I'm sorry, I didn't mean to be pushy."

"No. I'm sorry. I didn't mean to look as if I didn't want to go out with you. It's just I'm not posh, not like your mother. I'm not used to fancy places like that hotel where you had your wedding reception."

It's true it had been a very exclusive hotel. Mother had been deprived of an enormous show at Elaine's wedding, because of the need for haste and the bride's expanding figure, so she went to town on mine. Suddenly Rick's parents' attitude to me makes sense. "Is that why you never liked me?"

Tris seems startled by my bluntness. "It's not that I don't like you. Just you're so different from most girls round here. You're smart and clever and you've got a big career. You're always flying off places and having things written about you in the newspaper."

I nearly say, 'Only the local newspaper,' but I realise that will prove her point.

"Oh Tris, I'm not like that! At least I hope I'm not."

She looks embarrassed. "It's just the things you do seem very grand to me. You won't understand this, Annie, but I never had much life outside the home. I'd only left school a few weeks when I married Tom. I was seventeen when Martin was born."

I'd already known that, but she's right, I can't imagine being married to a man old enough to be my father and having two sons before I was out of my teens.

"Do you miss Martin?" Rick's brother lives and works in America.

"Yes, but to be honest, I feel a bit resentful. He's the one who insists his dad should stay at home and it's Rick and I who have to cope."

"And me," I say. "Please, from now on, don't shut me out."

She smiles at me. "Thank you."

"Do you ever regret marrying Tom?" I ask.

All gentleness vanishes. "Of course I do," she says.

I spend a pleasant evening with Tris and get home just before ten. Rick's not in and there are no messages on the answer phone. In the hope of finding out about his day I turn on the News. The appeal for information about Stacie Frewer is the first item up and I click record on the digibox. The young mother looks so fragile. Rick escorts her to her seat and looks down at her with courteous concern.

The fair-haired stepfather starts his appeal. Stumbling slightly he says, "Please, if anyone out there has seen Stacie or knows where she is, please let us know and bring her back to us. And Stacie darling, if you're listening, you must know that Daddy and Mummy love you very much." He pauses and runs a hand across his face. "Please, whoever's got her, send our lovely little girl home to us... I'm sorry, I can't go on."

He staggers to his feet and stumbles out. Rick ushers the mother after him while Superintendent Roebuck supplies information about the police phone line.

Most people would be concentrating on the parents but I'd looked at Rick and I'd seen the icy hardness in his face. I wonder where he's gone to, the man I'd known and loved, and what sort of monster has come to live within his skin.

Chapter 29: Rick

All through the appeal I watch Terence Frewer. Every cop knows it's possible the heartbroken parent begging for help is responsible for what's happened to the child. I watch Frewer parade his suffering and I remember Emma's father, who never made a show of anything. His buried grief has eaten him from inside. But Terence Frewer... I don't believe a bloody word he says.

After the appeal I take the Frewers home and spend some time with them. When I get back to the Incident Room all the phones are busy.

I've hardly got in the door when Roebuck's yelling, "DI Evans, in my office now."

I don't think the formal 'DI Evans' is a good sign. As I make my way through the Incident Room I see people watching and think this is Dead Man Walking time.

Bob says, "Good luck mate," as I go past his station.

Oh great! It's not just Roebuck waiting for me, DCI Lane's there as well and he looks like he'd take pleasure in throttling anyone who gave him the slightest aggro.

In contrast Roebuck appears remarkably calm. "Right Rick, suppose you tell us what this is all about?"

"About sir?"

"Don't play games with me. I mean this business with Terence Frewer. He tells me you were rude and provocative when you questioned him."

"And Mrs Frewer, did she have any complaints?"

"Well, no."

To my surprise Lane butts in, "She said you'd been very kind."

"That's not the point," snaps Roebuck. "It's Mr Frewer we're talking about. I saw the way you looked at him during that appeal. The whole country saw it. It's not the image we want to put across. We don't need a reputation for Gestapo tactics here... Are you all right?"

"Fine." The room is whizzing round in sickening arcs, the ceiling light has divided into flashing images and I can hear a lisping voice inside my head, *'Gestapo tactics, Richard? And I'd thought you were a civilised young man.'*

You'd better sit down." Roebuck sounds more irritated than sympathetic.

I subside into a chair.

"Look Rick, what problem have you got with Terence Frewer?"

"I think he did it."

Roebuck doesn't speak for a few seconds but when he does his voice is reasonable to the point of patronising. "Of course we've looked at him, we always look at family members. What do you have against him?"

All I have is an instinct I don't even trust myself.

There's a knock on the door and Roebuck snaps, "Come in."

Kelly enters. "Excuse me, sir, but there's a call you ought to hear on line three."

Roebuck says, "Right. You set DI Evans straight please, Chief Inspector."

He hurries out and I wait for the thunderbolt.

Lane glowers at me. "You cocky bastard. You reckon there's nobody can do this job apart from you. Well I checked Terence Frewer. I turned his past inside out and there's no sign of child abuse, no hint of criminal activity, not even a bloody speeding fine."

I take a chance and ask, "What do you reckon to him, sir?"

"He's too bloody smarmy for my taste, but that don't make him a murderer."

The phone rings and Lane answers. As he listens his face grows even grimmer. He raps out questions then says, "I'll be over as soon as possible."

Roebuck comes back in time to hear this. "What's going on Jim?"

Lane glances at me and says reluctantly, "That was a reporter from the Galmouth News. He's found a gold locket in his car. It's engraved with the initials SLF."

Stacie Lucinda Frewer. The world does a series of swivelling arcs.

"How long has it been there?" demands Roebuck.

Lane shrugs his massive shoulders. "God knows. He says it was on the floor."

"I think we'd better consider this journalist very carefully. Is he claiming he left his car unlocked?"

"He says he always leaves the window open an inch or so for his dog." Lane sounds regretful. Like most working cops he'd like to nail a journalist. "Anything useful on your call, sir?"

Roebuck frowns. "It was anonymous. A man claiming he's a member of a group known as the Apostles of Ernest Clift. He claimed they hold rituals in Elmwash Woods and they're taking children to start up a new mausoleum."

"Bollocks," snarls Lane. "It's some loony stirring it." His heavy hand descends on my shoulder, clenching tightly.

"Nevertheless it must be checked," says Roebuck. "Perhaps Rick should go. He knows more about Clift than anyone else we've got."

"No way!" snaps Lane. "I'll do it after I've seen this reporter. You ain't sending Rick back to Elmwash Woods tonight. I told you before, if I had my way I'd not have him on this case at all."

I'm drearily grateful to Lane for his intervention but I wish the old sod didn't rate me quite so low.

"Excuse me, sir, I got work to do." Lane's already at the door.

Roebuck gives a curt nod, his lips a narrow line. The door slams behind the DCI and I wait for extermination. "So what have you got against Terence Frewer, Rick?"

I fall into the trap. "A feeling, sir."

"Your feelings are not evidence. You are not psychic. You're an ordinary working cop. You had a feeling about Ernest Clift and we know how that ended. Tomorrow you'll apologise to Mr Frewer. Now get out there and do some work."

When I get back into the main room they're all looking at me. The room Roebuck's using for an office is only screened by chipboard, so they've heard every word.

"Alright, Rick?" asks Bob.

"Yeah." The room sways. No-one else seems bothered by the earthquake so I guess it must be me. "Kelly, how about you nip out and get me some chips?"

She looks up with a scowl. "I'm manning this phone."

Bob slams to his feet. "Bloody hell, when I was a Detective Constable if a DI said 'Jump' we said, 'Yes Guv, how high?' Don't bother, Kelly, I'll go. Don't want you to miss a chance to brown-nose round the SIO."

"That's enough!" Roebuck appears in his doorway. I guess they'd forgotten hearing through the thin walls goes both ways. "No-one's going anywhere. There's sandwiches in the kitchen. We're not running a take-away service for fussy gits."

He storms back into his office. I go into the kitchen, make a cup of coffee and exhume the sandwiches. They've curled themselves into cylinders.

From the hallway I hear DCI Lane's voice, "There's one thing DS Borrow got right. If a senior officer tells you to do anything, you bloody do it. I won't have no jumped up graduate cops being cocky on my team. You got that?"

"Yes sir."

Just what I need, Kelly with even more motive to stitch me up. Strangely, when she comes into the kitchen, she doesn't look angry.

"What's in these," I ask, pointing to the sandwiches.

"Those are cheese, that's the last two left, and those are

paste. They all taste shit. I won't order from the village shop again."

"What sort of paste?"

"I ordered beef paste. Why?"

"No matter." I take a bite. She's right they taste like shit.

"I'm sorry about before, Guv. Do you want me to go and get you something?"

"Better not. These'll do, as long as they're not fish."

I eat the two cheese sandwiches and three of the paste ones and drink two cups of coffee, and feel a bit more rooted to the ground.

An hour later I feel not so much rooted to the ground as ready to be put six foot under it. My headache's still there and I've got bad gut ache but what scares me is this pain right through my chest. It makes it hard to breathe. I wonder if I'm about to have a heart attack and which of these ugly buggers will give me CPR.

Chapter 30: Annie

I'm almost asleep when I hear the car pull up. Rick's footsteps sound unsteady and my tension mounts. I hear him on the stairs, hauling himself up, stumbling, waiting, then moving on again. I sit up, pressed against the steel bed head. My eyes are on the small cupboard I've used to barricade the door. He stops outside my room. I can hear his ragged breathing. *'Oh please God, not again.'*

"Annie, are you awake?"

I stay still and silent. The door handle turns, hits the obstruction and halts.

"Annie? Can I come in, please? Just to get something."

"What do you want?"

"To get to the medicine cupboard."

I'm dressed in the solid pyjamas I usually wear on winter lecture tours. I creep out of bed and shove the cupboard clear.

"Thanks." He passes me without a look and heads into the en suite.

I stand near the door and watch him fumble through the medicine cabinet.

"What are you looking for?"

"Something for indigestion. I'll be out of your way in a minute." He winces and rubs his chest. "Christ, it hurts."

I feel a tremor of fearful memory. "If you move out the way I'll find you something."

"You sure? I'm sorry I woke you."

"The sooner you get out of the way, the sooner I'll be able to go back to bed." The words come out sharper than I intend and I flinch, waiting for his anger and abuse.

"Sorry." If he takes it that meekly he must feel terrible.

I have to rummage deep into the cupboard to reach the indigestion cures.

Rick's waiting on the landing, leaning heavily against

the wall. Everything about him seems down, from the slumped shoulders to the lines beside his mouth. It's possible to recognise the cold-faced man I'd watched on television two hours ago but not the Beast of my recurrent nightmare.

"Go downstairs. I'll mix it for you."

"But you... thanks."

In the kitchen I dissolve the tablets and take them into the living room. He's sitting on the sofa with his jacket and tie off. His shirt is stained with sweat but he's shivering.

I hand him the fizzing mixture and turn on the fire, then I sit opposite him.

He gulps it down. "You don't have to stay up. I'm sorry I woke you."

"It's not like you to get indigestion."

Rick gives me a wary look, as if he can't believe I'm being nice. "It's been a stressy sort of day, loads of aggro and eating the wrong stuff on the run."

"Eating what sort of wrong stuff on the run?"

"These paste sandwiches, bloody awful things, tasted like they'd come via the mortuary."

"Would that be fish paste?"

"Could be. Kelly said not but they were beyond identification."

"You idiot."

"I know it was bloody stupid but I hadn't eaten all day. I asked Kelly to go and get me some chips but Roebuck said he'd got better uses for officers than running errands for fussy gits."

"It will serve the bastard right if you're off sick and he has to manage without you."

"I reckon he'd prefer my space to my company. I got the feeling he was glad of an excuse to send me home."

I don't pretend to misunderstand. "I saw you on television."

"The stepfather wanted to do it... fancies himself as a TV star." Rick looks like there's a bad taste in his mouth; it might be the fish paste repeating on him but I don't think so.

"You think he did it, don't you?"

"I was that obvious?"

"It was the way you looked at him."

"No wonder I got a lecture from Roebuck about the sympathetic face of modern policing and how I wasn't showing it."

"Why do you think it was the father?" I need to know what Rick's thinking, then maybe I can help.

"I've got this feeling he knows more about it than he's letting on."

"But you've got no evidence?" I try not to make the question sound arsey.

Apparently I fail. Rick slams his clenched fist on the sofa arm. "God, you sound like bloody Roebuck!" He must see my instinctive withdrawal. "Sorry, I didn't mean to shout. But can't you understand what I mean? It's like when you say some piece of art is good. I can't see it's any different from loads of others but you can because it's what you do and you've got an instinct for it."

The difference is that my art instincts, if wrong, might make me look a fool or lose a bit of cash, but when the police go with instinct instead of evidence some poor sod could get banged up for life.

"You must know what I mean, Annie. It's gut instinct."

I've known for years that Rick has a talent for saying the grotesquely appropriate but it still makes me smile.

"What's so funny about that?"

"If you provided the sound effects for your gut instinct quite so graphically I'm not surprised the Superintendent wasn't keen."

Rick stops glaring and looks embarrassed. "I hoped you hadn't noticed. Sorry."

"That's okay... Do you want to talk about it?" If I keep trying to build bridges maybe one of them will take our weight.

"Not much to tell. Just that I've felt crap all day. I reckon most of the people in Saronholt think I'm the Force's contribution to Incontinence Awareness Day. I've spent half my time in bloody loos... speaking of which..."

He drags himself to his feet and goes into the cloakroom. While he's gone I fill a hot bottle. "Thanks." He returns, sits down and leans back, cuddling the bottle to him. "Jesus, I feel rough."

"Do you want to talk about what's got you in this state?"

"Getting slaughtered last night you mean?" He opens his eyes and looks at me challengingly.

"I meant this case. It's getting to you isn't it?"

"Yeah, crazy isn't it? I mean after all the crap I've seen."

"I think that probably makes it harder. Why do you think the stepfather's responsible?"

He shrugs. "I don't know. It's like I said... a feeling. There's something in his attitude... it's there when he's talking to his wife... sort of possessive and controlling. But there's no evidence. Perhaps I've got it wrong and I'm pinning it on him because I can't face the truth."

"What do you mean?"

"That I let a child killer get past me. That Clift was a harmless nutcase and I hounded him into bloody topping himself. Every time I walk into the Incident Room I can hear them whispering about me." His voice gets faster and shriller. "Or it could be a paedophile ring. There's this new group of paedophiles. They call themselves *The Apostles of Ernest Clift*."

He breaks off, gasping for breath. I want to say 'nonsense' and dispel his nightmare with brisk common-sense, but I'm paralysed by the violence and increasing incoherence of his speech. Words like paranoia and delusions of persecution pinch at my mind. All instincts of self-preservation warn me I ought to run, but something stronger makes me stay.

Chapter 31: Annie

Slicing through my fear I hear Rick whimpering. He's leaning forward with his hand pressed against his chest and his colour is greyish-white. "What's wrong? Is the pain worse?"

"Yeah, it's going right through." He manages a twist of the lips, which I think is intended as a reassuring smile. "Don't worry, it'll pass."

I remember Dad. "I'm going to call an ambulance."

"No way. It's just indigestion. I'll look a bloody fool if you dial triple nine for that."

"Your street cred's going to end up pretty pear-shaped if you're dead."

"Thought that's the way you'd prefer it."

"What do you mean?"

"You'd be better off without me clogging up your life. No messy divorce. You could just get on with things."

Of all the cruel things Rick could say to me that must rate as the worst. Never, even straight after he raped me, have I wished him dead. Then I see the fear in his eyes and realise he really thinks I'd be happy with him gone.

"Don't be so stupid. Of course I don't want you dead."

He opens his mouth to speak then swallows and mutters, "I'm sorry, Annie, I'd better get to the cloakroom. I feel bloody sick."

"Stay there, I'll get a bowl,"

As I pass it to him our hands touch and I realise his is burning hot. Timidly I rest my fingers on his forehead. "Rick, your temperature's really high!"

He stares at me bearily. "Do you reckon that's why I'm talking so much crap?"

When he says that, my fear doesn't disappear but it does lessen considerably. "I expect so."

He gives me a wavering smile then leans forward,

elbows on knees, head cradled in his hands. For a moment I stand there uncertain, then I move behind him and lean over the sofa to slide my hand under his untucked shirt and rub his back between the shoulder blades.

He murmurs, "That's good."

"You'll be okay. Just give it a few minutes for the stuff to work." In parallel I hold a priority discourse with my God, *'Don't you dare let him be having a heart attack. You haven't done much for either of us recently so it's about time you started earning your keep... Please God.'*

After a minute I move round to sit on the sofa arm and get into rhythm massaging his back. The smooth elasticity of his skin is so familiar that touching him feels like coming home. And yet there's a difference, his back is bony and I'm shocked how thin he's got.

"Thanks love, that feels..." the words are cut off by a hefty belch.

"Better?" I supply the end of the sentence hopefully.

"Will be... in a minute... Oh Christ!" He grabs the bowl and it's several minutes before he manages to sit upright again. "Sorry. Didn't mean to gross you out."

"No problem. Has the pain gone?"

"More or less." Hiccups succeed the more harrowing sound effects. I fetch him a glass of water and after a minute he says, "Reckon that's it, no heart attack tonight."

"Thank God."

"You ought to go to bed."

"In a few minutes. I want to make sure you're okay. I was worried about you."

"Yeah, I was getting pretty worried about me too. Sorry to be such a bloody nuisance."

"How do you feel?"

"Better than I did but I've got a lousy headache. I can't shift it."

I stroke his forehead and he says gratefully, "That's nice. Your hand's so cool."

"Actually it's your head that's so hot. Would you like me to get an ice pack?"

"No, carry on doing that, just for a little while if you don't mind."

I massage his temples while he sits with his eyes shut.

I send a swift word of thanks to the Almighty, something along the lines of, *'Thanks God, that's a bit better, so how about you keep it up?'*

At last I whisper, "Are you asleep, Rick?"

"No. I wish I could sleep. I'm so bloody tired."

"Hang on a minute." I run upstairs to fetch pillows and duvet from the spare room and the sleeping pills Maris gave me from my handbag. Then I hesitate. I don't trust unlabelled drugs. I break a pill and take Rick the smaller bit.

He sits up to swallow it and his shirt and trousers twist round him.

"You'll be more comfortable if you undress."

"What? But you wouldn't like… I mean…" he stumbles to a halt and nurses his head between his hands. He's trembling with weakness and exhaustion.

I look down at him, probing my senses for fear, but I fail to find it. My Viking Warrior is incapable of rape and pillage tonight.

I help him to strip down to his boxers. "Lie down again."

"Yeah, I don't reckon I could make it up the stairs."

I cover him with the duvet, pull an armchair near to the sofa and sit beside him. "I spent some time with your mum today."

That startles him. "How come?"

"Your dad was being awkward about going into the respite place so I went and talked him into it. Why didn't you tell me how bad he'd got?"

"It's not your problem. But thanks for sorting it and for being good to my mum."

"I wasn't being good. I like her."

"What she really needs is a bloody good holiday. Next

time the old man's in respite I'll try and fix up for her to go somewhere."

Remembered happiness makes me ask, "Do you remember that place in Devon?"

"I'll never forget it. You had that red dress, the amazingly sexy one... You haven't worn that for ages." His voice is slurring and he keeps yawning.

"That was a good time, wasn't it?"

"The best." His fingers grope for mine and intertwine. "Don't leave me."

Chapter 32: Annie

When I wake, I'm stiff and aching. I fell asleep in the chair. The clock on the mantelpiece says seven-fifteen. It's an antique carriage clock bestowed on us by my mother, so it's more posh than accurate. I check my phone and find it says the same.

I don't know what he meant by *'don't leave me.'* Was it a plea to save our marriage or just that he didn't want to be left alone when he felt ill? For that matter what did I mean by replying *'I won't?'*

He was crying in the night. Still asleep, he begged that someone would let him out. It's happened before when he's been sick or stressed. I'd stroked his forehead and told him he was okay, and after a while he'd quietened into a deeper sleep.

I shower and dress, then cook myself breakfast. By half-eight Rick still shows no sign of coming back to life and I know I ought to wake him. I put the percolator on and gather up towel and sponge, but before I use ruthless methods, I kneel by the sofa and say, "Rick? Come on, Rick, wake up."

There's no response. His skin is sallow and there are lines on his face that shouldn't be there for another twenty years. I touch his forehead. His temperature's still up, although I'd guess it's lower than last night. He looks ill and vulnerable.

I take the sponge and towel back into the kitchen and phone him in sick.

The lecture I'm giving this afternoon is one of my major ones of the year and, mindful of Neil's tendency to panic, I ring through to College. Lucy's in the office and I ask her to tell him I'm taking my record-keeping time at home but I'll be in this afternoon. Then I turn the answer phone to intercept and get out my files.

It's amazing how much I get done without the interruptions of students and colleagues. By half-eleven I've finished and go through to the kitchen to check the answer phone. There's just one message, from Maris: 'Hello, Annie, it's me. I'm home and I need you. I thought you would have visited me by now.'

"Who's that?" asks Rick from the doorway.

"No-one important. How are you feeling?"

"Fine."

"Is that fine as in bloody awful or some other sort?"

He gives me a weary grin. "Yeah, fine as in bloody awful covers it. I'm tired and kind of achy and my head feels like it's been stuffed with cottonwool."

"Come and sit down."

He makes a groggy try for a stool and nearly falls.

"You'd better go back in the sitting room."

"Thought I'd trashed that already and ought to be moving on." He looks at the clock. "Jesus! Why didn't you wake me? Roebuck's going to slaughter me."

"It's okay. I phoned in and told Superintendent Roebuck you're sick."

"I can't go off sick when there's a childhunt on."

I'm tempted to point out he doesn't have a choice; he's only staying upright by clinging to the breakfast bar.

"Rick, I promise it's okay. Roebuck was quite sympathetic, especially as I told him you'd been poisoned by their fish paste sandwiches."

He slumps against the wall. "Thanks for sorting it. I still feel pretty rough."

"You look it. Go and lie down again and I'll get you some breakfast."

I make a pot of tea and a pile of toast and sit opposite him as he struggles to eat. He's shivering and I'm sure his temperature is rising again.

The doorbell rings and I go to answer it.

"Good morning, Arianne." Mother sails through the hall and on into the living room, brushing my cheek with a kiss as she passes.

"Hello Mother," I stammer, "I thought you were playing Bridge this afternoon." Mother always rests before social engagements and she takes Bridge very seriously.

"I am but something urgent has occurred. I telephoned the Art College and they informed me you were at home... Oh Richard, you're here."

Rick pulls the duvet closer round him. "Yeah. Sorry, I'm not dressed for visitors."

Mother arches her delicately shaped eyebrows. "But then you're not exactly dressed for the drawing room, are you?"

"Rick's not well," I say.

"Still ill? In my day people didn't have time to lounge around at home. In my generation people soldiered on."

If I wasn't so cross with her I'd have to laugh. 'Soldiering on' is not within my mother's terms of reference; in fact it rates somewhere below 'making the best of things.'

"Sit down, Mother. I'm giving Rick his breakfast. Would you like a cup of tea?"

"No thank you, dear, I prefer coffee at lunch time."

"I'll make you some when Rick's finished." I perch on the sofa next to him.

Mother takes the seat opposite. She sits beautifully, her legs crossed, displaying the elegant arch of her exquisitely shod foot. After a few minutes she gets out her cigarettes.

"Mother, do you mind not doing that in here?"

She looks offended. "You cannot expect me to go into the garden to smoke?"

"It's very nice out there. The Winter-Flowering Jasmine's looking great this year."

Mother's expression is bleak enough to freeze the hardiest flower in the bud. "No, thank you, you know how susceptible I am to the cold. Arianne, if you could spare me a little of your attention, I wish to talk to you."

Rick hauls himself to his feet. "I'll go upstairs and leave you two to talk."

He pads out of the room, the duvet gathered round him like a quilted Roman toga.

The door is hardly shut before Mother gives an affected shudder and says, "I do not know how you can live with that crude man."

"And I don't know how I could live without him."

The words come instinctively, with no desire to provoke, but Mother switches into martyr mode. "I cannot understand why both my daughters never consider me."

"Both of us?" So I'm not the sole offender this time.

"For Elaine to let me down like this is intolerable."

The more melodramatic she gets the less alarmed I feel. "What's happened?"

"Out of the blue, Philip has announced he is going away this weekend and Elaine will have to look after the children."

"Where's Philip going?" My brother-in-law's not exactly the wild roaming type.

"To a Marketing Conference. He has to fill in for a colleague who is unwell."

So why is that a problem? I'm still confused and obviously look it.

"Arianne, surely you haven't forgotten too? We are going to the ballet tomorrow. It's our 'Girls Night Out.'" She says the last few words with a sort of coy bravado. 'Girls' Night Out' is what she calls our monthly mother-daughter-sister bonding sessions, when she arranges for the three of us to go out for a meal and theatre trip.

"Can't Felicity look after the boys?"

"Apparently she's busy. She's always out when she should be studying. Of course it's Philip's fault, he has spoiled the children."

"It will have to be you and me, Mother."

She looks discontented. "But they are such good tickets. It's such a waste. I wondered if you had a friend who'd like to come?"

Again I hit the fact that I've got lots of colleagues but

not much to show for friends. "I'll try to think of someone."

"I did think of asking Maris."

"But she's just had a baby."

"Exactly. I thought it might cheer her up. She's back home you know but she had to leave the baby in hospital. It seems there's something not right with it, poor little thing."

"Have you been to see her?"

"Of course not. Don't be silly, Arianne. How could I get up that terrible track in this weather? No taxi driver would take me. Mrs Goodman's son drove her up there in his Landrover. She said Maris was very depressed. You ought to go and see her."

"Yes." If Mrs Goodman, half-crippled by arthritis, could manage it, I have no excuse.

After I've changed for work, I load a tray with a jug of fruit juice, a flask of tea and a plate of plain biscuits and take it up to Rick.

"Thanks. I didn't mean to make you late for work." He smiles at me but he's shivering violently.

I speak without thinking, "Go into our room, Rick. It's more comfortable."

He obeys me without questioning, which is just as well. If he'd asked for some sort of ground-rules I wouldn't know what to say. Against all sense and reason I've just invited Rick back into the bed in which he'd raped me less than four days ago.

Chapter 33: Annie

"Annie, thank God you've made it!" Neil pounces on me as soon as I walk through the door.

"Don't start that 'Annie you're late' business again."

He looks blank, then susses out what I mean and grins. "Well, you're not early. No, don't even joke about walking out on me. I've been terrified you weren't going to turn up and I'd have to give the lecture. With what I know about Post Modern Feminism we'd all be headed home by two-fifteen."

"Sounds good to me. But I don't know what the fuss is about, didn't Lucy give you my message?"

He walks with me towards the Lecture Theatre. "Yes, along with a sermon about running my department more efficiently and not allowing my colleagues so much leeway. I never thought I'd say it, but I'll be glad to have Maris back."

"I'm going to see her later."

"Lucky you."

"Rick's not well so I won't be able to stay long but I've got to go. Mother says she's depressed and the baby's very ill."

"I heard. I arranged for a bouquet from the department and I didn't know whether to put *'Congratulations'* or *'With Sympathy'* on the card."

"What did you put?" Neil has blank spots in tact with people he dislikes.

"*'Best wishes.'* I wonder, if the baby dies, if she'll want to come back to work fairly soon?"

This hits a raw nerve. Doesn't he realise the loss of a child is the ultimate bereavement? "You bastard!"

He stares at me in blank astonishment. "What?"

"You can't wish the baby dead because you hate Lucy and want to get Maris back."

His face goes taut with shock. "What the hell do you think I am?"

We've reached the lecture theatre but he grabs my arm to stop me entering. "Think about it logically. What would actually suit me best is for Maris to quit working and stay home permanently to take care of the kid. Then I could get Graphics on a par with the rest of this Department."

"But Maris couldn't afford to give up work."

The look he gives me mingles disbelief with contempt. "You're her best buddy, surely you know Maris' grandfather was a property developer, just about a millionaire. Maris' mother was his only child. Now she's gone bonkers and Maris is in charge of the lot."

I stare at him. "How do you know this?"

"It's no secret. That old Goodman woman told me years ago. You've known Maris since you were kids and you know nothing about her. And you call me a bastard! For God's sake get in there and give your bloody lecture."

He pushes the door open and I have no chance to apologise or reply.

It's a packed house. Not just Mainstream students but a lot of Access and Part-time. Women are in the majority. I stroll to the front and smile at them. "Good afternoon. I'm sorry I've kept you waiting. My husband is ill and I'm sure you'll appreciate that in some circumstances a woman's place is definitely in the home."

By the time they register this blatantly unfeminist provocation I'm into my lecture, outlining the Feminist role in Post Modernism. In the brief break before I take questions I phone home. Rick sounds subdued but assures me he's fine.

The question time becomes a hot debate. Lucy turns up trumps; she has strong views but she keeps the argument well short of abuse.

When it's over, I hunt for Neil, to try and make my peace. He's in his office and greets me with a perfectly friendly smile.

"Hi. Nice lecture. Sorry I couldn't stop for the questions. How did it go?"

"Okay. Look, I wanted to say sorry about before."

"No problem."

"How's your neck?"

"Better than it was. This typing's a killer though."

"Can't you record it for Sara to do?"

"It's for a lecture I'm giving in London next week. You know what a balls up Sara will make of it and I don't plan to look a total idiot."

"Dictate it on to one of the College recorders and I'll do it for you."

"You're an angel. I hate to be awkward, but could you take down that Hannibal Lecter monstrosity you're displaying in the Entrance Hall?"

I have no problem in identifying the piece of art he means. "Wesley's one of our most talented students."

"I know he is. I can practically see the maggots wiggle in that painting. But next week I've got tasters for the Art in the Community courses we're setting up. There's a drive to get retired people in and most of them want to paint pretty watercolours."

"Yuck!"

He scowls at me. "If we want to maintain the prestigious courses we have to do these bread and butter ones. It's not easy to set them up. They cost the students a fortune since the bloody Skills Council has cut funding for anything they call a leisure course. Do you know how hard I have to fight to keep us going?"

I remember what Neil was like fifteen years ago, so beautiful and confident and a charismatic teacher. I'm overcome by a sense of waste.

"Sorry. I know you work really hard and I wouldn't have your job for anything, but I could keep things running for a few weeks while you took a Sabbatical and concentrated on your own art."

"Thanks for the offer, sweetheart. If I get a chance I'll take you up on it. I'm hoping to do a series based on Chloe and the baby. That's if Josef will let her."

"Why shouldn't he?"

Neil looks cagey. "He got the wrong idea about the modelling fee."

"But why? I'm going to pay for the picture I've done of her, even though I did it from memory."

"Josef wouldn't mind Chloe taking a modelling fee from you."

"Then why?... Oh I see."

"My reputation." There's a surprising note of bitterness in his voice.

"Josef must be finding it hard to think straight at the moment. If you like I'll have a word with him."

"It's not just Josef."

I stare at him. "That's ridiculous. No-one with any sense would believe you'd hit on a vulnerable kid like Chloe."

"Then, judging by the snide comments I've been getting, there's a lot of people without any sense round here."

"I haven't heard anything." But I've been fully occupied with my own problems.

"Believe it or not, in all my teaching career, I've only ever slept with one of my students."

In that case I know better than anyone who that one student was. So where has Neil's reputation come from? As soon as I think about it the answer presents itself: the back-biting has come from Maris, Joan Hammond and a few other gossiping bitches who don't like having a handsome, flamboyant guy as their boss.

He mistakes my silence for disbelief. "Why the hell should I risk my job and professional reputation when there are so many non-students in the world who are up for sex with me?"

His naive egotism makes me smile. "Don't pretend you utterly hate the Casanova image, Neil."

He grins. "I can live with Casanova but I don't like being treated like I'm a sleazy predator. Anyway that's enough of my problems. How's the murder hunt going?"

"It's not a murder hunt yet. Not unless they've found her this afternoon?"

"Not that I've heard, but all the papers are tying it in with the Elmwash murders. You must know more about that business than me."

"I don't know much. Rick tries not to bring his work home."

"I recorded the documentary about Elmwash. Borrow the DVD if you want." He selects a DVD from a pile on his desk and pushes it towards me.

"Thanks." Neil did his PhD on Art and Images of Evil and he's retained his interest in criminology.

He glances at his watch. "I've got a meeting. See you." He hurries away.

I hesitate, then slip the Elmwash recording into my bag.

Chapter 34: Annie

"Annie, you've come at last." Maris' voice is flat and lifeless and so is her brown hair. Otherwise she looks quite fit. Her figure's gone back to what I remember it, a sort of doughy bulk.

"Of course I came. How are you, Maris?"

"All right."

"And the baby?"

"We'll know one way or the other in the next few days."

Another woman would say the words with tears or with gallant brightness, Maris says it in a monotone that I find as chilling as the musty dampness of the hall.

"I can't stay long," I warn her.

"No-one ever stays with me." There's still no expression in her voice.

In the kitchen I spot the bouquet Neil sent, lying on the draining board. "Shall I put these in water? Have you got a vase?"

Maris doesn't answer so I rummage through the cupboards, find a large earthenware jug and put the flowers in it. It's surprisingly effective with the rough kitchenware and the exotic blooms.

Desperate to make conversation I gabble about events in the department. I keep away from Chloe and Josef and their flourishing baby boy, but she asks, "What about that baby? The one you were so interested in?"

"He's doing fine and Chloe seems happier when she's at College. Of course Joey's too young to go in the crèche, so most times they take turns looking after him, but for my lecture this afternoon they smuggled him in. I didn't know until the end. When I was leaving I heard snuffling and realised it was coming from under Chloe's coat."

Maris doesn't smile. "It's against College rules."

"Don't you want to be at the hospital with your baby? I could take you there."

"There's no point in that."

"What are you calling him?" Giving him a name might anchor him to this world.

"I thought William, if you'd like that."

"It was my father's name."

"I know."

"But don't you want to call him after the baby's father?"

"I don't see why. He never considered us."

I'm not sure having a fatal heart attack three weeks after the child's conception makes the poor guy a seriously neglectful father. "I have to go. Rick isn't well."

"You're going to stay with him, aren't you? Even though he did that terrible thing."

"Please Maris, forget about that. He didn't mean to hurt me."

"You mean he's having a breakdown?" She sounds eager.

I'm not giving her any more rope to hang Rick. "He's fine. Just tired and worried about this missing child case."

"They had it on the News: how this murderer they thought was dead wasn't really. He feels guilty, doesn't he? Because it's his fault."

Maris has a numbing effect on me. I should feel angry but I just feel cold and drained. "No! He's just sorry for the child and her mother."

"She should have looked after the child better. People who don't look after things deserve to lose them."

I stare at her in disbelief. "How can you be so cruel?" I grab my coat and bag.

"Don't go. I didn't mean it." She wipes her hand across her trembling lips. "I'm not well. Please wait while I go to the bathroom. There could be bleeding. I'd like to know there's someone in the house."

"Okay." I can't refuse that appeal.

"Don't worry if I take a little while."

Eventually she returns and I say, "I've got a present for the baby but I don't know if you'd rather not have it until you've got him home."

"It doesn't matter."

I get out the package containing two matinee jackets and hand it to her.

"You like babies don't you, Annie? Having a baby is important to you?"

"Yes."

"That's what I thought. I was afraid if I didn't have a baby you wouldn't come."

"Of course I came." And now I'm going, much more eagerly.

"Don't leave me," she says as we walk through the hall.

"What?"

"I don't want you to go."

"Maris, I'm sorry but I must." The swollen panels of the front door make it stick. I wrench it open and hurry out into the rain.

I clamber into my car and switch the engine on. The steering wheel feels sluggish and there's a rumbling noise as I try to reverse.

"Oh God, you're kidding!" I say as I grab my torch and scramble out to peer at my tyres. Front and rear on the passenger side are both flat. I must have gone over a razor sharp flint. "That bloody track!"

I dig out my mobile to phone the RAC and stare at the blank screen. I'd forgotten there's no reception here.

My instinct is to walk down to the road and ring for a taxi. But I have to tell Maris what has happened. She'll worry if she finds my car abandoned outside her house. Of course it's perfectly simple, I'll go in and use her phone. Half an hour and I'll be heading home.

I ring the bell. No answer. I try again then bang upon the door. I hammer for over five minutes but she doesn't come, so I use my torch to pick my way round to the back. I turn my heel on the rough ground and thorny plants snag at my tights and skirt.

The back door isn't locked. I open it, step into the scullery and flash my torch around until I find a light switch. It's the bleakest place I've ever seen, grey walls and grey slab floor and sour damp smell. There are two doors. I guess the one in the corner leads down to the cellar, while the other goes into the house.

My stomach is clenched into a knot but I shake myself into action and call, "Maris? Maris, are you there?"

I hear a whispering groan that echoes my name. I push the door open and find Maris sitting on the kitchen floor, a knife in one hand, her other arm dripping blood.

"Oh God! Maris, what have you done?"

"Annie, you came back." A smile of remarkable sweetness lights up her sallow face.

Chapter 35: Rick

It's dark and damp and everything stinks of piss. I'm so cold. I've thumped at the door until my hands are raw. I lick them and the broken skin feels rough beneath my tongue. I can taste blood and tears, but I'm not crying now. I'm too scared for that. I curl into a ball. The concrete floor cuts into my nakedness and the walls are rough and covered with ice cold slime. Through the small vent beside the overhead cistern I can see a chequered pattern of moonlight. It's all I have to hold onto. A small rectangle of light from the outside world.

Suddenly I know I'm not alone. There's somebody else, whimpering in the blackness. It's a lost child.

My screams wake me but it takes some time to register that I'm lying in my bed. I'm shaking and shivering and yet the bed is soaked with sweat. That was one serious bastard of a nightmare, even for me. Although, on the bright side, I wasn't joined in my sleep by Ernest Clift.

I get up. I'm still shaky but fit enough to grab a shower and shave. I cling to the thought that Annie will soon be home. I'll tell her I'm sorry and I'll offer to go back to therapy if she reckons it will help.

I strip the bed and put fresh bedclothes on. Then I dress in clean jeans and sweatshirt and go downstairs to raid the freezer. I find Annie's home-made lasagne, defrost it in the microwave and put it in the oven to cook through. I lay the dining table, using our best tablecloth and the slim yellow candles that give a romantic light. When it comes to music, I opt for totally sloppy and dig out a song that goes back to our first date.

Before I do anything else I need to phone my mum and check everything's okay. Mum hasn't got anyone but me to look out for her. Martin's lived in America for a good few years and shows no sign of coming back. I'm glad he's not around. He's good at doing the oldest son thing when it comes to mouthing off. To hear him talk you'd think he did everything for Mum and Dad, but the truth is he's a selfish bastard who'll never get off his arse for anyone.

"Rick, how lovely to hear from you." Whatever she's doing Mum always seems pleased when I phone or come round. "Are you okay, love?"

"Yeah, I'm fine." No need to worry her. "You enjoying your free time?"

"Oh yes. Thanks to Annie. Did she tell you how she helped me yesterday?"

"Sort of." I hadn't really taken a lot of it on board.

"She's a lovely girl." Mum's voice is warm. "I just wish..." she breaks off.

"Wish what?" I ask.

"Nothing."

"What?"

As an interrogation technique it wouldn't wring a confession out of a six-year-old, but Mum's not really fighting all that hard. "Martin and Veronica have separated."

"Wow, didn't see that coming!" I'm being sarcastic. Martin is a vicious, control-freak. This is his third marriage and it looks like he's heading for his third divorce.

"I worry about the children. They must get hurt every time his relationships break down."

She doesn't add that it hurts her horribly that she has so little contact with the four grandchildren Martin's produced from his three marriages. I know she's longing for the time Annie and I have kids but she never says so; not like Annie's mother. I wonder why no-one seems to understand how terrifying the thought of having children is. Whatever you do, it's impossible to keep them safe.

"I'm sorry, Mum."

"There's no reason you should be sorry. None of it's your fault. I'm glad one of you has managed to make a good relationship. It makes me feel less of a failure."

The trouble is, she's not being sarcastic. She really thinks I'm not like my dad.

"Sorry, Mum, someone's just pulled up outside, I've got to go."

I'm expecting Annie but the doorbell rings. I open the door and Bob's standing there.

"Hi mate, can't stop, just wanted to check you're okay."

"Better than I was. Anything happening with the case?"

"Not a bloody thing. Just us chasing all the false sightings round the country. Sometimes these TV appeals are more trouble than they're worth."

"Tell me about it. How many sightings so far?"

"Over two hundred at the last count. And three crazy confessions. Talk about a waste of time. Roebuck asked me to check if you'll be fit for Court tomorrow?"

"Yeah, should be." It takes an effort to tear my mind back to a completed case. I must read through my notes later, to make sure I've got it wrapped up.

"See you tomorrow then."

He leaves and I go upstairs to sort out suitable clothes. When dressing for Court you have to walk the line, smart but not too flashy, and not too pricey or the jury think you're on the take.

There's no sign of Annie and I'm getting edgy. It worries me that she's driving at night on the wet lanes. The phone rings. I grab it and say, "Hello?"

"Rick it's me."

"Annie, are you all right?"

"Yes, well sort of... I've got a puncture."

"No problem, I'll come out and sort it. You're not hurt are you? You didn't come off the road?"

She speaks in the same tight tone, "No, I'm still at Maris' house. You can't sort it because it's two punctures and the tyres are pretty well shredded. Anyway I can't come home because Maris needs me... I'm really sorry Rick."

"Shall I come over and see you?"

She hesitates. "You'd better not. I don't think Maris would like it."

"Okay. Take care of yourself."

I start to put the phone down when she says something else that I half catch. I slam the phone back against my ear.

"Annie, what was that you said?" But she's already gone.

I want a drink but I know it's time I made a real effort to turn my life round. What was it Annie said last thing on the phone? I can't believe it's what I thought but I'm not going to blow it again.

I serve my dinner but I don't really fancy it. When the doorbell rings I think about ignoring it, but it peals again so I go to answer.

"Kelly, what are you doing here?"

"I was passing and thought I'd see if you're okay."

"Yeah, I'm getting there. Come in for a minute, you're letting the cold in."

She steps inside the hall. "I don't want to disturb you and your wife, Guv."

"My wife's not here. She's had to stay with a friend who's sick."

"Oh, I see." From the way she says it I reckon she's heard rumours about the way things are between Annie and me. "I wanted to say sorry about those sandwiches."

"Sandwiches? Oh them. Yeah, I can't eat fish."

"So everyone's been telling me today." She pulls a wry face. "DCI Lane told me if I couldn't handle catering he'd find a less demanding job for me."

"That sounds pretty moderate for the DCI. You're lucky you didn't poison somebody he likes." I see the look she can't quite cover up. "Okay, that was a stupid thing to say. DCI Lane doesn't like anyone. You can poison the whole bloody lot of us and he won't give a shit, except there'll be no-one left to do the work. Bob Borrow said there aren't any developments from the broadcast?"

"Nothing that looks much good. We're going for

151

Crimescene next."

"Terry Frewer will love that." Crimescene is the newest, most flashy, appeal-to-the-public programme on TV.

"I had another go at the babysitter, Guv."

"Vicki the teenage nymphomaniac? Any joy?"

She frowns. "I'm not sure."

"Have you eaten? Come in and have something and bring me up to speed."

She gives me a wary look and I guess she's trying to suss out whether she wants to eat with a senior officer, in his home, when she's heard his marriage is dodgy and his wife's away for the night. Then she says, "Cheers Guv, I'm starving."

I'm not sure whether I've passed the test or failed but I've no plans to score with Kelly so I guess I'll never know.

We eat our food out in the kitchen at the breakfast bar. She tells me how, when she thought about it, she reckoned I was right, and talked to Vicki again.

She sums up, emphasising her points by jabbing the pasta with her fork. "Vicki insisted Terry Frewer would never let Stacie go out in the garden wearing her best dress. If she was dressed up he'd make her sit inside. Apparently he created hell when Stacie's mum bought her a pair of jeans to go up to the animal sanctuary."

"You can't arrest a guy for wanting his stepdaughter to look nice."

"I still think there's something funny about her being out there in that dress."

"You humouring me?"

She gives me another wary look then smiles. "No Guv, I wouldn't do that. Except I'll be humouring your food requests in future."

"I'd like to know why Vicki hates Terence Frewer."

I see Kelly's expression change. "Do you think Vicki could have done something to Stacie? To spite Stacie's dad?"

"No."

"You can't be that sure, Guv."

"Yes I can. I had Mark Corrigan check out Vicki's whereabouts last Sunday. She was at a stables over at Millwash. They had an open day and she was helping."

I allow Kelly a few moments to process two unpalatable facts: one, I'd spotted a possible suspect long before she had, and two, I'd used another detective constable to look into Vicki's alibi.

At last I say, "Was there anything in that stuff you got from Stacie's teacher?"

"Just a load of the kid's drawings."

"I wouldn't mind taking a look sometime." Although I don't know what I'm looking for.

"I'll drop it in to you on my way home tonight."

Removing evidence from the Incident Room! Roebuck will go berserk if he finds out. "I can't get it back first thing. I'm in Court tomorrow," I warn her.

"I'll pick it up in the morning. I'd better get back, Guv. Thanks for the food."

As I show her out I think having Kelly on my side could be way more scary than her as an enemy.

Chapter 36: Annie

"You ought to go to hospital."

Maris ignores me, the way she's done the last five times I've suggested it. I guess she knows I want her to go there as much for myself as her. She's got a first aid kit and the wounds on her arm aren't bad, cuts rather than gashes, nothing that really needs a trip to A&E. Maris seems a lot calmer than me. She sits there smiling while I put a dressing on her arm. All the time her eyes stay on my face.

"Why, Maris?"

She doesn't answer. Instead she says, "You're cold, I'll find you some dry clothes."

"Don't bother. I'll see what I've got in the car."

Out in the rain I feel an absurd desire to run down the rutted lane into the darkness and hide from everyone. I don't. That would be a crazy thing to do. Instead I open the car boot. There's no clothes of mine but there are old jeans and a sweatshirt Rick dumped in there the last time he worked on my car.

I take them to the bathroom and put them on, using my skirt belt to tether the jeans. They smell of oil and Rick's deodorant and I feel safe when I'm wearing them.

Safe? What's wrong with me? Of course I'm perfectly safe. I'm here with Maris, whom I've known since I was a child. Okay, she's just done something really stupid but she's been through an awful lot. I shudder. If I hadn't happened to have those punctures and come back she'd probably be dead.

When I go down to the front room she's waiting for me and she's poured me a glass of wine. "I could have lent you clothes. You don't have to wear those awful things."

"They're fine."

I curl up in the armchair. I don't want the wine but, under Maris' gaze, I take a sip.

We sit for a long time in silence. Under my lashes, I peer at her and see a strangely familiar look, a mixture of greed and calculation. Recognition hits me. The first time I saw it was back in Junior School. It was the Top Year's Christmas play and I was Cinderella, the only time in my life I got the lead. An hour before lift-off, the girl who was playing the Fairy Godmother fell down a flight of stairs and broke her arm. Although she was two years younger, Maris had played the part. We didn't run to understudies and she was the only one who knew the words. I remember they'd given her a shiny cloak from my outfit because the Godmother's dress wouldn't do up. I also remember how the girl who'd fallen had insisted she'd been pushed.

Maris gets up and leaves the room. I tip the full glass into a nearby plant.

When Maris comes back she's dressed in a nightie, a pink, satin, frilly thing, like a refugee from a Forties musical. On Maris it looks grotesque.

She crosses the room and puts her hand on mine. "Are you coming to bed?"

"No, not yet. I'm not sleepy. But don't let me keep you up. I know where to go."

Instead she sits and watches me. This gets on my nerves. Exasperated, I go into the hall and collect the document case I'd brought in from my car. I sit down and mark my First Years' contributions to the interpretation of Minimalism. This means I don't have to look up and meet Maris' unwavering gaze, even though I feel it. I'm half way through my work when she leaves the room and I hear her go upstairs. This time she doesn't return so I guess she's gone to bed.

I finish the essays, although I'll have to scan through again and moderate some of my more savage commentary.

I curl into myself and watch the dwindling fire and wonder what Rick's doing, whether he's okay and if he's got drunk again. And I wonder why he didn't respond when I said I loved him. Was it that he didn't know what to say?

That he couldn't respond in kind because he doesn't love me any more?

After a while I feel my eyelids growing heavy. A glance at my watch tells me it's not yet ten o'clock, but I didn't get much rest last night.

The creak of floorboards warns me of Maris' imminent return. When she appears she has covered the negligee with a quilted dressing gown, which is a change without improvement. "Are you coming to bed yet, Annie?"

"No, not yet."

I realise I'd rather sleep down here, fully dressed, than upstairs near Maris. As a declaration of this, I get up and put more coal on the fire.

"Don't waste all the coal. It's got to last, you know."

"I'll buy you a bag." Memory of what Neil had told me about how wealthy she is adds a clipped note to my voice.

Determined to ignore her, I pull the curtains back and stare out of the window into the dark, damp night.

Chapter 37: Rick

When I met Annie it was on a night as dark as this but crisp and dry. I was off-duty but I spotted this girl sitting on the sea wall and thought she looked upset. I identified myself and asked if she was okay. I should have left her when she said she was fine, but somehow I couldn't.

"It's not safe, you hanging round here," I'd said.

"No-one will hurt me, I'm too unhappy."

Something in those quiet words twisted inside me. I sat down beside her and we talked and after a while I asked if she'd go out with me.

We felt so right together. Not like we were strangers. She was an art student, which was another world to me, but she seemed interested in my work, even though I was only a patrol cop at the time.

It's funny how much you can remember when you start thinking back. I asked her where she wanted to go and she said, "I don't care, let's drive." So we did for hours and we stopped at Services to get some food. There was a couple there with a baby and Annie couldn't take her eyes off it. But, with all the talking we did, then and all the years after, I never told her why I have the nightmares and I'm so scared of being shut in, and she never told me why she was crying on the harbour wall.

The doorbell rings again and I think Kelly moves bloody fast, but when I open it Neil Walder's standing there.

"Hi Rick, glad to see you're on your feet. Annie seemed worried about you. Is she free?"

"She's not here."

He looks surprised. "Where's she got to?... Sorry, that came out nosy, but she said she was in a hurry to get back to you."

"She's got caught up at Maris' house."

"Oh God, she's not let that selfish cow batten on to her, has she?" He fumbles a bulky envelope out of his pocket. "Could you give her this? It's some stuff she said she'd type up for me."

"Yeah sure. You want a drink?" Any company is better than my own.

"Thank you." He signals to a waiting taxi, which drives off.

"You got problems with your car?" I ask as he steps into the hall.

"No, just problems driving. Didn't Annie mention that I'd buggered up my neck?"

"No, I don't think so."

"I guess I'm not much of a priority in Annie's life any more."

I take him through to the sitting room and give him the vodka and orange he requests but I stick to orange juice. He describes Annie's lecture and how good it was.

As we talk I'm planning my line of attack but in the end I wade straight in. "Why should you be a priority in Annie's life?"

He looks startled then smiles. "Dear Rick, always so direct. I wonder if that's what attracts Annie, the brutal frankness?"

I'm not about to discuss what attracts Annie or what repels her in our relationship. "Why should you be a priority for Annie?" I repeat.

He hands me his glass for a refill. "Auld lang syne and that sort of thing. Annie and I go back a long way."

"Lots of people go back a long way but that doesn't give them special rights. Annie and Maris go back to infants' school."

"Yes, but the relationship has hardly been the same. At least one hopes not."

"What?"

He looks at me with a glazed but knowing stare. "Don't

be naïve, Rick, it doesn't go with the tough policeman image. You know Annie and I were lovers. She told me you've known from the start of your relationship."

"Yeah, she told me."

He must pick up on my tension. "You're not jealous, are you?"

"Should I be?"

"Certainly not of me. My thing with Annie was over years ago. We never got together again after the baby. Sometimes I think she holds it against me, even now."

"The baby?" I say numbly. "You and Annie had a baby?"

"You mean you didn't know?" A shrewd look battles with Neil's drunken smirk. "Well, well, secretive little Annie."

This knocks me off balance. Of course I'd known about Neil and Annie being lovers but that was before I was on the scene. I couldn't complain. Prior to Annie I'd screwed around a fair bit myself.

"Tell me about the baby. When was this?"

"When Annie was a First Year. Beautiful she was, but so bloody careless. How the hell did she manage to muck up with the Pill?"

"The baby?" I prompt him.

"There was no baby, she got rid of it."

"You mean she had an abortion?"

"Of course she did. She couldn't have had it. How could she have coped?"

"She could have managed with help from you." I cannot believe this guy.

From the look on his face neither can he believe me. "It would have wrecked both of our careers. I'd just had my first London exhibition. I was getting there."

"In that case you've been a bloody long time arriving."

He nods in agreement. "There's a lot of spite in the art world, you know."

The doorbell peals again. Since when did I become Mr Extremely Popular? This time it is Kelly. She hands me the file.

"Come in," I say. Things have altered and three is definitely company.

She follows me into the sitting room and stares at Neil lolling on the couch. "I didn't realise you'd got a friend with you."

"I wouldn't actually class him as a friend. His name's Neil Walder, he works with Annie and he can't hold his booze. I suppose I'd better get some shoes on and run him home." I take the file from her. "Thanks. Do you want a drink?"

"No thanks, Guv."

"Right." I shake Neil who has drifted off to sleep. "Come on, you loser, let's get you back to Corham."

"Corham?" Kelly sounds surprised. Corham's a dead-hole mini-village where even the pub's gone bust.

"Yeah, he's got this barn converted into a studio and flat. He's a sculptor."

"Really? Does he do the sort of stuff where you can see what it is or the usual garbage any kid could do?"

As the husband of a practising artist I tread carefully. In Artist World, what Kelly said is grounds for justifiable homicide.

"His stuff's pretty accessible." I'm proud of my response, Annie's taught me well. "He carved that wooden figure over there on the bookcase."

She surveys the eighteen-inch carving. "It's beautiful."

"Yeah." I can't deny that. I pull out one of Annie's reference books and hand it to Kelly to flip through. "That's got some of his early stuff."

Kelly seems impressed. "He's good."

I don't answer. I've never really looked at Neil's stuff before and now, in that book, I've seen something that hits me like a blow in the throat.

"I go through Corham, Guv. I can drop him off. It'll save you turning out. You still look white."

"You sure?" I use the tone that invites the reply 'no

problem.'

"No problem." With easy grace she hoists him to his feet. One thing's certain, this is a tough girl.

Neil opens his eyes and smiles at her. "You're very beautiful."

"And you're very drunk."

He considers, then comes out with the most mind-blowingly unoriginal chat up line in the world, "But in the morning I won't be drunk and you'll still be beautiful."

She gets him in her car and I shut the door on them.

Back in the living room I thumb through the book. My hands are trembling. The sculpture I'm looking for was sold to an American Gallery years ago. It's called *'Deathwalk.'* It's of a young woman, head bowed, arms folded across her breast. You can tell she's shuffling to her doom. I stare at the picture for a long time and bits of the pattern slot into place.

Chapter 38: Annie

I struggle along the rutted track, moving cautiously in the dismal, early light. The cold sleet soaks me and Rick's jeans chafe the insides of my thighs. My high-heeled shoes pinch my feet but the ground's too rutted and flinty to go barefoot. I'm heavily laden, carrying portfolio, document case and bag. Even now, out of sight of the cottage, I feel like Maris' eyes are following me. I hate myself for rejecting her when she's so unhappy but I loathed every second spent in that house.

It's a relief to reach the lane. If I'd had any sense I'd have phoned from Maris' house for a taxi to meet me here, but I was too intent on leaving. I get out my mobile and see I've got a signal. I could phone Rick and ask him to pick me up, but I don't want him driving if he's sick or stale drunk.

The taxi driver treats me like I'm eighteen. He grins and says in a fatherly sort of way, "Fancy dress party was it, luv? Tramps' Ball, that sort of thing?"

The rest of the journey is taken up by reminiscences of a Tramps' Ball he and his wife went to last year and how his wife hadn't fancied blackening her teeth. I tune him out and sit with my eyes shut. "Here you are, luv, home by turning out time."

I open my eyes and see Rick saying goodbye to the beautiful black girl I'd seen on the News. She's immaculate in dark trousers and a leather jacket. As she strolls towards her car she smiles at me and says, "Good morning."

"Hello." I shuffle across the drive to where Rick is standing by the open door. No way is he stale drunk. He's pale and there are shadows beneath his eyes but he's clean and freshly shaved and wearing a smart suit. I look from him to the girl and feel a wrench of jealousy that ties my guts in knots.

"You okay, love?" asks Rick. "Oh God, here's Bob. He's early for once."

Bob gets out of his car. As he looks at me a broad grin spreads across his face. "Hi Annie, been a rough night has it? You ready, mate?"

"I'll be out in a minute." Rick follows me inside. "Annie, are you okay?"

"Apparently not as okay as you."

"What do you...?" Bob's playing a serenade of impatience on his horn. Rick flings the door open and yells, "Shut it, you wanker! Annie, I've got to go, we're due in Court and I've got a meeting with the barrister first."

"Go then."

"Not until I know you're okay."

"I told you I'm fine, so go."

"You can use my car if you want, that's why I got Bob to pick me up."

"I'm surprised you didn't get that girl to give you a lift."

"Girl? Oh, Kelly. We're not going the same way. Are you sure you're all right?"

"For God's sake go!" Bob's into the opening chords of a fresh fanfare.

Rick leaves and I slam the door after him.

Turning, I see myself in the hall mirror. I don't think I've ever looked so horrible before. Shedding wet clothes I go into the kitchen and make a pint mug of milky cocoa. I open a pack of Jaffa cakes and sit at the breakfast bar to eat my illicit feast. It's a long time since I sat in the kitchen naked, although once I used to strip for Rick throughout the house. I stare down at my pale body as if it belongs to a stranger.

I open the dishwasher. Glasses, mugs and Rick's cereal bowl are stacked; not to mention two dinner plates, two sets of cutlery and a lasagne dish.

I go into the dining room. The table's covered with the lace cloth we bought in Belgium years ago, and he's set out my favourite onyx candlestick. I pick it up and hurl it across the room. It cracks the window and the burglar alarm screams into life.

Swearing, I stalk across the room to ring through and tell the local station it's a false alarm. I hear someone pounding on the front door and simultaneously a large, blue-clad figure appears in the garden, peering through the patio windows.

I think, *'Please God, let me die.'* I scream my explanation down the phone and gesture to the goggle-eyed cop to rejoin his colleague at the front. I grab the only cover I can see, the tablecloth, and drape it round me while I go to the door.

"There's no problem. Something slipped from my hand and cracked a windowpane. I was phoning through to cancel the alarm when you arrived."

"Oh I see. Sorry madam. We were in the lane when we heard the alarm and thought we'd get in quick." The older cop is keeping his eyes firmly on my face. His young partner isn't and it's obvious the thin lace swathing my body is having an effect. Usually I'd find this funny but at the moment it makes me cross.

"Excuse me, madam, but have you got any proof of identity? Just to establish you are the householder." The younger cop's pushing his luck in every way.

I know he's taking the piss and start to enquire how many naked female burglars he's met in his obviously short career.

The other cop chimes in, "Leave it, Sam. I know who this lady is. Sorry to have disturbed you, Mrs Evans."

I shut the door, uncomfortably aware that I've made Rick a laughing stock at work. I should be glad of the revenge but I don't want to feel I owe him in any way.

I go upstairs to shower and dress. In the bedroom everything is tidy and someone has changed the bedclothes. I wonder whether he had her in our bed.

Chapter 39: Rick

What the hell's she like? Turning up in that state when I've got half the police force on our drive? I've never seen her look like that before, the sexiest mess in the entire world. But she's way too pale and there's a lost look underneath all the snapping and bravado. Or perhaps it's just I know more about her today than I did when I saw her yesterday. That's a weird thought in itself.

I consider telling Bob to turn the car round and get me back to her, but I don't. We're giving evidence in a murder case. I scowl at Bob and he keeps quiet for a bit, then says, "What's Annie up to? Research for one of her arty-farty bits of crap?"

"Shut it, Bob, you know fuck all about art."

"I know as much as most of those wankers you see on the telly. I mean, take that woman who sells her dirty knickers and calls it art."

"Annie's art's not like that." I realise I sound defensive and hate him for it.

"You sure? Next thing you know you'll find a bed filled with your spunk on display in that Tate Modern place."

"Bob, I'm warning you, leave it."

"What's the matter? I'm not smart enough for you to talk to any more?"

I don't answer. My silence offends Bob and he sulks for the rest of the journey.

Most of our big criminal cases are tried at Winchester, and there's always a lot of hanging round. Bob sees some cops he knows and goes off to talk to them but I stay where I am. I'm still aching and my eyes feel gritty. My head's full of Annie and I don't feel sociable. It's weird; physically I feel crap but mentally I don't feel so isolated, as if knowing about Annie has helped me re-connect with the world.

While I'm waiting, Kaye Harrow comes and sits down next to me.

"Hi." I grin at her. Of all the psychologists I've met she's the most approachable. She's plump and down to earth and old enough to be my mum.

"How are you, Rick? You look tired."

"I'm okay. Had a touch of food poisoning, guess that's made me a bit white."

"Are you on this Saronholt business?"

"Yeah."

"Take it easy then. Try to relax when you're at home. How's Annie?" Kaye's been a guest lecturer at Annie's College.

"She's fine." The memory of her big blue eyes and white pinched face comes back to haunt me, along with the picture of that death camp girl.

We talk about a few things, stuff that touches on neither of our lives. At last I find the guts to say, "Kaye, can I ask you a sort of general question?"

"As long as you're satisfied with a sort of general answer."

"If a woman has an abortion, how's it likely to affect her mentally?"

"You mean a deliberate termination of a baby that's not damaged?"

"I guess so."

"It will have to be a very general answer. Everybody reacts differently according to their character and circumstances. Some girls seem to shrug it off, they put it behind them and get on with their lives. But other girls are haunted by loss. They mourn for their child and they feel deep guilt."

I hadn't thought it was possible for me to hate myself more than I already did, but now I do. "Do girls like that ever get over it?"

She shrugs. "I don't know."

"And is it usual for these girls, the ones who've really been hurt, not to tell anyone about it, even the people who love them best?"

The look she's giving me is way too knowing.

"Rick, have you ever told anyone about the things that have hurt you most?"

In Court I always swear not affirm. It goes down better with the Judge and old-fashioned members of the jury.

The Prosecution leads me through the case. It's pretty straightforward, a guy who killed his wife because she was having an affair.

The Defence woman goes for me hard, focusing her attack on my questioning techniques. "Tell me Inspector, is it not true that you kept hammering away at this poor man in the hope he'd confess? What did you say to him? What threats and cajoling did you employ on this distraught and shocked man who had just found his beloved wife murdered?"

I wait for the Prosecution to object but he's slow off the mark and it looks bad if you hesitate. "The defendant's solicitor was with him and he was given all the rights laid down by the Police and Criminal Evidence legislation."

"But isn't it true, Inspector, that having decided you'd got your man, you did not look for any evidence that might point to anybody else?

"No."

"Come now, Inspector. You must admit you have a reputation for selecting the person you think is guilty. And you hound them without mercy until you break them."

"No, that's not true..."

And he is here with me. 'You can't escape me, Richard.' I hear the screech of brakes, feel the shuddering impact, see the blood oozing down the crazed glass. My hands are clenched on the steering wheel so tight I can't peel them off.

My hands are clenched on the bar of the witness box so tight I'm not sure I can let go. The Prosecution guy's on his feet. I guess he's got off his arse and objected to this line of questioning. I wonder what else has happened while I've been away.

The Judge decides that I don't have to answer and the rest of the Defence questions aren't personal.

If Stacie Frewer gets tied into the Elmwash murders I'm going to get this every way I turn. Every case I work on is going to be looked at sideways to suss out whether I'm stitching someone up. And there'll be reviews of all the stuff I've headed. It'll be the end of my career.

Chapter 40: Annie

I take the Black Bear to work with me and let him loose to savage everyone. I know it's unprofessional to vent my personal problems on my students and colleagues but I enjoy every minute of it, in a viciously miserable sort of way. I shake up my students, then have a row with Lucy and a few stiff words with some part-time lecturers. It's mid-afternoon before I head for my office. I don't want company and, from the way everyone evaporates as I stalk down the corridor, I guess no-one wants to be with me.

I open my door and find Maris there. I don't want to believe my eyes but she's a pretty substantial fantasy. She sits, knees apart, feet planted solidly, a small rucksack on her lap clutched by both hands. She's sitting, just sitting, as if she's been there for hours and will be there for ever more.

"Oh God Maris! What are you doing here?"

"I didn't want to be at home alone. Who knows what I might do?"

I'm tempted to say, 'I don't care what you do as long as it's not near me.' I grab at self-control. "If you feel like that we ought to contact your doctor. He'll be able to prescribe something or suggest a therapist. You're with the Bellmead Medical Practice aren't you?" I pick up my phone.

"You don't have to phone. I've made an appointment already."

"Promise me you'll tell him what you did last night?"

"Yes."

I wonder if she'll need a lift to the doctor's surgery. "How did you get here today?"

"In my car of course."

"But I didn't see your car when I was at your place." I'd assumed she'd left it at the hospital and wasn't driving yet after the baby's birth.

"When the weather's bad I keep it in the barn."

So she could have offered me a lift this morning. I swallow disgust that tastes bitter as bile. "You can't stay here, I've got work to do."

"I'll have to. That woman's in my office and she was rude to me."

"At the moment it's Lucy's office. You're meant to be on leave."

I get the brick wall look. If I stay in my office I'll scream abuse at her, so I walk out.

It occurs to me I haven't seen Neil today. I could enjoy a really good argument with him. I'm passing Sara's office, so I look in and say, "Where's Neil hiding?"

Sara looks like she's expecting me to bite. "He's not in."

"Thanks for telling me. I'm only Deputy Head of this department. Why should I expect to be told the Head's not in?"

"I didn't want to make you cross."

"Cross? Why in the world should I be cross?" I slam the door behind me to emphasise how content with life I am.

Of course, if Neil isn't here, it means his office is unoccupied. The closed door summons me as if it has grown a neon sign flashing 'SANCTUARY.'

As I push the door open there's a scrabble of movement. Chloe's sitting there, baby Joseph at her breast. The noise was Josef getting to his feet.

"What are you doing in here?" I make an effort to speak pleasantly.

"Neil said I could use his office for feeding as long as he didn't need it."

"You mean Neil knows about you bringing baby Joe into College?"

"Yeah. Joey can't go into the crèche yet but I don't like it out at that house when Josef's not there with me." Little Miss Cocky has become painfully vulnerable. "There's this loony woman. She seems to have some sort of fixation about

Joey. She freaks me out. I told Neil how I didn't want to be there and he fixed up monthly bus tickets for us, so I could get out whenever I wanted to. And he wouldn't let us pay. He said he'd take it out of my next modelling fee." She makes the last statement with a defiant look at Josef.

"Josef, you don't have to worry about Chloe modelling for Neil," I say.

He nods agreement. "I know it is so. Chloe has explained it to me and now I understand that Neil gave her so much money because he was wishing to be kind."

"So much money?"

"Four times the usual fee," explains Chloe. "He said it was because pregnant women rated more and now he's saying nursing mums get paid it too."

I think Neil's a rare breed of hypocrite, one who conceals his good deeds more assiduously than his bad. "Of course he's right. I hope you don't mind, I did a picture of you too. So I owe you a quadrupled fee as well."

Chloe smiles at me. "Thanks."

After I leave Neil's office, I decide to cut and run and let the Art Department fend for itself. I make it to the Reception area unchecked, but then a plaintive voice says, "Annie, please could you give me a hand? I've got a seminar in five minutes "

I turn round and see Neil. He looks as if he's destined to expire under Wesley's maggot-filled painting, which could turn it into a very macabre installation piece.

I take his heavy document case and go with him back to his office. It's empty. The only signs of its recent occupation are the disposable nappy in the bin and a smell of baby lingering in the air.

"Thanks." Neil sits down and cradles his head in his hands.

"What's wrong with you?"

"Your husband's vodka. I was totally out of it last night. I wouldn't have made it home at all if the beautiful Kelly hadn't driven me."

"You mean DC Kelly? You saw her there with Rick last night?"

It's clear, even through his hangover, Neil's aware of the desperation in my voice. "She turned up with some papers while I was there."

I try to hammer down the blossoming of hope. Taking Neil home doesn't prove a thing, she could have turned round and gone straight back to Rick.

"I made a bloody idiot of myself, and she stayed all night to check I was okay."

"Would you mind repeating that?" I'm scared to feel too happy.

"When she was manhandling me indoors, my pills fell out of my pocket, and she realised I'd been mixing booze with painkillers. She was worried about me so she got me onto my bed and spent the night on the sofa to keep an eye on me."

There are birds singing in the room and I think Spring has arrived in late November. "So she was there with you all night?" I say, stupid with relief.

"That's right. Wonderful isn't it? The most beautiful woman I've ever seen and I'm too plastered to make any sort of move."

"What time did she leave?"

"Early. She brought me a cup of coffee and said she wanted to go home and shower and change, and she'd have to hurry because she had some papers to pick up."

"Papers?"

"Some stuff she'd left for Rick. She said she'd got to get them back first thing."

I know he's seen through me and, with a flash of gratitude, I realise that's why he told me where Kelly spent the night. "Thank you," I say

"You're welcome. I think I probably owe you anyway."

"What do you mean?"

There's a knock on the door. I open it and six seminar students sidle in. I have to postpone the interrogation but as I leave I wonder what Neil meant about owing me.

Chapter 41: Rick

At lunchtime the pub's crowded but Bob's girlfriend, Debs, has driven over to meet him and she's got a table saved.

Bob says, "Give me a hand to get the drinks in, Rick."

I follow as he shoves his way to the bar. "Gin and tonic, love, and a pint of your draught Guinness and two of your giant pasties. Rick, what you fancy? You want a pint or whisky?"

"Just coffee."

As we work our way back through the jostling crowd, I spot a group of our uniform boys standing near the bar. I guess they're giving evidence in another court. There's a lot of laughter and one says, "He swears he could see right through this lacy thing, bit of alright she was." Someone nudges him and they go quiet.

"What's that about?" I ask as we sit down.

Bob shrugs. "Don't ask me."

"I expect they're talking about the alarm call at your house," giggles Debs.

"What alarm call at my place?" Half my coffee splashes out the mug.

Bob gets in fast. "It's okay. Annie broke a window and one of the patrol cars was in the neighbourhood and got there before she could phone to cancel it."

"What's so funny about that?"

"Nothing. Small things please small minds."

When it comes to small minds I reckon I can get more information out of Debs. "That right?" I say and give her a lairy look.

She tosses her head. "Of course people find it funny when an upmarket bitch like her gets the cops in when she's starkers."

"What?"

"You heard, stark naked when the police came to the door."

"No she wasn't, she was wearing this lace thing," says Bob.

"There was nothing of it. She was really flaunting herself, that's what Sam Morris said." Debs knows most of the uniformed guys because she's a barmaid at their local, *The Running Fox*.

"I'll see about Sam Morris." I stand up and lean across the table so I'm right in Debs' painted face. "And don't you ever call my wife a bitch again."

Bob's evidence isn't finished, so he's stuck in Winchester. I manage to get a lift back to Galmouth and grab a moment to speak to the duty sergeant, a good mate. With the weekend duties we plan for Sam Morris I reckon he'll think twice before he mouths off about my wife again.

There's an air of depression out at Saronholt. I feel it as soon as I walk into the Incident Room but at least Roebuck seems glad to see me. "Ah Rick, are you better?"

"Yes thanks sir."

"Good. And they don't need you any more in Court?"

"They reckon not."

"Excellent. In that case you can take Kelly and go back to Galmouth. One of the sorters at the Animal Shelter Shop noticed a bag of Stacie's clothes that was left in their collection bin."

I go across to Kelly. "We'll have to take your car, my wife's got mine."

"No problem, Guv." She keeps her voice carefully neutral and I guess she's heard the gossip.

As we drive, I realise Kelly's not interested in discussing Annie, she wants to know about a totally different artist. Her tone is too casual as she says, "Neil didn't look like he's living with anyone. Is he married or anything?"

"No. So you went in with him last night?" I might as

well get my boot in if I can. Why should the other buggers have all the fun?

"I had to help him in. You shouldn't have let him mix painkillers with vodka."

"I didn't know he was on painkillers." What does she think I am? My wife's ex-lover's keeper? "You fancy Neil Walder, then?"

She looks self-conscious. "I like his sculpture. Artists are different, aren't they?"

"Yeah," I say. "They're different alright."

The shop lady has the stuff waiting for us. "I'm sorry. I handled it all before I saw the name label in the jeans."

I pull on gloves and put down a protective sheet before I accept the carrier bag. I note it comes from a local supermarket then I get out a sweatshirt and a pair of jeans.

"What's up, Guv?" asks Kelly.

"Nothing. I remembered about her stepfather not wanting her to wear jeans."

She shrugs. "He's old-fashioned."

I turn to the shop woman. "Do you know when and where they were donated?"

"It was in the collection bin outside the animal sanctuary but I'm not sure when."

I wonder if that means another full search of the animal sanctuary. I hope not, that donkey looked like the sort who'd hold a grudge.

We drop off the stuff for forensic testing and head back to Saronholt.

Roebuck is notably unimpressed by our report. "It's obviously nothing to do with Stacie's disappearance. She was wearing a pink dress not jeans."

"Do you want us to see the Frewers and ask about the stuff?" I say.

"Not tonight. I don't want them upset when they've got another media appeal."

So much for me liaising with the family. This is one trip I'm not invited on.

"You can speak to them tomorrow, Rick. There's a pile of reports on your desk that I need you to look at."

"Yes sir."

My discontent must show because he frowns. "I hope you're not getting one of your feelings about this? We've had enough of that sort of nonsense already."

My instincts tell me there's something wrong about those jeans being dumped, but I play it innocent. "Feelings? No sir, of course not, but, like you say, it's best to tidy up loose ends."

Chapter 42: Annie

I nip out to buy cream cakes and leave them in the staff room with a note saying, *'Sorry. Help yourselves.'* Then I head back to do some work.

Maris is still sitting in my office. She frowns at me. "Where have you been?"

Re-encountering her almost makes me cross again, but I hang on to the thought that Kelly had spent the night with Neil. "Have a cake, Maris." I present my unwelcome guest with an éclair.

She lays it on the desk in front of her and ignores it. "Are you coming home with me tonight?"

"No, I'm going out with Mother."

"Oh. What about your car?"

"I'll phone the garage. Rick lent me his car so I'm sorted for today."

She clutches her rucksack even more firmly and gets solidly to her feet. "Please come back to me tonight. It doesn't matter how late you are, I'll wait up for you."

"I may stay at Mother's. I often do if it's late." This is both truth and lie. I sometimes stay at Mother's because Rick has got this thing about me driving alone in the dark, but I don't plan to do so tonight.

"I suppose I might as well go home now. I'll see you soon."

As she passes my desk she puts her hand on my shoulder and gently squeezes. I sit rigid under her caressing fingers until she releases her grasp and leaves. I rummage my desk drawer for my key, unearth it and lock my office door.

I remember I need to contact our security firm about replacing the broken glass and do it before it slips my mind again.

Then I have a brilliant idea regarding Mother's spare

ballet ticket. I phone through to Rick's mum. "Tris, it's Annie. I know it's short notice but I wondered if you're free this evening? Mother has booked up for the ballet and my sister has had to pull out. Mother asked me to find someone to take her place and I'd love you to come with us."

There's silence then, in a wondering voice, she says, "Would you really?"

"Really, truly." I dip my finger into the chocolate éclair and lick at the cream.

"But what about your mother? Surely she wouldn't want me to come?"

"Of course she would." Even if she doesn't, Mother won't let her displeasure show until she gets me alone.

"I'd love to."

"Great. I'll pick you up about six. We usually have supper after the theatre."

As I ring off, it occurs to me that I'd never dare to pick at a cream cake when Mother was on the line, she'd hear me squelching no matter how discreet I was.

Waste not want not. I start into serious work on the éclair. The phone rings and I pick it up without considering the consequences. "Hello?" I say thickly.

"Annie? It's me, Rick. Are you okay?"

I swallow frantically. "Yes, I'm fine."

"You sure? You sound kind of odd."

"That's because I'm eating chocolate cake."

"No change there then."

We lapse into awkward silence.

"I'm sorry," he says, "I shouldn't have bothered you at work."

"You're not a bother." I'm scared he'll ring off. "Let's try again without the cake. Ring, ring, ring, ring, I'm lifting the phone. 'Hi you.'"

"Hi you."

"Are you okay, Rick?"

"Yeah, sort of. Are you?"

179

"I am now. Rick, I'm sorry about this morning."

"Me too."

"You didn't do anything to be sorry about, did you?" I hear my tone sharpen, suspicion is a hardy sort of beast.

"I shouldn't have buggered off when you were upset."

"Of course you had to go. Rick, I've got to tell you, I did something really stupid this morning. I'm sorry."

"Yeah, I hear you did a striptease for the uniformed guys."

He sounds casual, almost amused, and that hurts more than if he was angry.

"I didn't mean to."

"Didn't reckon you did. You going to tell me what happened?"

"I dropped something and it broke the patio window. I was phoning through to cancel the alarm when two cops arrived and one came straight round the back and I'd undressed because I was wet and cold and I didn't mean to make a fool of you."

"Calm down. It's no big deal. Were the guys who dealt with it polite to you?"

"Polite enough. The younger one was a bit cocky but nothing to fuss about."

"We'll see about that. What were you wearing when you opened the door?"

"A tablecloth. It was the first thing I could grab."

"A tablecloth? Not the lace one from the dining room? Jesus!"

"I'm sorry, Rick," I repeat dismally.

"It's okay. Do you want me to fix up about getting the glass replaced?"

"No, I've already phoned."

"That's fine. You're out tonight, aren't you? I saw it on the calendar."

"Yes. Elaine can't come with us to the ballet and so I asked your mum. She seemed pleased."

"Yeah she would be. She's always liked that sort of thing but she's never had much chance to go anywhere, my bloody father made sure of that even before he got sick. Give her my love and tell her to have fun."

"I will." I only wish he'd give me his love too.

Chapter 43: Annie

I go home in good time to change for the ballet. I select a low-cut, amber dress, teamed with a silky brown jacket and a gossamer scarf around my throat to hide the lingering bruise.

Five o'clock: I've got an hour to kill. Time in which I mustn't think of Rick and the gulf between us. I spend five minutes not thinking of Rick, then know I can't keep it up. What's more I don't want to. What have I got to lose? I know that physically he could harm me again but, in every other way, I can't be hurt worse than I have been. Where Rick's concerned, I've got no pride left.

I phone through to his mobile. "Hi you."

"Hi you."

"You busy?"

"Not really. There's a live appeal on that new Crimescene programme tonight but, for some reason, Roebuck doesn't want me anywhere near that."

"Does that mean you can get away early? Do you want me to pick you up?"

"You got time?"

"Of course."

"That would be good. I'm in the Incident Room in Saronholt Church Hall."

"I'll come straight away."

I'm about to leave when the phone rings. I answer it, hoping it's not Rick saying they've found more work for him and he'll make his own way home.

"Annie? It's Tris. I'm so sorry but I can't come tonight. They've brought Tom back early." She sounds near to tears.

"Oh Tris, I'm so sorry."

"Well it can't be helped. They often do it if they decide they're short-staffed. They don't want to pay the Temp agencies for extra staff, you see, and Tom can be demanding.

Have a lovely evening, won't you? And thank you for asking me."

I'm so preoccupied with feeling sorry for Tris that I'm almost in Saronholt before it occurs to me I'm going to have to outface the rumours. At least this time I'm equipped to deal with stares, wearing just enough clothes to give me confidence.

I expect to be stopped when I reach the Incident Room but the constable on duty recognises Rick's car and lets me into the car park. I pull up as Superintendent Roebuck and his entourage emerge. I get out and stand by the car. Roebuck notices me and smiles acknowledgement. The other cops turn to stare and I get some satisfaction from their obvious admiration. Rick comes across to join me and I don't even ask if he wants to drive.

"You look exhausted," I say.

"Yeah. You look gorgeous though. Hang on a sec, let these jokers clear first. Did you clock the way the randy bastards were staring at you?"

"They probably didn't recognise me with my clothes on. That was a joke, okay?"

"Not funny. I don't like it when..."

"When I show you up at work?"

"No! I don't like it when you get mixed up in all this shit."

The police cars drive slowly past on the way to the television appeal. In the back of one car I get a glimpse of a woman's face, set and white, a death mask of despair. I turn to look at Rick and see a similar pale tension in his face.

"Oh, Rick..." I wonder how I can get through to him that, if he's mixed up in shit I'm in it with him and that's the way I want it to be. "Your Mum can't come tonight. They've brought your father home unexpectedly."

"Typical! They've done it before. They say he's pining to go home but the truth is the old bastard's disruptive, so they'll grab any excuse to get rid of him. Still there's no reason Mum should miss out tonight."

He gets out his mobile and rings through. "Hi Mum. I'll be round in half an hour and I'll look after Dad while you go out. No, don't argue... What?... No, but that doesn't matter. I'll ring for a pizza if I get hungry."

He keys off. "That's sorted. You can drop me at Mum's and pick her up. At least she'll get one decent evening out."

He looks hideously tired and I want to object but I don't. I no longer feel I've got the right.

He squints at my petrol gauge, as if it hurts to bring it into focus. "You're nearly empty. You need to fill up soon."

"I'm sorry." It's good of him to lend me his car and he's got every right to object if I wreck the engine by running it dry.

"To hell with sorry, I don't want you getting stranded again."

I remember last night at Holy Cottage and shiver. "Nor do I."

I pull into a petrol station. As I pay, I see some bowls of violets and buy one each for Mother and for Tris.

At Rick's parents' house we're greeted by the smell of cooking and Tris with her apron on over a smart suit.

She thanks me for her bowl of flowers and then turns to Rick. "All that nonsense about a take-away. You need a proper meal. I've done you a mixed grill and chips." She pulls out a kitchen chair and Rick sits like an obedient little boy.

"Annie, I'm almost ready," she says apologetically. "I don't want to keep your mother waiting."

"No hurry, we've got lots of time."

"I'll try and get Tom settled. He's being awkward. He doesn't like it when he knows I'm going out." There's a thumping noise coming from the sitting room and she hurries to deal with him.

I stand in the kitchen and watch Rick picking at his food. It looks and smells delicious and I lean over and pinch a chip.

"Take what you want. I can't manage any more."

"But you've hardly eaten anything."

"I'd better get rid of it before Mum starts worrying that she shouldn't go out tonight."

I hear Tris coming. "Give it here." I tip the lovely meal in the bin and cover it with an empty carrier bag.

"Thanks." He gives an apologetic smile that's totally drained of any happiness. I can't remember when I last heard Rick laugh.

Chapter 44: Rick

This is going to be a lousy evening and I'm longing for a bottle to see me through. I sit in one corner of the room and Dad sits in the other. He's looking at me with watery, crafty eyes. He smells repulsive but I'll sort him later, just before Mum comes in. That way she might get a chance to change her clothes before she has to deal with him again. He always gets past the incontinence pad. I reckon he does it deliberately. Sometimes I think the only enjoyment he's got left is the pleasure of spiting us.

I get out my briefcase. There are reports I should check through. I use them like a screen against my father's gaze but my head's aching too badly to focus on the words. I spot the scanned copies I took of the pictures Kelly brought me, the stuff from Stacie's school. I'll shred them as soon as I get home. We don't need any tabloids getting hold of them.

I flick through the pictures. The kid's still in the primitive stage of art. There's one of a small round person and a big round person both wearing what I reckon must be trousers and, all over the page, there are lots of circles with four sticks coming out of them, which I guess are animals. It's highly coloured and both of the people and all the animals have smiles. There's another of a big man right in the centre of the page. He's been carefully coloured in and his smile has got a scary row of teeth. In the background there's a woman, judging by the triangle of her skirt and her long hair. Her lips curve down, she's not coloured in and she's much littler than the man. And in the corner, very small indeed, a tiny, round figure standing on some sort of box. She's got no colour, no clothes, no features, just an empty circle for a face.

I stare at it a long while, though the effort makes me squint. I'm really losing it. I don't believe in psycho-crap. All it means is the kid ran out of coloured crayons, or out of interest, or out of time.

Dad's looking at me. I ignore him. I ignore the stain spreading across his trousers. I ignore the smell. I flick through the TV channels and catch the Crimescene programme. It's one of those fast moving, ram-the-message-home jobs. Our case comes up and Roebuck explains matters before the Frewers make their appeal.

I watch Terry Frewer and try to be analytical. I want to work out why I don't trust him but it's nothing he does, it's the feeling the whole thing's an act. He stares into the camera and begs, "Please, whoever has got her, send our little girl back home to us."

They cut to Cindy Frewer. Her face looks like a mask and it's impossible to see the pain churning underneath.

Dad says, "Stupid cow. People shouldn't have kids if they don't look after them."

"Shut up, Dad."

He scowls at me. "Yeah, now I'm old you talk like that to me. Time was you wouldn't dare. I can still take this bloody stick to you!"

He waves his arm and the flailing stick knocks Mum's plant off the cupboard. Most of the contents dump themselves in his lap. He stares at the mess of earth and purple flowers and yells, "Look what you made me do!"

A strand of violets are lodged in his sparse hair, they frame his lined, pouting face.

'You won't forget me, Richard.' Ernest Clift is staring up at me. I grab the stick from his hand and raise it ready to smash down on the leering face.

Reality returns. I'm breathing hard and shaking. I look down at Dad. He's cowering in his chair, peering up at me in cringing terror.

I lower the walking stick and drop it on the floor.

"Come on," I say, then I clear my throat and start again several tones lower, "Come on, Dad, let's get you cleaned up before Mum comes home."

Chapter 45: Annie

To my delight Mother and Tris get on really well. They chat all the way to the theatre and carry on until the orchestra strikes up.

The ballet has an Ophelia based theme. A girl is date raped by her boyfriend, who then deserts her, which causes her to go ostentatiously insane in a wild flower meadow. I can't help thinking, in a well-ordered society, such a green space would have a conservation order, to stop mad women rolling on the rarer specimens. She wears a garland of wild flowers, rosemary for remembrance, pansies for thoughts, and there are poppies too, poppies for pain and the imminence of death.

As the curtain falls I say, "Back in a minute," and leave before the general exodus to the bar. I discover a sheltered place outside the entrance doors and get out my mobile.

Rick answers quickly, "Annie?"

"Hi you," I say softly.

"Hi you. You okay?"

"Yes, just checking you're all right."

"Yeah."

I catch the tension in his tone. "What's wrong?"

"Nothing."

"Rick, tell me."

"Hang on a sec." I hear him moving and the sound of a closing door. "It's the old man, he's driving me crazy. I don't know how Mum puts up with it."

"I guess she's used to it," I say helplessly. "I'll try and get back as soon as I can."

"Thanks love." He rings off on the words.

I feel mean hustling Mother and Tris through supper but I do it anyway. I drop Mother off first and it's eleven-thirty when I get Tris back home. Rick's dad is still sitting in his chair. He looks at me and says, "Hello Mummy, you're looking very beautiful tonight."

"Thank you." I turn away to help Rick gather up his stuff.

I try to ignore Tom's petulant muttering but as we're leaving it becomes an audible whine. "Mummy, don't leave. Nasty man, don't take Mummy away."

Rick looks worried. "Are you going to be okay?" he asks his mum.

"Of course I will."

"I've never seen him as bad as this."

She kisses him. "Don't worry. You get on home."

In the car we're silent. He's totally shattered and there's no hope he'll be able to talk things through tonight. We're almost home when Rick's mobile rings.

"If that's Roebuck tell him to sod off," I say.

He answers and I hear a woman's sobbing voice, though not the words.

"Jesus! We'll come straight back. Have you sent for an ambulance? That's good." He rings off and snaps, "Annie, get us back to Mum."

I attempt to turn in the narrow lane. Rick says, "Shove over love, I'll drive."

I don't argue. It's his car, his mum and dad and he's the one who has done fast response driving. "What's wrong?" I ask as we hurtle back towards town.

"It's Dad, there's been some sort of accident."

The house is quiet and from outside you'd never guess anything was wrong. Rick has his key ready. He opens the front door and I crowd in after him. Rick's mum is sitting on the stairs that lead up from the hall. She's about half way up, holding a mobile phone and looking down at Rick's dad who's lying at the foot of the stairs. There's a cut on his head and one leg is twisted at a sickening angle. His eyes are open but he doesn't seem to be focusing. His moans sound like an animal in pain.

Rick goes down on one knee beside him. He doesn't speak or touch and I think this must be how he looks when he's at a scene of crime, checking out a corpse. But this is different, this is his father and he isn't dead.

"Talk to him, Rick, tell him it's going to be okay."

He looks at me and opens his mouth but no words come. I kneel beside Tom and murmur reassurance. I reach for Rick's hand and his fingers clench on mine.

At the sound of an approaching siren, Rick jerks free and scrambles to his feet. He hurdles his dad's body, stumbles up the stairs to Tris and grabs hold of her upper arms.

"Mum, listen to me, they're going to ask how this happened. You've got to tell them how he gets confused and forgets he's not supposed to go upstairs. He slipped and fell and you were nowhere near him. You've got that, haven't you? It was an accident, he slipped and fell."

Her vague eyes leave the old man on the floor and turn to Rick. "He slipped and fell. It was an accident."

"That's right." Rick straightens up and helps her to her feet.

The movement dislodges something on the stairs that slithers down to where I'm crouching beside Tom. It's a narrow leather belt.

I take the car to the hospital while Rick goes in the ambulance with his mum and dad. When I get there his dad's being treated and Rick and Tris are in the waiting area. I go to join them. "Does anyone want coffee?"

Tris says, "No thank you, dear."

Rick says, "Yes... no... I don't know."

I get him a coffee from the machine and he says, "I don't want that." Then he drinks it. "I feel sick." He goes into the loo.

I sit with Tris and hold her tense hands. "Are you all right?"

"Yes thank you, dear."

"What happened?"

"He fell... on the stairs... it was an accident."

Rick comes back, looking green.

A plump, middle-aged nurse comes over to him. "Hello, it is you. I thought it was. What are you doing here again?"

"My father's had a fall, he's pretty bad."

She makes a sympathetic, clucking noise. "You have had a week of it."

She moves away and I ask, "What was that about?"

"Nothing."

After a while a doctor tells us Tom's being taken up to ITU. Only two visitors are allowed beside the bed, so Rick and Tris go in to see him. Then the doctor says he needs to talk to them and I go to sit with Tom.

He looks very frail lying there in the middle of all the machines. He opens his eyes and focuses on me and one side of his mouth twitches, as if he's trying to smile. His voice is slurred but I make out the words. "Stay with me, Mummy."

Eventually Tris comes back. "Sorry to leave you here for so long, Annie."

"That's okay. Where's Rick? Does he want to come back in?"

"I don't think so. He isn't feeling well."

She sits down next to me. Tom looks straight at her and says, "Fuck off you stupid bitch." His voice is much clearer than before.

She puts her hand over her lips. "I'll go outside for a while."

I stand up to follow her but Tom grabs my hand. I could break free but I'm scared of dislodging the tubes and drips, so I crush down my panic and stay there until Rick comes in. "You okay, Annie?"

"Yes. How about you?"

"Yeah fine." That would be more convincing if he didn't look like he'd been coated with primer.

I put my untrapped hand on his forehead. "You've got a temperature."

191

"People do have, unless they're dead."

"You know what I mean. You're ill."

"Just stressed… and knackered."

"Your mum's upset. Take her back to our place and make her go to bed, and for God's sake get some rest yourself. I'll stay here."

"You can't do that."

"Of course I can. I promise you, it's fine."

The fight drains out of him and his shoulders slump. "I'll leave the car for you."

"Yes, I don't think you should drive."

As he leaves I take a step after him, thinking that I'll wait with him until the taxi comes. Tom's grip on my hand tightens. I look down at him and he speaks with great satisfaction, "That's got rid of them. Now it's just Mummy and me."

Chapter 46: Annie

I sit in the shaded cubicle full of the machines that maintain life, but it's Tom's voice that makes it crowded. It becomes a green-baize installation over-brimming with memories; a flimsy container for so much anger and malice.

In the early morning the doctor orders me to leave while he examines Tom.

When he allows me in again, he says, "He seems to be holding his own but it's early days. We're going to move him to a side ward, he's disturbing the other patients when he yells out like that."

"I see." The things he's been shouting appalled me and I feel ashamed, as if some secret dirtiness has been exposed.

"We don't anticipate any immediate change in his condition. I suggest you go home for a while."

"Thank you." I turn to my father-in-law, "I'll be off now, Tom."

He stares at me with hollow, unfocused eyes and the thin, cracked voice cries, "Mummy, don't leave me! Don't go away. I promise I'll be good."

The house is still. I creep around the kitchen, trying not to disturb Rick or his mum. No luck. The door opens and Rick comes in. He looks appallingly ill; still dressed in yesterday's clothes and stinking of stale whisky. My heart sinks.

"You should have gone to bed, Rick. Didn't you sleep at all?"

"A bit. Is Dad okay?"

"There's no change. They don't seem to think he's in any immediate danger so the doctor sent me home. Come and sit down."

He moves unsteadily across to a stool. As he clambers onto it the bottle he's holding clangs against the breakfast bar.

He stares at it with surprise, as if he's wondering how it got to be almost empty or maybe what it's doing in his hand. Then he looks at me like he's a naughty kid, pleading for forgiveness but with defiance lurking in the back of his dark eyes.

I don't feel mad with him but I'm scared. I'm sure it's when he's stressed and drunk he's likely to lose control.

I take the bottle. Then I dissolve two Alka Seltzer and put the glass down in front of him. "It's okay, love."

"It's not okay. I'm sorry, Annie. I don't know what's happening to me."

"You're exhausted. Why don't you go to bed?"

"No can do. I've got to be in work. We're short of manpower this weekend. The trouble is I ought to go to the hospital with Mum. You reckon I can manage two places at once?"

"With or without the headache?" That makes him rub his forehead and grin in rueful acknowledgement. "I can do the hospital with your mum."

"But you've been there all night."

"I'm fine. Is your mum okay?"

"I think so."

I go to the stove. "I'll make porridge, you're more likely to keep that down."

"You're a star." He puts his arms on the breakfast bar, his forehead on his arms, and doesn't move until I stir in milk and syrup and say, "Here you are."

The porridge gets cold before he hits the bottom of the bowl. I pass him a paper napkin. "I'll let you off the rest."

He wipes his mouth. "Thanks. I feel better for that."

I put a mug of tea in front of him. "Rick, tell me what's worrying you."

He stares at the paper napkin and tears it into strips. "Has Dad said anything?"

"A bit."

"It's not true!" His vehemence startles me and I can't help looking sceptical. "Don't look like that, Annie! You can't believe she'd do anything like that."

"She? What are you talking about?"

He counters with his own question, "What did you mean about Dad saying stuff?"

I flinch at the violence in his voice. "I'm sorry but he was talking about when you were a kid. They've moved him to a side ward so nobody can hear."

He stares at me, then shrugs. "Talking about me? I see. That doesn't matter."

"What did you think he was saying?"

"Nothing." The napkin has been through a fine-gauge shredder.

Suddenly it all clicks into place. "Rick, your dad had a stroke."

"What? You've got that wrong. He fell down the stairs and banged his head."

"No, he had a stroke and they think that's what made him fall."

Rick's staring at me like he doesn't understand. I reach over the breakfast bar and get hold of his hands, papier-mâché napkin and all.

"It was nobody's fault, Rick. That's what the doctor told your mum last night. I'm sorry, I thought you knew."

He shakes his head slowly, like he's trying to clear his muzzy brain. "I guess I wasn't listening. I was feeling bloody sick... Yeah, I see." He stands up so abruptly that the stool clangs sideways onto the floor. "I'll go and grab a shower."

While he's upstairs I pack a lunch-box. At least I can make sure that he won't be forced to eat fish paste or starve.

When Rick comes back he's looking pretty good, if you discount the deeply scored lines around his mouth and the stains of exhaustion under his eyes.

"You might need the car. I'll get a patrol car to pick me up." He glances at the clock. "I'd better make it a fast response vehicle. Roebuck will bring back public executions if I'm late again today."

Chapter 47: Annie

I keep out of sight when Rick's lift turns up. This sexy dress has had a hard day's night and I don't want any more rumours causing him grief at work.

I cook and eat my breakfast, then go to tidy and air the living room. The smell of stale whisky is overpowering. There's a stain on the floor and I realise Rick must have spilled his booze. It's a large stain and I'm glad. I'd rather whisky soaked into the carpet than into Rick. I clean it, then move an occasional table to cover the mark.

Upstairs I shower and change into clean jeans and top. When I come down I find Tris sitting in the kitchen, drinking coffee and eating toast. To my surprise she's wearing fresh clothes that are obviously her own.

"I hope you don't mind me making myself breakfast, Annie."

"Of course I don't. Was I staring? I didn't mean to. I was wondering where you got the clothes."

"Rick told the taxi driver to go to our house last night. He said he had to make sure everything was sorted out, so he got the suitcase I keep packed for emergencies."

"Tris, what happened last night?" She looks at me in silence. I say, "Rick's worried sick. I'm sure he thinks you pushed Tom."

Even that doesn't crack her calm. "Poor Rick. How stupid of me not to realise he'd think that. It really happened like Rick said. Tom was angry that I'd been out having fun and he came after me to take his belt to me, but he collapsed and fell."

I try not to react to her calm acknowledgement of Tom's violence. "I'm sorry, Tris, I'd no idea how bad he'd got. The way he calls me Mummy gives me the creeps."

"Tom adored his mum. And you do have a look of

her." She must see my recoil. "That's no bad thing. She had beautiful blue eyes and a smile that lit up her face. She was a nice woman, bright and generous, and never had a bad word for anyone."

"Not like me then."

She considers me, then smiles. It's the same sweet smile she's passed on to Rick. "You'll do," she says.

The doorbell rings. I'm afraid it might be Maris, but it's Mother standing there. She signals to a taxi, which drives off. "Arianne dear. We had such a pleasant evening that I thought I'd see if you wanted to visit a gallery and then have some lunch."

"I'm sorry Mother, Rick's dad's had a stroke. His mum's here. I spent last night at the hospital and we have to go back soon."

"Oh how terrible! Where is she? In the kitchen?" She sweeps through and enfolds Tris in a perfumed embrace. "My dear, I will go to the hospital with you. Arianne can stay here and rest in case she's needed tonight."

"I can go by myself. I don't want to be a nuisance," falters Tris.

"I wish to come with you. I know what you're going through."

I remember Mother's grief when my dad died and think she has no idea what Tris is feeling now. Tris goes to get her coat and I follow her. "Are you sure this is okay? Mother can be rather overpowering."

"I like her." Tris smiles. "And I expect she'll be good at dealing with the doctors."

I laugh. "They'll be scared stiff of her."

I'm tired but not sleepy. In that restless, itchy mood nothing will hold my interest, except one thing. I drag myself up the studio stairs.

Over the years I've taken thousands of photos but I know which ones I've got to look at now. I pull out the record of sixteen years ago, then I go across and rummage through my old taped music, the stuff that goes back to when our relationship began. I don't find the song I'm looking for, the one that goes back to our first date, but there's other music that will summon back that time. I kneel on the floor and spread the pictures out.

Memories are potent; they reawaken love. I start at the beginning. Not photographs but sketches done from memory that first night. It was late evening and I was at the harbour, looking out to sea and thinking about being dead. I wasn't planning to kill myself, just drifting into oblivion.

"Excuse me, miss, are you all right?"

He didn't startle me. It was as if his voice belonged inside me, had always been there as some part of me. I said something about being fine but, instead of leaving, he showed me his ID and sat down beside me. We chatted for a while and then he asked if I'd go out with him.

That first evening we drove for miles and talked for hours. I wanted to explain about my baby and the emptiness inside me that ached more every day, but he was talking about his work, about a child neglect case and how some people didn't deserve to have kids. So I didn't tell him that time, or the next, and so it drifted on.

On the way back he stopped on a headland and we stared at the rippling darkness broken by golden lights. I heard the shush of the water and music from Rick's car radio. After a while the sound of my own name made me listen more intently. The announcer said, "And now, in our *Sounds of the Seventies* slot, a special request for a special lady. This is *Annie's Song*."

Rick grinned at me. "You see, special request for a special lady."

"You blagger, you didn't know you'd meet a girl called Annie tonight."

"True. I never thought I'd get as lucky as this." He pulled me into his arms and we danced in the darkness, closely intertwined.

Chapter 48: Rick

What a bastard! What sort of person believes his own mum would do a thing like that? Not that I thought she did it deliberately. I thought she got frightened when he came after her.

Sitting in the car, heading to the Incident Room, I feel so ashamed I don't know how I can face her again, or Annie who knows the lousy things that were going on in my head. Suddenly it occurs to me, if Dad had a stroke, it's probably down to me frightening him. I shove that thought away. I'll have to deal with it later but, at the moment, I've got to keep my mind on the job.

As we approach Saronholt I spot some posters and rouse myself to ask my driver, "What's going on here?"

"Fun Run. Cross-country. Six miles I think they said."

"Strange time of year to hold that sort of thing."

"They always hold it now, in memory of some Councillor who sponsored it. They reckon they usually get a good turn out. Don't know how it'll go this year. I wouldn't want my kids running through them woods. They asked the Frewers if they should call it off but her dad said no, Stacie would have wanted it to go ahead."

I doubt Stacie would have cared, but it's the sort of thing people say and it's not reasonable for me to suspect the worst just because Terence Frewer made the choice.

There's total frustration in the Incident Room. We all want Stacie to turn up alive but no-one believes she will, so we want a body: we want Forensic evidence; we want to know it's murder. The Crimescene appeal has dredged out a lot more crap and we've got to go through it all. It's afternoon before Kelly and I call on the Frewers.

Cindy's curled up in an armchair. I swear she's shrunk since I saw her last. She doesn't turn her head to look at me or answer my greeting. Terry looks better than before, although his sleek expression slips when he sees me.

"Inspector, I thought you were off the case."

"I've been on sick leave."

"Sick leave? Oh, I must have misunderstood."

"My Superintendent tells me I owe you an apology. When I last saw you I was feeling pretty ill."

I see Kelly look approving, while a smile spreads over Terry's face. "So that was it? I see. You know, when you looked so sour, I began to think you suspected me."

"I certainly didn't mean you to think that."

"You still don't look a hundred per cent."

"You know what they say, 'It never rains but it pours.' My father had a stroke last night and he's pretty bad."

This gets reactions from them all: Kelly seems shocked, Terry displays concern and even Cindy turns her head to look at me.

"I'm sorry to hear that," says Terry.

"Yeah, well these things happen. The important thing is your little girl. We don't want to upset you, but we need to ask you about these."

I hold out the sealed evidence bags of clothes, retrieved from the lab after the fast-track forensic tests turned up empty.

Terry's face twists with distaste. "Yes, what about them?"

"They were left in a charity box. What day was that?"

"Let me think... Thursday. Stacie and I went for a walk and put them through."

"In all that rain?"

"Why not? A bit of rain never hurt anyone. Children spend far too much time sitting at home watching television or playing computer games."

My eyes go to the piano and I wonder how long Stacie was forced to sit practising.

Cindy curls into a tighter ball, her hand pressed against

her mouth. I speak directly to her, "Mrs Frewer, did you always give to this animal charity?"

She nods. "Stacie loved to go there. She loved the animals."

"I wondered why you'd passed on the jeans and sweatshirt when they look like they'd still fit her."

Cindy looks surprised. "I didn't."

"Stacie decided to, darling. She knew they didn't suit her, not like her dresses do." Terry speaks softly, resting his hand upon her arm.

Cindy doesn't reply. She moves away from her husband but she retains her grasp on the bag holding the jeans.

I nod towards the photo on the piano. "The dress in the photograph, the one Stacie was wearing on the day she disappeared..."

"No!" says Terry, cutting across my question.

"Yes," says Cindy, clearly bewildered.

I turn to her, "Mrs Frewer?"

"I thought... I'm sure I put out Stacie's bridesmaid's dress for her to wear."

"No, you didn't, dear," insists Terry.

She stares at him. The frown that wrinkles her forehead makes her look like a puzzled child. "But I'm sure..."

He smiles down at her and takes her hand, squeezing it gently. "I thought you were going to but it wasn't that one you put out. It doesn't matter, she looks beautiful whatever she's wearing."

"The next door neighbour said Stacie was wearing her bridesmaid's dress," I say.

"Well she was wrong, her sight isn't very good," Terry snarls the words.

"Sorry. I'm just trying to get things straight."

"Well get this straight, Stacie is not wearing her bridesmaid's dress, she's wearing another pink one. Her bridesmaid's dress is still hanging in her wardrobe. It's not surprising the police can't find her if they can't even get that right. It's like that other case a few years ago, the one the Press are linking with Stacie. They said that investigation was mucked up by police inefficiency, preconceptions and prejudice."

The more provocative he is, the easier I find it to keep my temper. "Perhaps I could see the bridesmaid's dress, sir?"

He leads me upstairs into Stacie's room and opens the wardrobe. How many pink dresses can one small child wear? He jerks out a soft, flounced, silky-looking one, pink flowers on a pink background. It's definitely the dress in the photograph.

"Satisfied?"

"Thank you, sir."

Cindy has followed us upstairs. She waits until her husband and Kelly go back down then asks, "Do you have to take Stacie's jeans away again?"

"I'm sorry. For the moment we've got to hang onto them but I'll see you get them back."

"She loved wearing them. In them she felt like any other child." Her head is bent and I can't see her face but I'm sure I hear resentment in her voice. "He used to call her Podge when she wore them." She goes across the room, gets the teddy bear out of the cupboard and hugs it to her as she shuffles back towards the door.

As I come alongside her she says, "Are you better now?"

"More or less. Sorry if I was out of order the other day."

"You were kind. I'm sorry about your dad."

"That's the way it goes. He's nearly eighty. He and I aren't that close, it's my mum that's the special one for me."

She goes down the stairs very slowly, one foot on the stair then the other joining it, like a small child. "My mum was my special person too. She's dead now. She died before Stacie was born. I've been wondering these last few days, if her granny sees Stacie up in Heaven, will she recognise her, sort of know by instinct who she is?"

"We don't know Stacie's dead." Heaven talk is definitely

not my thing. Hell I can do, but there's nothing I can tell Cindy about that.

At the foot of the stairs Cindy says, "Thank you."

"We are doing our best to find her, you know."

She stares at me with empty eyes. "You'll find her, when He decides it's time."

"He? Cindy, do you know who took Stacie?"

Her gaze drifts past me and she walks into the living room and curls up in a chair. In a sweet, high voice, she sings a lullaby to the bear.

Chapter 49: Rick

As we turn into the village street, Kelly says, "Do you really think Terry Frewer did it, Guv?"

I shrug. My instincts are useless; I can't even get it right about my own mum.

"He talks about Stacie like he's sure she's still alive but Cindy acts like she's certain Stacie's dead."

I'd noted their different reactions some time ago. "You reckon it's mother's instinct or the difference in their temperaments?"

"Or she knows."

"You think she killed her kid?"

"I didn't say that, but the only fingerprints that the Forensic people could pull off those silk poppies from under Stacie's swing were Cindy's." Kelly's not only on the fast-track to promotion, she's also fast-track to any information that lands on Roebuck's desk.

"Meaning the other fingerprints were too degraded to identify?" I say. Roebuck's inclined to pick and choose his evidence to suit himself and I can see Kelly falling into the same mind-set if she's not pulled up before the habit forms. Maybe Cindy's guilty, maybe not, but that's nothing like conclusive evidence.

"Yes, Guv." I can see she knows where I'm coming from.

"Cindy told us she'd picked up those poppies when they blew away from the War Memorial and put them in her back garden. Was it possible to get prints off the rock she says she pinned them down with?"

"Yes, it was a smooth surface. There were hers and some smudges, like someone had handled it wearing gloves. They were superimposed on her prints."

This time she goes the extra step herself and I don't need to ram the message home. Instead I ask, "You know of any

204

motive for Cindy to hurt her daughter?"

"As much as for the father. Everyone says how he adored Stacie. The mother could have been jealous. After all, she suffers from depression."

Did I miss that? Or did nobody bother to mention it to me?

"Has that been checked with her GP?"

"Yes, she's been treated for depression but no-one seems to think she's dangerous."

"How's her alibi? Someone must have seen her if she was helping at Church?"

"It's not foolproof. She's vague about timings and no-one seems to have noticed her. She's that sort of person. Of course, her husband could be covering for her."

"True." That might explain the act Terry Frewer's been putting on.

"What do you reckon, Guv?"

"I reckon she's pretty near the edge." When it's Cindy Frewer in the frame I can't think in terms of guilt or innocence, all I can feel is her overwhelming pain.

It's late afternoon when Roebuck calls me into his office. Again Lane's in there and again he's scowling. It's evident something has rattled his cage... or someone... I review my actions but my conscience is relatively clear.

"I'm off duty tomorrow," says Roebuck, "DCI Lane is in charge."

To my surprise I feel relieved. Lane doesn't faff around with PR and Politics; if a thing needs doing he makes sure it's done.

"Any news on the paedophile ring you were looking at, sir?" I ask.

"No," snarls Lane. "I don't know if these Apostles of Clift are for real or if it's some bastard jerking us round, but, if they do exist, they're experts at hide-and-seek."

Roebuck butts in, "If there's a serial killer out there,

we've got to get him fast."

"I don't reckon it is a serial killer," says Lane. "In my experience there ain't many serial killers around, not like on the bloody detective shows."

Roebuck looks annoyed at Lane's disagreement. He shrugs and turns back to me, "I've got a job for you." I see Lane scowl and shake his head but Roebuck carries on, "I want you to take a couple of uniformed lads and get over to Elmwash Woods."

"What's happening in Elmwash, sir?" Roebuck should do something about shoring up this room. Every time I'm in there the bloody place spins round.

"It's nothing to do with Stacie Frewer," says Lane. "Bloody souvenir hunters are getting through the wire and taking the hut apart."

Again Roebuck wrests the interview back, "I need a senior officer there to send the message that we won't have this sort of thing."

I want to say, 'Oh God, do I have to?' but I manage, "Yes sir. Is it okay if I go home after I've sorted it?"

Roebuck frowns and I add hastily, "My father's in hospital, sir."

"Oh yes, of course. You can go off duty after you've been to Elmwash Woods."

"Thank you." I leave before he can change his mind and head to my desk to gather up my stuff.

Bob says, "You look terrible."

"Cheers. I'm back over to Elmwash. Some bastards are taking the hut apart."

"Jesus, you get all the crap jobs, don't you? You want me along?"

I don't need Bob doing his Rambo act in Elmwash Woods again. "No that's okay."

The woods are dark and damp and full of ghosts. I inspect the hut, which, in the twilight doesn't look much different than before. The uniformed guys aren't happy about being stationed here and they're taking their resentment out on me.

One says, "You mean we've got to stay out here without a car?"

"Yeah." The track's too narrow to get a car up unless it's essential, especially when the ground's boggy from all the rain. Anyway Roebuck wants to keep it covert so we can collar some of the bastards and make an example of them. "If any buggers try and get in, grab them, but don't rough up any genuine mourners. Emma Brown's father hangs round here a lot."

I pause to make sure no-one's going to give me a back answer then say, "I've arranged for pizza delivery later on. Don't jump them either."

That gets grins, "Cheers, Guv."

I flash my torch over the hut once more and turn back down the path.

I wait to see Ernest Clift, to hear his soft voice whispering through the trees, but he's not here. Instead my head is filled with images of my dad. I see him flexing a belt around his hands and moving steadily forward, the way he always used to do before he beat me and locked me in the dark.

Chapter 50: Annie

It's six o'clock when I come back to the world. I've got the idea for a body of conceptual work blazing in my mind. I envision it as a background of continually shifting images: the story of a relationship screened through two pairs of eyes, one blue, one brown. The trouble is I don't yet know the end.

I'd texted Rick and Tris to contact my mobile if they needed me and I've ignored the numerous calls that had flashed up *Maris Home*. I go downstairs and check out the landline answerphone. There are five new messages. One is from Neil saying that he's sorry to hear about Rick's dad and to contact if I need to take time off. The rest are all from Maris; she sounds petulant and aggrieved. I'm sick of Maris hounding me and I'm embarrassed by the avoidance strategies she's pushing me into. I feel like she's blackmailing me with her threats of suicide.

My mobile beeps and I bring up a text message from Rick's mum.

DEAR ANNIE. TOM NO WORSE. I AM FINE. GOING HOME WITH SONIA FOR NIGHT. BEING WELL LOOKED AFTER SO TELL RICK NOT TO WORRY ABOUT ME. LOVE TRIS.

I read it with relief, text an acknowledgement, then I go upstairs to wash and change before Rick gets in. I flick through the wardrobe and select dark trousers and a high necked jumper. Towards the back I spot a flare of wine red and get out the dress Rick mentioned. It's part of a special time in our lives and I wonder if I'll ever wear it again.

I look at the bed. It was here he raped me a week ago. Deep down I'm still afraid of him. I've done some Internet research and know counselling and medication can help him fight his way back, but only if he'll agree to it. If we can't get past this, we've got to separate. We can't continue in this stress-filled half-relationship.

I hear the front door open and go to the head of the stairs to peer down. He's hanging up his coat and he looks cold and tired. As I watch he presses the palms of his hands against his eyes. He must sense me looking because he moves his hands away from his face and smiles at me. "Hi."

I walk down the stairs to meet him. He makes no move towards me, just stays leaning against the door frame.

I draw his head down and kiss him. For a moment I think he's responding but then he draws back and mutters a hoarse, "Sorry."

So it's all over and I have no choice in the matter.

"It's okay. I understand. It's not your fault that you don't love me any more." My voice sounds high-pitched but remarkably clear and cool.

"Not love you?... me... not... but you mean?... you can't.... not after what I did..." His voice trails away and I see his grip on the door frame tighten, his knuckles gleam white.

There's so much we've got to deal with and at some point we'll have to talk it through. The sense of betrayal, the violation and the fear exists, no-one can wave a magic wand and make them disappear, but there's something I've got to say, here and now. "I love you."

He stares at me. His face is chalk white and emotionless.

"Rick, please say something... anything."

"I'd better sit down." His voice is as expressionless as his face. He makes his way carefully into the sitting room, aims for the sofa but slides down to sit on the hearthrug in front of the fire. "Sorry." He ducks his head forward until it rests on his bent knees.

Suddenly despair turns into something else. I can't sort out exactly what I feel, but outrage, irritation, worry and a tinge of amusement are all there.

"Rick, you can't faint now."

"You got any evidence to back that up?" He slurs the words.

I sit on the sofa and wait.

After a few minutes he pushes himself upright. "Why not now?"

"What?"

"Why did it matter whether I passed out or not?"

"I was trying to talk about us."

"Is there any us?"

"I don't know, but I want there to be."

"Did you say what I thought you said? Before everything started fading out."

"I said I love you. But if you don't feel the same I understand, I know nobody can help falling out of love. I wanted you to know I'm here for you, if you still want me."

"If I want you? Sweet Jesus, Annie! I love you more than anything in the world. But I know there's no way I can ever make it right. No way you'll ever want me touching you again."

I slide down to sit beside him. "Make love to me."

He turns his shadowed face towards me. "What?"

"Make love to me."

Slowly he raises a shaking hand and strokes my cheek, then his fingers move down the side of my neck, reach the jumper and hesitate. I drag it over my head and toss it aside.

"Oh Jesus!" I realise he's focusing on the bruises on my neck.

"It's okay."

He strokes the marks. His lips are quivering. In all our time together I can't remember ever seeing Rick cry. He shows no signs of undressing and so I reach across and unbutton his shirt. Obediently he pulls free of it and I nuzzle against his chest. Again I'm assailed by the familiarity of his body, the comforting intimacy of its feel and smell. I wrap my arms around him. Instinctively I tense as his hands trace down my backbone but I hug him more fiercely when he attempts to draw away.

The removal of our other clothes lacks finesse. We strip

ourselves hastily, without making eye contact.

When we're both naked, I climb on top of him and feel his fingers stroke down my bum and along my thighs.

His nervous approach is not just painfully slow, it's positively agonising in its lethargy. In all our years together, Rick has never been a rough lover, apart from that one cruel time, but he's always been assertive and inventive. Now he's so tentative, it's as if he's afraid to touch me. If I'm scared of him losing control, then he's terrified of the same thing. Raping me has disempowered him.

I hurt for him so much there's no room left for self-pity or for fear. His pain is my pain. I cannot be whole if he is maimed. I guide him home and his release is immediate. When his orgasm is over, it's me who gently disengages. I lie with my cheek pillowed on his chest and hear his tumultuous heartbeat. I move to sit beside him. "Are you okay, Rick?"

"Yeah. Annie I'm sorry. I couldn't hang on."

I giggle. "I think that could be classified as catching you as you came."

He doesn't laugh. "Not much in it for you."

"My turn next time." I speak before I think the implications through. "We're going to make it, Rick. At least we will if you want to as much as me."

"If I want it? I don't want to live if I can't be with you. Oh Annie love, I'm sorry for what I did."

"And I'm sorry for what I put you through."

His voice is sharp with tension, "Annie, I'm so scared."

He doesn't say what he's afraid of. He doesn't need to.

"We'll get through it together." I wrap myself round him and cradle him.

He curls against me and starts to cry. I hold him until he finally quietens down.

"I'm sorry."

"It doesn't matter. You needed to let go." He looks even more exhausted than before and he's shivering violently. I kiss his forehead and move gently away. "I'll make some food."

I pull on trousers and jumper and go into the kitchen and put together a bowl of spaghetti and a platter of garlic bread. Then I run upstairs and change into my red dress.

When I go back to Rick he smiles at me, "You look beautiful. I've always loved you in that dress. It's like a miracle, I keep expecting you to disappear."

I find that heart-wrenching. Rick's usually so matter-of-fact. I sit down beside him on the rug. "You've got to eat. Did you manage any of the sandwiches I made you?"

"No. Sorry."

"No wonder you turned faint. You're going to try and eat this."

"I'd rather have a drink." He looks guilty as soon as he says this. "Annie, I think I'm an alcoholic."

"We'll beat it together. We'll both stop drinking and get it sorted." I kiss the furrows on his forehead where the skin is pinched into a pain-filled, squinting frown.

We share one pasta bowl, the way we did when we were first together and we're almost finished when he miscalculates and spills a forkful on my lap.

"Oh God, I'm sorry."

"No problem."

"But your dress, I've ruined it."

"It's fine. A run through with biological detergent and a tumble dry and it'll be as good as ever. In the meantime..." I stand and strip it off. I'm dressed only in knickers and a lacy black chemise but I don't feel the slightest tremor of fear.

"Do you fancy some music?" I go across to put it on.

"Put on the tape that's in there. I got it out for us the other day."

I glance at it and tears well in my eyes.

"Sentimental sod, aren't I?" he says.

"You're my sentimental sod." I turn on the tape I'd looked for earlier and hold my hands out to him. As he scrambles to his feet the shadowed room is filled with *'Annie's Song.'* The fireside rug clogs between our toes as we cling together.

I kiss him and feel his penis move against my thigh, so I run teasing fingers down to linger at his groin. We tumble back onto the rug.

"Annie, ease off. I'm not sure I can come again, not yet."

I laugh, suddenly filled with joy and confidence. "And I'm sure you can."

Chapter 51: Annie

I wake before Rick and lie, curled into the curve of his arm, watching him. This time last week my life had fallen apart. I can't believe we're starting to rebuild.

At last his eyes open, although he still looks dazed with sleep. "Hi you," I say.

"Hi you."

"How are you feeling?"

"Better."

"I'll get some breakfast." I go downstairs and return with my favourite snack.

Rick stares at the laden tray. "What the hell's that?"

"Tea and doughnuts."

"Doughnuts! You can't eat doughnuts for breakfast."

"I can, for breakfast, lunch or dinner and before and after sex." I sit cross-legged on the bed and take a bite. Raspberry jam squirts out. "Have one, they're yummy."

"No thanks, love."

"I'll make you a proper breakfast before you go into work."

"I don't want to think about work." He starts to shake.

"Hey, it's okay." I wind myself round him, rocking him gently and making soothing sounds. "What was that about?" I ask when he calms down.

"I don't think I can do it any more. Oh Annie love, I'm so sick of shovelling shit for everyone. I don't reckon I can carry on. Every time I go into the Saronholt Incident Room no-one will look at me. They're certain I screwed up and Clift wasn't the killer. And if I got it wrong, then it's all started again and Stacie's death was down to me."

I hate the way he's blaming himself. I lean forward and rest my face against his. "It wasn't down to you. You were part of a team and you weren't even the SIO. But if you feel like that, don't carry on. Take some leave and, if you still can't face it, quit."

"If I quit what else could I do?"

"I don't know, but we can't go on like this. You were dreaming last night."

"Was I? I don't remember."

"I cuddled you and you stopped crying."

"I'm sorry I woke you."

"That doesn't matter. Rick, could you bear to tell me why you're so scared of being shut in? It was something your father did, wasn't it?"

He looks past me and focuses on a blank piece of wall. "When I was a kid I used to pee myself, not just at night in bed, but in the day as well. If Mum wasn't round, Dad used his belt on me and made me stand in the corner, naked, and he wouldn't let me get clean or anything."

I feel sick with horror. "How old were you?"

"Seven. They took me to a child psychologist the school welfare people recommended, but it wasn't any use. I think Mum must have guessed what Dad was doing, because it got so she never left me alone with him and, after a while, I stopped doing it in the day. At night it wasn't so bad. Mum used to cover for me and she bribed Martin so he didn't tell." He stops talking. I cuddle him and wait.

Eventually he takes a deep breath and says, "When I was twelve, Mum had to go into hospital and Dad found out about me still peeing the bed. The first two nights he just took his belt to me, but the third night he put me outside in the old lavatory, the one at the bottom of the garden. He locked me in and he left me there all night. Ever since I can't stand not being able to get out of places."

I'm trembling as much as he is. "I'm sorry," I whisper.

"You're sorry? What for?"

"I should have been more supportive."

"You've been bloody wonderful."

"If you'd told me I could have helped more."

"I've never told anyone before."

"Not even your Mum?"

"Especially not Mum. She always blames herself for not protecting me better."

"But it's not her fault. She did the best she could." She was hardly more than a child herself when Rick and Martin were born.

"I know, but victims often blame themselves. It's sort of guilt for being so unlovable. I see a lot of it in my work."

I wonder if he realises it applies to him as well. Rick's no fool and I'm sure he does. I move on and say, "I phoned your mum when I was downstairs. She's fine and there's no change in your dad."

"Thanks love." He sighs and pushes back the duvet. "I'd better get into work. Roebuck's buggered off for the day."

"Why don't you phone Bob's mobile and see if there's any developments? If not perhaps you won't have to go in. You told me DCI Lane wanted you to take some leave."

I expect him to argue but he picks up the phone. "Bob, it's Rick. Do you need me in today? I'm feeling pretty crap."

"Skiving bastard." Bob speaks loud enough for me to hear. "No, cut that, I didn't mean it. There's nothing doing here. The Super's gone up North to his niece's christening and the DCI is dealing with a clubbing assault in town."

"Okay. Make sure you call me if anything breaks." Rick rings off but he still looks edgy. "I'm sorry, love, I'm so uptight, I don't know what to do with myself."

I stretch on top of him, rubbing myself against him. "I'll think of something."

This time he makes a better job of it and I enjoy it very much. For the past six months I'd been so devastated by the loss of our emotional closeness that I hadn't realised how much I missed sex. All the same, there's something worrying me.

Rick must spot my troubled face. "What's wrong, love?"

I look down, pleating the duvet cover between my

fingers. "Rick, I swear I wasn't setting a trap for you but, if I'm pregnant, please don't ask me to get rid of it."

He stares at me. "I'd never ask you to do that."

"Thank you." The lump in my throat threatens to choke me.

He puts his hand over mine. "Annie, I know about you and Neil and the abortion."

"What? How?"

"Neil told me."

"The bastard!"

"Calm down, love. He'd been mixing booze and painkillers and he was pretty out of it."

"You must despise me." It's been an emotional sort of morning and I can't stop myself from crying.

His hand under my chin tilts up my face. "This is me, Rick. Remember me? I'm the guy who loves you."

"Well I hate myself." I grab a box of tissues, wipe my eyes and blow my nose.

"Annie, can I ask you something?"

"Of course."

"How could you bear to go to work with Neil at the College?"

"It wasn't hard. After all we'd seen each other all the time while I was finishing my degree. He'd probably had a hundred women since we split up and I'd got you."

"But how can you forgive him for what he did to you?"

"It was me who mucked up taking the Pill. He'd never pretended our relationship was anything permanent. Anyway, if he'd stood by me I'd never have met you."

"Better for you if you hadn't."

Indignation banishes any remaining wish I have to cry. "Don't say that! Don't ever say or think it again."

"Sorry."

"So you should be. What would you say if I said you'd be better off without me?"

He makes a show of considering this. "I'd say it might

be true. I'm married to a woman who eats doughnuts for breakfast and leaves sugar in the bed."

Over an hour later the phone rings and I answer it. Bob says, "That you Annie? Can you tell Rick to get in as soon as possible? There's been a major development."

"He's here."

I pass the phone to Rick. As he listens his face grows grim and tautly focused. "Okay. Send someone straight over to pick me up. Annie might need my car."

He puts the phone down and says, "I've got to shower and change, the car will be here pretty soon."

"It's bad news, isn't it?" Sorrow for little Stacie mars my own, newly recovered happiness.

Rick nods. "Yeah, they've found her."

Chapter 52: Rick

The patrol car stops at the edge of the village next to a stile guarded by a young constable.

"Through there, Guv," says the driver.

Just what I need, another body in a wood.

They've put boards down to walk on. They're slippery with rain and mud and the path's churned up. I guess this is where the Fun-Runners hit the village yesterday. Saronholt Wood is damp and bare and strangely hushed, considering the large police presence.

In the clearing, the Scene of Crimes people are about to erect their tent. They're wearing their white suits and, in this desolate landscape, I think they look like space travellers just set down. I pull myself up sharply. This is not a bloody X File.

The SOCO team become aware of my presence and move aside to let me see, although I can't go close until I'm suited up.

Stacie is lying a few yards from the track. She's naked and laid out neatly, but death is not pretty and her little body is bloated and oozing, decomposition is well underway. Her fair hair is loose and tangled and her corpse is adorned by a scattering of rain-swept flowers.

They're all staring at me. Trying to suss out my reaction. And the weird thing is there isn't any. I don't feel anything.

"Any idea how long she's been dead?" I say to the Crime Scene Manager.

"Quite a while. The pathologist's on his way but we're sure she wasn't killed here."

"We know that! We searched these woods last week when she went missing. And they had a Fun Run through here yesterday. She must have been put here last night or early this morning. Who found her?"

"Couple of village kids going up to the Animal Sanctuary." Bob nods along the track to where Kelly's standing with two girls. "They're pretty shook up. The bigger one's been sick."

She's still being sick, doubled over and retching. The other kid's hysterical and Kelly's got problems restraining her.

"What the hell are they doing hanging round here? And why haven't you got another female officer along to help?"

"I hadn't got round to sorting it." He scowls at me. "I was kinda busy. The guy in charge took the morning off."

"Don't push your luck, Bob. Call a doctor to examine those kids, and do it now."

I go over and put my arm round the older girl's shoulders. "It's okay. Calm down and try to take deep breaths."

She hangs limply for a minute, then she straightens, turning in the shelter of my arm. As I offer her a wad of clean tissues I recognise Vicki, the kid from the village shop. She looks much younger with the make-up washed off her face.

"Oh it's you," she says. "I must look awful." Then in a bewildered tone, "Stacie's dead." She begins to cry.

"Come on, let's get you home." I half carry her along the track and Kelly follows with the smaller girl.

At the stile the constable is struggling with a plump woman whose orange hair makes a cruel contrast to her white, anxious face.

"For God's sake! She's this kid's mother, let go of her." I lift Vicki over the stile.

The constable complains, "She assaulted me."

"That's nothing to what I'll do to you if you don't shape up. Clear those bloody reporters out the way." I speak to Vicki's mum, "As far as we know she's not hurt but she's badly shocked. Let's get her somewhere private and the other kid as well."

We hurry them into Vicki's mum's shop, away from cameras and staring eyes. Vicki's mum slams the door and bolts it.

Kelly says, "Okay if we go in here?" and takes the other kid through to a separate room.

Vicki's still holding onto my hand. I haul a chair from behind the counter and sit her down. "Is it alright if I talk to her?" I ask her mum. "Or would you rather wait until the doctor's checked her out?"

Her mum's sharp eyes go from my face to Vicki's. "Better get on with it. Always knew no good would come of it, hanging round those bloody animals."

"What?"

"Up the animal sanctuary, riding Mrs Rutherfield's horses."

If I was Vicki's mum I'd have reckoned a horse was the safest thing to keep between her legs, but of course I don't say so. I get out my notebook and crouch down in front of Vicki's chair. "What time did you start off for the sanctuary?"

"'Bout half-nine, maybe a bit later."

I glance at my watch, it's ten-thirty.

"That was you and the other girl? What's her name?"

"Lisa. Her mum and dad don't mind as long as I look after her." She's speaking between sobs but she's doing well.

"Good girl. Now was it always just you two who went up?"

She nods.

"Never Stacie?"

This brings on a fresh bout of sobbing but in between she manages to get out, "Not lately... I used to take her... she loves the animals... I mean she loved them... I can't believe she's really dead."

I think of Vicki's cocky attitude when I'd first interviewed her, but that was play-acting, now she's found out what violent death is like.

"Why did Stacie stop going up to the sanctuary with you?"

"Her dad moaned she came back smelling of animals."

"Don't blame him," says her mum.

221

Vicki ignores her, "And he don't like the people up there."

"Why's that, Vicki?"

She grows calmer as she thinks this through. "Connie... Mrs Rutherfield... she's the one what runs the place, she's nice, but she can be stroppy, she always tells people what she thinks of them, and Wayne, who works there, he's kind of disabled."

"What do you mean disabled?"

"Not right in the head," says Vicki's mum.

"In what way?"

"He looks funny and he likes touching girls," explains Vicki.

"What? Why didn't you say?" Her mum's voice rises to a screech. "Come on, tell me, what did he do to you?"

"Nothing! Don't be thick, Mum. He likes little girls, not ones as big as me."

Jesus! There's a mental defective wandering round the area perving on little girls and we're the last to know. I've been worse than useless lately, but has the whole bloody police force been on go-slow?

"Wayne lives up at the sanctuary does he, Vicki?"

"Yeah, he's got a caravan."

"Did Stacie go in this caravan with Wayne?"

"Yeah. She liked him... she said he used to cuddle her and give her sweets."

There's the sound of rapping on the door. I open it and let the doctor in, followed by a worried looking woman who says she's Lisa's mum.

"Thanks for getting here so fast, Doctor," I say. "Vicki, is it okay if the doctor sees Lisa first?" The kid's still bursting our eardrums with her screams.

"Yeah."

I show him where to go and return to Vicki. "Now, let's get back to this morning. Did you see anyone in the woods?"

She shakes her head.

"Which of you saw Stacie first?"

"I did." The tears are speeding up.

"And did you or Lisa touch anything?"

"No!" She shudders. Her mum puts an arm round her and glares at me.

I ignore the warning look, "Vicki, when you found Stacie, exactly what did you and Lisa do?"

"At first I couldn't believe it. I just stared. Then Lisa saw and she started screaming. I wanted to run away but Lisa wouldn't move. So I got my phone and dialled 999 and after a long while some people came and I was sick."

Her mother says, "That's enough."

"More than enough. Thanks, Vicki, you've been very helpful and brave. The doctor will see you soon and I expect he'll give you something to calm you down."

Next door the screams have stopped. My head has been thumping in time to Lisa's hysteria and it carries on even now it's quiet.

I say in a low tone to Vicki's mum, "Thanks for letting me talk to her. Try not to let her dwell on it but listen to her if she wants to talk."

"And then report back to you lot?" she says resentfully.

"I assume if she remembers anything to help us catch this bastard you'll let us know." I moderate my tone, "Actually I meant don't let her keep it all inside. If you start clamping down on bad things, it can really mess you up."

She seems to suss out that I'm not blagging. "Alright."

The door opens and Kelly appears. "The doctor's given Lisa an injection and she's asleep." She looks at me warily, as if she expects me to complain that I wanted to speak to the kid before she was put out of it.

"That's fine. Did you manage to get anything useful out of her?"

"Not really. Sorry Guv."

"It can't be helped. Anyway Vicki's put me in the picture."

My phone rings and Bob says, "The pathologist wants to move the body."

"Has the CSM given the go ahead?" The Crime Scene Manager has a lot of clout and things get screwed up if you don't allow the SOCOs enough time to do their job.

"Yeah. The CSM's waiting on you."

"Tell the pathologist to move her and I'll catch up with him and the CSM as soon as possible. And you can get back to the Incident Room, I'll need you there."

Outside the shop we force our way through reporters and cameramen. They hurl questions at us: "Is it true you've found a body?... Can you confirm it's Stacie?... Is it another Mausoleum killing like Elmwash?"

Chapter 53: Rick

We reach the Incident Room and I turn to the reporters and yell, "Thank you. Listen please. All I can tell you is that a child's body has been discovered. We'll have more details for you later."

Inside I say to the uniformed guy on the door, "Make sure those bastards are kept well back."

I go to the middle of the hall. "Okay, folks, settle down. We'll have a proper briefing in a couple of hours. By then we'll have formal identification, but it's definitely Stacie. There was a Fun Run yesterday and everyone's got to be checked out, especially the stewards or anyone who came along after the race. What time did the call come in from those two girls?"

"Nine-thirty-eight, sir," a constable replies.

"And we were on the scene when?"

"Nine-forty-three," supplies Bob. "Control called straight through here."

Vicki said they'd taken ages to arrive. Five minutes is a good response time, but when you're standing in a wood with a murdered child any time seems long.

"Start house to house. Find out if anyone's walked that path this morning and what they saw. We need to narrow down the time the bastard dumped her there. Bob, you sort that. That animal sanctuary, who interviewed the people up there?"

There's silence, then Kelly goes to a computer and checks. "Jeff Hiller, Guv. He's off today."

"Then get him in, I want to talk to him." I nod dismissal to the rest of the team and Bob and I go over to join Kelly. "Anything useful in Hiller's report?" Knowing DC Hiller I don't hold out much hope.

She shakes her head. "Nothing special."

"Nothing on a guy called Wayne who lives up at the sanctuary in a caravan?"

"That would be Wayne Jones? Says here he didn't see or hear a thing and the woman who runs the sanctuary said he was up there all the time."

"I want that alibi checked out."

"You got something on Wayne Jones?" asks Bob.

"Word in the village is that he's mentally handicapped…"

"That's the worst sort of prejudice there is!" protests Kelly. "Just because he's disabled doesn't mean he's a paedophile…"

I continue over her, "The village kids reckon he's into touching up little girls and Stacie's been in his caravan a lot and he used to give her sweets."

That shuts her up.

Bob scowls at her. "You ought to get all the facts before you start sounding off." He adds under his breath, "Lairy cow."

She rips back at him, "I'm going to report…"

I out-yell both of them, "That's enough! I don't need this sort of crap from either of you. Any more aggro and I'll have both of you out of here… Got it?" I receive two sulky nods. "Bob, do the DCI and Superintendent know what's going down?"

"I let the DCI know straight off. He said he'd get over here as soon as he could, but he's pretty tied up, so can you handle it until he or the Super get back?"

"No problem. Is he still working that clubbing assault?"

"Yeah. Only the victim died, so it's murder." He glances at Kelly and adds, "Word is a gang of black kids knifed an Asian boy. It's a sort of racism roundabout, ain't it? Us poor white gits haven't got a chance."

"Shut it, Bob, and get the uniformed teams sorted. Kelly, you come with me."

"Where you two skiving off to?" Bob meets my look and adds hastily, "In case I need to contact you, Guv."

226

"We're going to talk to Stacie's family and if you call that skiving you've been in this job too long."

"Sorry, Rick."

"Whatever."

I head out of the main hall and Kelly follows me. She slams the door behind her. The noise feels like a clenched fist battering my brain. I haul her into a small side room and say, "Get one thing straight, today you haven't got the Super to run to. Today it's my team and you can cut the attitude."

"Me cut the attitude? What about him?"

"Yeah, him too. I'm not taking any more crap from either of you. Understand this, I'm not prejudiced against disabled people, I'm not racist and I'm not sexist. In fact, of the two of us, I'd reckon you were far more guilty of that sort of stuff than me."

"What do you mean?"

"How about giving us guys a chance to work with you, without being scared you're going to slap in a complaint every time we say something dumb?"

She considers me, then smiles. She's quite a stunner when she looks like that. "That's okay for you Guv, but what about DS Borrow? He's got it in for me."

"I can deal with him a damned sight better if you don't answer back." I know Bob's not a racist, he's got plenty of black and Asian mates, but he loathes Kelly so much he'll use any weapon to lash out at her. "Bear in mind he's pretty stressed at the moment. He was part of the Elmwash investigation too." Everything shifts out of focus as I speak. I lean against a big photocopier while the dizziness washes over me and away. "Let's go and talk to Stacie's family."

There's been a lot of action along the street and the Frewers must know something's going on. They're sitting together on the sofa... no, that's wrong, they're both sitting on the sofa but they're not together in any way.

"What's happening?" says Terry. "For God's sake tell us."

I'm finding problems with the words, I open my mouth but nothing comes.

Cindy looks straight at me and says, "You've found her haven't you?"

I choke out, "I'm sorry."

"A child's body has been found," says Kelly. "We believe it's Stacie but we'll need formal identification. I'm sorry to ask you, sir, but…"

He falls to pieces. Covers his face with his hands and starts to moan, "No! You can't ask me to do that! Oh Stacie! Stacie!"

"I'll do it," Cindy's small, cold voice slices through the room.

"No Cindy you mustn't!" wails Terry. "What if she's disfigured? What if they've done terrible things to her? It's like those other ones with all the flowers and stuff!"

"It doesn't matter what anyone's done to her, she's still my little girl." There's no emotion in her words. It's like she's dead, out there in the wood, with her daughter.

I can't bear to look at her. I stare around the room and focus on the plant, wilting in its shady corner. Cindy stands up and walks towards the door. "I'm her mother. It's up to me to look after her now. I didn't look after her when she was alive."

"Cindy!" screams Frewer, "Cindy, where are you going? Cindy, don't leave me!"

She doesn't look back and I follow her into the hall.

She holds out her hand as if it's the end of a formal party. "I'll be in Stacie's room. Please call me when you want me to go to her."

Chapter 54: Annie

So now I know his secret, my sexy, streetwise husband with his deeply-buried fears. I wonder if that's why Ernest Clift focused on him. Did his predator's instinct help him to see through the tough cop persona to the abused and vulnerable child?

After Rick leaves I get the Elmwash DVD out of my briefcase and shove it in the machine. As I watch my senses are stretched to have some warning if Rick returns unexpectedly. I feel as if I'm doing something wrong.

It's strange to see the news clips. Rick looks tired and stressed but much younger than he does now, without those deep-etched frown lines on his face. The report starts as a reasonable retelling of the case but soon the emphasis shifts. The reporter speaks of police inefficiency, preconceptions and prejudice, as if Rick and his colleagues were the villains in the case. I think Rick has told it how it is when he says the police may dig the shit but it's the reporters who spread it.

The programme examines the case against Ernest Clift. His picture appears and I shudder. I'd forgotten how loathsome he was: in his mid-sixties, pale and paunchy, a white slug of a man. My disgust turns to rage as the reporter brushes aside the Coroner's verdict and implies that Clift was the victim, harried to his death by police persecution. With gritted teeth, I watch to the end. Then I remove the DVD and put it in its case, resisting the temptation to hurl it into the rubbish bin.

I switch to the midday news in time to hear, '... *the main news story in the South today. Police investigating the disappearance of seven-year-old Stacie Frewer have discovered the body of a child in Saronholt Woods.*

I hesitate before I pick up the phone. Rick won't be happy if I interrupt him when he's in charge of a murder case, but the worry is overpowering and I dial his mobile. It rings for a while then the answer service cuts in.

"Hi, Rick, it's me. Just checking you don't need your car or anything. Love you." I put down the receiver but, after ten seconds, I pick it up again. Impelled by an instinct too strong to be denied, I ring the same number.

On the sixth ring there's a croaked, "Yeah?"

"Darling, what's wrong?"

I hear him sobbing. "I told you I couldn't do it any more."

"Oh my poor love! Where are you, Rick?" For a full minute he doesn't speak. "Rick, where are you?"

"Sorry... I was trying to work it out... I'm in the woods... by that animal sanctuary place."

"Stay where you are, I'll be there."

I'm out of the house in seconds and driving fast down the lane. I have to brake and shift into a gateway to let a car coming towards me get through. It maintains the inexorable pace of a driver who has no intention of backing. As it passes I see it's Maris. She spots me and stops but I'm already accelerating away.

I don't go through Saronholt. I drive to the far side of the sanctuary and take a trespassing short cut through a field. All the time the fear is gnawing me. *What if I can't find him? What if he's not there? What if he's done something terrible to himself? Please God let him be all right.*

I find him huddled against a tree and kneel beside him. "Rick, I'm here."

No answer. I try again, "Rick, it's Annie."

Still nothing. I hold his face in both my hands and make him look up. His eyes meet mine. I force a smile. "Hi you. Remember me?"

He manages a nod, then he starts to shake.

What can I do? I can't get him out of here by myself, but if I phone for help I finish his career. I wonder what hope there is of discreetly contacting Bob.

I hear the sound of someone trampling through the soggy

leaves and move to shield Rick. The woman approaching is elderly and wearing wellington boots, cord jeans, a thick jumper and a grubby body warmer.

"What's wrong?" She's got a husky voice, as upper-class as any I've encountered in my mother's drawing room.

"It's my husband, he's not well."

She asks no further questions. "You'd better come inside."

I get up and, miraculously, Rick scrambles to his feet, using me and the tree trunk for support. We follow her out of the wood, through a gate, across the yard and into the kitchen of a small bungalow. Everything is neat and clean, except the floor, which bears a trail of muddy footprints. The air is heavy with the smells of damp animals, percolating coffee and boiling sugar.

A young man is standing by the stove. He's large and flabby and, as he turns a reproachful gaze upon the woman, I see he's got beady eyes and thick rubbery lips. "It's got too dark again. You shouldn't have gone away when you saw the Art lady."

The woman peers into the saucepan. "Move out of my way." She tips the thick brown goo into a greased tray. "Leave it alone and roll out the gingerbread."

She pours coffee and takes a whisky bottle out of the cupboard, interrogating me with one raised eyebrow. So much for Rick quitting drinking, this is definitely not the time. "Not for me, thanks, but please put some in Rick's."

She pours a generous shot into the mug and hands it to him. I hear his teeth chattering against the rim.

I take mine. "Thank you. This is kind of you. You must think it's very odd."

She smiles. "I admit it's not what one expects of the police."

Rick manages to say, "You know who I am?"

"I may live outside the village both literally and metaphorically, but I still hear the gossip." Now her smile is distinctly mischievous. "You, I believe, are the Detective Inspector I had described to me as 'really gorgeous and completely up himself.'"

"That was Vicki, I guess." Rick sounds washed out but in control.

"I hope you don't expect me to reveal the names of my informants?" Then suddenly serious, "Have there been any developments?"

Rick nods. "Stacie's dead. Vicki found her body in the woods."

"Poor little Stacie." She turns to Wayne, who has an anxious, puzzled look on his face. "Wayne, remember I told you Stacie had gone away? Well I'm sorry, dear, she won't be coming back."

"Not ever?"

"No, I'm sorry, Wayne, she's dead."

He stares at her then the bewildered look clears. "You mean she's dead in Heaven like Emma and Kate?"

Chapter 55: Annie

When Wayne mentions two of the Elmwash girls, I gasp and see Rick stiffen, but the woman seems unmoved. "Yes, like them. Wayne, please go and muck out the horses."

"Vicki didn't come today, that was bad of her."

"Vicki isn't well."

"Poor Vicki, I'll take her some sweeties."

"Perhaps later. Now do the horses for me."

As he shambles away Rick says sharply, "What was that about Emma and Katie?"

"Emma and Kate were Wayne's sisters. They and their parents were killed in a car crash five years ago. They'd left Wayne with me while they went out for the day."

"I see. I thought... of course they're popular names... You must think I'm really weird."

"Not at all. My husband was a military man. He saw some dreadful things. He had nightmares for the rest of his life."

"Thank you," says Rick as she pours him another cup of coffee. "No whisky this time. I've got a job to do. You understand I have to check on all angles?"

"Indeed, what 'angle' is it that you're referring to?"

There's a bite in Rick's voice as he replies, "There have been reports that Wayne likes touching up small girls."

Her face freezes into anger, then it relaxes. "This village gossip. Yes, it's true that Wayne likes holding little girls on his lap, he likes watching cartoons with them or looking at picture books. He used to do that with his sisters."

"What was his relationship with Stacie?"

"They were friends."

"Why did Stacie's stepfather stop her coming here?"

"There were several reasons. For one thing, he didn't like her getting dirty, he's very involved in music and preferred the poor child to do that."

"It wasn't anything to do with Wayne?"

"He didn't care for Wayne but he stopped Stacie coming here because of me."

"Why you?"

"We had words about Vicki and the gate."

"What gate's that?" Rick glances at me and seems reassured that I look bewildered too.

"Mr Frewer was taking a group of children on a nature walk and Vicki was assisting him. He left a gate open and a brood mare got out. Afterwards he denied it was him and blamed Vicki. It upset her very much."

"Why are you sure it wasn't Vicki?"

"Vicki was born and brought up round here. She's good around horses and very responsible. But if she'd made a mistake she'd have said so. Although she can be very silly, I've always found her a truthful child."

"So you quarrelled with Terence Frewer?"

"I gave him a piece of my mind. It would have happened sooner or later anyway."

"Why's that?"

"I don't like people who always demand the centre stage." She smiles at me. "Your mother can be like that but Sonia has a genuinely kind heart."

"You know my mother?"

"Of course, my dear. How silly of me, you don't recognise me in my working clothes. I'm Connie Rutherfield, your mother and I were at school together."

"Oh yes, of course." My mother's words drift back to me, 'poor Constance, sometimes I think that she's completely mad.'

"About Terence Frewer." Rick kicks the ball firmly back into play.

"He's not a man I care for. I would wager good money that, at the moment, he's more grief stricken than anyone has ever been before." I can see from Rick's face she's got this right.

"How's Stacie's mother?" she asks.

"Being incredibly brave."

Connie nods, as if this confirms what she'd already guessed. "Poor girl."

A commotion outside takes her attention. "Excuse me a moment, the pot-bellied pigs have got out." She strides out, yelling, "Wayne! Emergency!"

Rick starts to get up. "Do you think we ought to help?"

I push him back into his seat. "No way. The only Pig I'm rescuing is you."

He grins at this, then rubs his forehead. "Thanks. I really lost it."

"Want to talk about it?"

"There's not a lot to say. There's the kid's body in the woods sprinkled with flowers and everyone thinks it's another Mausoleum killing. It hit me how it's my fault. If Clift wasn't the killer, there's been some other bastard out there all the time, waiting to kill again, and it's down to me we stopped looking and my fault Stacie's dead."

I search for a succinct way to convince him he is wrong and come up with the word, "Bollocks!" which I say.

It's not an expression I've used before but I like it, it has a nice solid sound. It startles Rick into focusing on me and I push my advantage, "Stop whinging and start thinking logically. Why do you think Stacie's death is a Mausoleum-type murder?"

"I didn't, not at first, but would someone else lay the kid out naked in the woodland and sprinkle her with flowers?"

"Why not? Surely lots of killers copy other crimes? And there was a TV documentary about Elmwash recently."

"Shit! How the hell did I miss that?"

"I don't know, but it's probably just as well." I consider pointing out there are several other cops in Galmouth CID and surely one of them should have realised?

I see Rick's expression sharpen as his brain grinds into

gear. "It'd be useful to have a copy of this programme. I'll have to find a fast but discreet way of getting one."

"I've got one, I borrowed a DVD from Neil."

"You've watched it?"

"This morning. I wanted to know... to try and help you."

He cups my cheek in his hand. "Oh Annie, love." Then briskly back to business, "Can you get it for me?"

"Of course. But Rick, I don't think you should watch it."

There's a wry twist to his lips. "It'd probably finish me. Don't worry, I won't, unless I've got you around to pick up the pieces."

The door opens and Wayne comes in, bringing with him the smell of pig. He goes across to wash his hands.

"Wayne, when was the last time you saw Stacie?" says Rick.

The boy stares out of the window. "Dunno."

"Did you see her last Sunday?"

"No!"

"Wayne, look at me. That's right. Now answer me. Did you see Stacie last Sunday?"

Wayne's nose is running. He wipes it with the back of his hand. "I didn't see Stacie. I didn't do nothing bad." He's not a good liar.

"Wayne, I want the truth."

Wayne stares at him. Slobber dribbles from the corner of his mouth. "I didn't do nothing bad!" He backs away until he's pressed against the work surface.

"Wayne, I know you're lying. You saw Stacie last Sunday, didn't you? If you won't talk here, you'll have to come to the Police Station." Rick steps towards Wayne.

"No!" Wayne fumbles behind him and I see his hand come round in a heavy swing. He's holding something and it's lunging towards Rick's head.

"Look out!"

Rick's left arm comes up to block the blow but it makes him stagger. Wayne shoves past me and heads out of the door.

"Shit!" Rick cradles his arm as he starts after him.

"No! Rick please!" I grab his undamaged arm.

He stops and grins at me. "Don't worry, chasing loonies round farmyards has never been my scene."

"Did he hurt you?"

"Too fucking right he did. What the hell did he hit me with?"

"The rolling pin. It's marble."

"Bloody felt like it. Anyway, I've got a suspect." He pulls out his phone and calls the Incident Room. "It's DI Evans, get me DS Borrow quick. Bob? I need men up at the Animal Sanctuary fast. I've had trouble with Wayne Jones. I want the entire area searched and him picked up. Tell them to take care, he's violent. And I need someone to pick me up."

He rings off and looks at me. "It's all right, love."

I ask through chattering teeth, "Do you think Wayne killed Stacie?"

"He certainly knows more than he's letting on."

We wait in silence until the squad cars arrive. As I scurry across the yard I see Rick pointing to the barn. A few moments later, uniformed officers head towards the sound of Connie's voice, which is still upraised, scolding the pot-bellied pigs.

Chapter 56: Rick

When we get to the Incident Room I make Annie come inside with me while I grab a couple of uniformed guys. "You two are going to drive my wife home and one of you is going to stay with her while the other brings the DVD she gives you back here."

Annie protests, "You can't think I'm in any danger, Rick?"

'I know where you live. I've seen your pretty wife. I've friends, good friends who will carry on for me.'

"That animal woman's a friend of your mother. She'll know where you live. It's not likely Wayne will come after you, but with loonies you can't be sure."

"It's a waste of manpower," says Annie. "Is there any problem with me coming back here with the DVD? I'll keep out the way but you'll know I'm all right."

Who does she think she's fooling? What she means is she'll be here for me.

Bob draws me aside and mutters, "Lane'll go crazy. It's against all the rules."

Since when has DCI Lane's mental health been a priority for me? I'm more concerned with my own, and I'm so near the edge the rulebook isn't relevant any more.

"Okay Annie, but you'd better wait in here during the briefing."

I show her into the small room the SIO's using as an office. The walls are paper thin, so this is discretion being seen to be done rather than actually happening.

I go into the Main Hall and yell to the cops waiting in the Incident Room, "Right you lot, gather round. First off, what's happening with formal identification and the post-mortem?"

"We've got the formal identification, Guv," says Kelly. "The mother did it. I went with her."

"How did she cope?"

"Very quiet and controlled."

"Thanks for sorting that, Kelly."

She gives me her swift smile.

There's a sort of cautious blankness in most of the faces looking back at me, like a lot of them are waiting for me to crack and a few who think they'll enjoy watching the show. Sorry to disappoint you, arseholes, but that's over for today. The adrenaline's pumping and briefings have always been my thing. Will Newton once told me I was the best DI for briefings he'd ever known and then, in case I got too cocky, added it was because I loved the sound of my own voice.

I say to Bob, "Any reports of the people using that path?"

"One of the Fun Run stewards went through about seven last night. And there's this old guy who walks his dog at six-thirty every morning. Neither of them saw anything but it was dark both times."

"You checked these guys' alibis for last Sunday?" Sometimes Bob can miss the obvious.

"Yeah, they're both in the clear."

"Keep at it, I want to know when Stacie was left there."

"Taking a chance, weren't they? Dumping her under our noses."

"How many people are out in the woods before daylight on a wet Sunday in winter? And if he's local he could know people's routines."

I go back to the incident board. "So we've found Stacie. We've got to wait for the pathologist's report but, from the state of her body, I'd guess she's been dead a good few days."

I see Bob's nod of agreement and carry on, "So what happened to her and where's she been stashed for the last week?"

I give a swift recap of Cindy and Terry's stories, mentioning the hole in Cindy's church alibi and that Terry's got no significant alibi at all. "I thought it was odd, him getting Stacie dressed up and letting her play in the garden in the rain. But the next-door-neighbour says she saw Stacie out there."

"Everyone says her parents were devoted to her," says Kelly.

"Yeah, I know, but it's hard to tell with families. A lot of crap goes on behind closed doors. Anyway we've got a hotter suspect. Or rather we haven't got him, at the moment he's still out there. I've been talking to Constance Rutherfield, the animal sanctuary woman, and her helper, Wayne Jones. There was something between him and Stacie and he's a very strange guy."

I see Kelly's protesting look and add, "And, when I questioned him about whether he'd seen Stacie last Sunday, he assaulted me and took off."

"You alright, Rick?" demands Bob.

"Yeah, just got a banged up arm." The pain is sharpening but I manage to grin at him. "Anyway, we've got to find him. Don't take any chances, he's scared and violent. I'm going to apply for a search warrant for the animal sanctuary. I've got a feeling that Mrs Rutherfield's unlikely to be co-operative this time. Is Jeff Hiller here yet?"

There's a moment's silence then a reluctant voice says, "Yes Guv."

"Jeff, when you did the routine interviews, how did Wayne Jones seem?"

It's a stupid, unfocused question but Jeff does his best to answer it. "He was odd and jumpy and a bit upset. To be honest, Guv, I didn't know whether he was always like that. It's easier to read the signs on a normal bloke, if you know what I mean?"

"Yeah, I know. And if you'd pushed the questioning too hard you'd get someone moaning about contravening a disabled person's rights."

"That's it, Guv." Jeff still sounds nervous, as if he can't believe I'm not going to bawl him out. "And that woman... his boss... she insisted on being there all the time I was talking to him and she kept saying how she had lots of important friends." He looks flustered. "I know it shouldn't make any difference but…"

"It doesn't make it easy," I finish for him and he flashes me a grateful look.

"What gets me is the way no-one in the whole bloody village pointed a finger towards Wayne," says Bob. "All of them claiming to care so much about Stacie and not one of them gave us any real help."

"That's villages for you," I say. I'd been brought up in a town and moving to the country had been a revelation to me.

"Right," I continue, "Let's pull together what we know about Wayne."

I make a summary of our findings, then add, "Quite a few of the people we spoke to said Stacie wasn't the kind of kid to go off with a stranger."

"They always claim that," says Bob.

"I know, but sometimes it's true. She'd trust Wayne. Does anyone know anything else about him?"

"We've got nothing on him. I'm trying to access the Benefits and Education information but it's not easy," says Kelly.

"Keep on that when you've got time, but Connie Rutherfield should be arriving in a patrol car soon and I want you talk to her in one of those side rooms. We need anything she can tell us about Wayne and a photo of him as soon as possible."

"Right, Guv."

"You all know Stacie's naked body was found in the woods this morning, sprinkled with flowers. Put this with the flowers left when Stacie disappeared and the locket in the reporter's car and the resemblance to the Elmwash killings is pretty clear. We've got some alternatives to consider." I brace myself and put forward the fear that has been haunting me all week. "The first option is that we wound up the Elmwash investigation prematurely." I swallow and force myself to say the words, "That would mean Clift wasn't guilty and the Elmwash killer's still alive and out there, ready to kill again."

Chapter 57: Rick

When I suggest the Elmwash killer's still with us there's a low buzz of agreement. It's hard to pin down, but I'm sure it doesn't come from Bob or, strangely enough, Kelly.

I raise my voice, "Yeah, I've heard the murmurs about the sloppy way we investigated Elmwash. Well, it was a bloody sight better than the crap work that's gone on here this last week."

It hits me that the reason the over-all investigation has been so weak is because Roebuck assumed from the start that this crime was tied to Elmwash and all the investigation was pushed that way. If the SIO goes charging along one path, most junior cops will follow, and when it's a juicy story like Elmwash, the media jump on the bandwagon, baying for blood.

Of course there's no way I can say that, so I continue in a moderate, reasonable tone, "We've got to suss out if this is the original Elmwash killer and, if it is, we've got to get the bastard. But if Clift was the original killer, we have to work out whether it's a copycat and if he's got any special knowledge. Remember Clift had pals amongst the kid-abusing dregs and the DCI's been checking out rumours of a paedophile ring. But there's another possibility. It could be someone trying to cover up a crime by making it look like the Elmwash ones. Any of you see that documentary about the Elmwash killings that was on a few weeks ago?"

Silence. No-one plans to incriminate themselves until they see where I'm heading.

"Me neither, but I'm getting a copy of it, discreetly, because we don't need the reporters to know what we're thinking. When you get a chance sit in and watch it and try and see whether Stacie's killer knew anything that's not told in this programme. Bob, if you've spotted any differences between Stacie and the Elmwash girls you can share them with me, either here or in private."

"The Elmwash kids were indoors. I mean the pathologist reckoned he'd killed them in that hut and kept their bodies there afterwards to carry on... doing things."

"Good point. The Elmwash killer would have set up another nice little hideaway by now. He kept the bodies for a reason and he wouldn't have dumped them in the woods. Anything else? Bob? Anyone?"

"The flowers were scattered over her not tied together like Elmwash," says Kelly.

"That's right. One of the things we traced back to Clift was that he used to go round the markets and buy flowers and he'd done a floristry certificate, so he knew how to wire the flowers up. We know the flowers under the swing had been dumped in the Frewers' back garden... another difference from the original Elmwash crimes. Not to mention the fact that the hair ribbon and cheap bracelet weren't the Elmwash killer's style. So the question is where did the person who dumped Stacie get the flowers? They weren't artificial ones, like the ones left under the swing. We need to check out anywhere that sells flowers."

"How about the tributes outside the house?" suggests Mark Corrigan.

"That's an idea. You stay on the flower angle, Mark. Use the local florists and news footage and photos of the house."

I need to wind up. My arm hurts like hell and the faces in front of me are beginning to sway and blur. "Bob, get Forensics to do a sweep of the ways into the wood from the village, in case they can work a miracle. And tell them to pay close attention to the stile out of Stacie's back garden and the routes from that Animal Sanctuary. If anyone needs me I'll be in the office."

As I close the door I think again this office must suffer from underground erosion or perhaps a poltergeist. The floor's shifting under my feet and I'm viewing things through a haze of swirling lights.

I hear Annie say, "Rick?" She guides me to a chair.

The room settles down and I mutter, "This arm's a bit worse than I thought."

"Let me look." She helps to ease off my jacket, then rummages in her bag and produces a pair of scissors to cut the sleeve of my shirt. My arm's badly swollen and moving it makes me so woozy I have to lean against Annie to stay in the chair.

There's a bang on the door and Bob breezes in. "Rick, I wanted to... sorry, didn't mean to barge in on a domestic moment."

I'm struggling through the fog to tell him to piss off when I hear Annie say, "Shut it you wanker." I think her language is going downhill fast. "Bob, look at the state of his arm. And he pretended it was just bruised."

"Yeah, he always was a stupid bastard about stuff like that."

Great, now the pair of them are ganging up on me.

"Tell you what, Annie, I'll give the doc a call. Unless you reckon he ought to go straight to hospital?" That's all I need, Bob's moved into helpful mode.

"I'm okay," I protest. "It's lucky it's not my right one."

"Yeah," agrees Bob, "Otherwise you might not be able to sign off on our overtime."

"You call the doctor while I get some First Aid stuff." Annie bustles away.

Bob starts to say something but I interrupt, "Hang on, I've got to speak to the DCI." I phone through to Lane's mobile. "Sir, we've got a new suspect, a mentally handicapped lad called Wayne Jones. He's on the loose and I want him picked up fast. I could do with more manpower."

"I'll borrow some more men from other divisions." This is an aspect of Lane I respect, there's no arsing around about budgets or politics.

"And I need a search warrant for the animal sanctuary."

"I'll see to that. You alright, Rick?"

"Yes sir."

"Well you don't bloody sound it, make sure you keep me informed."

"Yes sir." As I ring off I wonder why I didn't tell him about my arm. He's going to crucify me when he finds out.

Chapter 58: Rick

I put the phone down, lean back, and look at Bob. "You want something or is this a social call?"

"Just checking you're okay. You look bloody awful."

"Yeah, but at least, when we find this guy, we can hold him for assault while we're checking him out. Can you get things moving for me? But Bob, get one thing straight, any more racist crap and I'll have you, and I mean the whole disciplinary scene."

Bob gives me a sour look but he nods acknowledgement. He leaves as Annie returns. She dumps the First Aid box on the desk and rummages through until she finds a sling. Manoeuvring my arm into it is agony but, when it's supported, the pain is bearable.

"I shouldn't have let you in for this, Annie."

"You couldn't keep me out." The ferocity of her kiss makes me gasp.

Bob arrives back, again his warning knock comes after he's through the door. "Sorry, First Aid is it?"

"No, this time it's a domestic moment," retorts Annie.

Bob grins but says to me, "Kelly said to tell you she ain't having any joy with the old girl. The old bitch is going on about harassment and she won't give us any information or photos of Wayne."

"Rick, maybe I could help with that," says Annie, "I could phone my mother."

"Why?" Life's tough enough without my mother-in-law getting in on the act.

"If she's a friend of Connie Rutherfield she'll know everything about her life, including Wayne. It sounds awful, but I can't believe Wayne or his family were really Connie's friends."

"You mean he's as common as me?" I tease her.

247

She sticks her tongue out. "No, commoner than that."

"Common like me then," says Bob. "She may have a point, Rick, we can use any info that's going. No offence, Annie, but can we trust your mum to keep quiet?"

"Yes, if you ask her to keep a secret she's completely reliable."

I know that's true so I nod towards the phone and say, "Okay." I switch on the speaker so we can all hear what Sonia says.

I'm impressed by the way Annie cuts through all the crap, "Mother, it's me. Please bear with me and don't ask any questions, but tell me everything you can about Connie Rutherfield and Wayne Jones."

"Constance Rutherfield?" Sonia's majestic tones sweep round the office. "I assume it is Richard who wishes to make this enquiry? Tell me, is she in trouble? I fear she has become very peculiar."

"Why is that, Mother?"

"Her husband died seven years ago. He was a most distinguished man and such good company. Then, soon after, her daughter died and Constance became so odd."

"How did her daughter die?"

"In a car crash. Constance only had one child, very late in life, and so, of course, she spoiled her. She allowed her to visit a theme park with her cleaner's family, so unsuitable, and poor Constance certainly paid for it."

"Her cleaner's family? Would that be something to do with Wayne Jones?"

"Yes indeed, dreadful uncouth boy."

"So Connie took in Wayne when her daughter and his family died in a car crash?"

"Yes, that's correct. Arianne, what is this about?"

Annie looks enquiringly at me and I nod agreement. "You're right, Mother, I am asking for Rick, this is police business and anything I tell you is confidential."

"I may have my faults, Arianne, but I am not a gossip.

What does Richard think that boy has done?"

"He may have had something to do with what happened to that little girl."

"Goodness! How dreadful!"

"What do you know about him, Mother?"

"Very little. He must be about twenty and I know he was born like that."

"Does he have any friends? Anywhere he's likely to run to?"

"I cannot say, but I suppose he may have friends amongst the other gardeners at your establishment."

"My establishment? You mean the College?"

"Of course. He has a sheltered work placement there."

I remember Wayne had said something about Annie being the Art lady but I hadn't taken it on board.

"Excuse me a moment, Mother, please hold on." Annie turns to me, "If he works at our place there should be records on him and a photograph."

"I'll get right on it," says Bob.

"Dig out Annie's boss," I suggest. "Let him have some Sunday grief as well."

"Dr Neil Walder." Annie supplies Neil's phone number. "Be warned, he'll try to photograph you at work and pump you about murderers you have known."

"Just what I need, a groupie," says Bob and hurries out.

"Thank you, Mother, you've been a great help," says Annie. "Is Rick's mum still with you?"

"I left her at the hospital. Richard's father is quite rational today."

I chip in with, "Thank you."

"Is that you Richard? You don't sound like yourself."

Annie looks at me and again I nod, so she explains, "Wayne Jones attacked Rick and hurt his arm."

The door opens and Connie Rutherfield storms into the room, followed by Kelly. "Sorry Guv, she wouldn't wait."

Connie's dressed the same as before but now I'd have

no problem placing her among my mother-in-law's more snobby pals, this is one old bat with attitude.

"Come in, Mrs Rutherfield. Kelly, you stay, please."

Connie Rutherfield sits down in the chair opposite mine. "This is discrimination and harassment and I'm going to make you sorry you tangled with me, young man." She turns her glare on Annie. "You should be ashamed of yourself. It's always been common knowledge that you married beneath you, but what your poor mother will say about this disgraceful behaviour I hate to think."

The swift heat of Annie's anger makes Connie Rutherfield's outrage pale into insignificance. "Why don't you ask her? Mother, Mrs Rutherfield wishes to complain about me encouraging Rick to find a child killer."

Sonia's tones put a few layers of frost on the already chilly office, "Constance, kindly stop talking such offensive nonsense. I've told you for years that you cannot control that boy, this is what comes of your arrogant irresponsibility."

Connie Rutherfield tries to interrupt but Sonia rides straight over her, "Be quiet, Constance. I am disgusted by your behaviour. It's bad enough that you permit that boy to attack a police officer but when that officer is my son-in-law it's indefensible..."

Annie grins at me. "Welcome to the family," she murmurs. "I'll get that DVD."

She rats and leaves me to it, just as Connie gathers her wits and starts answering Sonia back.

The two old girls argue in circles until they run out of steam. I cut in to say, "Sonia, I've got to get on now, thanks for your support."

"You're welcome, Richard."

"I'll get Annie to ring you when things have quietened down."

I end the call and say, "Would you like coffee or tea, Mrs Rutherfield?"

She gives me an upmarket glare. "I do not require

refreshment. I require an explanation and apology. How dare you harass Wayne in this manner? It's because the poor boy is handicapped. You wouldn't dare bully him if you didn't think he was defenceless and vulnerable, but you'll soon find out that I am not without influence."

"Wayne's wanted on serious charges. Assaulting a police officer for starters."

"That means he's in big trouble," says Kelly.

"You obviously frightened him."

I try a gentler tone, "Mrs Rutherfield, no-one wants to hurt or frighten Wayne, but a child's been killed and we're going to find out who's responsible. DC Kelly and I didn't know Stacie but you did. It's strange if we care more about finding her murderer than you do, isn't it?"

She stops trying to out stare me. "Wayne wouldn't harm Stacie. He'd never hurt anyone."

I don't point out my arm hurts like hell. "Do you know why Wayne should turn so nasty when I asked him if he saw Stacie last Sunday?"

"No."

"Do you really know where he was all the time last Sunday?"

She hesitates. "I saw him around the Sanctuary a lot of the time."

"But not all of it?"

"No."

"So he could have slipped off down the village?"

She nods.

"Has Wayne ever been violent before?"

"N-no."

I pick up on the hesitation in her voice, "You're sure about that?"

"Sometimes he gets upset, if people tease him or are rude to him or frighten him."

We've seen what Wayne does when people upset him and I'm a full-grown guy not a little kid. "Did he get upset or cross with Stacie?"

"No! He thought the world of her."

"How did he take it when she wasn't allowed to go up to the sanctuary any more?"

"He was upset. He cried."

"And was he angry?"

"Not with her!"

"Who with? Her dad?" Reluctantly she nods. "Did he make any threats?"

She doesn't answer.

"Mrs Rutherfield, do you know where Wayne's gone? It'll be better for him if we find him soon." She purses her lips and looks stubborn. "In that case we won't trouble you any more for now. Kelly, show her out."

After a couple of minutes, Kelly returns. "The doctor's here to see you, Guv."

"Fine. Kelly, see if you can find out the gossip in the village about what Wayne threatened when Stacie's dad wouldn't let her go to the animal place any more. And check out if anyone knows why Frewer stopped her going up there. But be discreet, the last thing we need is a witch-hunt after him."

Chapter 59: Annie

In the patrol car I make an effort to chat to the uniformed officers. I don't want them to think I'm too stuck up to talk to them. I'm glad I've got them on my side when we pull into the driveway and see a car parked outside my house. Maris gets out of it and moves towards me.

"Damn!" I mutter.

"Problem?" asks my driver.

"No. At least nothing for you to worry about." I go across to where she's standing. "Hi Maris. I hope you haven't been waiting long because I can't stop."

Her gaze fixes leech-like on my face. "Are you in trouble?"

"Of course not."

"Has something happened to him?" There's a gloating eagerness in her voice.

"Rick? No, he's okay. I came back to get something. These officers are waiting for me, so I mustn't stop." I cross the driveway and go into the house. Maris sticks to one side of me and one of the cops stays in close attendance too.

I pick up the DVD, turn and collide with Maris, who's standing in my way. "Maris, I've got to go. You shouldn't hang round here by yourself."

"What's wrong?"

"The police are looking for someone who might be dangerous and Rick doesn't want me here alone."

"You can come home with me."

"No!... Thank you, but I must get back to Rick. It's essential I deliver this myself."

Maris doesn't move. "Other people need you as well as him."

"He's my husband."

"If you're ready, Mrs Evans, we ought to be getting on,"

intervenes the constable.

"Come on, Maris, outside please, I've got to set the alarm."

Sullenly she obeys.

I climb into the patrol car and say, "Thank you," to my escort.

"No problem. She's a persistent sort of lady isn't she?"

"Very."

"I'll wait and make sure she's cleared the premises," says the driver. He makes a gesture to Maris, inviting her to pull out first. Her expression is hostile but she accelerates away.

Back at Saronholt Church Hall, the patrol car draws up next to Superintendent Roebuck's Mercedes. He's sitting in it talking to Constable Kelly. As soon as he sees me, he gets out and hurries across the car park. "Mrs Evans, I've heard about what happened this afternoon. I'm sorry you had such an unpleasant experience. Rick had no right to involve you in this investigation or to take you into a dangerous situation."

How dare they never give my guy a halfway-even break? I long to slap the Superintendent's smug face. As for Kelly, Rick's right, she's a despicable little snitch.

I smile at the Superintendent. "You've got that completely wrong. I was there because Mrs Rutherfield is a friend of my mother and I thought I'd check she was all right. Rick arriving to question Wayne was a coincidence. It was lucky he did, imagine if Wayne had turned violent with just us two women there."

"Oh, I see."

"If you'd asked for Rick's report before judging the matter, you wouldn't have fallen into that foolish error."

As we walk inside, Kelly says quietly, "Mrs Evans, could I speak to you?"

"No." I'm sticking with Roebuck while I try to work out how I'm going to get Rick alone to brief him on the story

I've fed his boss.

Roebuck and I reach the office neck and neck. The door is opened by a middle-aged man. "I'm glad to see you Superintendent. I was beginning to wonder if DI Evans was the only senior officer left in CID."

Roebuck looks annoyed. "Not at all, Doctor, I'm here to take charge."

"About time too." The doctor blocks me as I attempt to slip through. "And where do you think you're going?"

"To check Rick's okay. I'm his wife."

The stern look is replaced by a smile. "Come in, my dear. He turned very faint when I examined his arm."

Rick's still sitting in his chair. His face looks white and drawn, with deep bruise-like shadows under his eyes. He smiles at me. "I'm okay love."

Roebuck squeezes into his office and says, "How are you, Rick?"

"The doctor wants me to go to A&E. He reckons the bastard's broken my arm."

"Then of course you must receive medical treatment. Are you up to briefing me about developments before you go?"

"Yes, sir."

"Excuse us, Mrs Evans." Roebuck holds the door open.

I can't refuse but, as I follow the doctor out of the room, I pray that Rick's alert enough to prevent Roebuck and Kelly from stitching him up.

Chapter 60: Annie

When Rick finishes talking to Roebuck, the Superintendent offers to send him to the hospital in a patrol car, but he says he'd prefer me to drive him there.

It's hard to tell from Rick's manner how his interview went, so, after a few minutes, I venture to ask, "Did the briefing with the Superintendent go okay?"

"Yeah, funnily enough it did. Kelly offered to do all the talking and, believe it or not, she made me sound pretty good."

"You are good," I say warmly and he grins.

"Kelly told Roebuck you being up at the animal sanctuary was a coincidence."

I wonder exactly what game Kelly's playing. "I'd already told him I was calling on Connie because she's a friend of my mother," I explain. "He was waiting for me outside the Incident Room. I think it was to try and trap me into saying something he could use against you."

"Yeah. If I'm an embarrassment he'll throw me to the wolves."

"I guess so." It would be scarily easy for a ruthless superior to disgrace Rick.

"I left the Elmwash DVD with Roebuck but I don't think he'll bother with it."

"He's that sure Wayne's the killer?"

"Pretty sure. Kelly's been asking round the village, the way I told her to and a few people told her that Wayne's odd about death. When any of the animals die he lays them out and makes a coffin for them, then he gives them a big funeral and has a party with sweets and cakes for everyone who goes along. Apparently they had a real carry on when the Shire horse died."

"That's creepy."

"Yeah, but he didn't bury Stacie, that's one point in his favour. But the thing that convinced Roebuck is that Kelly talked to the stepfather again and he said he stopped Stacie from going up to the Sanctuary because she was afraid of Wayne. He claimed Wayne was obsessed by her and she'd told him Wayne was always touching her and wanting to do dirty things."

"If that's true, why didn't the stepfather mention it straight away when Stacie disappeared?"

"That's what I said to Roebuck but he told me not to get obsessive, the way I had about Elmwash."

"But it was him who said this was the Elmwash killer, surely he doesn't think those killings were Wayne as well?"

"Rule Number One, the SIO can move the goalposts any time he wants, but, whatever he says, this Wayne business doesn't hang together."

"You mean Wayne's not bright enough to watch the television programme and then make Stacie's death look like an Elmwash killing?"

"Yeah."

"Do you think Roebuck's planning to stitch him up?"

"No. Roebuck's a slimy bastard but he's not going to deliberately leave a psycho out there to kill more kids. Or worse, lots of psychos, if there's a paedophile ring. Oh God, Annie! Imagine if there's a group of sick bastards out there who reckon Clift was the next best thing to God."

We have to spend some time in A&E, waiting for the results of the X-ray and then getting Rick's broken arm strapped up. The doctor doesn't seem worried about the break but he expresses concern about Rick's blood pressure, which is much too high. He advises him to stay home and rest for a couple of weeks and to consult his own GP. I'm glad of this reprieve, although I know it will take longer than a fortnight to put Rick right. I refuse to acknowledge my fear that he might never be well again.

As we emerge from A&E, a voice yells, "Hang on." A fat middle-aged man steamrollers towards us.

"Yes sir?" says Rick and I realise it's Detective Chief Inspector Lane.

"I need a word." The DCI leads Rick away but I hear him say, "I wanted to know whether you think this paedophile ring's the real thing."

They move out of earshot before I can catch Rick's reply.

When they return the DCI looks even surlier than before but he says, "Thanks, I'm glad to have your opinion. You go on home now." He yawns and runs a hand over his darkly stubbled chin. "I need a shave."

"Have you been on this clubbing murder all night, sir?"

"Yeah. But that ain't your problem. You take leave, as much of it as you need." He gives me a brief nod of acknowledgement and stomps away.

"He's keen to get me sidelined," comments Rick.

"Actually I think he was trying to be kind. He's a lot nicer than I thought."

Rick gives me a startled look. "I worry about you sometimes, you're the sort of person who'd think Godzilla would make a good house pet."

I ignore this interesting insight into my character. "Are you ready to go home?"

"While I'm here I ought to see Dad."

I wonder despairingly why I had to get the only guy in the world with a hyperactive conscience but I don't argue, his physical needs are still less urgent than his emotional ones.

It takes ten minutes for Rick to toil up the stairs. As we reach the third floor, the lift doors open and a voice says, "Arianne." Mother and Elaine join us.

"We came to collect Richard's mother, but I presume we're not needed if you're here," says Mother, obviously put out.

I speak quickly to placate her, "Actually, we were here for Rick to have his arm set, and afterwards he thought he ought to come up and see his dad. I want to get him home as soon as possible, and it would be a great help if you took Tris."

Rick surfaces from pain and exhaustion to say, "I'm really grateful for all you've done for Mum."

Mother smiles at him, a kind smile, not her social one. "I'm glad to help, Richard. They've moved your father's ward, he's over here." She leads the way.

As we follow, Elaine whispers, "What's got into her?"

"She's pleased because I let her know a friend of hers has hit the problems Mother always said she would."

"Is that why she's being so smug and secretive? Six times she's said, 'my lips are sealed.' It's driving me mad."

"I'm sorry but I can't tell you either."

"I never expected you to. You and Mother are good at keeping secrets, not being able to is one thing I get from Dad."

"You can keep secrets if they matter enough."

"Maybe. Rick looks really ill."

"I know. It's not just his arm, he's totally stressed out."

She looks ashamed. "When he didn't come to Mother's lunch party I thought he had a hangover."

"He did have a hangover but he's been drinking too much because of the strain."

"Is there anything I can do?"

"Well, there is one thing. You couldn't possibly check on Maris for me, could you? She's being a bit clingy."

"Oh God Annie, she's always been clingy! She's been obsessed with you since we were kids. She's an absolute cow and a total bloody pain."

"She's got post-natal depression."

"For someone who's supposed to be clever you can be very thick." She sighs. "Okay, I'll go and see her tomorrow."

"Thanks." I hug her.

Tom's bed is the first one in the ward. Rick has joined his mum by the bedside while Mother, mindful of the two-beside-a-bed rule, hovers by the ward door. Tom opens his eyes and smiles at his wife. His gaze moves on to Rick and he doesn't look as vague as before. "Hello, old chap, you been in the wars?" His voice is less slurred.

"Broke my arm."

"That's hard luck." He summons a passing nurse and says, "This is my boy, Rick. He's a policeman. Done really well, he has."

"Hi there, Rick." She smiles and hurries on.

"I'll be off now, Tom," says Tris, "Sonia's going to give me a lift home."

"That's right, you need your rest."

She bends to kiss his cheek. "I'll be in again tomorrow."

"That's good. 'Bye son. Take care of your mum."

"I always do," says Rick.

As we walk towards the exit, Mother says to Tris, "It must be wonderful to have Thomas back to being his old loving self."

"It makes visiting much pleasanter," agrees Tris.

I drop back slightly and Tris stays in step with me. "But?" I ask.

She smiles. "It won't last. He was like it before ever he got ill, one moment I'd be the best wife in the world, the next he'd be knocking me across the room. Some people are like that, they think people belong to them and they have to be in control."

"Not Rick," I say, terrified she's giving me an oblique warning.

She gives me a radiant smile. "No, not Rick," she agrees.

Chapter 61: Annie

I'm cooking breakfast when the doorbell rings.

"Check who it is before you open it," says Rick and follows me into the hall.

"I planned to." I look through the side window then open up. "Hi Bob, come in."

"Didn't mean to butt in, just wanted to check Rick's alright."

Rick grins at him. "I'm okay."

"The bastard broke your arm then?"

"Yeah, could have been worse, I suppose."

"Too right it could, he could have smashed your head in."

"Shut it, Bob." Rick gives a swift, protective glance towards me.

"What?" Bob looks puzzled. "Oh yeah. Sorry. Me and my big mouth."

"That's okay, you didn't say anything I haven't been thinking," I say. "Come on through. Do you want coffee or tea?"

"Didn't mean to interrupt your breakfast."

"Have you eaten, Bob?"

"No. I'll get something back in Saronholt."

"You tired of life?" says Rick.

"What? Oh you mean Kelly and them bloody sandwiches. Well, when you live by yourself it don't pay to be too fussy."

I take my untouched plate and dump it in front of Bob. "Eat that."

"But that's your breakfast."

"I'll cook some more."

Rick mouths a silent, "Thanks love," behind Bob's back and I smile at him.

Bob does as he's told; his plate's clear before I've

finished cooking a fresh breakfast for myself.

"Have they found Wayne?" I ask.

"Not that I've heard. But he's definitely our man," says Bob.

"You reckon?" Rick doesn't sound convinced.

"When they searched his caravan they found beads and elastic thread, exactly the same as the bracelet that was left under Stacie's swing. What more do you want?"

Rick shakes his head. "Giving her a bracelet doesn't prove he killed her. It's already been established that Wayne and Stacie were friends. You know, Bob, I don't think Wayne's got the brains to cover up Stacie's murder by linking it to the Elmwash killings like that."

"You reckon he's got an accomplice? Guess it'd have to be the old woman?"

"No way!" I say. "She may be an opinionated old bat but she wouldn't help a child-killer get clear."

"And if she'd been up for that she'd have given him an alibi," says Rick. "If he's got an accomplice it'll be one of the local paedophiles, there's plenty of cunning bastards willing to sort things for one of their own kind."

Bob nods. "That's the line Lane's been working on. I'd best be going. Thanks for the food, Annie."

"You're welcome." I'm halfway through my own meal.

Rick sees Bob out but he doesn't fully shut the kitchen door. I hear him say, "Let me know if anything happens. You can get me on my mobile. I'm taking Annie into work. Is there anything in from the pathologist yet?"

"Yeah."

The rules say I shouldn't listen to police business but I want to know.

"How bad is it?" says Rick.

"It's not that bad, I mean apart from being a dead kid and someone hanging onto the body for a week. They reckon she'd probably been kept in a bin liner somewhere reasonably warm. But it's weird, no sexual assault or anything like that, just some bruises on her upper arms like she'd been restrained..." To my frustration they open the front door and move out of my hearing.

A minute later Rick comes back into the kitchen. He's looking puzzled.

"Are you okay?" I ask.

"Yeah, but there's something buzzing round the edge of my mind and I can't bring it into focus."

"Something about Stacie's death?" I see the old stubborn expression. "Rick, I'm not a child. I won't tell anyone but I want to know."

"The pathologist says Stacie choked to death on some kind of toffee. It wasn't the sort you usually get in shops. It reminded me of something but I can't pin it down."

"Oh God!"

"I'm sorry, love, I shouldn't..."

"Rick, don't you remember? Yesterday, when Wayne was cooking, he said it was going wrong like it had last week. I'm sure it was treacle toffee. And when Connie said Vicki was ill, Wayne said he'd take her some sweets."

"Shit!" He grabs the phone and dials straight through to the Incident Room.

It's after ten when we get to College. In the last week I've taken more scraps of time off work than I've done for years. I see Josef sitting under the trees that border the car park and go across to speak to him, "Hi, what are you doing out here?"

He indicates the shabby carry-cot beside him. "Neil does not want the baby in College today. There are people come without warning to inspect the department."

Oh wonderful! What's that about? As far as I know, unless you're on Special Measures, OFSTED don't call totally unannounced. I'd have noticed if we'd been scheduled a visitation; the mountains of pointless paperwork and the coaching sessions on 'how to deal with your inspector' would have given the game away.

"Where's Chloe?" I ask.

"Inside. She wanted a little time to call her own."

"What are you going to do this morning?"

He points to the journal on his lap. "I will write up my work if Joseph permits me to. No, please, do not wake him."

Obediently I draw back from the carry-cot. The baby's invisible; the hood is up and a plastic raincover keeps him snug. "I'll check when Neil will let you in."

"I would be grateful. It is important that I telephone the immigration people, there is a problem and we have no credit on our phones."

I thought he seemed unusually uptight. "Take my mobile and phone them straight away, and let me know if there's anything I can do, write letters or give references or stuff like that."

"Thank you, Annie."

"Josef, do you know the gardener called Wayne?"

"The one who looks different?"

"Yes. He's in trouble. If you see him, take Joey and go inside and tell someone straight away."

"What has he done?"

"They think he might have hurt a little girl."

"That is bad. It seems that Wesley was correct."

"Wesley? What's he got to say about anything?"

"This Wayne, he used to hang round when Wesley was working. Wesley said that he gave him the creeps."

I can't see how this is relevant but I mention it to Rick as we walk towards the Fine Art reception area. We've hardly got inside the door when we meet Neil. "It's about time you got in," he says to me.

"Sorry. What's happening about the surprise inspection?"

"Oh that! Just the Principal doing one of his spot checks. He's gone again."

"Everything okay?" The College Principal does not like Fine Art and has developed a whole new department that he claims is more relevant to the 21st Century. He's a supporter of Business Studies, Media & Business Studies, Foreign Languages & Business Studies etc. I've suggested to Neil we tack the title Business Studies onto the end of all our courses, but for some reason he wasn't keen.

"Not bad." Neil grins. "Thank God it wasn't last week or he'd have walked into Wesley and his maggot-ridden bird."

"Can Josef bring the baby back inside?"

"Leave it a few more minutes in case the Principal runs a double-bluff." He turns to Rick. "I'm glad to see you, I need your advice. In fact I was about to phone your people. Our chief gardener came back today, after a week off, and I heard him moaning that someone's been digging out there behind the gardeners' hut."

"What? Neil, you'd better show me."

"Okay. Annie can take my students along with hers."

"I'm coming too, I'm not scheduled to teach for another hour."

"You're staying here," says Rick.

"Please Annie, don't be difficult," begs Neil. He and Rick walk away.

I stare after them in deep frustration. I'm tempted to abandon Neil's students, but that's risky when the Principal could play sneaky and turn up again.

"Annie, where's that wretched man buggered off to now?"

Never before have I been so pleased to see Lucy. "Neil? He should be back soon."

"He'll have to do something about that woman, I won't have her turning up whenever it suits her. Either I'm in charge or she is."

I stare at her blankly.

"I'm talking about Maris. Why, for pity's sake, can't she stay on maternity leave?"

"She's depressed."

"Don't talk to me about depression! She depresses everyone who comes near her."

I edge towards the door. "You're quite right, I'll go and talk to Neil. Could you take over his students for a few minutes, please?" I'm out and running as I utter the last words.

I catch up with Rick and Neil and they both give me unwelcoming looks, which I ignore. The gardener shows us the place behind the shed where the earth is newly dug; a neat rectangle just large enough to accommodate a child.

We all stare at it.

"I don't get it. There are no more kids missing, are there?" says Neil.

"Not that we know of on this enquiry but there are lots of lost kids out there." Rick dials through on his mobile. "DI Evans here, I want to speak to Superintendent Roebuck... Sir, it's me, Rick. I'm at the Art College where Wayne Jones works. There's been some digging in the gardens. It's probably nothing but we should get a SOCO team to take a look... Yeah, I'll stay here."

As he rings off, Neil says, "Do you still need me?"

"No, we'll take it from here." Rick sits down on a nearby bench to wait. "You take Annie back for me, will you?"

Men! Does he really think I'm going to leave him here alone? I sit down next to him. "I'm not a package, you know."

"Please love."

"No."

"I'll leave you to it then," says Neil. The gardener has already taken himself off.

We sit in silence until Rick says, "You stubborn woman," and puts his arm round my shoulders.

"Rick, what are you afraid of? Who do you think it is?"

"I've always been scared the Elmwash three weren't the only ones."

"But who else?"

"There was a kid went missing eight months before the first of the Elmwash girls. Her name was Kyra Hamilton."

"Tell me about her."

"Not much to tell. She was fourteen and she'd spent her life in Care. That made her pretty streetwise. She'd done runners before, so no-one was surprised when she went off, but this time she didn't turn up again. That was one of the reasons I kept interviewing Clift, he said there were other bodies and he could tell me where they're hidden."

"But what's that got to do with someone being buried here?"

His grip tightens on my hand. "What if Wayne's some sort of accomplice? A sort of junior partner? What if there's been another mausoleum somewhere we never found? What if Wayne's panicking and started to bury the rest?"

As he speaks the sun goes behind a cloud and the SOCO van turns in at the gate.

Chapter 62: Rick

There must be better ways of earning a living than this.

I send Kelly into the tent with the SOCO team while Annie and I wait outside. I try to do my usual trick and numb off all feeling but having Annie here makes it hard.

The three Elmwash kids had all been pretty but not Kyra Hamilton. She had sharp features and protruding teeth. Not a nice-looking kid, not a nice kid come to that. She'd been caught a few times shop-lifting and been on the game since she was ten.

It was in the squad car bringing him in one day that Clift leaned close to me and murmured in my ear, "You never ask about the other ones."

"What other ones?" My guts tied themselves in knots.

"You didn't think there were just three? How foolish of you. Those were the best. There were plenty of others."

"I don't believe you."

"Don't you? I think you do."

"You're bluffing, you bastard. Otherwise you'd name them here and now." Despite the rough words I found myself lowering my voice to match Clift's whisper.

"Really Richard, I'm ashamed of you. You sound like your friend, the sergeant. Still, I'll forgive you, no doubt you're upset. All those lost children and no-one even noticed. I'll give you a clue, to start the game, how about Kyra... Kyra Hamilton?"

Of course I looked her up. Kyra Hamilton: abused, abandoned, shoved in countless foster homes. When she went missing, the police kept an eye out but no-one really looked.

'You like children, don't you, Richard?' The guilt washes over me again for Kyra and all the others. How many did the bastard really take?

Annie squeezes my hand. "There's no reason this should be Kyra's body. No reason it should be a body at all. There's no real connection between Wayne Jones and Ernest Clift."

"Oh shit!" Kelly's words ring out from the tent. Then she appears; she looks sick and her lips are curled in revulsion.

The lurking dread engulfs me. "What have you got?"

"A bird."

"What?"

"A bloody big bird." She gives a wobbly laugh. "We were expecting to find a kid and instead we find this maggot-eaten bird." She draws a hand across her mouth.

I head towards the tent but Annie's there before me.

"Annie, don't!" She ignores me. I follow her in and we look down into the hole. It's a mess of white feathers and white maggots and it stinks. A second look shows me the bird's been laid out like a human corpse, wings crossed on its breast.

Annie's voice is calm, "It's Wesley's goose."

My stomach churns and I make a dash for the fresh air.

Annie comes after me. The Scene of Crimes team trail out and gather round as she explains, "One of my students, Wesley, was painting a dead goose. When he'd finished he wrapped it up and put it in the bin. My guess is that's what's in the hole."

"When did this kid dump the bird?" I ask.

She considers. "Tuesday evening, the day we had the visiting artist."

"And was Wayne around?"

"I've no idea. I didn't know he worked here."

"I checked the work rotas," says Kelly. "Wayne works here Tuesdays and Thursdays, but the head gardener was off last week and no-one's sure if he turned up."

"Right." I turn back to the SOCO team. "Sorry, false alarm."

"Better than finding another body," says Bryn Davis, who's a good mate of mine.

I reckon, what with this fiasco and getting clobbered by a rolling pin, I'm going to be a bloody laughing stock. But it'll blow over, it always does. Anyway, I'm not done making enemies. "I hate to tell you this, but you'll have to shift the goose and check there's nothing underneath." They groan. "I know, but I'm not going to risk missing evidence because it's buried underneath a maggoty goose. Sorry guys, we'll leave you to sort it and clear up. Kelly, you come with me."

"I'm okay, Guv." She looks embarrassed. "Sorry about before. It was the odd way it was laid out."

"I know." It hits me as weird that two experienced cops could have their guts turned by a dead goose while Annie's so calm. "You okay?" I ask her.

She smiles at me. "Yes, I'm fine, but I'm used to Wesley's art."

"Must be a psycho, painting stuff like that," comments Kelly.

Annie's smile switches off. "Why don't you leave art criticism to those who know?"

As we walk back towards the College building I phone through and report to Roebuck about our wild goose chase.

When I stop talking, Kelly asks, "No sign of Wayne, Guv?"

"Not yet." I'm curious about whether she's still running with the pack. "What do you reckon? Do you think he's our guy?" She gives me a doubtful look. "Go on, completely off the record, what do you think?"

"I don't know. He must know something, the toffee and the way he clobbered you proves that, but all this clever stuff with flowers and jewellery and leaving no forensics, people like him can't usually plan like that."

"I know nothing about people like him and what they're capable of."

The shyness deepens. "I've got a brother who's learning disabled. I'd have thought he's got more going for him than Wayne but he wouldn't be up to covering his tracks like that.

But Wayne's a sick bastard, witness that goose."

"Remember this is the guy who insisted on burying all the dead animals at that sanctuary. If he saw this Wesley kid dumping the goose in the bin he probably couldn't resist giving it a decent burial."

"Jesus!" Kelly shudders.

"Do you reckon Wayne killed Stacie?"

This time her hesitation is longer. "I'm not sure."

"Is it because you feel sorry for him? There's no problem with that, I'll feel sorry for the bugger myself when the pain in my arm eases off."

"No Guv, it's not that. It's to do with Stacie's stepfather's evidence."

"Yeah? What's your problem?"

"I think Terry Frewer knew what we wanted to know and why."

"Why do you think that?"

"When I got there I saw Stacie's teacher walking away and the guy on the door admitted he'd let her in to visit the Frewers. He said he'd had no orders to keep them isolated. The chances are she told them about Wayne and our enquiries."

"Shit! Did you tell the Superintendent about this?"

"No. I knew he'd blame you for any slip-ups and it's not fair."

"It's fair enough. I spread myself too thin. I should have got DCI Lane to come back. It was a judgement call and I got it wrong. What Terry Frewer said helped tilt the scales against Wayne, so make sure you tell the Superintendent."

My arm hurts and I'm tired. I've had enough. It's as if Annie reads my mind, she murmurs, "Why don't you give it a go?"

"Give what a go?"

"Stop pedalling and see if the world keeps turning anyway. I think Josef's asleep. I'd better wake him and tell him to come inside."

She runs across the grass towards the boy she'd spoken to before and bends over him. She shakes him and he sits up.

Annie crouches over the carry-cot, then she jerks upright and screams, "Rick!"

The panic in her voice makes me run. "Annie, what's wrong?" I skid to a halt beside her.

She stares at me, her face bleached. "The baby's gone!"

"Sweet Jesus!" My mouth is dry and my stomach's in a knot. I look in the empty carry-cot. As I turn the covers over I see a few spots of colour flutter onto the grass. The petals of a flower.

Chapter 63: Rick

"What's happening, Guv?" Kelly sprints over to join us.

"Baby's gone missing. May be a false alarm but get that SOCO team up here fast. We need the area cordoned and covering put over this scene to keep off the rain, and nobody's to leave the College grounds. I'm going up to the building. With any luck some do-gooder thought the kid was getting cold and took it inside. If so the SOCO lads can have another laugh at our expense."

"If the kid's okay they're welcome to," says Kelly and sets off fast.

"Come on, let's go," I snap. Josef takes no notice. He stands there staring blankly. "For Christ's sake! Let's see if your girlfriend's got the baby."

Still no response. The boy's eyes are frantic but no words come.

Annie says, "Wait a second, Rick. He was brought up in a Romanian orphanage. English is his second language and he's in shock."

"Can you get through to him?"

She grips Josef's upper arms. "Josef, the police will look for your baby. We must go to the College and find Chloe. Perhaps she's taken him inside."

Comprehension and hope flicker across his face, he nods, wrenches himself free and runs back towards the building. We follow him.

As we race through the corridors, I phone through and tell Roebuck what's going down. "It may be a false alarm, sir, but it doesn't look good. I'd like as many people here as soon as possible."

"Of course. Get things moving and we'll be along straight away."

We discover Chloe, in a sculpture studio, laughing and

chatting with a group of students. As we arrive, she hastily stubs her cigarette and drops it out of the open window behind her.

Josef finds speech as he reaches her, "Chloe, baby Joseph, where is he?"

The laughter still lighting up her face, she answers casually, "You've got him. It's your turn." The meaning of his question hits her and her expression freezes. She lunges forward to grab Josef's arm. "Where's my baby?"

"I do not know."

"Oh God! How could you? You've left him out there in the rain!"

As she hurtles towards the door she rams into Neil. It's clear he's heard the news. "Chloe!" He grabs her arm and stops her mid-flight.

"Let me go!" She lashes out at him. "I've got to find my baby! I can find him. I must."

"Chloe, stop it. The police are looking for your baby. If you go out there you'll get in their way."

Amazingly she stops struggling. She throws herself at him and sobs, "Neil, my baby! I want my baby back."

Neil looks white and tight-lipped. "Calm down, there's a good girl. Come into my office and sit down."

In the studio Chloe's friends are lingering, indecisive and anxious. Josef is standing apart from them, leaning against the wall. He slides down to sit on the floor, his face cradled in his hands. Annie crouches down beside him, her hand resting on his arm.

I say, "Annie, where's the best place for everyone to go?"

"The Main Lecture Hall's the biggest place."

I raise my voice to the huddled students, "Right you lot, Main Lecture Hall, and gather up any stragglers. This is urgent."

They drift away and only Annie and Josef are left.

I kneel beside them. "Josef, listen to me. What time was

it when you went to sleep?"

All I get is a slight shake of his head.

"No idea? Come on, Josef, think. Did you see the action by the gardeners' hut?"

Another head-shake. I sharpen my tone, "Josef, this is your kid we're looking for."

The effort he makes to regain control is painful to watch but he manages a choked, "I will try."

"Thank you. So you've got no idea when you went to sleep?"

"I am sorry. When you are almost asleep it is hard to know how time moves."

"While you were awake did you notice anyone hanging round?"

He considers then shakes his head again. "No-one special. It was only Annie who came to speak to us."

"What was the baby wearing?"

"A blue coat and a blue baby-suit."

"Have you any pictures of him?"

"I have started a picture but it is not yet complete."

I imagine presenting Roebuck with a Picasso-style painting and saying, *'There you go, that's a likeness of the missing kid.'* "No," I say hastily, "I mean photographs."

"We have some photographs at our house."

"We'll have them collected. Whereabouts do you live?"

"At Elmwash."

"Jesus!" The name takes me unawares and I feel my colour drain.

"I have said something bad?"

'You can't escape me, Richard.'

"No, it's nothing, just my arm hurting. I broke it yesterday."

That may fool the kid but not Annie; she transfers her comforting grip from Josef onto my good arm.

"Thanks Josef," I say. "You can go and join Chloe now."

"Chloe does not want me."

"Of course she does."

"I have lost our baby." He turns his face towards the wall and cries.

Annie draws me to one side and says quietly, "Do you think Wayne's taken Joey?"

"I don't know." None of this makes any form of sense. "It's crazy taking a kid when you're on the run but I guess that's what Wayne is. I'm going to take you and Josef to your study. I'll get one of the SOCO guys to stay with you while I scout around." I walk them down the corridor.

"Can't you wait for the others to turn up?"

"No."

When we get to the study Annie pushes Josef gently into a chair.

Bryn passes the door and I snap, "Any joy?"

"No."

"Bryn, do me a favour and keep an eye on the baby's father. This is my wife, she's a tutor here. Okay Annie, Bryn will look after you."

There's something else I've got to know, although I'm certain Annie won't like me asking. I beckon her into the corridor. "Annie, when you were talking to Josef earlier, did you look in the carry-cot?"

"No. Josef asked me not to wake Joey."

"So you didn't actually see the baby in there?"

"No." She stares at me. "What are you thinking? That the baby wasn't in there at all? That Josef has hurt him?"

"It's a possibility you know. Or the girl has and Josef's covering for her."

"No way!"

"These kids have no money and no home. They're sleep-deprived, out of their depth and Josef at least hasn't had a chance to learn parenting skills. What's more likely than one or both of them decided to lose the baby? I've got to look at all the options, that's my job."

"Then your job stinks!"

"Tell me something I don't know." I leave on the last words.

Chapter 64: Rick

It's spooky searching an empty building and this art place is the pits. The studios with life-size sculptures really get to me. I imagine the dust-sheets being thrown off and someone creeping out, knife in hand. I'll have to stop watching mystery-horror films, they're not good for my nerves.

Roebuck and the rest of the team turn up and we make a proper sweep of the place. Pretty soon Roebuck has the entire College, apart from Annie, Neil, Chloe and Josef, crammed into the big lecture hall. He fights his way up on the stage and makes an appeal for anyone who has seen anything to tell us immediately.

There's silence then Kelly says, "There sir," and points to a middle-aged woman at the back of the crowd who has got her hand up.

"Yes, madam?" says Roebuck. There's a faint squeak but no words we can hear. "Get her out."

Bob shoulders his way through and escorts her to the front. She's a dismal looking woman, drab and droopy just about sums her up.

"Name, please?" says Roebuck.

"Joan Hammond, Lecturer in Graphics." Even close to she's got a wispy voice.

"Is that Miss or Mrs?"

"Ms. I'm a firm believer in women's equality."

I hear Bob choke but Roebuck says, "Well, Ms Hammond, what have you got to tell us?"

"I saw him."

"You saw the baby? Where and when was this?"

"No, I didn't see the baby. I wouldn't have looked if I had, that baby shouldn't be in College, it disrupts routine."

"Then whom did you see?" asks Roebuck and I admire his self-control.

"I saw the man, the one you're looking for. We always said it was a mistake employing somebody like that."

"When was this and where was he?" Even Roebuck's finding it hard to keep his temper now.

She looks at him as if he's a backward student. "Halfway through this morning. He was out there in the bushes, lurking, waiting for his chance."

The moment I've been ducking from is here. There's a mentally deficient psycho running wild on a kid-killing spree, and I could have taken him out of the game yesterday if I'd been sharp enough. The flower petals in that carry-cot must have been grabbed from the border by the car park. Ernest Clift wouldn't have liked that, it doesn't show respect.

The meeting ends and Roebuck says, "Rick, I want a word."

I brace myself for aggro but he asks, "How are you? How's the arm?"

"Okay," I answer both questions with one lie.

"We'll need your statement and your wife's, then I suggest you go home."

"Do I have to, sir?" Sitting at home won't deal with my guilt.

He hesitates. "Are you fit enough to go over to Elmwash House? You can take those kids back with you to have a look around. You're the best man for the job, you're good with people."

I can think of several kinds of torture I'd rather undergo but I say, "No problem."

"I know you'll play it gently, Rick, but don't let this Wayne Jones business make you forget these cases are often down to the parents and both of these parents have been in trouble before."

"They have?"

"The girl got caught with recreational drugs when she was a minor, but, as far as we know, she's been clean for three years. A few days ago, her boyfriend was dismissed from the supermarket where he worked. They caught him stealing and they always prosecute."

"What did he pinch?"

Roebuck calls across to Bob, "What did that boy, Josef, steal from his work?"

Bob pulls a sour face. "A padded all-in-one suit for his kid. It was torn anyway, so it'd have gone in the bargain box."

"Hardly the crime of the century," I say.

"I know," agrees Bob, "And immigration may decide to boot him back to his own country, no questions asked. It's a bloody shame."

"It's the Law," says Roebuck.

"Sir, is it okay if I take my wife along with me?" I ask. "She's these kids' tutor. I know they're over eighteen but I reckon they need someone appropriate with them."

"Yes, that's a good idea," says Roebuck.

When he's gone I pinch Bob's notebook. "This the supermarket that's going to prosecute the kid?"

"Yeah, why?"

I shrug. "Just want to nominate them for the Scrooge of the Year Award."

Neil's room is thick with cigarette smoke. I grope my way through to where Chloe's sitting on the couch. Her face is white but she seems calm.

"You okay?" I ask.

"Yeah."

"Josef's in a bad way."

I expect indifference but she demands, "What do you mean?"

"Sort of withdrawn."

"Oh God! He got like that before when…"

"When what, Chloe?"

"Last year he thought he'd tracked down one of his sisters. He was so excited he'd got someone of his own but then he found out it was a mistake. He got depressed. Is someone with him? You haven't left him alone?"

"Annie's with him. They're in her office. But it's you he needs."

She gets jerkily to her feet and heads straight out the door. I follow as she bursts into Annie's office, runs to Josef and puts her arms round him. For a moment, his eyes stay blank, then he sobs and buries his face against her. I wonder if their love will survive if baby Joseph turns up dead or doesn't turn up at all.

"Thanks Bryn," I say, "I'll take over here."

He leaves and Annie comes across to me. "Sorry."

"Sorry for what?"

"For being a stupid cow."

"Oh Annie, love." I'm going to tell her I understand the way she feels when there's a knock on the door and Kelly yells, "You ready, Guv?"

"Yeah. Annie, I'm going out to Elmwash House. Are you up for coming, to take care of the kids?"

"You're supposed to be on sick leave."

"I know, but I can't just walk away. It's my fault the bastard's still out there."

"You don't know it was Wayne."

"One of the tutors says she saw him hanging round."

"Really? Who?"

"Joan Hammond." Annie frowns and I say, "Is there anything wrong with that?"

"No, I guess not." But she doesn't sound very sure and I wonder what's going on in her mind.

Chapter 65: Annie

I travel with DC Kelly and the kids, while Rick follows in a squad car driven by an uniformed officer. As we drive I think of Joan Hammond's claim to have seen Wayne hanging round College today. My instinct is to disbelieve her. Why would any responsible person see Wayne and not raise the alarm? But Joan is almost totally spineless in a mildly malicious way and I can believe any stupidity of her. It's possible she's telling the simple truth and Wayne's got Joey. That makes me shudder.

"Do you want the heater turned up?" asks Kelly.

"What? Oh, no thank you, I'm fine."

"I thought you were cold."

"Just a bad feeling. Someone walking over my grave, that's what my dad used to say." I babble to a halt.

"My granny used to say a goose was walking over her grave." It's her turn to shiver. "I can't believe I said that."

"What? Oh I see, Wesley's goose."

Kelly stares straight ahead, then she glances at me, looks away, then back to me again. Unable to stand the strain I say, "What's wrong?"

"I was wondering, are all artists really strange?"

"I beg your pardon?"

"Oh God! I'm sorry! I didn't mean it like that. I wasn't talking about you. I…"

"Oh I see. Neil."

She nods, her eyes fixed fiercely on the road ahead. "Neil seems nice."

Nice isn't the first word that springs to my mind when I'm describing Neil but I don't bring out the best in him, any more than he does in me. "He can be," I agree.

"I was wondering if he'd said anything about me?"

Rick said Kelly had watched his back with Roebuck and

one good turn deserves another. "He said you were the most beautiful woman he'd ever seen."

Kelly gives me a glowing smile. "Thanks."

"You're welcome." I mean it, she's entirely welcome to Neil.

At Elmwash House, Kelly's annoyed because the squad car hasn't kept up with us. At last it turns up. The driver gets out and Kelly snaps, "Where have you been?"

"Had to stop at a supermarket, the DI's orders."

I try to keep my expression disinterested but inside I'm terrified, I pray he hasn't bought himself more whisky.

Rick comes across to join us. He's moving briskly and I can't smell any trace of alcohol on his breath. "Let's go inside."

We trail through the damp corridors to the icy rooms. Josef gets out the photographs and Rick takes them. "Mind if we look round?"

"What you think you're going to find?" asks Chloe. She guesses the answer and her pinched little face flushes scarlet then drains of all colour again. She shrugs. "Go ahead, we've got nothing to hide."

Nothing but their painful poverty. Efficiently the police officers take apart the room and put it back again. Chloe, Josef and I watch.

"What about your neighbours?" asks Rick.

"There's that strange woman who wanted to cuddle Joseph," I say.

Chloe shrugs. "This kind of place runs to nutters. It can't be down to her, we lost him at College."

"It's still worth checking," says Rick. "Where does she hang out?"

"The room along there, second on the left."

"Kelly, you come with me. Pauline, you keep an eye on things here."

All the others obey him but I sidle out to linger in the corridor, I'm worried about Rick and I want to be near in case the strain's too much. I hear a door open and Rick's voice, "I'm Detective Inspector Evans of Galmouth CID and this is Detective Constable Kelly. We're making enquiries about a missing child."

There's a crash. I sprint along the corridor to see what's happening. An overturned table lies in the open doorway and the woman with haunted eyes is backing across the room. There's a hypodermic syringe held like a weapon in her hand. Rick and Kelly are circling her, keeping out of range, while Rick talks softly to her, "Now calm down... no-one's going to hurt you... drop that and we can talk..."

She reaches the edge of the room and grabs something from a crib. Straightening she drops the syringe, leaps through the veranda windows and sprints across the grass.

Rick and Kelly plunge after her and, thinking only of the baby, I join the chase. Rick is slowed by his arm but I'm nearly up with Kelly and she's closing on the woman. The ground is soggy as we near the lake. Kelly slips and falls. I'm scared but I can't stop, not when Joey's life's at stake. The woman glances behind and sees me almost upon her. With a scream she hurls him into the grey water.

I leap into the lake and strike out towards the child. It's so cold I can hardly breathe. I hunt the water. Dive down under it. Surface and try again. My groping fingers find a fold of material, I haul it in, clasp the limp body and thrust him clear of the water. I'm not certain where the edge of the lake is any more.

I feel an arm around me. "It's okay Annie, I've got you."

I'm shaking and my legs are weak. The water drags me down but Rick's support gets me to dry ground. "The baby's not crying," I whimper, "I think he's dead."

The baby is taken from my grasp.

"Annie, it's not a baby, it's a doll."

The world swirls in a whirlpool of grey lights. I fall to my knees and scream, "I hate you, God!"

I feel Rick's arm around me, lifting me to my feet and

urging me back towards the house. I'm shaking so much I can hardly stand.

Kelly is heading in the same direction, hustling the woman along.

The woman screeches, "You bastards! I want my baby."

Kelly passes her the doll. Her hands are like claws as she snatches it.

The kids and Constable Harmer are waiting for us by the cars.

Rick's grasp on me is gentle but his voice is hard, "Kelly, I'm pissed off with fucking round. We need a proper search team in here." He hands Constable Harmer a waterproof bag. "Pauline, the baby's photos are in this evidence bag, give them to CID straight away. You can drive Kelly's car and take my wife and the kids back to the Station, make sure you take good care of them."

"Yes sir." She gets two First Aid blankets from the boot of her car, passes one to Rick and wraps the other around me.

Rick leads me to the car. "Okay love? I'll be back as soon as I can."

I grip his uninjured arm. "No, please, don't make me go."

"Get in the car, love."

"Please come back with me."

"I can't. There's things to do out here. Someone has got to secure this bloody place and I'm the only cop here who can't drive."

"Then let me stay with you."

"No! Please, Annie, don't make this harder than it is."

I remember I mustn't show him up in front of his junior officers. "I'm sorry. I didn't mean to make a fuss." I get into the car.

Chapter 66: Rick

They drive off and I say, "Kelly, are you okay escorting the prisoner in by yourself?" The woman's cuffed securely in the patrol car but she's still shrieking abuse. I can see people peering through the windows of the house and I want her out of here fast.

"Yes Guv, but are you going to be all right out here alone?"

"Someone's got to keep an eye on things and there's no way I can drive. But I need to borrow your mobile, mine didn't like the bath I've just given it."

"No problem, Guv. I've got a radio in the car." She hands it over and leaves.

I ring through to request a team to take Elmwash House apart. I warn them to keep the approach low-key, no sense in starting a panic amongst the rest of the squatters.

I order a quick check on the woman's previous. She's got a load of psychiatric sectionings but she doesn't seem to have any connection to Wayne Jones or Ernest Clift. I reckon she's just some weirdo we've stirred up. When you start sieving shit you always end up with more crap than you bargained for.

Lights flashing, sirens screaming, the squad cars screech to a halt outside the house. I yell, "What part of low-key don't you lot understand? Some of you jokers get round the back and head off any sod that's doing a runner. Then do a thorough search. At the moment I don't give a shit about finding illegal substances or dodgy Benefit books, we're looking for the baby or any sign of him. Okay, move!"

Bob has brought me dry clothes from my locker. He follows me inside and waits while I get changed. It takes some time because my arm's killing me.

"Roebuck says you're to leave this to me and get back

straight away." There's something edgy in Bob's attitude.

"Fair enough. I'm meant to be on sick leave. You got a problem with that?"

"Course not."

"Then why the sour face?"

"Word is there's trouble back there."

"What sort of trouble?"

"Trouble with your bloody wife."

"What do you mean? What's happened to Annie?"

He scowls at me. "The fucking cow's trying to screw you over."

My punch takes him on the chin and knocks him off his feet.

He staggers up and wipes blood from his lip. "Listen, you wanker. Word is she's complained to Roebuck. She's claiming you raped her."

Chapter 67: Annie

"Raped me?" I glare at Superintendent Roebuck, hiding my panic behind a mask of indignant outrage. "That's ridiculous."

The Superintendent looks surprised. "But our informant..." he trails to a halt.

"What informant?"

"I'm sorry, I can't tell you that."

"Oh, wonderful! Any stray lunatic can walk in here and make slanderous accusations and you won't even tell me who it was."

"This was somebody with facts and circumstantial evidence."

"What evidence?"

He looks embarrassed. "For a start there's the bruising on your throat."

I put my hand to my neck and realise the sweatshirt I've borrowed from the police driver doesn't cover the lingering discolouration. I launch into attack, "We like rough foreplay and I mark easily. What business is that of yours? Do you enjoy prying into your officers' sex lives?"

I see him flinch. "Please calm down, Mrs Evans. I want to make this enquiry as low-key as possible, that's why I'm speaking to you off the record like this."

"The enquiry you should be making is why someone's told you these lies."

As I speak, my brain runs in circles. Has Rick told anyone what he did? Does Roebuck believe this informant because it's a fellow cop? The only person I can think of is Bob. He's the most likely person for Rick to confide in.

Superintendent Roebuck backs off from confrontation. "I assure you this will be thoroughly investigated. Please do not worry, Mrs Evans, you can consider the matter closed."

He escorts me to his office door. "I've sent word for Rick to come back here. I'll have a talk with him and then you can take him home."

I spin into panic. If Roebuck springs his accusations on Rick he'll probably confess. How can I warn him? "Does he have to come back here? Couldn't I meet him and take him straight home?"

"I'm afraid not, I need to speak to him. Thank you for your co-operation, Mrs Evans, I hope I haven't distressed you too much."

"You haven't distressed me, just made me very angry."

Despite his secretary's disapproving glare, I sit down in the Superintendent's outer office. It's a prime position for intercepting Rick. The second he appears I'll hurl myself passionately on him and whisper, 'Deny everything,' in his ear. Unfortunately I've mislaid my handbag, so I can't phone his mobile and warn him.

Five minutes later Kelly comes through and goes in to speak to Roebuck. When she comes out she says, "Do you want to go for a cup of coffee?"

"No thanks."

She still lingers. "Thanks for helping out today. Are you all right now?"

"I'm fine. Have you got everything sorted?"

"We've done all we can until she's been seen by a doctor."

"Do you really think she had anything to do with baby Joe's disappearance?"

"Who knows? The DI's the one for instinct, the rest of us make do with facts."

This backhanded comment fuels my smouldering temper. "And what 'facts' have you reported to Superintendent Roebuck while you've been spying on my husband?"

She stares at me. "Who told you that?"

"My husband of course. He's not stupid. He sussed you ages ago."

She sits down beside me and says quietly, "Off the record, at the start of the Frewer case, the Superintendent did ask me to report back to him on how the DI was coping, but it wasn't to get him into trouble or give him grief."

"No?" I'm beginning to have an inkling of what's coming next.

"The Superintendent has been worried about him. He wanted me to let him know if I thought the stress was getting too much."

I'm still furious. Roebuck had no right to undermine Rick with his subordinates. "And what did you report back?"

She matches my bluntness with her own, "The beginning of last week I thought he was a liability, but the last few days he's been brilliant."

That startles me. Do I really make that much difference to Rick's professional life?

Kelly must misinterpret my silence because she says, "That's the truth."

I probe a little deeper, "Have you heard what Superintendent Roebuck wanted to talk to me about?"

"Yes. It's all over the station. God knows how. The Superintendent told me he wanted it kept quiet."

"Did he ask for your opinion?"

"Yes, but not until he realised everyone had heard."

"And what did you tell him?"

"I told him it couldn't be true. Why should the DI rape you? He wouldn't need to, it's obvious what you think of each other."

"Is it?"

She seems flustered, all her tough, cool image gone. "Anyone who sees you together must realise you adore each other."

Slowly I smile. "Yes, that's true," I say.

I stay in Roebuck's outer office for over an hour. I get funny looks from people passing through but I don't care. All

I want is for Rick to walk in, to be where I can see him, hold him, keep him safe. Every time the door opens my heart gives a hopeful jump that withers into disappointment when it isn't him.

At last Bob comes through and goes into Roebuck's office, ignoring me in a very pointed way. My tension notches up.

It seems like forever until the door opens and Roebuck says, "Mrs Evans, please come in. Thank you, sergeant, I'll speak to you when I've decided what's best to do."

Bob brushes roughly past me. With his back to Roebuck he mouths the words, "Fucking bitch." His jaw is swollen and I wonder who hit him.

Roebuck pulls a chair out for me. "Please sit down, Mrs Evans. I'm afraid we've got a bit of a problem with Rick. Something seems to have upset him and he's taken himself off."

I stare at him. "But where's he gone?" I say stupidly.

"We're not sure. He walked away from Elmwash House. Sergeant Borrow tried to get him to come back but he refused. I'm sure he'll be fine. He'll take a good long walk and calm down."

"You could ring his mobile. Isn't he answering that?"

"DC Kelly tells me his mobile is out of order after the wetting it received earlier today and he left the one she lent him at Elmwash House. It's important you get home quickly in case Rick turns up. Indeed he may already be there."

I don't waste time protesting or asking what's upset Rick. In the light of Roebuck's story and Bob's insult I've already worked it out.

"I haven't got my car and Rick's is still at the College."

"A squad car will take you back and a police officer will stay with you."

"I'll be glad of the lift but I don't need anyone to stay." If Rick turns up in a state I don't want any witnesses.

I leave the Superintendent's outer office and say to the

young constable designated to escort me, "I want to see DS Borrow before I leave."

We find Bob in the CID office. He's with Kelly, apparently doing the listening for once. I march up to him. He stands and says, "Annie, I..."

I keep my voice low-pitched but my anger lashes through it, "Did you tell Rick I'd complained he raped me?"

"Well yes. I thought..."

"You bastard! You destroyed your own marriage and now you're trying to ruin ours. From now on you can stay away from both of us." I leave without giving him a chance to have his say.

At home there's no sign of life. There's a delay getting into the house, because my mislaid bag contains my door key. The long-suffering cop collects a spare from a neighbour in the nearby farm cottages. He offers to check the house for intruders but I refuse in case Rick's here.

I prowl around, nerves twitching, but the house is empty. I turn the phone's ring tone to maximum while I shower and change. It remains silent.

Back downstairs, at last the phone rings. '*Oh please God.*'

"Hello?"

Neil says, "Annie? Do you know what's going on? Have they found the baby?"

"No, at least not that I know of. Neil, you haven't seen Rick have you?"

"Rick? No, not since you left. Why? What's wrong?"

"Nothing."

"You left your handbag in your office. I thought you might be worried about it."

"That was stupid of me. Thanks for keeping it safe. Rick's car's at College as well, but I'll have to leave it for tonight."

"Didn't you say yours is at Maris' house? You might need a car. Do you want me to bring Rick's over?"

"Would you? That would really help. The keys are in my bag."

"No problem." He rings off.

Half an hour later he arrives. I go out and say, "Thank you. Do you need to phone a taxi to get back?"

"No. Kelly turned up just after I phoned you and she's giving me a lift."

Kelly's car pulls into the drive and I fight down my instinct to demand why she isn't out looking for Rick and baby Joe. "Thanks for bringing the car back, Neil."

"Are you sure you're okay?" asks Neil. "Kelly told me about Rick. I'll stay if you need me."

"No thanks. I'm fine."

He leaves and I'm glad to see him go. My life has honed down, there's just one voice, one step, one presence that I need.

Where can he be? I ring through to the hospital to check he isn't there with his mum. The staff nurse must realise it's an emergency because she lets Tris come to the office phone.

"Tris, Rick's a bit stressed. He's taken himself off. He's not there is he?"

I know my casual tone doesn't fool her. "No, love, I'm afraid not. I'll go home in case he turns up there and I'll ask the nurses to keep an eye out for him, though it's not likely he'll take a fancy to visit his dad."

"Thank you." I key off quickly as tears start to gush. I'm scolding myself into calmness and mopping my eyes when the phone rings again.

Chapter 68: Annie

"Rick, is that you?"

"It's me."

I wonder, not for the first time, how anyone can have a voice so like a dollop of cold porridge. "Maris, I'm busy so…"

"I want you to come round."

"I'm sorry, I can't."

"There's something here you ought to see, something you wanted."

"Maris I can't, I told you…"

"You must come."

"I can't. Look I've got to go."

I put the phone down. After a few seconds it rings again. I hesitate then pick it up.

"We got cut off."

I say through gritted teeth, "Maris, I can't talk to you now."

Again I put it down. Again it rings. Again I daren't leave it. "Hello?"

"You must come round tonight."

I slam the phone down and switch on the answer machine. In the next ten minutes Maris rings back six more times.

If only I'd skived off work today, then Rick would have stayed with me and he'd be safe. By now we'd be curled up in front of the fire, with the curtains drawn.

Surely he wouldn't kill himself, not Rick. But what do I know? I'm the wife who lived with his Post-Traumatic Stress without recognising it.

I remember him cowering in the woods. Perhaps that's where he'd go, to Elmwash or Saronholt. I write a note: 'Rick, darling, I've gone out to look for you. Please stay here. I'll be back soon.' That's not enough. What if he phones instead? I record a loving answer phone message begging him to come home. I don't care what anyone else who rings through thinks of us.

I search through my handbag for my mobile but it's not there. Then I remember I'd lent it to Josef and, in the panic, forgotten to get it back.

I hurry through the woods at Saronholt. It's still and silent, the police presence must have moved on. I watch every tree, scared that Wayne is going to lunge at me. When I lock myself back in the car I'm trembling, and I know the worst is yet to come. I've left Elmwash until last because it's the place I dread the most.

I park in a lay-by off the main road and go in on foot. It's dusk and Elmwash is a brooding place. Evil lingers. It curls itself around the trees like smothering ivy.

I walk the beaten pathways with all senses prickling. Then I stumble into a run. "Rick?" My voice is trembling. "Rick? Rick, are you here?"

I stand at the perimeter wire and stare at the hut. It looks so ordinary, that's what frightens me.

"What are you doing here?" It's a man's voice.

I scream.

"Shut that noise! I said what are you doing here?"

"I'm looking for Rick." I move the light of my torch away from the hut to shine on him.

"What?" He's staring at me with fierce intensity.

"I'm looking for Rick Evans, my husband."

"Rick Evans the cop?"

I nod, choked with fear, and wonder if there are any police on the outskirts of the wood to hear my scream.

"He's not been here that I've seen." The man's voice is quieter now, less challenging.

I realise he's not as old as I thought, although his hair is grey and his face lined. Something clicks into place, "Are you Emma's dad?"

"Your husband told you about me, did he?"

"Yes."

"Nice bloke, the best of that lot. He hasn't been here in the last three hours. I've been trying to keep off the souvenir hunters. Last night they had police here but that didn't last long."

"There's another child missing, a baby, so I guess they need everyone on that."

"A baby? Oh Jesus, no!" Then in a gentler tone, "You shouldn't be here. You could run into some of the bastards who come and pinch bits off the hut."

"It's sick."

"Yeah. The souvenir hunting died down until this new kiddie got killed, then it all started up again. It'll be worse than ever if a baby's gone."

"I guess there's no way to stop it, not while the hut is here."

"No, you're right, it won't be over while that place still stands. You want me to walk you back?"

"No, I'm fine thanks." I want to get away from this man and his overwhelming, irredeemable pain.

He leans forward to light a cigarette, the flickering yellow flame makes his face look jaundiced. "Do you think anything would ever grow here after this?"

I seem to be drifting, floating far away. "Poppies... poppies would grow here."

That seems to focus his attention. He stares at me then says, "Poppies? You reckon? Perhaps if we could let in some light."

There's a man waiting on our doorstep. For a second my heart lifts, then plummets when I see it's Bob not Rick.

"What do you want?"

"Just to say I'm sorry and to let Rick know we've picked up Wayne. Rick called it right, he went to give Vicki some sweets."

"Rick's not turned up yet." I go into the house but I don't stop Bob when he follows me.

"Annie, I'm sorry."

"It's a bit late for that."

"Yeah, I guess it is, but Annie, I've been thinking and I've got to tell you this. Today, Rick told me what he did the other night. The thing is, before that, we were at this Mexican restaurant doing shots of Tequila."

"So?"

"It didn't occur to me at the time but one of the guys was saying how some people go crazy on that stuff. I thought you ought to know… that it might help."

A week ago it might have helped a lot but now it doesn't matter all that much. But if… when… Rick comes back it might ease him to have a reason.

I glare at him. "And you told Roebuck what he'd done?"

"No! I wouldn't! Anyway I swear I didn't know until it was all over the Station. I warned Rick what was being said when I went over to Elmwash. I thought you'd turned him in."

I think I believe him, even though he's done his best to turn Rick against me in the last few years. "Bob, why do you hate me so much? We used to get on okay."

I think he's not going to answer but then he says, "I guess I've been mad with you since Pat left. I blamed you for telling her."

"Telling her what?"

"About me and Debs."

I stare at him. "I didn't, it was Pat who told me."

"What? But Debs said it was you who stitched me up… that you told Pat I was screwing Debs when I wasn't."

"You weren't?" That surprises me.

"Not then. My thing with Debs didn't start till after Pat left."

I shake my head. "I'm sorry, Bob, but Debs is lying. A girl Pat knew was working in the pub and Pat warned me that Debs was making a play for Rick. So I went in there and enquired if she wanted to be the most battered barmaid in Town. Debs backed off but I know she hated me for it."

His face is hard. "And that's when she turned her attentions onto me?"

"I guess."

His mobile rings. He listens then says, "Jesus! I'll get right on it." He rings off.

"Is it news of Rick?"

"No, at least I don't reckon so. Someone's torched the hut in Elmwash woods. They've burned it to the ground. Annie, you don't think it was Rick, do you?"

I remember Emma's father's haunted face, illuminated by the flickering lighter flame. "No, I'm sure it wasn't Rick."

"I must go. Annie... please... let me know if there's anything I can do."

He leaves abruptly and seconds later I hear him accelerating away.

There are three messages on the answer phone. They're all from Maris, telling me to come and visit her, I think her voice sounds triumphant, almost gloating, and I wonder why.

Chapter 69: Annie

Again I sit down beside the phone to wait. There's nothing else to do and I'm afraid there'll be nothing else to do for all my life. It's a long while before it rings again. It makes me jump. I snatch it up and gasp, "Hello?"

"Annie?"

I swallow hard and say, "Hi, Elaine."

"Is something wrong?"

"No." My denial's instinctive but, even as I say it, I realise I need to share my fear. "Yes, something's very wrong. Rick's gone missing."

"What?"

"Someone told his boss that he'd done something and it's upset him."

"This something he did, was it something to you?" There's a strange note in Elaine's voice.

"What do you mean?"

"It's something Maris said when I saw her today."

Things start slotting into place. "What did Maris say?"

"It's nonsense. Maris being spiteful."

"Tell me what Maris said Rick had done to me."

She says reluctantly, "Raped you."

"I see." My mind whirls into overdrive. "But why did she tell you?"

"Spite."

"Spite?"

"Yes." She seems to sense my bewilderment. "You don't get it, do you? It's just not in you, envy, spite, maliciousness, all that sort of stuff."

"I don't know what you mean."

"Maris told me Rick had raped you because she wanted to score over me, to show me it was her you confided in. She's always envied me because I'm your sister... Are you still there?"

I struggle through a labyrinth of confusion. "I hear what you're saying but I don't understand."

"Surely you know how she's always felt about you?"

"No."

"When we were in junior school she used to tell people she was your sister. It used to drive me mad."

"She used to say she was our sister? That's crazy!"

"Your sister, not mine. At one time there was even a rumour going round that I was adopted... It's not funny!"

"Sorry. But it's ridiculous, you're the image of Mother. What was the idea? That having had two failures in me and Maris, mother decided to adopt a beautiful blonde child to make up for her disappointment?"

Elaine's voice sharpens even more, "You were never a disappointment to Mother, she's incredibly proud of you."

"Tell me what Maris said when she claimed Rick had raped me."

"I went round to see her this morning like you asked, she didn't seem pleased but when I said you'd sent me she let me in. She was talking about you and how you ought to leave Rick and I said that was nonsense, you and Rick had your ups and downs but you weren't going to leave him."

"And?"

"She said he'd raped you, and you'd got bruises on your throat, and you'd cried with your head in her lap and you'd been afraid to go home."

"What did you say?" I'm burning with shame but my voice sounds ice cold.

"I told her she shouldn't tell lies like that. It was bad enough about anyone but especially harmful to a cop." I hear her in-drawn breath as she works it out. "Do you think she went to Rick's boss? To get him into trouble?"

"I don't know what else to think."

"Oh God! I'm so sorry, Annie! I never thought she'd do anything like that."

"It's not your fault."

"Shall I come round to keep you company?"

"No, there's no need. I'm fine."

I put the phone down and try to conjure back the past. It seems as if, throughout my life, Maris has haunted me, a solid, prosaic spectre. During village events she'd be there, attaching herself persistently to my side, or if that proved impossible she'd stare unwaveringly. Everyone noticed and I found it embarrassing, especially when Mother hissed at me, *"Arianne, don't encourage her."*

I was halfway through my Fine Art Degree when Maris came to the same University. She was doing Graphics but it was remarkable how consistently she turned up. When Lucy retired from the Art College I was lecturing in America for a month. I returned and found Maris established as Head of Graphics. If I'd thought about it, I'd have assumed she'd grown out of me. As many people who are fond of me have pointed out, in some ways I'm pretty thick.

What the hell does she want of me?

I stop and start again. As Rick would say, 'To hell with what she wants, she's got no right to anything you don't want to give.' I remember she'd told Elaine about me crying with my head in her lap and wonder if she'd told Roebuck that detail too. Embarrassment fuels my anger. On cue the phone rings, I snatch it up, "Hello?"

"It's me."

"I thought it would be."

"You're being very silly, Annie."

"Maris, you are the most interfering, aggravating cow in the entire world."

She continues as if she hasn't heard, "You should come round. You'll regret it if you don't."

Suddenly I want to tell her what I think of her, face to face. "Okay, I'll give you five minutes." One last encounter and our pseudo-friendship will be officially closed.

I bang on Maris' front door hard enough to cave it in. She opens it and I stalk inside.

"Come into the living room, I've made supper." She moves nearer and murmurs intimately, "Fish pie."

"I've not come to supper."

"You're so impatient," she says reprovingly. "Very well then, follow me."

She starts up the stairs. I grab her arm and haul her back. "Maris, did you tell Rick's boss that he'd raped me?"

She stares down at my hand until I release my grip then she rubs her arm. "Really Annie, there's no need to be rough."

"Did you tell Rick's boss?"

"Of course I did."

"But why?"

"Someone has to look after you."

"Look after me! Maris, you had no right."

"How can you say that? I have every right."

Standing on the third stair she's taller than I am. It gives her an advantage but not so great as the power of her calm assumption that she has some authority in my life.

I speak every syllable loud and very clear, "You have no right."

Her face doesn't change, neither does her voice, "How can you say that after all we've been to each other for so long?"

"You're nothing to me. You never have been."

"You came to me for help. You cried in my arms."

"I shouldn't have told you. I was upset and stupid. I'm sorry I told you anything you could use to hurt Rick."

"You've always been too soft, that's why you need me."

My fingers twitch as I restrain the desire to slap her, to wipe that smug certainty from her face. "Look Maris, I know we'll have to meet at work but apart from that I want you to stay out of my life, and don't ever phone me again."

"Don't be silly, Annie. You can't walk away from me."

"Watch me."

For the first time she falters, "But the baby, you've got to come upstairs and look at it, then you won't want to leave."

"I don't want to see your baby."

I wrench open the swollen front door and run out to Rick's car. Maris stands in the doorway watching me, but when I get in the driver's seat she goes back inside. I'm shaking with frustration. Most of the things I wanted to say are still boiling in my mind.

I see my own car, still marooned although it's been repaired. A painting I'd promised Wes I'd get framed is lying on the back seat and I know I shouldn't leave it to the danger of Maris' spite. I cast a nervous glance at the cottage but there's no sign she's looking out. Nevertheless, as soon as I open my car, I switch off the interior light.

As I haul the canvas out my hand encounters an unpleasant stickiness and I swear. What has Wes been experimenting with as a painting medium? I switch on the internal light and stare at my stained fingers. I'm sure it's blood. Of course it could be goose blood but surely that would have dried by now. Anyway, this is a seascape; one Wes produced in answer to my challenge to paint something that wasn't gross. I see a small puddle of dark stickiness behind the front passenger seat. And, on the seat itself, my mobile phone.

I gaze at it uncomprehendingly. I know it's my phone because of the blob of paint I'd spilled on it that looks like a dinosaur. But I'd lent my phone to Josef and he couldn't have put it in my car, the only person who could have done that is…

"You'd better come inside." Maris is towering solidly over me. I drop the phone and back slowly out of the car, wiping my sticky fingers on my jeans. "You always were too inquisitive," she says.

I feel bewildered. And uneasy. I could exert my will power and drive off. But I don't leave because of the blood and the phone and the fear that isn't for myself. What has happened to baby Joseph? What has Maris done?

I wonder if Maris' baby is dead. Maybe that's why she's acting so oddly. It's crazy and nasty and I feel sick. I should hurry home in case Rick's trying to contact me, but I think of the baby and allow Maris to lead me back into the house.

"Maris, can I see the baby?"

She smiles smugly. "I knew you wanted to. Come upstairs."

She leads me to Mummy's mouldering room and there, in the middle of Mummy's fusty bed, is a tiny figure lying face down, still and silent. Now I'm desperately, despairingly afraid.

Chapter 70: Rick

There's stickiness in my eyes. It's blood, his blood, his blood blinding me. He didn't die immediately he hit. I don't know how long he lived, seconds, minutes. It seemed like time had stopped. We looked into each other's faces and I swear he could see me, even though one of his eyes had wrenched free of its socket. We stared through the crazed windscreen. His lips were twisted into the mockery of a smile and I'm sure he could smell my terror. I guess that's what he's followed ever since, the stench of fear.

I force my eyes open but it's still dark. My feet are tied together and my arms are fixed behind my back and the broken one hurts worse than any physical pain I've ever known. I'm lying face down in shallow, stinking water, spluttering and retching. I force myself to roll over onto my good side. That jars my arm and makes me go woozy.

I try to remember what happened, how the hell I got here, wherever here is. I remember walking away from Elmwash. I kept going until I came to my senses and realised I had to talk to Annie. I needed to know she was okay, even if she had given up on me. I'd left the phone Kelly lent me at Elmwash House but, after I'd walked a while, I found a phone box. I tried to phone Annie but the landline was continually engaged and her mobile went straight to answer service, so I left her a message telling her which way I was walking home. If I'd had any sense I'd have phoned for a taxi but I wasn't thinking straight. I carried on walking along the narrow country lanes until I heard a car coming. I started to turn to flag it down and ask for a lift but I heard it accelerate and then... nothing. I guess it ran me down.

The waves of pain die back a bit and I look around my prison. It's a damp, dark room with the windows covered.

No, that's wrong. It's underground, somewhere that's got flooded with the rain. No wonder it's so cold and dark and smells so bad.

I fight against panic. If I start screaming I know I won't stop.

'You won't forget me, Richard.' As if things weren't bad enough, Ernest Clift is there, twisting through my mind. Suddenly I know there's only one thing I can do, I've got to face what I've been running from.

It's not his death that's the blank spot. I've died with Clift a thousand times in my head. After it happened I replayed it every time I went near that bloody bridge. The time I've never gone to is the bit before, the hours that led up to Clift jumping.

I edge my mind towards it. After all there's nothing else to do, lying here in the dank darkness, hurting like hell, without a clue what's going on, and frantically fighting claustrophobia. In a weird way, thinking it through is like taking control.

Ernest Clift liked playing power games. That's what we're doing in the interview room. With Clift's permission we're recording the interview. He says he's delighted to co-operate. The room is a khaki coloured dump and I find it hard to stay in there at the best of times. Today the only way I can cope is by continually telling myself I can walk out at any time.

Ernest Clift sits one side of the table, me at the other; Bob has got this tendency to prowl. It's not a formal interview, no caution or charges and no solicitor, we've done all that and come out the other side with no result. Now it's just Clift, turning up and asking if he can be of any help to us. And I can't resist these interviews. At the end of every one I swear I'll never do it again but I know I will. My DCI has warned me off, not made it an order but given strong advice: "Leave it alone, Rick, the sick bastard's jerking you round."

"Let me try a bit longer, Will. I swear he's going to

break. I know there's something he wants to tell me."

He doesn't turn up every day or at the same time. He keeps me guessing. And when he's not there I wonder what he's doing and whether some new kid is being tortured and killed.

Bob says, "Tell us about the girls."

"The girls?"

"Hannah, Emma and Katie, you know what girls."

"Ah those poor girls. Quite beautiful, weren't they?"

"When did you see them? How do you know they were beautiful?" Bob jumps in too quick.

Clift smirks. His voice sounds like he's about to purr. "I've seen pictures in the newspapers. Such lovely girls." His pink tongue slithers out and circles his thin lips. "So sad to think they died in agony." He's smiling directly at me, I feel his foot pressing down on mine and jerk out of his way. "You like children, don't you, Richard? Now why would anyone do that to such lovely girls? What sort of monster would do that, do you think?"

"You tell me."

He leans back in his chair and places the tips of his pudgy fingers together on the table. "A collector," he says, like he's giving some sort of lecture. "Someone who assembles and preserves the best. But, of course, there are the others, the inferior specimens used for practising. Tell me Richard, have you located Kyra Hamilton?"

"You call him Mr Evans," says Bob.

It coincides with my demand, "Tell us about Kyra Hamilton."

As always Clift responds to me, "Kyra Hamilton, such a pretty name, what I'd call evocative. Not a pretty child though, not one of the better specimens."

"What did you do to Kyra Hamilton?"

"Me? Really, Richard, I don't know what you mean."

"Did you kill Kyra Hamilton?"

He shakes his head reprovingly. "You shouldn't ask me

that, Richard, you have no proof that she is dead."

Bob slams his hands on the table and leans right over it. "Okay, you want proof, how about the bodies we do have? Hannah Summers, we have her body. Did you kill Hannah Summers? And Emma Brown. Did you kill Emma Brown? And Katie Cavendish. Little Katie, did you kill her?"

Bob's never been the subtlest of guys; he bangs his fist down on the table next to the tape machine. I switch it off. For the first time I see unease on Clift's face. I've never been keen on beating up suspects but those girls in Elmwash Wood were put through hell before they died. And there are the others, the lost kids, Kyra and the ones who don't even have a name.

Clift forces a thin smile. "Gestapo tactics, Richard? I thought you were a civilised young man."

There's a tap on the door and a constable sticks his head into the room. "Sorry Guv, but the DCI wants Sergeant Borrow straight away."

"Shit," says Bob. "Sorry, Rick, I'll have to go."

The door slams behind him and Clift relaxes. He wriggles his shoulders beneath his peach coloured shirt. He's sweating and the underarms are stained. "What an exceedingly violent young man." He leans towards me, "Unlike you, Richard."

"Don't count on that."

"Oh but I do. I want to tell you how much I appreciate the tact and persistence with which you've arranged our meetings and, of course, this delightful tête-à-tête." He reaches across the table and strokes my hand. I stare, too shocked to react immediately.

I snatch my hand away and jump up. My chair smashes to the floor. "Get out!"

He stares at me with shielded eyes, then he stands. "Until tomorrow then?"

"You won't be seeing me tomorrow or ever, any further interviews will be carried out by other officers." I keep the words coldly official but my voice is trembling.

I wait for him to cross the room, keeping my distance, but at the door he pauses and turns back to face me. "You can't escape me, Richard. I know where you live, I've seen your pretty wife. I've got friends, good friends, who will carry on for me. Every time you say goodbye to your wife or those children that one day you think you'll have, you'll ask yourself, 'Is this the last time I'll see them alive?'"

I feel something snapping in my head, like an elastic band when it's pulled too far. I twang forward and my hands are at his throat. It's soft and puffy, like strangling a slug. I hear his breath rattle.

And then a voice, "For Christ's sake, Rick!" Bob hauls me off and pins me against the wall. "Are you crazy?"

Clift slumps back, clammy and gasping. After a few moments he braces his shoulders and straightens his collar and tie. His face is totally expressionless. He clears his throat and says huskily, "I will see you later, Richard."

"I told you, never again."

He sidles towards the door. "You won't forget me, Richard."

Back in the office, Will Newton takes one look and pours me a large whisky. He doesn't ask me what went on down there, just says, "Leave it to me, Rick."

He makes me stay in the office for the rest of the day. I feel sick and edgy and I keep finding excuses to phone Annie and check she's okay. Clift comes to the station three times that afternoon. Each time he asks for me and each time the duty sergeant says I'm not free. The last time he says he'll wait and does so, until the DCI goes down in person and sends him on his way.

When I leave, Bob walks me to my car.

"I don't need a bodyguard," I say, but I'm grateful and Bob knows it.

I turn left out of the car park to take the direct way home. I'm driving extra carefully because I'm tired and tense and, although I'm not drunk, I did have that whisky a few hours ago. As I come to the pedestrian footbridge I don't look up, I've got no reason to, so I don't see Ernest Clift charting my progress through his binoculars. I don't see him climb the parapet. I don't see him jump.

At the inquest, eyewitnesses said he dived as if he was trying to fly straight into me.

Chapter 71: Annie

I reach out a trembling finger to stroke the baby's cheek. The dark eyes open and he gives a cross-sounding yowl. Weak with relief I pick him up and he snuggles against my neck. "It's all right, darling, I'm here."

Maris eyes us with distaste. "It's noisy and it smells."

"He must be hungry, have you fed him?"

"I've got this stuff." There's a carton of baby milk and a bottle on the dressing table along with a disposable nappy.

"We'll have to sterilise the bottle." Bottle in one hand, baby in my arms I make for the door.

Maris blocks my way. "Where are you going?"

"The kitchen, at least we can try to get this sterile with boiling water."

She looks discontented. "It should eat what it's given. It wasted all that other packet. Oh all right. You stay here, I'll bring the kettle up."

She backs out of the door and slams it in my face. I hear the key turn in the lock. I cuddle Joey until she comes back with a steaming kettle, then I put him on the bed, empty the bottle and rinse everything in boiling water in the china wash-bowl.

"Mind you don't crack that basin, it's valuable," says Maris.

I ignore her and fill the bottle with the made-up milk. Then I pick up Joey and nurse him as I put the bottle in his mouth. "It's okay, sweetheart, Annie's got you."

He's hungry and guzzles the milk down.

"It's made a wet mark on Mummy's bedspread," Maris complains.

"I'll change him when he's fed."

She stands over us, arms folded, legs slightly spread. Her eyes are on little Joseph and I think there's nothing soft about her, nothing motherly. Her gaze shifts to my face, the sullen look disappears and she smiles with great tenderness.

"Maris, what happened to your baby?"

She says cautiously, "That's my baby."

If she's delusional I could push her over the edge. I tense, ready for evasive action. "No Maris, it's not your baby, it's Joseph, Chloe and Josef's baby."

She looks blank and then a sly smile spreads across her face, like the Mona Lisa on her way to the funny farm. "You're cleverer than I thought. How did you know?"

"I recognise him."

"Really? They all look the same to me."

"Maris, what happened to your baby?"

The sly look deepens and then, terrifyingly, she giggles. "Don't you know?"

"Know what?" My mouth is dry.

"There was no baby."

"You mean you had a phantom pregnancy?"

Her laughter becomes quite wild. "You could say that."

I clutch baby Joe so tightly he whimpers. "I don't understand."

"You don't really think I'd let a man do those disgusting things to me?"

"You mean you weren't ever pregnant? You were pretending? But why?"

"I enjoyed it. It wiped the smirk off Neil Walder's face and made people treat me with respect. And it made you notice me."

"But how? I mean the guy told Neil he'd slept with you."

Neil's comments when he'd reported the matter to me had been profane, amusing and cynical and I'm sure Maris knows this by the way she smiles. "It's easy to say things. He was old. Doing it to me was a feather in his cap. He tried, you know." I shake my head and she elaborates, "He tried to paw me, I had to deal with him."

"Deal with him?"

"There's all sorts of pills in Mummy's medicine box. Over the years I've saved up lots of them. But you know that, I gave you some of the strongest ones for that Beast you lived with. They were special ones. I used to visit Mrs Munro when she was dying, I gave her disprins and took her tablets home. I knew they would come in useful, but you didn't use them properly." She sounds reproachful. "Three or four of them washed down by whisky would have saved me so much trouble. It was very thoughtless of you."

Horror engulfs me. I could have killed Rick with those pills. I realise she'd drugged my wine on that first night and tried to do so again after she'd punctured my tyres. She'd never intended to kill herself, just schemed to make me stay.

At least now I understand what happened with the visiting artist. "You mean you drugged him and when he woke up the next day he thought he'd made love to you?"

"Not love. It was nothing to do with love. He thought he'd screwed me and he was proud of it. After all he was over sixty. He boasted that he was the one who'd screwed the Virgin Maris. Don't look so shocked, Annie, did you think I hadn't heard them call me that?"

"Not me, Maris."

She steps closer and strokes my cheek. "No, not you." She resumes briskly, "Of course, I only knew it was safe to invent a baby after I was certain he was dead. Otherwise he might have wanted to see it."

I stare at her. "Certain? Did you do something to him?"

She smiles at me. "Don't look so shocked, Annie. It served him right."

I scramble back to the safer ground of the pretend pregnancy. "But how could you fake it? Surely there was paperwork you had to give in at College?"

"It was easy enough. That Sara girl is so inefficient. I told her I'd given everything to her and she'd lost my papers. She apologised and begged me not to report her." Again that thin smile. "She was grateful when I told her I'd sort it out and she needn't worry about it."

Baby Joseph has finished his milk. I put him against my shoulder and pat his back.

"But I felt the baby move." Although I think I've worked that out.

"I used a little battery toy, I put it in the padding. I'm clever, you know. People don't realise."

I'm seriously scared. Post-natal depression is one thing but this is lunacy.

"Of course I didn't plan to have a baby. I was going to have a stillbirth, then everyone would have been sorry and made a fuss of me. You'd have been kind to me then, wouldn't you?"

"I guess. But why did you take Joey?"

"It seemed as though it was meant. Surely you see that? There was that stupid immigrant boy asleep when everyone said the child murderer could be hanging around. I went across to point it out to him and then I saw your phone and knew he'd stolen it and should be punished. Then I had a wonderful idea. I took the phone and the baby and put them in the boot of my car and I even remembered to leave a flower, so everyone would think it was the same as those other children. I liked doing that because I knew your husband would be blamed. I've read the papers and I knew they'd say it was like those other killings. It was clever the way I thought of everything when I had to plan so fast. Then I went inside, collected my bag, had a word with Joan and left."

"Joan didn't see Wayne through the window, did she? You told her that she had."

Maris nods approvingly. "I knew you were quite clever even though you hide it well. Of course Joan didn't see that murdering moron, he wasn't there to see."

Baby Joseph burps and spews milk down my back. Maris looks disgusted.

"But why take Joey? It's obvious you don't like babies."

"For you, of course. You wanted a baby and that was the one thing he could give you that I couldn't."

At last I can't avoid her motivation and it makes me feel sick.

"Why are you looking so surprised? Surely you knew we were meant to be together? Ever since we were children I've known that."

She unfastens her silver locket and opens it for me. Mother had chosen it as a childhood gift to Maris when we'd attended her birthday party, but now it's engraved with our names, *Maris & Annie,* intertwined. Inside there's a picture: Maris and I, aged eight and ten, taken at that party years ago. I remember Maris' mummy gave Mother a copy, only that picture was postcard size and Elaine was in it too.

Maris fastens the locket round my neck. She leans close and rests her cheek against mine. She smells musty, like the house.

"Maris, we don't need this baby."

"But you want one, you won't be happy otherwise."

"I want my own baby. I'm pregnant."

Her eyes are riveted on my face. "Are you sure?"

"I did the test today." I smile as I tell the lie, the pregnancy testing kit is still unopened at home.

"Our baby." She kisses me upon the lips. "I'll take good care of you." She looks at Joseph and frowns. "What a nuisance. If I'd known I wouldn't have taken it. Still, it can't be helped. I'll get rid of it."

She puts her hands out to take him and I know she's going to do something terrible. "No, don't hurt him." I clutch him to me.

"It's all right, you won't have to hear it cry."

"What are you going to do?"

"I thought the well… it's deep."

I'm numb with horror and yet my brain works fast. "No, don't do that. There's no need to kill him and it would be a bad omen for our baby. We'll drive him over to the hospital.

I'll run in with him and leave him in Casualty."

"I don't know. Can I trust you?" Her eyes scan my face and I sustain her gaze.

"I don't want a relationship with you if you don't trust me." Before she can object, I carry Joey out of the door and down the stairs.

Chapter 72: Rick

So at last I've faced it, the whole bloody day. It's funny that it took being kidnapped and imprisoned to make me deal with it.

After Clift landed on my car, the paramedics had to give me a tranquilliser shot so they could unclamp my hands from the steering wheel and take me to hospital. They cleaned me and patched me up and treated me for shock. I was shaking and throwing up for days and it took three weeks for me to get feeling back in my hands and sometimes, even now, they don't work perfectly. I remember, the feeling didn't come back until after I'd given evidence in the Coroner's Court and sworn I had no idea why Clift had done it or why he'd chosen me, and the Coroner decided none of it was my fault. Annie had tried to get me to talk but it was locked up tight inside me and trying to get it out hurt far too much.

They sent me to a psychologist but I found her too patronising to talk to and she made it clear she thought I was bloody rude. She said I was in Denial.

"So what?" I said. "Denial's not a bad place to be."

But I realised she'd got the power, so I played the game until she let me return to work. Will Newton wanted me back and pulled some strings.

As I lie in the cellar, the damp and the darkness and the smell take me back to a time long before Clift, when I was a kid. *'It takes one to know one.'* There's a lot of truth in that. As a cop there's been a good few times I've gone into a house and felt the balance of power is distorted and I've been surprised no-one else seems to have noticed. It was like that the first time I went into Stacie Frewer's home.

It's like a light switches on in my brain. I try to block out my present pain and fear and piece together what happened to Stacie. It's extraordinary how it all comes together. Typical of my luck. I've worked it out now, when I'm a prisoner and can't tell anyone, much less take steps to prove it.

I'm so deep in thought that when the door opens it takes me by surprise. I focus on the triangle of light, then realise that it's at the top of a flight of steps and I'm lying at the bottom of them. A woman picks her way down using a torch. I can see her outline silhouetted by the light.

"Help me, please."

She rams some sort of tape over my mouth. I try to squirm away.

"Don't make that silly fuss. I need you quiet until I've got time to dispose of you." It's a cold, flat voice, the sort you don't forget.

She goes up again, much faster with the light in front of her. The door shuts and I'm left close to suffocating in the dark. Why should Annie's terminally dismal friend, Maris, capture me and keep me prisoner?

I try to wriggle up to the top of the steps. I have some hazy hope that if I can get there perhaps I can kick out and trip her the next time she comes through. Not much of a chance but the only one I've got. I get about halfway. I hurt all over and the tape over my mouth makes it hard to breathe. I slip and bang my bad arm. I roll down again, taking out some shelving as I land.

Chapter 73: Annie

"What's that noise?" I ask as we go through the scullery.

"Rats in the cellar, I'll go down later and get rid of them. Come on, we haven't got all day, we'll take your car." She has the keys ready and goes to the driver's side.

On the passenger seat I sit on something hard. Keeping a wary eye on Maris, I feel under my leg and locate my mobile phone. Discreetly I pocket it.

Maris sings during the journey. She sings me love songs. Her voice is tuneless. It makes Joey cry and I ask her to stop. So then she talks. She talks about how wonderful our life together will be. We can sell up and live abroad. She's got plenty of money. She's been preparing for this all of her life.

Once I get inside the hospital with Joey I'll stay there and phone the police. Then it will all be over. *'Please God let Rick be home when I get there.'*

"You're very quiet, Annie."

"Sorry."

"Are you worried about your husband?"

"Yes." I'm startled by her mind reading.

"You don't have to worry about him, he won't stop us, he can't bother us any more." She switches from reassurance to a boastful tone. "Why don't you believe I'm clever? I've looked up about Forensic Evidence. If they can't find a body it's hard for them to prove anything. I think the best thing would be to drive your car away and set it on fire. The police will think it's joyriders. That will get rid of the blood. It was careless of me, I should have planned it better, but I was improvising and on the whole I did very well."

I feel dazed. Is she really saying what I think? It makes no sense. How could she have got hold of Rick? But I've checked and there are no wounds on the baby.

"Here we are." She pulls up outside the hospital. "Wait

319

until I've turned round." She positions the car for a quick getaway. "Leave your bag here. I'll be watching you."

There's some sort of trouble by the reception desk. A gang of teenagers are brawling with the security guards. The public phones are near the doorway, within Maris' view. With my hand shielded I get out my mobile and turn it on. It takes a lifetime registering and when it does the battery is low. Swiftly I check the messages and realise there's one in the memory. "Annie love, it's me. I'm sorry about everything. I'm walking home. I'm on the road that leads out of Millwash and I'm knackered. Is there any chance you could pick me up?"

I feel numb, then fear cuts in, sharper than even the worst moments of this truly hideous day. The message is timed at four-twenty this afternoon. Even without a lift he should have got home before I left. Maris must have accessed it but she didn't delete it. I wonder why. I guess she was saving it to use for some sick purpose of her own.

The whole story comes into focus hideously clear: Rick alone and exhausted on Millwash Lane; his disappearance; the blood in the car; the crash in the cellar; the deep well where she had threatened to dispose of the baby, and Maris promising *'he can't bother us any more.'* If I call the police now could they get to Maris' cottage before Maris can drive back? Desperately I key in 999 just as the battery dies.

The quarrel between security guards and yobs has turned into a full-scale battle. In the distance I hear a siren. Maris is going to take off and I've got to go back with her to stop her hurting Rick. I drag the silver locket over my head and stuff it inside the baby's all-in-one. I dump him on a chair and drop my phone beside him.

The car's already moving off. I sprint towards it, pull open the door and fall inside. Maris accelerates away as a squad car turns in.

"What happened?"

"There was a fight… drunks in Casualty." I play the only

card I have. "You were going to leave me." Incredibly I get an injured whine into my voice.

"I thought you weren't coming back."

"I trusted you and you tried to run out on me."

"I'll make it up to you."

Neither of us speaks again until we turn off the lane onto her rough track and she stops to shut the gate.

"I'll do it," I say.

I wait until we've been in the kitchen about three minutes and say, "Oh, my locket's gone. I must have dropped it by the gate."

"Are you sure it was by the gate?"

"I think so. I felt it pull but I didn't realise what it was."

"We'll get it tomorrow then."

"No, I want it now. Please go and get it for me Maris, I'm so tired."

She hesitates.

I stand up. "Okay, I'll go, and afterwards I won't bother to come back."

"Don't say things like that."

"Why not? You've already shown how little you care about me. I'm going now."

"No, I'll go." She pulls on her coat.

I wait until I hear her drive away, then I bolt the back door. I run to the front door but there's no bolt and all the furniture is too heavy to shift. I can't waste time searching for something to block the entrance.

The key to the cellar is hanging on its hook. I'm surprised Maris left it there with me in the house. *'Oh please dear God let Rick be alive.'*

Everything is happening in slow motion. My fingers are clumsy and the lock is stiff. I need both hands to turn the key. It clicks and my heart jumps with it. I pocket the key and drag the door open. I have no torch but the scullery light pours in. There's a huddled figure at the bottom of the steps. I creep downwards. "Rick?"

He moves slightly and gives a muffled moan. I travel the rest of the distance fast, despite the poor light and my trembling legs. As I kneel beside him I see there's tape over his mouth. He winces as I pull it free. I rummage in my bag, find scissors and cut the binding around his wrists and ankles.

"Can you move, Rick? We've got to get out of here."

"Give me a sec... I'm kind of numb."

"Did she hurt you?"

"Reckon she must have run me down... Sorry, I'm really woozy."

"Please love, try to hurry." I hoist him to his feet.

And then it's too late to run. There's a click and a dim light bulb flickers into life. Maris is standing at the top of the steps, holding a hunting rifle.

"You shouldn't be down here, Annie."

"Maris, don't do anything silly."

"I'm sorry you had to see this, but it's your own fault for being so inquisitive." She moves down the steps towards us.

"No, Maris." I put myself in front of Rick. I feel him try to regain pole position but he's too shaky to push past me.

"Don't be silly Annie, you know he has to die."

I'm improvising in a bad melodrama; nothing I do or say seems real, and yet I speak the truth, "Then kill us both."

"I can't kill you, Annie."

"If you want to kill Rick, you'll have to kill me first. Anyway you won't get away with it. I left a message for the police."

"I love you, Annie."

"But I don't love you."

She stares at me, silent and expressionless, and, in that moment, I feel her desire for me turn into hate. I see the rifle shaking and brace myself, expecting her to shoot. I should be afraid but I've gone past that and all I can do is wait for her to act. She backs slowly up the stairs and slams the cellar door.

I'm trembling so much I can hardly stand, but Rick's leaning on me and I mustn't give way. His voice, soft and steady, speaks close to my ear, "Sweetheart it's okay. Come on, give me a hand. Let's see if she's locked us in."

"I've got the key. But what if she's up there waiting for us?"

"We'll have to chance it. With any luck she's run for it."

"Do you really believe that?"

"No, but we haven't got much choice." He pushes the door open.

We step into the scullery. Maris is standing there. Her eyes are fixed on me and she's smiling as she levels the rifle. "Goodbye Annie," she says quietly.

Chapter 74: Annie

"No!" I feel a swirl of movement. Rick's momentum staggers me aside. He leaps at Maris and the gun goes off. The crash stuns my senses. Rick goes down, wrenching the rifle from Maris as he falls. She stares at him, her face twisted in fury.

I scream and I hurtle at her, screeching, clawing, biting, kicking. A groan from Rick brings me to my senses. I must help him. I shove Maris away, the anger still buzzing like a cloud of black flies in my head. She edges towards the kitchen, then through it and away. I hear the front door squeak open and then slam. I check the back door's still bolted. Then I hurtle into the kitchen, shut the door and upend a table to keep it closed.

Rick's lying on the stone floor, writhing and making guttural, groaning sounds. "Hang on, darling. I'll dial 999."

"Cops... and... ambulance... no Fire Brigade... unless she tries... to burn us out."

"Oh God! You're dying and you're making silly jokes."

"Not dying... just winded... help me... sit up."

I help him and soon his breathing eases. "Sorry to frighten you. I got the side of the barrel as it went off. What is it, a bloody elephant gun?"

I stare at the weapon, lying beside Rick on the stone floor. "It looks big enough. Are you really okay?"

"Known times I've felt better but I'm not dying. You'd better make that triple nine call. Keep low in case she's lurking outside, from what you said there are plenty more guns in the other room."

I crawl into the kitchen and ring through, then we sit huddled together on the scullery floor. As we wait I tell him everything I know until the sound of sirens informs us our siege is at an end.

In Casualty they take Rick away and won't let me go with him. They put me in the visitors' room and leave me. After a few minutes, Bob comes in, looking harassed.

"Bob, where's Rick? I want to see him."

"You can't see him yet, Annie."

A thousand questions crowd in on me. Why can't I see Rick? How badly is he hurt? I get slowly to my feet. The lights dazzle and turn to blackness.

I travel up from darkness to grey and white, then colour and sound slot in and synchronise. I'm lying on a hard, high bed and Mother's standing beside me, looking old. I think it's odd she's got no make up on.

"Rick? Is Rick okay?"

A nurse bustles over. "He's all right. Lie still. You fainted."

I slide my legs over the side of the bed and sit up. The world sways then settles down. "I want to see Rick."

"Later." The nurse turns to go.

I clamber from the bed. "Mother, please, I want to see Rick now."

"One moment." Mother's voice stops the nurse in her tracks. "I will not have my daughter subjected to any more distress, kindly take us to her husband immediately."

The nurse pouts but does as she's told. She struts on ahead and we follow at the fastest shuffle my shaky legs can manage. Mother holds my arm. "Don't worry, Arianne, his mother is with him and she'd send for us if there was any danger."

My eyes are fixed on the Resuscitation Area but the nurse jerks back the curtain of an ordinary cubicle. "You'll have to leave when the doctor comes."

She's drowned out by Rick, "About bloody time. If we did that you'd call it unlawful detention." He holds out his hand and I run to him.

"Don't mind us, will you?" says Bob. "Reckon you could cut the mouth-to-mouth resuscitation for a while?"

We surface and look at him. He's given Mother his chair and she's sitting next to Tris, they're all watching us but even Mother doesn't seem put out. Rick grins and pulls me up to lie on the bed next to him, curled into the circle of his arm.

"I told Annie she couldn't see you yet. Roebuck's going to be furious I haven't kept you two apart till we've had your statements," complains Bob.

"Fuck Roebuck," retorts Rick.

"No, thanks he's not my type." Bob and I say the same words at the same time.

Tris giggles and Mother gives a reproving cough. "How badly are you hurt, Richard?"

"I'm fine."

"Rick, tell me the truth," I beg.

"Well they've got to reset my arm and I've got a lot of scrapes and bruises and a bang on the head but I'm okay, love, I promise."

"And Maris really did those dreadful things?" says Mother. "She always was a peculiar girl. They say that her mother is much brighter now she's in the Care Home."

"Maris probably drugged her," I say.

"I'll see her mother's doctors realise that." Mother's voice is troubled and unnaturally hesitant, "I fear... her brother and sister died when she was ten... poisoned by an overdose of medication. There were rumours... people thought perhaps their mother... but now I wonder if Maris did something."

"Have they caught her yet?" I ask.

"No, she took her car and headed off," says Bob. "She'll be miles away by now. Tell you what, Annie, next time you're kidnapped try to leave a clue that us thick bastards can figure out. We were still trying to work out the reason for that locket when we got your triple nine call."

"I was in a panic. I'd only just realised she'd got Rick

and I had to go back with her, otherwise she'd have..." I can't say the words.

"Bob, get Roebuck down here will you?" says Rick.

"He's already on his way. You two ladies off?"

"Arianne and Richard need some privacy. We'll wait outside," says Mother.

Tris and Mother kiss both Rick and me, then Tris kisses Bob. "You'll have to come over for a meal, you haven't been taking care of yourself properly."

I consider him. Tris is right, in his florid, heavy way he looks wrecked.

"There's a big match on Saturday," I say. "If you come round and watch it with Rick, I'll make you both a sumptuous post-match meal."

He looks puzzled. "Thought you wanted me out of your lives?"

I think of Maris. "Who am I to choose people's friends?"

Chapter 75: Annie

A few minutes later Kelly turns up and takes me away to make my statement in a doctor's borrowed office. When I emerge Neil's hanging around.

"Hi, are you waiting for Kelly?"

"No, for you. I wanted to check you and Rick are okay."

"Not bad." Apart from the nagging fear that Maris will come after me again.

"Chloe and Josef want to see you. The hospital has put them in a side ward for the night while they check the baby."

He leads me along a maze of corridors and ushers me through a door that's guarded by an uniformed cop. It's amazing how cosy a hospital room is compared to the squat. Chloe is curled up on the high bed, baby Joseph in her arms.

She greets me with a radiant smile. "Thank you."

"Thank you, Annie," echoes Josef.

"You're welcome. Is baby Joe all right?"

"Fine. Neil told us what happened. Is your husband okay?"

"Yes, thank God."

"Would you say thank you for us. He's alright for a cop."

I smile at her. "I'll tell him that."

"No really, he was good. That woman cop, the driver, told us how he put pressure on the supermarket so they're not prosecuting Josef after all. And the Social Services are going to get us a flat." She gives me a mischievous look. "And I've told Josef I'm going to marry him."

"Really? Does he get any choice?"

Her grin widens. "No."

By the time the police have finished with me, the doctor has reset Rick's arm and he's been put in a single room for the night. I rejoin him and say, "I've just seen Chloe, Josef and the baby, they're doing fine."

"That's good, three less destroyed lives is a bonus in this business. I've been thinking, I don't want Wayne Jones prosecuted for the assault on me. There's been enough victims already without adding that poor bastard to the score." He grins at me. "And I've got no great ambition to go to Court and explain how I panicked a mentally disabled guy into assaulting me with a rolling pin."

"But Bob says Roebuck's still working on Wayne to confess to Stacie's murder."

"Well I hope he doesn't succeed because Wayne didn't do it."

"You got anything to back that up?" The rough voice from the doorway makes us jump. For a big man DCI Lane moves very quietly.

"I think so, sir."

DCI Lane pulls a chair up to Rick's bedside. As he sits down both he and the chair groan. He looks exhausted.

"I came to let you know there's nothing in this paedophile business, Rick. It was all a con. Some bastards getting cash from reporters for an inside story about a paedophile ring. And now the reporters are whinging to us to get their money back."

"We'll make it top priority," says Rick, and DCI Lane laughs.

"The only thing I can't work out is how Stacie's locket got into that other reporter's car." The DCI's shrewd eyes hold Rick's. "Or maybe I can. I had a look at that Elmwash documentary and it gives all the details any copycat could want."

"I think I know what happened, sir."

"But you'd rather run it past the Superintendent first? Fair enough, it ain't my pigeon anyway. The Superintendent's told me to concentrate on the clubbing murder."

"I've got a few informers… if you need any input…"

"Not from you! For God's sake, take some leave and get

sorted before you bloody kill yourself. I should have come and dealt with it meself when they found Stacie's body. Truth is I thought the Superintendent would be back quicker than he was."

He drags himself to his feet. "I got work to do. I'm glad that baby's safe."

"That's thanks to Annie, sir."

"Mebbe, but I'd keep quiet about that. The Superintendent is getting fidgety about you dragging your wife into this business."

"Rick didn't drag me," I say indignantly. "What happened with Maris was my fault, not his."

He looks at me cynically but not unkindly. "You don't have to convince me about that but it's still a case of least said soonest mended." He turns back to Rick, "You did alright, in fact you did bloody well. I've given orders there's to be a guard on you and your wife and surveillance on your house until that loony bitch is caught." He leaves.

"Annie, I'm worried. If Lane's being that nice I must be hurt worse than I thought."

That makes me laugh. "I think he's rather sweet."

Rick shakes his head. "You know, there's times when I wonder about your taste in men." Then suddenly serious, "Go home, love, and get some sleep."

I know it will worry him if I hang around here. He's gearing up for Superintendent Roebuck's arrival and I don't want to distract him. It's important to him he finishes this case right.

"Okay. Mother's coming home with me for the night so I won't be lonely."

"That's good of her, I hope she doesn't mind."

"She insisted." When I'd tried to tell her I'd be fine by myself, her lips had trembled and she'd dabbed at them with her lace handkerchief and said, 'Please Arianne, I'd like to. I won't sleep if I'm not with you. I'd be too worried about you. Please, let me stay with you until Richard comes home.'

"You'll be safe now Lane's set up a guard for you." Rick interrupts my thoughts.

"Yes." Although he knows as well as I do that neither of us will feel safe until Maris is caught.

The guard cops are very kind and agree to go via Mother's house so she can collect her things. By the time we get home I'm so tired I can hardly stay on my feet and, as soon as the policemen have checked through the house, Mother urges me up to bed and makes me a hot milky drink. I feel myself sliding back into nursery days.

"Arianne dear, I wondered if you'd find this comforting." She delves into her overnight bag and produces a hefty, wrought iron candlestick with a slender, pale pink candle protruding from the top. "I collected it from my bedside cabinet when I was fetching my night clothes."

I'm puzzled. "Have you got any reason to expect a power cut?"

"The candle is just for show. If you hold it like this it makes a very satisfying weapon." She swings it casually. "A woman who lives alone has to be prepared."

She smiles at me, serenely unaware of how much she has startled me, then places the candlestick within my reach. "Drink your Ovaltine while it's warm, Arianne."

"Aren't you having one?"

"Goodness no! Milk drinks are much too fattening. Try to get a few hours sleep, you'll want to be up early to visit Rick."

It's five minutes later, when I'm sneaking into the en suite to tip the loathed Ovaltine down the loo, that I realise, for the first time in my married life, Mother had called my husband Rick.

Chapter 76: Rick

It's after midnight when Roebuck, Bob and Kelly troop into my room. Roebuck says, "Are you all right, Rick?"

"Yeah, thanks sir."

He scans the statement Bob took from me. "So this woman, Maris Clarke, abducted the baby, and it was nothing to do with any other crime?"

"Nothing, although what happened to Stacie gave her the idea." Annie's filled in a lot of the blanks for me and I tell them about Maris' escalating violence.

Roebuck seems horrified. "You really think she'd have killed you?"

Bob chimes in, "She's a nasty piece of work. The house is falling apart but every gun in the place is well cared for and loaded. None of them are licensed. Someone's head ought to roll about that."

"Yeah," I say. "But I don't think she planned to shoot me. Annie reckons she'd have shoved me down the well."

Great place for a claustrophobic bastard like me to end up. I wonder if she'd have killed me first, or whether I'd have been conscious as I went down the narrow hole and the black water closed over me. I clamp down on panic, I've got to keep control or Roebuck won't listen to what I've got to say.

"Anything new on the Stacie Frewer case?" I ask.

Roebuck shakes his head. "We've questioned Wayne but all he'll do is cry and say he didn't do anything bad."

"If you want sense out of him, reassure him, and tell him that he didn't do anything wrong in sneaking Stacie that toffee."

"What?"

"I think Wayne doesn't have a sense of scale when it comes to right and wrong, a minor act of disobedience or a serious crime both measure the same to him."

I see Kelly's nod of understanding but Roebuck and Bob look blank.

"I'm not sure what you're getting at," says Roebuck.

"Stacie and Wayne were friends, just friends, nothing sinister or queer. Stacie loved sweets but her stepfather said she was too fat. Wayne makes toffee on Sunday mornings but that week it went too hard. Wayne sneaked down with some toffee for Stacie and gave it to her in the garden. And he gave her a bracelet that he'd made. I'd guess she crept outside to play, because I still can't see her father letting her out there in that fancy frock. Anyway Terry Frewer must have brought her in to practise the piano."

They're all frowning but I don't get the feeling of disapproval, more like they're trying to remember and collate the evidence. "Go on," says Roebuck.

Now I'm starting on the dodgy bit. "The thing you've got to understand is that Terry Frewer is a liar."

"Now Rick..."

I hurry on, "Not an ordinary liar. He's the sort who cons himself. The sort that has an image to keep up. He couldn't even bear to admit he'd left the gate to a horse field open, he had to blame the kid who was helping him."

"Vicki?" queries Kelly.

I nod agreement and think Kelly at least is with me.

"Frewer had his image. Half that bloody village will tell you how wonderful he is. But his problem is everything belonging to him has to be perfect too. Cindy was seventeen and pregnant when he married her. He dominated her and crushed the life out of her and he did the same with Stacie. Trouble was, when he'd done that, they didn't do him credit. Cindy's been depressed for years and Stacie was a mess, overweight and shy and slow at school. But he had to keep up the image of the perfect husband and dad."

"There were bruises on the child's arms," says Roebuck. "But no sign of sexual interference. There's nothing to bear out your claim that Frewer abused her."

"I don't think it was physical abuse. There are other ways of taking a person apart, especially a kid who's in your power."

"You mean mental cruelty, Guv?" says Kelly.

"Yeah, and what do they call it? Emotional violence."

"So what was he like at home behind closed doors?"

"I don't know, only Cindy Frewer can answer that."

"What do you think happened that last day?" asks Roebuck and there's less scepticism in his voice than before.

This is where I put myself a hundred-per-cent on the line. "I think he brought her in from the garden and sat her down to practise the piano. But she wet herself. There's this embroidered cloth over the piano stool but under it the padded seat is stained. That would make Frewer angry. It was his piano. It came from his family. I think he stripped her and put her dress in the washing machine. There are clothes that look posh but are easy to wash and tumble dry, I only realised that the other day when my wife got some spaghetti on her dress."

"I'm still confused about which dress she was wearing," admits Kelly.

Join the club. I just hope, if this ever comes to Court, I'm not the cop who has to be cross-examined about pink dresses. Nevertheless I say, "There was only one dress, the bridesmaid's dress that the next-door neighbour saw. That was the one Cindy put out for her. Stacie was naked when she died. I don't know if Terry couldn't bear to dress her again when she was dead, or thought it wouldn't look like the Elmwash killings if he did, or he just panicked and overlooked the dress, but afterwards he simply bluffed it. With the number of pink dresses that kid had in her wardrobe, no-one could be certain whether one was gone or not."

I wonder, after we'd asked about the clothes, if Cindy had tried to work out whether any of Stacie's other pink dresses were missing and how she'd felt if she'd decided they were all there.

"It must have been a nasty moment for him when you started focusing on the bridesmaid's dress," says Kelly. "So the jeans had nothing to do with it?"

"Only that it showed what a domineering bastard he was to make her give them up. She loved those jeans because, wearing them, she fitted in, she wasn't an old-fashioned doll in pink frills."

"But where are you getting the idea she wet herself?" Roebuck hauls us back to the main plot.

I think, *'It takes one to know one.'* I say, "There's lots of signs: what her teacher said, the plastic sheets in her bathroom cupboard, the way her mum was always changing her clothes, the sort of scared little kid she was and a kind of smell that had stayed on in her room."

"Yeah," says Bob. We all look at him and he turns red. "My boy had a bit of a problem. He's over it now but I know how the stink used to hang round the place."

"Go on, Rick," says Roebuck.

I draw on Stacie's pictures and the memories of my own childhood. "I don't know, but I'd guess he stood her in the corner as a sort of punishment. There's a plant stand in the corner of their room. It's a lousy place for a plant, right out of view of the windows. I'd guess that, under it, the carpet's stained."

"You mean she wet herself again and he killed her?" Roebuck's voice is hushed.

"I think he lost his temper and shook her, but she had a bit of Wayne's toffee in her mouth and she choked to death."

Chapter 77: Rick

There's a deep silence until Roebuck breaks it with a whispered, "Oh my God."

"But if it was like that, it was an accident and he didn't mean to kill her. Why hide the body?" Bob sounds bewildered.

Kelly answers for me, "Like the DI says, he's not the sort of guy who could admit he'd done anything wrong. If his kid's dead, he's got to be the victim. And he's malicious. I'd guess that's why he left the bracelet Wayne made by the body. I think he realised who'd given it to her and hoped it would incriminate Wayne. If nothing else, it deflected attention from Frewer. "

"And he enjoyed playing the bereaved parent, being the centre of attention," admits Roebuck. "You said that, Rick, and you were right."

"We've still got to prove it."

Kelly opens the file. "They did that Forensic sweep you wanted, checking out the routes from the gardens into the wood. Terry Frewer said he hadn't been out there all week but there's one of his shoe prints on a stile. It's identifiable by a wedge-shaped crack. Unfortunately there's been too many Fun-runners through to find much."

"No wonder the bastard wanted the Run to go ahead," says Bob bitterly. "It gave him the ideal opportunity to put the body in the woods and decorate it to look like the Elmwash kids."

"Ernest Clift was the Elmwash killer," I say.

"We know that, Rick," says Roebuck soothingly.

"Yeah, you know it until some other kid turns up dead and some other arsehole tries to fuck us round with flowers. When that happens you'll start again about how I'm a loser who got it wrong or a bent bastard who only cared about getting a result."

That's about as insubordinate as anyone can get but I don't care any more.

"I know you've got a genuine grievance, Rick. I'm sorry for what you've been through."

You won't get fairer than that, certainly not from a Superintendent to a DI. I can hardly believe it's all over. Lane's right about letting things go. Ernest Clift and Elmwash are finished, at least as far as they ever will be for me. I feel limp and exhausted and the room is swaying round me like I'm drunk. I look at Bob and he gives me a lop-sided grin. I guess he's feeling much the same as me.

It's Kelly who brings us back to business, "Mark Corrigan established the flowers left with Stacie's body came from the tributes outside the house, so Frewer got that wrong as well."

"We'll have to work out what he did with the body for a week," says Roebuck.

I've got that covered too. "I don't see how he could get her off the premises. I'd tell Forensics to try the attic, over on the neighbour's side. There's a partition wall between but it's got a door that gives him access. The neighbour mentioned he went through at Christmas to fix her TV aerial."

Roebuck frowns. "It all fits but there are a lot of coincidences."

I expected that and I'm ready to fight it. "I don't reckon so, sir. I mean Frewer didn't need to have any special motive to watch that Elmwash programme on TV. In a way it was natural he should, those killings were big news round here. Then, when he was looking for a way of hiding his crime, it would come into his mind. And it was easy enough for him to slip out and slide that locket into the reporter's car. The only thing he couldn't get were the formal flowers, and he probably thought that didn't matter, most people would accept it as an Elmwash killing however sloppy he was."

"You've made your point Rick," says Roebuck stiffly.

"As for Maris, she'd take an interest because she was looking for any way to get at me. The only real coincidence was Wayne working at the Art College and us getting focused on that bloody goose so Maris saw her chance to snatch the baby, and that sort of coincidence does happen."

"That's true," says Roebuck. "You've done a good job, Rick. I don't know how you've put it together so clearly."

I guess it stimulates the brain to be tied up in the dark, cold, hurting and terrified.

"But, of course, it's all circumstantial, nothing the CPS will take to Court," continues Roebuck

"There may be new physical evidence in the house now we know what we're looking for," suggests Kelly.

"We'll get SOCO back in there first thing in the morning," says Roebuck. "And this time they'll check out the neighbour's attic as well. And I'll have Frewer in and question him."

I know there's only one certain way we're going to nail Terry Frewer. "I think when we showed the mother those jeans it brought it home to her. Until then she'd tried to fool herself into believing her husband wasn't a tyrant. She practically told me she knew he'd had something to do with Stacie's disappearance but I was too thick to understand. I'd guess she's worked it out by now and, if you level with her, she might come across with something that could help."

"Rick, is there any chance of you questioning her? I mean tomorrow, after a night's rest. She trusts you. Anyway you deserve the credit."

I know I ought to say, 'Sure, no problem.' That's the way to get promotion and I reckon it's nearer than it's been for years. And I could do it, I'm not hurt that badly, but the thought of Cindy Frewer's martyrdom flows over me like a tide of pain. "Sorry sir. I'd rather leave that to you."

Chapter 78: Annie

I jump awake while it's still dark and lie for a moment, trying to work out what roused me. Then I hear it again, the creak of my studio door. It must be my nerves playing tricks on me. After the guard cops had checked it last night, they'd locked it and given me the key. But I'm sure I'm not mistaken, I know that sound.

There's someone moving along the corridor towards my room. I slide slowly up to press against the metal bedhead, it's cold against my shoulders. I reach out for Mother's candlestick and hold it concealed in the folds of my duvet.

The door opens, slowly and quietly.

"Hello Annie," says Maris.

The nightmare engulfs me again. I think perhaps I'm dreaming, all my trauma bubbling to the surface while I sleep. She looks the same as always, the same drab clothes, limp hair and pasty face, but there's a line of scratches down her cheek and a slight swelling beside her mouth, evidence of my anger.

"How did you get in?"

"I was here all the time. I came straight here after you behaved so badly at my house. I was waiting for you in your studio. Those stupid policeman were very negligent, they hardly looked at all." She opens her left hand and reveals a set of keys. "I've been collecting these for years, getting them duplicated whenever you left them lying round. You're so careless."

"You mean you've been in my house before?" Even in this crisis that repulses me.

"No." She sounds resentful. "I couldn't get the setting for your security code, not until the other day, when you broke that window and made such an exhibition of yourself. I was listening outside your office when you phoned about the repairs."

"What are you doing here, Maris? There are police downstairs, I've only got to scream and they'll be here."

"Don't be stupid. I told you I'd been here for hours. Do you really think I'd waste my time? I've been busy in your kitchen."

"You've drugged them?"

"Of course, in the milk, sugar, coffee and tea. They're unconscious in the hall. They won't wake up for hours, if at all. No-one will hear you when you scream."

Hiding in my attic studio, she doesn't know that Mother's in the house. I've got to keep it that way. Maris is crazy and she wouldn't hesitate to kill Mother while she slept. "What do you want, Maris? Why have you come here? Do you still want me to come away with you?"

"No! You disgust me. I loved you and you betrayed me."

"That wasn't love. It was an ugly thing, like greed."

"Ugly!" She plucks out the word and screeches it at me. "You've always thought I'm ugly. You and your fancy mother and bitch sister. I wanted to kill you at my house, to make him watch you die, but I like this better. We'll see if he still wants you when you're scarred and sightless." She brings a knife from concealment in the folds of her skirt and steps closer to point it at my face.

I bring the candlestick round and crack it against her wrist. The knife clatters against the wall. Maris shrieks and leaps upon me, trying to wrestle the candlestick from my grasp. I hang on to it. If she gets it she'll smash my face in. We struggle. She's screaming profanity and shaking me from side to side.

Suddenly she's not fighting any more. She lies limp and heavy, smothering me. I carry on struggling, certain it's a trick. Then the weight is lifted from me and Maris clumps onto the floor.

Mother stands there, immaculate as ever, although pale and breathless. She's holding something wooden in both hands and, after a blank moment, I identify it as one of

Neil's carvings, which stands on the bookcase in the living room. She follows my gaze and examines it anxiously, as if concerned she might have damaged it.

"How did you know I needed you?" My throat feels scratchy.

She looks up and smiles at me but I can see she's near to tears. "I don't know what awoke me but I had a strong sense something was wrong. I came to see if you felt unwell and I heard Maris' voice. Of course, I went downstairs to summon our police guard. When I realised they were indisposed I telephoned for assistance and then picked this up and came to protect you." Her composure crumbles. "I've never hit anyone before."

I scramble across the bed towards her and she receives me in the warmest hug she's ever given me. "It's all right, Arianne, you're safe now. I would never let anyone hurt you. Now we must be practical, it would be best if we found something to secure Maris and then we must help those unfortunate policemen."

"Yes, of course." Maris is stirring. I look around desperately for something to tie her up. I have a bad feeling neither Mother nor I are good enough with knots to keep someone as dangerous as Maris properly immobilised.

"Doesn't Richard possess handcuffs?" Mother is thinking more clearly than me.

"Of course!" I don't need to find Rick's when I've got my own. I rummage through the clothes drawer where I'd hidden them. By the time I find them, Maris has her eyes open and is sitting up, while Mother stands guard wielding a threatening candlestick.

"I don't want her in here," I say. The only place solid enough to cuff her to would be the steel bedhead and that would hold too many parallels.

"Quite right. We do not wish the police to draw erroneous conclusions when they arrive. Stand up, please, Maris, and go down the stairs. Yes, that will do nicely."

Mother's tone is the one she uses when shepherding guests at a tricky social event. She sounds amazingly brisk and holds the candlestick with casual ruthlessness. Maris staggers down the stairs and stops without protest at the point Mother indicates.

"Sit down on the step, Maris. Now Arianne, please secure her to the banister support." Obedient as two small girls at a tea party we do as we are told.

I go downstairs and check on the two cops. One stirs when I shake him and shows signs of coming round but the other one is deeply unconscious and breathing in slow, deep, drawn out gasps. I'm relieved to hear the distant sound of a siren.

"Go outside and wave them down, Arianne," orders Mother. "Even a minute could be vital and we don't wish them to miss your drive."

I run outside in time to see a police patrol car coming, followed by the ambulance. I wave them into my driveway and gasp an explanation. As cops and paramedics hurry into the house another car barrels its way onto the drive and screeches to a halt.

DCI Lane emerges ponderously from the driver's side. Rick jumps out and overtakes him, sprinting towards me. He holds me close.

I'm shaking with relief but there's still practical stuff to be done. "I'm fine and so is Mother, but Maris drugged the cops and one of them looks bad."

Inside the house we find DCI Lane standing next to Mother and staring in bemusement at the scene in front of him. One of the drugged cops is sitting up and taking bleary notice while the paramedics work on the other one.

Maris is still sitting halfway down the stairs, watching the scene with her usual flat indifference. DCI Lane glares at her and roars, "Get her back to the Station and don't take no chances, she's a slippery, dangerous bitch."

"Yes sir." One of the uniformed officers accepts the

key I silently hold out to him. He releases Maris from my handcuffs and fits official ones in their place. I think she's going to leave without a word but, as she's led out, she resists for a moment and halts beside me. "You're wrong, Annie. I did love you."

"Oh Maris, why didn't you stop before it was too late?"

Maris' face retains its accustomed emptiness. "It was always too late," she says.

Chapter 79: Annie

It takes hours for the forensic officers to do their stuff. At last they all leave, apart from two new cops on guard duty, and we go slowly and wearily up the stairs. Rick sits in a chair by the open window while I change our bed. I've already dumped all the food the SOCO team didn't take, just in case Maris had got to it.

"Rick, what will happen to Maris? She'll go to prison, won't she?"

"It depends if she's found fit to plead. It'll be prison or a secure mental hospital."

One day, she'll be free again. "Do you think, when she's let loose, she'll still be obsessed by me?" I struggle to control the tremor in my voice.

"I suppose she could be, she's good at fooling people, but it's no good meeting trouble before it comes." He grins as the irony of his words strikes home. "That's weird, me saying that to you."

I smile back at him and smooth out the freshly-made bed. "All done."

The phone rings. I move to answer it but Rick gets there first. "Yes, speaking."... "Yes sir." He listens intently for a minute or two and asks, "Is she okay?" Again he listens, then says, "Thank you for letting me know."

He puts the phone down and turns towards me. His expression frightens me, it's so rigidly controlled.

"Rick, what is it?"

"That was Roebuck. SOCO found evidence that Stacie's body had been stored in the attic belonging to the old lady who lives next door. As soon as they interrogated Frewer, he confessed. He claims it was an accident and he panicked."

"After all the games he played, he simply gave up and admitted it?" I find that incredible.

"As soon as they found evidence of where Stacie had been kept, his wife walked out on him. She told Kelly that she was sure she'd put out Stacie's bridesmaid's dress for her to wear and that Frewer got angry when Stacie wet herself, although never when there was anyone but her around."

I shiver. "It's scary, what goes on behind closed doors."

"Yeah. Roebuck says Frewer fell to pieces when he realised Cindy was leaving him."

"Is she somewhere safe?" I ache with pity for Cindy Frewer. She must feel like she's living in hell.

"Yes, they've taken her to a hotel and a Bereavement Counsellor is staying with her." He gives a shuddering sigh. "It's over."

"Yes."

I hear a car pull up on the gravel drive. "Oh no, who's that?"

"Just your mother in a taxi." He leans out of the window. "She says she's not coming in but she's left us some food with one of the uniformed guys."

"Bless Mother."

"Yeah, I take back everything I've ever said about her, I can't believe she clobbered Maris the way she did."

"Even the most elegant Siamese turns into a tiger when her cub's threatened, but I'm worried she'll have a bad reaction later on."

"That's why I phoned my mum. She's here too, passing more food out of the taxi."

I go to the window to watch our mothers leave. The cop on the drive is the young one who answered the burglar alarm.

"Oh what a nuisance," I say, "The tablecloth's still in the wash. What shall I wear when I'm answering the door?"

"Behave yourself, woman, and come to bed." Rick's trying to fumble his way out of a lager lout tee-shirt that I suspect belongs to Bob.

I go to his rescue and liberate him from his borrowed clothes. His body is a mass of bruises and shallow cuts. "I'll

345

get some arnica cream."

In the medicine cupboard I spot my pregnancy testing kit and think I'll have to use it later on today. It's strange, but now I hope I'm not pregnant. Rick and I need time alone together to heal ourselves and our relationship.

Back in the bedroom I make Rick lie down and smooth the cream over him.

"Better treatment than you get on the NHS," he remarks.

"So I should hope." I have just reached his groin.

He laughs at this, but his voice is serious as he says, "Annie, I love you, but I'm so tired and so scared I won't be able to get myself sorted."

The image of the poppy field is vivid in my mind. All experience is universal and I wonder if this is how generations of women have felt when their men returned from battle. They were happy and, at the same time, confused, sad and lonely; for their lovers were not as they'd set out, now they were scarred in body and maimed in mind. Then I remember my father's words, *'Love looks like it's so easy to destroy but it always comes back again, just like the poppies.'* And, for the first time, I see the frail, glowing flowers through his eyes, as a sign of regeneration and of hope.

"What are you thinking?" asks Rick.

I lie down beside him and cautiously cradle him, mindful of his bruises and broken arm. He smiles at me and raises his good hand to stroke my face.

I offer my half-formulated thoughts, "I'm thinking about the poppies..."

Made in the USA
Charleston, SC
24 June 2016